Trigger Warnings

Physical Assault
Murder/Death
Drugs
Emotional Abuse
Violence/Blood
Kidnapping
Misogyny
Physical Abuse
PTSD/Depression/Flashbacks
Sexual Harassment
Anxiety
Hospitalization (brief)
Arson
Talk of pregnancy (very brief)

Content Warnings:

Sexually Explicit Scenes (consensual)
Adult Language
BDSM dynamics

Raised by Shadows

E. Abraham

Copyright © 2024 Emilia Abraham

All rights reserved.

This is a work of fiction. Any similarity to places or persons, living or dead, is entirely coincidental. All ideas and characters are that of the author and should not be reproduced, stored, or transmitted in any form without the written permission of the author.

Generative AI has not been used in the making of this project in anyway, shape, or form.

Sharing is caring, but not for pirates. Be a friend, not a pirate.

Cover Artist: K.B. Barrett Designs

ISBN-13:978-1-961802-08-7

For anyone who's ever wondered what it would be like to be fingered against a tree.

Prologue

Emma

Nine Years Earlier

My body vibrates with anticipation and nerves. I shouldn't be standing outside his room. Then again, I shouldn't be having any of these feelings anyway, but I can't push them down anymore.

After all these years, I'm still chasing after a guard who works for my brother. Doubt runs through my mind as I wring my hands together. This is going to be a disaster.

First, I'm only fifteen and he's twenty. This is arguably the biggest reason I should keep my damn mouth shut. I glance over my shoulder to make sure none of my brothers are hovering. They might not be able to know I just cussed in my head, but they'd *know*.

They'd also kick my ass if they knew I was about to tell a man, because he's actually a man and no longer a boy, my feelings for him. Actually, they'd probably tell Sam, and she'd ship me off for another round of training in the mountains. I shudder at the thought.

The second point is almost as bad, yet it's more personal and I doubt I'll ever share it with anyone. If I tell him how I feel and he laughs...it'll change me forever. I'm at a crossroads, anxiety riding me hard. His reaction will determine which path I'm forced down, and I hate it. Logically, I know he doesn't have that kind of power over me. But I can't keep these emotions from bursting out of me.

I'd rather tell him now while we're alone than randomly when he picks me up from school. Being chauffeured around is embarrassing enough as it is. Add in the gawking from all my classmates and I'm fucked. Completely and royally fucked. He'll never see me as anything other than a kid. Which is exactly what I am to him—a damn child. No one in their right mind would think any different. *I* don't think any different, either.

This was a really, really bad idea. I shuffle back, holding my breath while I pray the handle stays still. I don't even make it two feet before I freeze. My eyes widen as the door swings open, revealing a shirtless Titus.

Shit, shit, shit. He's no longer the gangly eighteen-year-old who could barely hold his gun steady. This right here was why I shouldn't have come. I don't even have boobs yet. Not really. They hardly fill *my* hands, much less the ones hanging at his side.

"Emma? What's wrong? Did something happen?" He turns, probably to grab a shirt, and my palms itch to stop him.

When he reveals his muscular back, I figure this isn't such a bad view, either. I shake my head to center myself. Drooling over his body is not okay. Then again, I'm not doing anything other than admiring. I bite my cheek, then do it again for good measure.

"Nothing's wrong," I rush out as I take another step back. "I was just bored and wandering."

It's not a great excuse and from the look on his face after he pulls on his shirt, he knows it.

"If nothing's wrong, why do you look like you've seen a ghost?"

"Creepy house?" I wince. "I'm just going to go."

"Obviously something is on your mind. Why don't you spit it out, Emma." He says it like a command, not a question, and I'm opening my mouth before I've made the conscious thought to answer.

"I need someone to train with." The words spill out of me and my mouth gapes open and closed. I'm pretty sure I look like a fish, but I'm baffled why my mind picked *that* particular lie.

Confusion contorts his face as he hangs off the top of the door frame. "Isn't Miss Sam training you?"

Why does he have to keep doing things that are hot? It's like he's got some type of manual—the hot guy's guide to driving a woman wild with desire. I bite my lip, glancing away so he won't notice me staring.

"Uh, yeah. That's not...you know what? I'm just going to go." I throw my thumb over my shoulder, kicking myself the entire time. So awkward.

He tilts his head before he glances behind me and straightens. "Sir?"

I spin around, spotting some guard I can never remember the name of. He's constantly glaring at me and telling me what to do. As if I don't have three other men fully capable of keeping me in line. I haven't said anything about him to Shane, though I should. I keep thinking I can handle shit myself. It's becoming clear I can't.

"Get her inside. Shit is going down. We've got enough to worry about without wondering where the fuck she slipped off to," the guard growls before pivoting and prowling down the hall.

My phone buzzes right then, and I glance at it. Shane demands to know where I am, what I'm doing, and find my handler. He doesn't call Titus my handler, but that's what the man wrapping his hand around my arm is.

"What the hell, Titus?" I snap, forgetting for a minute who I'm talking to. I've been stumbling over my words for years whenever he's around. Except when he pisses me off, apparently.

He doesn't respond, manhandling me into his room. When he pushes me to the side, I stumble over his boots. Not that he notices. He's too busy peeking out the door, then slamming it shut. I've never been in his room and it's making me sweat. I suddenly understand why Sam wears hoodies all the time. Hiding my hands in a pocket would be perfect right about now.

"Don't have a place for you to sit," he mumbles as he kicks a pile of clothes to the side.

The bed looms in front of me, taking up most of the room. A small dresser sits next to his open closet, though there's nothing hanging inside. Most of his clothes are scattered on the floor. He's worse than I am.

"You know we have a maid service, right?"

"*I* did. Didn't realize *you* did." His lopsided grin sends butterflies fluttering in my stomach.

"I like you. I mean, I love you."

The butterflies die one by one and a chill snakes down my spine. My chin quivers as I cast for a way to take the words back. They just tumbled out without my consent. And now I'm pretty sure I'm having an out-of-body experience.

I sway and my wide eyes bounce around the room. Anywhere but directly at him. I don't want to see his expression or know what he's thinking. He's better at hiding his emotions now, but we've spent so much time together over the last couple years I notice more than others.

When I finally muster up the courage, he's staring at his bed. "Back at ya."

"That's not what I—"

"I know what you meant." He sighs, running his fingers through his hair. "You're a nice girl and all..."

I huff, shaking my head. I didn't expect him to fall to his knees and profess his undying love for me. The recitation of generic responses to let me down easy, though, is weak.

"I don't need you to respond. I just had to get it out. These feelings were eating me alive." I snap my mouth shut, close my eyes, and take a deep, calming breath. "I just wanted you to know. And now we can pretend I didn't say anything."

He snorts, and my gaze snaps to him. "There's no stuffing this cat back in the bag, Emma."

"We can. And things will go back to normal. I told you what I needed to and now this conversation can be over." I move to the door, but he blocks my way. "Are you going to move?"

"Nope." He leans away like I'm going to jump his bones, and I roll my eyes. "Hep said you have to stay put. Which is why we're not going to be able to ignore your little outburst."

My mouth drops open as my cheeks burn. "It's not like I crawled through your window while you were sleeping. I didn't shout it from the rooftops. I made a statement."

His head tips back and he laughs. I've heard him laugh before, yet there's an edge to it now. It's not carefree or light. It hits me then that he's laughing at my explanations. At my feelings for him. At me. I swallow hard, stepping back.

"What did you expect to happen, Emma? Did you honestly think I would say anything other than you're too young?"

"I didn't think—"

"No, you didn't. You never think." He chuckles again as he leans against the door.

"Stop laughing at me. This isn't fucking funny."

He straightens, a cruelness pulling at his mouth. "It's laughable to think I would do anything with you."

He's right. I'm too young. Doesn't mean he has to be so hurtful about it. He's never been this cruel. Annoyed, sure. Upset, absolutely. But even when he was forced to follow me to school or go to some party or drop me off in the middle of bumfuck nowhere, he never took it out on me. I thought we were friends. If we couldn't be together because of the age difference, fine. We were friends, though.

"I thought we were friends," I whisper, fighting back tears.

He snickers, the sound stabbing at my already battered heart. "We're not friends, and we never will be."

My body vibrates, anger washing away the heartache. "Fuck you, Titus. Go to fucking hell."

"Real mature."

He rolls his eyes, glancing away, and my anger turns to rage. How fucking dare he treat me like a little kid!

"When did you become such a goddamn bastard?"

His eyes narrow, and for a split second, I wonder if I crossed the line. I shove away the feelings of guilt and my muscles tense. I swear if he tells me to grow up, I might throat punch him.

"Even if you were old enough, I wouldn't fucking touch you with a ten-foot pole. If I didn't have to babysit you, I'd run as far as I fucking could from you. The only reason I'm putting up with your bratty ass is because if I don't, your brother will float me. You're a fucking job, darling. Nothing more."

"You can't mean that," I murmur, all while trying to school my face into some semblance of normalcy. I'm not Sam, though. I don't have a ready-made mask to slide over my features so no one knows what I'm thinking—what I'm feeling.

"I'm not surprised you didn't notice. You're so self-centered, you rarely notice anyone who you think is less than. A spoiled fucking brat who doesn't give two shits about anyone but herself. I could excuse that, blame it on your upbringing, if you weren't such an insufferable bitch. No one fucking cares if you don't have friends. No one cares how goddamn *hard* you think your life is. Hell, even your brother barely pays attention to you. You're a liability to the King family. And you always will be."

My body jerks with each revelation. He did a damn good job keeping me in the dark about his true feelings. I never suspected a thing. Pressing my lips together, I seal away my emotions, locking up the love I thought I had for him. If only I could erase them completely. Either way, I refuse to give him my tears. I refuse to give him anything other than my distain from now on.

Titus Prince is fucking dead to me.

Chapter 1

Emma

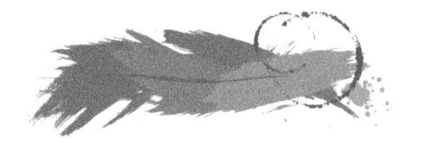

I'm pretty sure I'm about to die.

Either my demons will catch up to me or Shane is going to summon my ass back home to bury me. Instead of dealing with everything, I ran. It's not my usual way of handling problems. I've been trained better than that. Sam would probably kick my ass if she saw me right now. Rightly so. Which is why I'm staring at a small pond that reminds me of home. No one has ever found me here. It's like a little sanctuary made just for me. No one else comes this far out of the city and there's only one bench.

Daisy, my best friend since I left Synd, plops down beside me and I scowl. She probably followed me, trying to suss out all my secrets. She huffs, flipping her copper hair over her shoulder, smacking my face in the process. Bitch does that shit on purpose.

"It's cold," she murmurs, staring at the pond.

"Huh?" I glance at her out of the corner of my eye.

"It's cold."

"No shit, Sherlock. It's the middle of winter. What'd you expect?"

She snorts, shaking her head. "I see you're in one of your moods. That why you disappeared to this random-ass lake?"

"There's usually ducks. And I am all about the ducks." I gesture to the empty pond.

I close my eyes, a shiver rolling down my spine. Either someone is watching us or I'm freezing my ass off. I should go back to my apartment, do my last few papers, then sleep. Maybe this feeling of despair will flee in the face of a routine. If I keep going, I can ignore the doubts and fears that plague me, but I'm exhausted. It's more than finally finishing college. It's more than the prospect of moving back to Synd. I just can't put my finger on it.

I sigh. *A little longer won't hurt.*

"You going to tell me why you're hiding from the world?" Daisy asks, breaking me out of my thoughts.

"I've been lying to you," I whisper.

She nods, but doesn't bother turning to me. "About what? Because if you tell me you're about to be married off or some shit..."

I laugh, despite knowing I might lose her in the next couple minutes. "Nothing like that. My family wouldn't pull that with me. They know better."

The image of my old guard flashes across my mind before I violently shove it away. I'd love to say it's been years since I've thought about him. I'd be lying. He crops up at the most inopportune times—usually right when I'm about to sleep with someone. It's fucking annoying.

"Well, get it over with so I can figure out your penance."

She's kidding, though she might very well drown me in the pond. My phone buzzes in the pocket of my sweatshirt. I don't bother to answer it since it's been going off all day. I'm not ready to face Sam. Or Alex. Even Ren would be terrible. I'd put my money on Shane, my older brother. I stopped checking after the first three times he called. It's not an emergency. We have a protocol for that sort of thing and repeatedly calling me on my personal phone isn't it.

"You know how I never talk about my family?" I wait until she nods, then I stare at the nearly frozen water. "It's not your typical dynamic."

"Were you raised by two moms? Or two dads? Ooh, grandparents?" She smacks my leg, then squeezes my knee. "You realize those things are completely normal, right? Hell, *I* was raised by my aunt and uncle who were better to me than my own parents were. I call them Mom and Dad, for fuck's sake. Shit like this isn't a big deal, Emma."

"You think I would have kept from you that I had gay parents for five years?" She shrugs. "Some people would. Although, I thought you'd knew me better than to worry about that."

"I do. I was raised by my older brother and his two friends...who were like my brothers, too. Samantha didn't come into the picture until I was thirteen, but I suppose she raised me as well. She was more like a big sister, though. She taught me a lot." My chest aches whenever they cross my mind, which is every day. I miss them. And Synd. And my life there. I miss it all, but I'm terrified of going home.

"Okay, that's still not all that strange. Wait, are they hot?" The giddiness in her tone is too much for the anxiety rolling through me.

"Hell if I know. That's not the...no. You're not meeting them. Ever."

She squawks, pressing a hand to her heart. "For shame. You don't trust me? Am I not good enough for them?"

"They're with Sam. Like deeply, madly in love with her. You don't stand a chance," I say, grinning.

Realization dawns on her face and she nods sagely. "So you thought if I knew they were sharing a woman, I'd judge you. I don't really give a flying fuck, Emma. As long as they're happy, what does that matter to me?"

"Stop interrupting and I can actually get this out. Because this is all background shit. You just have to understand who they are to each other to fully grasp the other things I'm about to tell you." I scootch a little farther from her.

"Fine." She waves her hand regally. "Continue with your deep, dark secrets that probably won't matter to me anyways."

I suck in a deep breath, steeling my nerves. "The city I come from is run differently than Ridgewood. Synd is..."

"Wait." She scrambles to her feet, blocking my view of the pond. "You're telling me you grew up in Synd? Where all the shady shit goes down, but no one can tell what because there's so much fucking money flowing around no one bothers to find out?"

I nod, glancing over my shoulder to make sure no one else is around to overhear us. When I turn back, she's pacing in front of me. She keeps rubbing her hand over her forehead and muttering to herself. I'm sure she'd figure it all out soon enough, but I don't have it in me to wait for her to catch up.

"The city is divided into three sections. To the north is Reaper territory." She raises an eyebrow at me. "They're a motorcycle club. Then to the east of the river is Byrns territory. They're a mafia family. To the west is the other mafia family. It used to be pretty segregated, but things got better after some shit went down. We live in harmony, as cheesy as that sounds."

"The other family...the ones to the west...what's their name?" She already knows, yet she needs my confirmation.

"The Kings. Shane, my brother, officially runs it, but Ren and Alex are pretty much interchangeable with him. Everyone respects their role in the organization. And no one crosses Samantha. She can be scary when she wants to be."

I can't tell Daisy about Sam being the Wraith. I'm surprised she's still standing in front of me. If I told her my pseudo-sister was secretly an assassin, I'm pretty sure she'd shit her pants. Plus, it's not my secret to tell. Sam loves seeing people's faces when she reveals it. Daisy probably wouldn't have the reaction she'd like.

"Let me get this straight. You grew up in the mafia, raised by your brother, and obviously changed your last name. Then you came *here*. Out of all the places you could be, you came to this boring-ass town to go to college."

"Sounds about right. There's more to it, but honestly, you don't need to know my life story before I got here. Just the basics will do." I bite my cheek, worrying the soft flesh. "You don't look like you're about to run away."

"Why would I run away? This is the coolest shit ever," she exclaims, delight stamped across her face.

"It's not nearly as cool as you'd think. I grew up *very* sheltered. There was always a threat hanging over our heads, which made Shane terrified I'd die. It wasn't until Sam came around I was able to get even the slightest bit of freedom. By then, no one at school wanted anything to do with me. It was pretty lonely, actually."

Samantha Byrns falling in love with my brothers was probably the best thing to ever happen to me. Once she started influencing Shane's decisions and telling him he was an asshat who wasn't doing me any favors by isolating me, he eased up. It wasn't a normal childhood by any means. The perfect sitcom families didn't exist in my world. But it was better after she moved in. At the very least, I got trained to fight. Now I can protect myself.

"So, do you know how to, like, hurt someone? If you needed to?"

I chuckle, not at all surprised that's her first actual question. "I can kill a man twice my size six ways to Sunday."

She grins and then her face drops. "Have you been kidnapped?"

Flashes of memories scroll through my mind. Most of them are hazy, the film of childhood obscuring the details. The ones from when the Guild swept through almost over ten years ago, though, are fresh. They're stamped in my mind in invisible ink, only revealing their hideous secrets in the dark of night. It wasn't even what they did to me that was so frightening. No, it was the fear for my family that overrode every other emotion—including regret. And guilt which remains to this day. My shitty decisions led to so much pain and suffering—so much death. It's something I hope never to repeat, if only so those I love never have to feel that pain again.

I swallow hard, my gaze fixed on the shoreline. "A few times. Which is partly why I'm telling you this now."

"Shit, you're not going to get kidnapped are you? Wait, do kidnappers usually announce their intentions?" Her head whips back and forth as if men in ski masks will jump from the bushes.

"No, but I fucked up. Pretty badly, actually. I fucked with the wrong people in town, and I'm afraid they might come for me. Actually, I'm afraid they might come for *you*, which is why you needed to know all this. To keep yourself safe. We need to figure out a way to distance ourselves from each other."

I don't want to lose Daisy's friendship, but I'd rather have her hate me and be alive rather than love me and be dead.

She waves away my concerns and frustration hits me hard. "I'm sure it's nothing. I'll just be extra vigilant or something. And the fact you'd think I'd abandon you in your time of need is insulting, Emma. Honestly."

My stomach turns as I realize this is how Sam must have felt when the Guild came through. She didn't mean for me to get mixed up in their troubles. It's exactly what Shane strived to keep me from for years. I never took the threat seriously. Now that I'm in the same position, the one protecting someone I love, I'm hyperaware of how essential it is to keep her away from my world.

I slowly get to my feet and cross my arms. "You're going to have to trust me on this, Daisy. This isn't the movies. This isn't a book. This is real life. Not everyone gets out alive and many don't get their happily ever afters."

She rolls her eyes and I realize I'm going to have to be harsher. "You can't convince me to abandon you."

"Your loyalty is commendable, but it won't keep your guts in your body. It won't stop someone from cutting off various parts of you, hoping for a tidbit of information on my family. It won't prevent them from doing despicable things to you while they claim their own loyalty to whomever they're working for. You're not prepared for the hell you'll walk through if you stick by my side. And I won't allow you to be used to get to me." I try to keep my mask in place, to seem unaffected and emotionless like Ren or Sam. I never fully mastered it with those important to me.

Her wide eyes find mine as the blood drains from her face. "Did that—"

"I'm not telling you the shit I've been through. You wouldn't sleep for a month if you knew. Just trust me when I say I can't protect you and deal with the shit coming my way. I won't make you pay for my mistakes."

"What did you have in mind?"

Exhaustion pulls at my bones as I sink onto the bench once more. She settles next to me and I go through the plan I've been concocting in my head while I waited for the sun to set. It's not perfect and there's still a chance she'll get caught up in my schemes, but it's better than nothing. It's better than keeping her in the dark. Mostly it involves her tucking tail and running back to her parents' suburban house in a city seven hours from here. It's the best I've got.

When she finally stands, she peers at me as if she's trying to see straight into my soul. "You should call your family. Tell them what's going on."

"I will. When I've figured out how to fix shit, I will."

"You're not a little girl anymore, Emma. You're strong and capable and grown. They'll understand."

I shake my head, not bothering to refute her claims. My brothers love me. I know they do. They won't let me forget how much I fucked up, though. They'll tell me all the ways I went wrong. And they'll insist on riding to my rescue. When they save the day, Shane will demand I come home and I'll be under lock and key once more. I can't live like that anymore.

"Just think about it," she whispers as she hugs me.

I hold her close as long as possible. Then she's gone—back to her life with a little more burden than she came here with. I need to go too, especially with the last of the dying sunlight streaking across the sky. The temps will plummet and I'll end up freezing to death. Eventually, I'll have to get my shit together and deal with the problems I created. Or I could sit on this bench and wait until my world sinks or swims. All I need is a little time.

Just a little longer.

Chapter 2

Titus

As I stalk through the halls of the Kings' mansion, my mind races. It's not unusual to be called to my boss's office, yet I can't shake the feeling that this meeting will be different from others. Tensions have been running high lately. I've been doing my best to mitigate the issues that keep popping up. I'm only one man, though. And I haven't been in this position long enough to actually *know* what to do in these circumstances.

I raise my hand to knock on the heavy wooden doors to Shane King's private office, and my phone buzzes. Gritting my teeth, I pull it out and read the message before pivoting to head to the conference room two floors up and what feels like a half a mile away. The house is massive, taking up at least three city blocks. I could take the secret tunnels this place is riddled with, but they're technically only for emergencies. When I was guarding Emma…

I shake my head, unwilling to go down memory lane. I may have spent several years trailing after her, making sure she wasn't put in any danger, but those days are over. Even if I still wanted the job as her handler, which I don't, she'd pitch a fit about it. After our disastrous last meeting, we barely spoke even though I was still following her to school, to dances, to the mountains.

Before I knew it, I was being reassigned, terrified the Kings would float me. They didn't, but the threat hung over my head until Emma left for college. It was painful when she was in high school. When she took a gap year, it was torture. Stopping myself from protecting her after I was promoted was harder than I anticipated.

I nod to one of my men guarding the conference room, and he scrambles to open the door. He reminds me of myself when I first started working in the mansion. I fucked up more than once, but the worst was when I got duped by Samantha King, although she was Samantha Byrns back then. She grins at me from the other side of the massive table, then goes back to cleaning her nails with a dagger.

"Titus, what's with the lower gangs down south? Byrns keeps talking about a possible infiltration or some shit," Shane King says without looking up. As the head of a mafia family, he doesn't need to subscribe to the niceties of polite society, I suppose.

"There were some rumblings, but it's not as dire as we believed. I sent Wright down there to keep shit from boiling over. He'll be able to calm the tensions bubbling up." I cross my arms, then drop them to my sides again. I shouldn't be nervous doing this shit.

"Wright's got too much time on his hands. And he smiles too much," Alex King grumbles. Technically, he's not the head of the family. Neither is Ren King, but they're close enough. Their orders hold as much weight as Shane's.

"You're just upset he's funnier than you," Ren murmurs, not bothering to look up from his tablet.

"The fuck he is. Plus, he's got that pretty boy air about him. Thinks he's hot shit. One of these days, he's going to get himself into trouble and Titus is going to have to save him."

Sam clears her throat, then nods to me when the others glance her way. Thank fuck there's only them in here. It's probably the only reason they're talking shit about Wright. Unless they're trying to prove a point, they're pretty respectful to those underneath them. It's one of the reasons I was so keen on working for them when I was younger. They may be in the mafia, but they're not tyrants.

Shane leans back in his chair, leveling me with a glare. "Titus won't be able to save his ass. I've got an assignment for you."

"Whatever you need, sir." I clasp my hands behind my back, trying to seem like I'm capable of whatever he requires.

Shane's eyes fall closed as he grinds his teeth, and Sam snorts. "You won't be saying that when he tells you his plan."

"We've been over this, Sam," Shane growls, running his fingers through his dark hair that's started greying at the temples.

She holds up her hands, then glances at me. "Just remember, I'm on your side in this. However, I'm on her side more. Keep that in mind if you try to throw me under the bus."

I have no idea what the hell she's going on about. I nod my head anyway. It's the only reasonable response when it comes to her. Sam King has always been more than meets the eye and I know better than to cross her. If she's on my side, then I must be doing something right.

"We need you to go on a little mission, which clearly Sam thinks is unnecessary. One of us would do it, but that might make things worse. So, we're sending you. You're one of the few people we trust right now," Alex says, completely serious for once.

"Just tell me when, where, and what, and I'll make sure it happens." Nerves turn my stomach and set my veins on fire.

There are a great many things I'm sure they keep from me. I may be the head of their security now, but they're a seamless unit. I'm not privy to their inner conversations. The fact that they're hopelessly in love with Sam helps too, I'm sure. Part of me wishes they would at least talk to me about the shit I need to know instead of waiting until the last minute. It makes my job so much harder than it has to be.

Ren sets down his tablet and I focus on him. "We've received some threats and while *some* of us believe it's nothing to worry about, others feel we should take precautions."

My mask slips as confusion swirls through me. I haven't heard even a whisper about this. "Threats?"

"This is clearly someone from our past rearing their ugly head. Someone we didn't take care of when we should have. They've made threats against Synd and its leaders, as well as those in Rima. We're not taking any chances with those important to the future of our city."

"Of course, sir. I can put out some feelers—"

Shane's hand slashes through the air, cutting me off. "That won't be necessary. Byrns has that under control for the most part. We'll have you assign some of the men under you to help him and Lacey, but other than that, you won't be available."

A chill runs down my spine and I blink slowly. He's going to fire me. No, they don't fire people from the mafia. He's going to float me. Send me straight down the river to be stripped by those living in the Barrens that border the water. Hopefully, my years of service will afford me a quick death.

Mentally, I shake my head to snap myself out of my panicked state. He said I had a mission. He wouldn't say that if he had plans to kill me. They don't beat around the bush when someone has fucked up.

"What exactly will I be doing?" My anxiety loosens my tongue and I immediately regret it. I still haven't learned how to keep my fucking mouth shut, apparently.

Alex winces, and I know I'm fucked. "We need you to go retrieve someone. Most of the kids are sequestered in Reaper territory. They'll be safe up there. We're missing one, though."

"Who?" The question pops out without thought.

I may be head of their security, but I spent a lot of the last few years protecting the various children the leaders have had. They may not see me as family, but those kids don't know anything different. Hell, a lot of them call me uncle. No one stopped them, so I didn't say anything either.

"Shit, no. Not like that." Alex straightens as Sam's head drops into her hands. "Obviously, Helms and Hawk have their kids with them. We sent Pip up there, too. If we need to send them out of Synd, we got a contingency plan."

"Would you shut the fuck up? You'd think after twenty years we would be better at this shit," Ren mutters. "We need you to go get Emma. We've been trying to get ahold of her, but she's screening our calls."

Sam starts talking and the others join in, but their words are muffled. It's as if all the air has been sucked from the room. I've seen Emma since she went to college. She came home every holiday and for breaks. She was here when Hawk and Willow got married. She traveled back to Synd every time someone popped out another baby. It's been well over a year since I've seen her, though. Escorting her prissy ass back here will be a disaster.

My instinct is to say no. I don't have that option. It's not my job to question them. They must be asking me for a reason. I can't even ask them what the fuck that reason is. They don't owe me an explanation.

"You know she's capable of coming back on her own, Shane," Sam mumbles.

"If she'd answer her damn phone, I wouldn't have to send him. I'm not any happier about this than you, Sam."

I clear my throat, hoping I can still find a way out of this. "I have several men who could—"

"I don't trust anyone but you, Titus. You've been here for years, proven yourself. Also, Emma knows you." Shane's eyes darken, his expression at odds with his words. I wonder what the hell Emma told him about what happened when she was a teenager.

"Perhaps I can try to get ahold of her," I say, attempting to infuse my voice with my previous confidence. It doesn't work.

Alex shoves to his feet, absorbed in his phone. He drops a kiss on Sam's head, then disappears into the hidden panel behind her. I'm surprised they all gathered for this, anyway. Alex was my best bet to help solve this dilemma no matter what Sam said earlier. I don't know why they're making me do this. The last thing Emma will do is listen to me.

"You're welcome to try." Ren leans back as well, and now I have two mafia men staring me down. "Though I doubt she'll answer. Besides, we need to make sure she gets here safely."

"She's capable of doing that herself," Sam mumbles.

Shane slams his hand on the table, face flushing a dangerous red. When he drops his head in his hands, I wonder how exhausted he is. He's been running his half of Synd for over ten years now. Being the head of a mafia family, raising

Emma since she was three, and dealing with an organization attempting to overthrow them is sure to take it out of a guy.

"Sorry," Shane mumbles, and my spine snaps to attention. "Old habits. Listen, Titus, you earned your position here, and I know you and Emma had your...issues. Despite the past, you're the only one I trust to send after her since the rest of us have to stay here. They're having their own problems in Rima, and Emma doesn't know any of our other contacts."

"And what if she won't listen to me?"

There lies the ultimate issue. Emma hates me, and for good reason. She's not picking up any of her family's calls. If she's not answering them, I doubt she'll give me the time of day. Unless King gives me full control to do whatever is necessary, I'll fail at this assignment.

"Then toss her over your shoulder and force her. You have full authority, and it wouldn't be the first time you've had to do it," Sam says, a small smirk on her mouth. Shane opens his mouth, then snaps it shut when Sam puts her hand on his arm.

I swear my throat closes and I swallow hard. "That's not what—"

"I know. Remember, I'm on your side. Just don't hurt her and we'll be golden."

"When do I leave?"

"Tomorrow. Alex will fill you in on the specifics later. You can go," Ren dismisses me.

Sam smacks him as I turn and make my way out the door.

Sam's voice floats behind me, chasing my footsteps down the hall. "You're putting a spark to a powder keg by sending him. Emma is going to blow. And I am *not* going to be in the path of that explosion."

I shake my head and it hits me. I'm completely fucked. Shane may have been joking when he suggested I throw Emma over my shoulder, but it's entirely possible that's exactly what will happen. When I became head of security, I thought I wouldn't be in this position again. I thought I'd washed my hands of dealing with Emma King. She's been a pain in my ass and she doesn't give a shit about anyone other than herself. Now that she's being forced into my orbit again, I'll have to deal with her attitude.

Whatever happens, I'll do my job. I'll get her prissy ass back to Synd and get back to what I've been working toward for years. She won't derail me again. As long as I can keep my emotions in check, I'll be back within the week and everything will go back to normal. As normal as life can be in the mafia.

Chapter 3

Emma

"For fuck's sake, Daisy. You can't be following me around. Especially here. Go home." I keep walking down the dark alley while Daisy trails me.

She skips next to me, swinging her hands. "I get that you've got shit going down. But what kind of friend would I be if I didn't stick by your side?"

"You'd be alive," I growl, nervously checking the gun at my hip.

I've been training for this type of shit for years now. The first time I went to training in the mountains, I naively thought it would be fun. Shane kept me from learning anything for so long, thinking he was protecting me. He was right. At least partly. Being in the mountains was its own special kind of torture. I wouldn't have survived if it weren't for Sam. She did more than wrap my wounds and keep up with my training during the school years. She became an emotional support—the missing piece of our family.

"Okay, I don't want to put you in a position where you have to protect me. But I thought I could be your getaway car. You can't do everything by yourself, and I think you should stop trying." Her breath clouds in front of her, and I smirk, trying to imagine her being a smoker.

"This is my problem. I got myself into this mess and I need to be the one who gets myself out of it. You can't help me, Daisy." I sigh as I stop and turn toward her. Dammit. She looks so fucking hopeful. "I'm sorry. I've been through too much—seen too much—to put you in danger. Hell, I shouldn't have befriended you in the first place. You're at risk of being associated with me, and I might not to be able to protect you."

Her face falls the longer I talk. I hate having to push her away, but I don't have a choice. She's become a liability, which makes me feel like a terrible friend. It's not her fault I am who I am. I should have kept to myself when I first started college. Or kept everyone at arm's length like Shane. He's constantly pushing people away, and I never understood why. Now I do. It's easier to cut people off if they're threatened when you have no connection to them.

"I just want to help," she whispers, then clears her throat. "If you're not going to accept my help, then at least call someone. Your brother or his girlfriend."

I wrinkle my name at Sam being called my brother's girlfriend. She's so much more than that. They might not be legally married, but all of them went through a ceremony. The law might not recognize their union, but she belongs to my brothers as much as they belong to her. Hell, she even changed her name from Byrns to King.

"I'll make you a deal. You promise to finish your last class and then get the fuck out of Ridgewood. And I will call Sam."

She gives me a bored look. "We both know that's not good enough. You could call her and tell her about the effing weather. Promise you'll tell her the trouble you're in."

I grit my teeth, glancing down the hallway. "Fine. I promise I will call Sam and tell her what's going on. But I'm not asking her to come here. She's got other shit to worry about that doesn't include saving my ass."

She shuffles back and forth, a nervous habit she picked up freshman year. "Will you at least tell me what kind of trouble you're in? Or how you even got into this mess?"

"Let's just say I should not be left to my own devices."

"Why not?"

"Because they come with prices."

It took another ten minutes to convince Daisy to go home. She kept asking if she should get a gun and whether or not she should shave off the serial number. It was exhausting, but I think I finally got her to understand the danger.

It's not just the current situation. It's all of it. My entire life, really. Shane tried so hard to shield me, and at my first moment of freedom, I threw all that protection away. What he never saw was a realistic future for me. If I want my family in my life, I'll never escape the threats. I'll always be at risk.

I shove the thoughts of my family away, burying them deep within my soul. I'll deal with it all later when I'm not about to burn down a building. Part of me wonders if I should kill the men inside first. I could block the other exits and funnel them out the front door, pick them off as they run from the fire. If any of them get away…

I've snuck all the way to an old shed, leaving a long empty stretch between me and the abandoned gas station. They don't seem to have anyone on lookout, which isn't very smart, but it works in my favor. I'm counting on there being some gas cans I can use to help move along this little endeavor. Blowing up the building won't eliminate my larger issue. Can't hurt, though.

Or this could spiral my life in the worst way. This little stunt could land me in a heap of trouble. Worse than the one I'm already in. I shouldn't have fucked with the local gang. I should have talked to Shane long before it ever got to this point. And now I'm paying for my hubris.

Ducking my head, I run doubled over across the cold tundra. It feels like the space elongates the farther I run. Rationally, I understand it's my mind tricking me, like a dream I can't get away from. Doesn't stop my heart from racing, though. Thankfully, I make it to the corner of the building without much fanfare. The rest should be easy.

A shiver runs through me at the thought. Sam's warnings roll through my head. She always told me not to get too cocky, don't get ahead of myself, don't focus on the end result, focus on where I currently am. All things I struggle with, apparently. Shane calls me reckless. Ren says I don't think before I act. And Alex says I rush into things. Sam's way sounds so much better, even though they're saying the same things.

I peek into one of the windows. A soft light filters through, yet I can only make out shadows through the haze covering the glass. If I lived closer to Synd, I'd have swiped something to drop into the building. Then again, if I lived closer, I probably wouldn't be in this mess. Actually, Shane would have figured out what the hell I've been up to and stepped in long before it got to this. Blowing up buildings would definitely not be his first step. I guess it wasn't mine either.

Muffled shouting rings out from within, and I duck. I can't make out what they're yelling about. At least they don't know they're about to go boom. Grabbing a half-full can, I adjust my grip twice before tipping it. I splash the gasoline along the base of the wall as I walk to the back. I drop the empty can by the far corner and search the area for another one. Fifty feet isn't enough to make the whole thing go up. I'll need to slip inside and hope there's something I can use to my advantage.

"Bitch doesn't know what's coming. I know we're supposed to wait for orders, but I say we go have some fun first. What they gonna do, take us out?" I can't place the man's accent. It's not from around here.

"They *will* kill us, no questions asked. We're expendable, which you would know if you grew up in this life. I don't know what you mean by 'fun,' but you'll end up six feet under if you go within thirty feet of Baker." The other man coughs after his little tirade.

I jolt, wondering who the hell they're talking about. Then I remember that's the name they know me by. Lacey suggested an alias to keep my connections to Synd secret. I didn't like it at the time. I'm not ashamed of where I came from. Lacey convinced me after she said it would protect my family. No matter what it takes, I'll always choose their safety above my own. So I took the name Baker and prayed no one would connect the dots.

"We could just scare her a little. Doesn't look like it would take much to have her scurrying for cover like a scared little rabbit." The first man laughs raucously.

I snort, then cover my mouth to smother the sound. I'm not surprised they think I'm a docile creature. Taking a page from Sam's book, I cultivated a personality to make me seem less than I am. Hopefully, no one will remember me when I finally go home.

I find another can and spread it along the back of the building. It's not nearly enough and I'm kicking myself for not thinking ahead. I didn't plan on blowing it up when I set out. Maybe I should abandon this whole endeavor. Bouncing on the balls of my feet, my mind races, contemplating what to do. I could walk away, call Shane, and beg for him to come help me. I could call Sam—she'd be here before we got off the phone.

My gaze lands on a chain coiled next to the back door. Quietly, I unravel the links, pausing to make sure they're still talking inside. It's not easy to secure the length around the handles of the door, but it should block the way out. Another cluster of gas cans sits a few feet away and I skip toward them. Armed with two plastic containers, one slightly heavier than the other, I finish splashing old gasoline on the perimeter of the station. It's not large, thank fuck, or I would have run out. Actually, I have no idea if this will even light. I probably should have done some of Sam's homework when she told me to.

When I reach the front, I realize I won't be able to sneak in to rig up anything else. The men are clustered in the back where cars were worked on, yet there's a huge bay door facing me. I won't be able to close and secure it quickly enough if they're chasing after me.

I sigh, leaning against the stone wall. The cold seeps into me and I close my eyes. This would be a lot easier if I had someone with me. Daisy wouldn't have been any help, but at least I'd have someone to talk to.

I double back and find the side door I've already secured. Undoing my work is much harder and I wish I would have thought it through. I scowl, the lecture from one of my brothers running through my mind on repeat. Finally, I get the chain off and set it on the ground. I'm hoping the room I'm sneaking into doesn't have an open view to the men.

Slowly, I ease the heavy metal open enough to slip through. The space is cluttered with shelves holding random car parts I can't name. Tucked away in the corner is an old water heater. I'm too short to see the top, but I doubt it matters. Searching the small area, I find some tools. I'm not about to bludgeon them to death.

I close my eyes, attempting to channel my trainers or Sam, or hell, even Alex. They'd be able to find something to use. Instead, I'm left with a whole bunch of gears and a rusty old water heater. None of which will help unless I can find a pipe bomb mostly assembled within this mess.

Sighing, I resign myself to lighting the outside of the building on fire and hoping the propane tank sitting just outside will blow too. Why did I ever think this was a good idea? Fucking hubris always fucking up my plans.

I turn to slip out the door again and pause when I catch a whiff of a familiar cloying smell. Glancing to my left, I pull in a deep breath, the pungent aroma of gas filling my lungs. It's not as potent as I'm used to, but it's enough to have me shuffling toward the corner.

My arm brushes the pipes on the water heater, rust flaking off as it rattles. Gross. I freeze, closing my eyes to hear better. The low rumble of voices from behind the door continues without a beat.

I sniff again, trying to pinpoint the source of the leak. That's the only thing it could be unless someone dumped a can right here in the corner. The entire place has a faint scent of gasoline. I'm surprised I even caught this. I crouch, finding a metal pipe jutting from the base of the tank. I know next to nothing about these things, but I'd put cash money on this being a gas line. A large nut holds the metal in place, and I bite my lip. I might not be strong enough to get it off completely.

"I really should have done that fucking homework," I mutter. Sam probably didn't think I'd be using a water heater, though.

A block of C4 would be perfect right about now. Or that random pipe bomb. I'm sure if I was smarter, I could use some of these parts to create a makeshift bomb so I don't blow myself up, too. A gas leak doesn't do much good if I can't set it on fire without killing myself in the process.

Raised voices inside have me whipping my head around.

"Get the fucking beer while you're up there," someone yells.

As the footsteps approach, I scramble behind the wooden door. With no window, I'll have to rely on my other senses to gauge where he is. I hold my breath and slip my knife from the sheath at my wrist. Hiding and not being spotted would be infinitely better than stabbing him. Bottles rattle right outside and I jump when something hits the wall by my head.

"There's only one bottle of vodka left." His muffled voice seeps under the door.

With one more kick against the wall, his footsteps fade away. I wish I could sit around and drink. The thought pulls me up short, and a grin spreads across my face. Vodka isn't the best for the idea that just popped into my head, but it's a bottle. I swallow hard before sidling along the wall and wrap my hand around the knob.

It creaks as I spin it, then clicks, and I ease the door open. No shouts, no gunfire, no pounding feet. Thank fuck they didn't put their shit in my path or the wood would have sent it flying across the concrete. I snatch up the bottle and quickly shut the door again. My heart hammers in my chest and I press my fist between my tits. I should have worn a bra. Maybe that would have helped.

My smile returns as I empty some of the alcohol onto the floor, leaving a trail from the side door to the water heater. I wrinkle my nose, then take a swig. My throat burns as the liquor slides to my empty stomach. I'm not a big drinker, but I need the extra confidence it'll give me. I take one more shot before setting about finding the rest of the shit.

Two grease-stained cloths and some tape later and I have a makeshift Molotov cocktail. It's one of the first things Sam taught me how to make. It's not perfect, but I don't have any napalm handy. It'll do and that's what matters. I set it gently next to the side door, hoping I don't knock it over.

I spend the next several minutes searching for a wrench that might loosen the nut. I find one I hope will work and rush back to the corner. It's a little too big, but I don't have any other options. I can't exactly hammer the shit out of it. The men would hear that for sure. Fucking gang members. If they just would have left me alone, none of us would be in this situation. We'd be living our best lives and they wouldn't have to die. Fuckers.

I'm sweating by the time I loosen the nut more. The leak whistles, filling the room to an intoxicating level. If I don't get out of here, I'll pass out before long. Shuffling to the door, I glance around once more. This might not be enough to harm them, especially if the gasoline outside is a fail.

Eyeing the shelf next to me, I huff. I hold open the door with my ass, thanking whichever god decided to give me a little extra padding in the back. I hold the Molotov as far away from the room as possible, then set my foot on the middle shelf. I pull in a deep breath, letting the tension flow from me, mixing with the accelerant filling up the room. Maybe it'll give it that last little nudge.

Flicking the lighter, I count to three, then set it to the rag. As soon as the flame catches, I toss it into the room, then shove away, using the shelf as momentum. I trip, almost landing on my knees as the shelf tumbles to the ground and the glass shatters. The door slams shut, cutting off the men's yells of alarm. A deafening boom quickly overtakes everything else.

I don't stop, my arms windmilling as I attempt to stay upright while stumbling away. The metal door flies off as another explosion hits and the force sends me flying. I can feel the skin being filleted from my palms, and I grit my teeth against the pain. My leggings rip away as my knees slide along the gravel. Thank fuck I took my last test earlier today. It'll be a good long while before I can write again.

The ringing in my ears should worry me, but I'm too focused on trying to get away. The water heater and Molotov might not be enough. I need to get far enough away so I can pick them off.

The farther I stumble along, the less sure I am of my plan. It was a piss-poor one and now I've opened myself up to retaliation. Unless they assume it was an accident. They *were* hiding out in an abandoned gas station.

I reach the shed, ducking behind it when the trail of gasoline I splashed along the outside catches. Peeking around the corner, I fixate on the front door, willing the chains to hold. There are only a couple lights illuminating the area, one shining directly over their escape route. I mumble under my breath, begging whoever will listen to stick with me just a little bit longer.

A clicking sound ringing through the night is my only warning. I hide once more behind the shed as the sky lights up.

"Shit," I breathe, gaze on the sky as it turns a brilliant orange.

We may be a fair ways away from town, but someone is sure to notice a fucking fireball rolling through the night sky. I need to get away. I can't tell if the ringing in my ears has protected me from what I'm sure was a ridiculously loud boom. Or maybe the heat distracted my other senses. Whichever it is, I start to jog toward the tree line.

"Big bada boom," I murmur, then giggle.

A shadow detaches from the darkness, stepping from behind a tree. I jolt to a stop, reaching for my weapon. Maybe it's the way he stands, or the tilt of his head, but I'm pretty sure I know him. As soon as he opens his mouth, I'm scowling.

"What the fuck did you do, Emma King?"

Chapter 4

Titus

The entire ride to Ridgewood, I sulked. The last thing I want to do is schlep Emma fucking King around the goddamn state, attempting to get her to come home. According to Ren, she's still not answering her phone. He's been tracking her, because of course he has. She hasn't left the city, but he noticed her lurking in some seedy places. Despite that, I didn't expect to find her walking away from a burning building.

My palms itch to grab and shake her. She merely stands there, gaping at me as if I'm an illusion. Part of me wants to throw her over my shoulder right now. No discussion. No excuses. No chance for her to explain herself. My bosses—her family—wants her home and my only job is to get her there. It isn't to clean up her goddamn messes. I'm not a fucking babysitter, though that's exactly what I was relegated to for years.

I can't act on those impulses. She'll use them against me later, just like she did when she stood in my room and...

I stop the thought in its tracks, refusing to relive that night. "Answer the fucking question."

She rolls her eyes as she loops around me, trying to keep a healthy amount of space between us. I'm sure she thinks I'll grab her, but the last thing I actually want to do is touch her. It would be a very bad idea for several reasons I'll never fully acknowledge.

"You can't just run away from your problems, darling," I growl as I pivot and follow her. She doesn't even slow, merely slipping between the trees.

If she keeps stomping in this direction, we have at least a mile of walking before we reach the road. She glances over her shoulder and her brows pull low. Whipping her head back, she almost trips over a fallen log. I'm reaching out before I even realize, but she rights herself and hops over it.

Something's not right. I'm not surprised she's ignoring me. This is more than that, though. It was almost as if she didn't know I was still here. I crash after her, purposefully making as much noise as possible. Not once does she turn around. She doesn't even flinch when I toss a rock right behind her.

When I snatch at her arm, she startles, then swings her fist around. It connects with my jaw. I hate to admit it's a good hit, solid enough to loosen my grip. She spins, readying to hit me again, and I hold up my hands. We've only sparred once and I don't plan on repeating the experience. Confusion splashes across her face and alarm bleeds into me. Something isn't right.

"Why are you following me?" she shouts, and my spine snaps straight.

"Shit," I breathe, running my hand through my hair. "You can't hear me, can you?"

Her gaze fixates on my lips and her eyes narrow. "Course I can. What the fuck do you want, Titus?"

She responds just a beat too late to be believable. I shake my head and sigh. There's no point talking to her, much less in the middle of the forest with only the moon lighting our way. I gesture for her to lead the way, and she scoffs before continuing. We walk in silence for at least ten minutes. My hand hovers between us the entire time, ready to catch her. She's swaying and stumbling her way forward.

The blast must have affected her much more than I expected. I should have helped, stepped in long before she blew shit up. But I couldn't bring myself to do it. I got to Ridgewood an hour before she left her apartment and waited for her to appear. I was going to confront her then, but when she finally graced the world with her presence, she wasn't dressed for a party or a last-minute study session. Honestly, she looked like Sam on her way to bring vigilante justice to our enemies as the Wraith.

We reach the dirt road and I resign myself to another five-mile walk. I should have brought a car. Emma was walking, though, so I was as well. I'm used to exercise and work out in the basement of the King house regularly. This is excessive—walking almost twenty miles in a night. I'm surprised Emma isn't struggling, especially since I'm pretty sure she's injured. She keeps batting at her ears, though she's trying to be subtle about it.

I sigh, stopping at the edge of the forest. Tipping my head back, I stare at the stars. They look the same as back home. I don't know why I expected them to be different. It's the same night sky, the same stars marching through the night, the same moon lighting the way. We're not that far away from Synd, yet it feels like a completely different world.

When I glance back to the road, Emma has disappeared. Whipping my head back and forth, I search for where she could have gone. My chest tightens and I pull in a deep breath to calm myself. No fucking way am I going back to Synd saying I fucking lost her.

I rush across the road to check the ditch. If she hit her head at the gas station and has passed out now, I need to figure shit out. The last thing I'm going to do is take the fall for her ridiculous choices. I'd be better off running than returning. I ignore the stab of pain in my chest at the thought.

The ditch is empty, because of course my life wouldn't be that easy. I widen my search, never straying far from the road. After ten minutes, I have my phone in my hand, ready to call someone. Who the hell am I supposed to reach out to? Anyone I'd normally call will float me merely because I lost Emma within an hour of finding her. I could reach out to one of the other leaders, but they've got their own shit they're dealing with.

I pull up Emma's number. I've never used it, though I was tempted when she was younger. The number of texts I started and erased before they were ever sent isn't something I like to think about. I shake my head, then call her. It rings over and over while I keep half an ear for her phone vibrating in the area. She might be passed out in the trees and her phone might be the only way to find her. I wish I had her location, but she turned it off when she went to college.

I end the call with a curse, then curse again when the rumble of an engine splits the night. I slip behind a tree, peeking around the trunk to see who appears. If it's someone who escaped the blast, I'll be forced to take them out myself. Fuck Emma King for dragging me into her drama.

Headlights appear from the direction of town, and I duck into the shadows. Someone is probably coming to investigate the fireball Emma sent into the air. I have to find her and get us the fuck out of here before they widen their search. A four-door sedan whips around, then idles on the other side of the road, right where Emma disappeared.

When the passenger door pops open, I hold my breath, gripping my phone so hard I'm worried it might crack. I slip it into my pocket and scowl when Emma's blonde hair catches the moonlight as she rounds the trunk. Stepping from the shadows, I bite my cheek to keep from cussing her out. I scramble up the embankment with as much dignity as I can muster while slipping on the wet grass.

She smirks, leaning against the car as I approach.

"What the fuck is wrong with you?" I growl.

She rolls her eyes, then hooks her thumb over her shoulder, and makes her way back to the passenger seat. The woman behind the wheel gives me a half-hearted wave. At least the car is warm. Wearing just a sweatshirt and jeans wasn't my best choice tonight. My hands are icicles and I stuff them into my front pocket in my desperation to warm them up.

"Hi, I'm Daisy," the driver says as she pulls forward. Emma's grip on her leg looks painful, and I smirk. "Are you from Emma's hometown?"

"Don't talk to him," Emma yells, and Daisy jerks the wheel, then straightens out.

"Why are you yelling still? Seriously, girl. Get a grip."

"I believe she injured her hearing," I murmur, my eyes fixed on Emma.

"What the hell? Seriously?" Daisy shrieks. At least this time she keeps the car mostly on the road. "How the hell did she do that?"

Emma glances between us, desperately trying to follow the conversation. She narrows her eyes at me and I flip her off. It's juvenile, but I'm done playing games with her.

"I suspect she was too close to the blast when she blew up the abandoned gas station back there."

I turn my head, watching the trees give way to a few houses. Ridgewood isn't very large compared to Synd. It'll probably be a while before someone from a neighboring city comes out to figure out what the orange glow in the sky is. I'm surprised more people aren't on their porches with their eyes fixed to the east. I've heard small-town folks do that sort of thing.

Daisy grumbles under her breath, sorting through her emotions. Ignoring Emma isn't as easy as I thought it would be. I keep glancing out the corner of my eye at her. I thought after all these years of barely being around one another, of not seeing her every day, her effect on me would dull. Unfortunately, it hasn't. I've succeeded in burying it under years of bitterness, yet it still lingers.

When she was just a kid, I didn't mind hanging out with her. Sure, she was naive—what kid isn't? And when she confessed her feelings, there was no fucking way I was going to say anything other than no. I always admired her, though. No matter what I told myself, I could never fully hate her. Which is something I'll have to live with. Hating her would be so much easier.

"Are we going anywhere particular?" Daisy practically screams and I jolt.

"Why the hell are you yelling?" Emma asks, her brows pulled low. Thank fuck she's not screaming anymore. "Just drop me at the spot."

I grit my teeth, glancing out the window again. Clearly, Emma is going to go to her apartment. And she doesn't want me there. Too bad she doesn't realize I've already been to her place. It's amazing how much of her other life she's erased. I thought I'd be able to pick up the subtle ways she brought Synd to her life at college, but there was nothing. Not a spare blade or a single piece of black clothing. It's as if she's living two different lives.

Daisy pulls up to a curb about three blocks away from Emma's apartment and taps her fingers on the steering wheel. Her eyes keep darting to the rearview mirror. I push from the car, unwilling to explain to some random woman who the hell I am or what I'm doing. Slamming the door, I make it three steps before I pivot and knock on Daisy's window. Her gaze widens as she rolls down the glass, but not too far. I resist the urge to roll my eyes.

"Thank you for the ride. Hopefully, we won't cross paths again." I walk away before she can respond.

I don't need to trail after Emma. She'll probably end up chitchatting with her friend for a while. I'm not going to hang around waiting for her. My job is to get her back to Synd. The sooner I do that, the sooner I can wash my hands of her. The more time I'm forced to spend with her, the more she'll worm her way in. She has that way about her. Which will only make me hate her a little less with every interaction. I won't be sucked into her orbit, only to lose myself.

"You're a fucking asshole," Emma bellows as I slip into the shadows.

"Tell me something I don't already know, darling."

Chapter 5

Emma

I wave at Daisy's retreating car, wondering how much I've damaged our relationship. She didn't have a problem picking my ass up. I've put her in a precarious position, but I didn't have a choice. I wasn't about to walk the entire way back to Ridgewood. Not with Titus following me. I would have told him off, but I couldn't hear a damn word he was saying. The less I spoke, the less likely he'd figure out how bad it was. My right ear still has a muffled block in it, but the left has a ringing that isn't going away.

I'll have to call Ink, the doctor for the Reapers, if it doesn't go away after a few days. At least my palms aren't as bad as I thought they were. I doubt Ink would rat me out to anyone unless I catch him in a bad mood. Then he'd inform MacKenzie, who would turn around and tell Sam and I'd be in the shit. She'd probably come up here herself to drag my ass back home.

The thought has me jolting to a stop on the empty sidewalk.

"What the fuck," I breathe.

That's why Titus is here. I assumed he was merely checking up on me, or Shane got pissed off enough that I wasn't picking up my phone. I knew if I talked to my brother, he'd notice some inflection in my voice and realize I'd gotten myself into trouble. Part of me was hoping Titus got fired. He'd probably be dead if that happened. He wouldn't be randomly following me around.

"Not so fucking random. Fucking bastard thinks he can come here and just march me home like I'm some kid," I grumble under my breath as I climb the emergency stairs at the back of my building. They don't quite reach my window, which was by design.

I sigh, shaking out my hands before I climb onto the railing and inch along the lip of the bricks. I hum a soft tune to take my mind off the image of me falling to my death. Three stories might not actually kill me, and I've been doing this for almost four years now. I still sing to distract myself, though. No use fucking with something that's worked thus far.

The wood groans as I push the sash up, and I hold my breath for ten seconds, waiting for one of my neighbors' lights to flick on. They stay dark and I slip inside. I breathe a sigh of relief at being home. The apartment is small and not nearly as fancy as the mansion, but at least it's comfy. And safe. That's the most important part. Lacey installed the security system and showed me how to check for hidden cameras. I thought it was overkill at the time. Now I'm just thankful I have people in my life who care.

I strip off my black sweatshirt, tossing it in the corner of my bedroom. My long sleeve shirt is next, blending into my dark comforter. I'll regret not taking care of them right away, but most of my muscles ache and I can't be bothered. Thankfully, I know my apartment like the back of my hand and can navigate the space with my eyes closed. Otherwise, I'd be banging into every piece of furniture I've acquired since I got here. Shane wanted to set me up in the posh apartments by the college with brand-new everything. He wasn't happy when I refused, saying I needed to make my own way. Our compromise was him sending me a stipend for rent, which always seems to be triple what I actually pay. I suspect Sam talked some sense into him, but she can only do so much.

I stop in the doorway and shimmy off my pants, leaving me in only a pair of underwear and no bra. Thick curtains cover the windows and I'm in the top apartment, so I'm not worried anyone is spying on me. I crack my neck as I shuffle through the living area. Exhaustion weighs me down and I swear my shower is whispering sweet nothings to me.

The lamp next to my couch flicks on and I jolt, reaching for a weapon I no longer have on me. It takes a few seconds to process what I'm seeing—Titus fucking Prince sitting on my couch, an emotionless mask over his features as he stares at me. I plant my hands on my hips, glaring at him. The fucking audacity of this man. His gaze travels the length of my body, probably filing away images for his spank bank.

"Have you seen enough or do you want me to pose?" I snarl, raising my eyebrow.

"You shouldn't walk around your apartment naked. Anyone could have slipped in and now you're at a disadvantage." There's no inflection in his voice. He could be imitating an emergency broadcaster.

"First of all, if you think this"—I wave my hand down my body—"is naked, then perhaps it's been too long since you've been laid. Second of all, the only way you could have gotten in was if someone gave you the code. And if you still think you could have broken in without me knowing, perhaps you'd like to go out and try again without that little addition."

I pray he takes the bait. Lacey showed me how to reset the code if I needed. It would take me thirty seconds, tops. If I can just get him out, I can pretend this night never happened. Titus waltzing back into my life was not on my bingo card for this year. I thought I'd have to deal with him at Christmas, but I've gotten pretty good at avoiding him.

Despite my hatred toward him, my body still reacts as his heated gaze skips down to my chest. I won't delude myself into thinking he finds me attractive. He made himself perfectly clear I wasn't anything close to what he was looking for and I never would be. I wouldn't have blamed him if he would have said I was too young. *I* knew he was too old for me. I made a mistake telling him anything. He didn't have to go scorched earth on my entire existence. Bastard. He tore me down so completely it took me years to rebuild myself into who I am today. I won't let him make me feel inadequate ever again.

"Put some fucking clothes on. I'm not doing this while you flaunt your body."

"I'm in *my* apartment, fucker. If I want to walk around in a goddamn clown costume, I will. Whatever you need to say, just fucking spill it out so I can take a shower." I cross my arms, not to hide anything from his view because he can deal. I'd rather he didn't notice the trembling in my hands, though. The adrenaline from earlier tonight is bleeding from me faster than I thought it would.

"It's spit it out, but fine. Pack your shit and let's go. We're leaving tomorrow morning." He pushes from the couch. I'm sure he's trying to be smooth about it, but that thing is more sunken than an air mattress with a slow leak in it. Part of me wants to laugh. I won't give him the satisfaction of taking any of my joy, even if it's at his expense.

"Unfortunately for you, I have plans. So I'll pass."

"The fuck you will. Your brother wants you home. And apparently you're too much of a bitch to pick up his phone calls. So, we can do this the easy way or the hard way. Either way, your ass is going back to Synd tomorrow. The sooner we get this shit over with, the sooner I don't have to deal with your spoiled ass anymore."

Each one of his insults chips away at the wall around my heart. I carefully constructed it day after day, hoping to give myself time to heal. All it did was temporarily seal it behind a flimsy sheet of glass—always waiting for the right moment to shatter. I refuse to go back to that meek little girl who didn't know how to defend herself. His words can only hurt me if I let them.

He won't leave my apartment until I agree, though. It's not that I want to stay here. I planned on going to Synd in a couple months, anyway, as long as Sam said Titus was gone. I miss home no matter what my current behavior suggests. Explaining to Titus I have things to do, loose ends to tie up, won't deter him. He's nothing if not efficient and endlessly loyal to Shane—to the whole family, really. He'll tie me up and force me into a trunk if need be. So, I'll play along, act like the meek, scared girl he's expecting. And then I'll disappear.

"Why?" I ask, because I can't just give up easily. He'll see right through me.

"Whatever you need to know, your brother can tell you. I'm not a fucking carrier pigeon." He saunters to the kitchen, his arrogance on full display. Ripping open the front door, he pauses, then glances over his shoulder. "Be ready by eight. Or does her highness need more beauty sleep than that?"

"As a matter of fact—"

"Too fucking bad. Be ready or I'll take you just like that," he sneers, waving his hand at my state of undress.

My nipples harden and I tell myself it's from the chill in the apartment and not his statement about taking me. "Bold of you to assume I'd be upset about that."

There's a glint in his eyes, but he turns before I can read him. I used to be so good at reading him. No, I *thought* I was good at reading him. I *thought* we were friends. Apparently, we were nothing more than two people shoved together in an impossible situation. I'll never be anything other than a spoiled bitch who needed someone to babysit her, and he happened to draw the short straw.

"Keep whatever kinky shit you've engaged in to yourself. You want to be a whore here in Ridgewood, be my guest. But don't fucking bring that shit back to Synd."

He's gone before I can respond. Not that I'd know what to say. He doesn't even have the decency to slam the door. He had no expression on his face—no inflection in his voice—the entire time he was here. Even when he was insulting me and bossing me around, there was nothing. Not until the very end, and it wasn't even enough for me to fully understand what he was thinking. He's too in control to slam the door. Completely unfazed by anything I do.

I shouldn't have to deal with his bullshit. The fact that Shane sent *him* of all people baffles me. I wonder if Sam knows. She's been the one to subtly shift Titus away from me when I'm home. All through the years, she was there. She's the one who talked me through when Titus broke my heart.

Marching toward the bathroom, I spot a small cake on the tiny island in the kitchen. Titus must have brought it, but it isn't a gift from him. Marie must have made him bring it. I'd dig into the culinary perfection now, except Titus's words still linger in the air, making my stomach twist.

"He didn't break your heart, Emma. Because he never actually had it. You had a silly little crush. Nothing more, nothing less. You're a grown-ass woman and you're not going to let him affect you." My pep talk doesn't help.

It wasn't a silly little crush. At its core, it was so much more. At that moment in my life, Titus was my only friend. He was my confidant, my rock, my shadow. I couldn't imagine a world without him. Because he was always there.

And then he wasn't. As embarrassed and upset as I was at him, ultimately it was my fault. I imploded my own world. I fucked up my own life so completely by spilling my guts about something I knew would never happen. He shouldn't have been such a dick about it, but I brought it upon myself. If I would have kept my mouth shut...

I sigh, stepping into the shower and turning the water on. The cold spray hits me, chilling me to the bone. Numbness spreads through me and I shut off my thoughts, concentrating on my blood racing through my veins, my heart pounding in my chest, and my breath heaving from my lungs. Titus Prince doesn't matter. Not in the grand scheme of things. I have more important issues to worry about. As the water warms, I close my eyes and start to figure out how to dodge Titus tomorrow.

By the time I slip between my sheets, I have a plan. I smile into the dark. If everything goes as expected, he won't know what hit him. He may not have been totally at fault for my downward spiral ten years ago, but he did enough. The more I can fuck with him before he drags me home, the better.

Chapter 6

Titus

Emma's scream catapults me off her ridiculously uncomfortable couch. My elbows hit the ground, saving me from bashing my nose. My balls aren't so lucky. Somehow, the right one gets pinched between my thigh and the floor. I groan and roll, kicking my leg out. My foot connects with an end table, sending the lamp crashing to the floor.

"What the hell are you doing?" she yells as a pillow hits me in the face.

"Shut the fuck up," I gasp, rubbing at my crotch.

"I swear to all that is fucking holy," she growls and her bare foot jacks me in the side. "Who the hell do you think you are? And how did you get back into my apartment?"

I grab her foot and tug, expecting her to fall, but she twists. Because of course she knows how to get out of this shit. Her hands slap against the floor, and she breaks free. Her heel slams into my ribs again and I grunt. I'm not about to get into a physical altercation with her. It's not worth it. I'm not worried she'll beat me, but if I bring her home with a bunch of bruises, Shane will have my head.

She kicks me one last time, and I launch to my feet. "Knock it the fuck off, Emma. I told you, we're leaving today."

"So you decided to crash on my couch? What are you, a drunk frat boy? For fuck's sake." She swats her hair out of her face. The frizzy strands fall over her forehead and she huffs. I refuse to be distracted by her in any way, shape, or form. No matter how enthralling she is.

"We both know you were going to slip out the window or some shit. Where's your bag?" Just like I'm not going to get into a fight with her, I'm not going to argue either. She can do that on her own time.

"I'm not rushing just because you got your panties in a bunch. Why don't you go get some coffee and—"

"As if I'll fall for that shit. Get your shit together and let's go. You've got"—I check my phone, ignoring the two dozen notifications—"thirty-seven minutes. Use it wisely."

Her nose flares as she glares at me while I plop on the couch once more. She opens her mouth, then snaps it shut when she thinks better of arguing with me. She marches toward the kitchen and snatches up the cake I brought.

Stomping to her bedroom door, she shakes her head erratically and I smirk. She may piss me off a majority of the time, but at least it's fun riling her up. A frustrated noise leaves her before she traipses through.

"And don't escape out the window," I call.

The door slams behind her, and I roll my eyes. It's been more than ten years since I met her and she's still a fucking brat. A minute later, a scream erupts from her bedroom, and I grin as I work through my text messages. I brace myself for her to come out and berate me, but the knob doesn't move. Emma may be able to slip in and out of places she shouldn't be, but it's a lot harder when her path is interrupted by a bunch of grease smeared everywhere. She can't complain I didn't warn her not to go out the window.

My phone buzzes and Ren's name pops up. I ignored all their calls yesterday when I was tracking Emma, and I'm sure he's not happy about it. I heave from the deep cushions, vowing to never sit in the death trap again, and wander to the small kitchen.

"King," I mumble, hoping Emma can't overhear me.

"Prince, what's your status?" Ren isn't one to beat around the bush, thank fuck. He's also not one to scold me like a child because I didn't get permission to go off-grid for a bit. Out of all of them, he trusts me the most. At least I think he does. He's not exactly easy to read.

"She's packing now. Should be back in Synd by the afternoon." I pace back and forth, my stomach flipping as it always does when I'm talking to one of the Kings.

The silence on his end stretches until I'm glancing at the screen to make sure the line is still connected. His pause could mean a million different things, none of which I fully understand. I know better than to break the stillness, though. I'm acutely aware of my position within their organization and it doesn't permit me to interrupt or demand things.

He clears his throat. "We've had more threats. While the others feel as if bringing her back to Synd is the best course of action, you will protect her at all costs regardless of whether you return her. I understand that. Make sure whatever shit she's involved in gets resolved before you bring her back."

The line goes dead before I can respond and I slip my phone in my pocket. I brace my hands on the counter and hang my head. Ren knows more than he's letting on, which pisses me off. I don't want to get involved in her bullshit. It isn't my fucking job to clean up her messes. I don't particularly enjoy him dropping all he did in just a few sentences, either. The only reason I would protect her is for the family. Why Ren thinks it's common knowledge doesn't make sense. Unless it's merely our past. I did spend several years putting my life on the line for her.

If I'm expected to take care of whatever the fuck she's mixed up with before bringing her home, I'll need to get what the problem is out of her. That feat will probably be harder than actually dealing with anything else. Especially if I can get her to not blow up anything else while I'm here. From her little display, I doubt she'll listen to reason.

A firm knock at the door has me straightening, every muscle in my body tensing. I doubt those who threatened the Kings would knock if they came after Emma. I'm still not willing to risk it. I slip my gun from the holster at my back and tuck it into the front pocket of my hoodie, then sidle toward the small entryway. There's no peep hole and I don't have access to the hidden cameras yet.

I glance over my shoulder before opening the door. The smile on the other man's face dies when he sees I'm not Emma. Neither of us speaks as we size each other up. Or maybe that's just me. He looks like he's still deciding whether to shit his pants or blow a gasket. My money's on him shitting. I tower over him by a good six inches. His cardigan sweater-vest and khaki slacks aren't helping him in the slightest.

"Can I help you?" I ask after a full minute.

"Uh, is...uh...Emma. Is Emma here?"

What a twitchy little fucker. "Emma who?"

Confusion splashes across his face. "Emma Baker?"

"That a question or an answer, Twitch?" He doesn't pick up on my insult as he tries to peek around me.

"Who the fuck are you?"

I smirk, amused at his sudden backbone. Too little, too late. I'd love to fuck with him some more, but I have more important things to do—like get Emma to confess what the hell she's been up to. I swing the door shut and his foot shoots out, wedging his expensive loafer into the opening.

"What the hell are you doing?" Emma hisses, shoving me out of the way. She's a lot stronger than I gave her credit for. "Devon, what are you doing here?"

He shuffles from one foot to the other, eyes bouncing to me. He fixes his gaze on Emma and crowds into her space. It's subtle, but she tenses, her body leaning away. Whoever this fucker is, Emma clearly doesn't want him around.

She glares at me, gesturing with her head for me to back up. I huff out a chuckle, but it's more annoyed than I wanted. If she wants to deal with Twitch on her own, so be it.

I stalk to the kitchen to make some coffee. I should be making sure she's actually packing instead of cleaning off the grease from her window. Being close in case Twitch makes a shitty decision is more important. We're clearly not heading back to Synd today, so it doesn't really matter if she's got her shit together.

"The better question is, what is *he* doing here, Emma? And at this time of the morning," he mutters.

"First of all, you know I hate it when you avoid my question in favor of your own. And second of all, that's none of your business. What do you want? And why did you bring flowers?" Her tone wavers between annoyance and anger.

He runs his fingers through his light brown hair, yet it falls back into place, perfectly coiffed. Little prick probably styles it to within an inch of its life. I wonder how long it takes him to get ready in the morning.

His entire demeanor changes, going from a jealous asshat to perfect frat boy in the span of two seconds. "You took your last test and I wanted to congratulate you. I'm so proud of you."

He goes in for a hug, but she pulls back even farther and whispers, "We're not together anymore, Devon. You can't just show up and bring me flowers."

"You said we could still be friends."

"Yes, but not if you don't respect my boundaries. Which means you have to text if you want to stop by."

I narrow my eyes, studying his features. He seems crushed—utterly heartbroken by her rejection. It's almost undetectable, but the tightening around his eyes says something else. It's as if he's playing at being the distraught ex-boyfriend rather than actually grieving the loss of their relationship.

I didn't even know she was seeing someone, much less someone who would bring her flowers. Twitch is the exact opposite of every man Emma grew up around. Maybe that was his appeal, though. Growing up in the mafia, she's seen some shit. Devon here is probably the safest option out there.

She sighs, taking the flowers he holds out. "Thank you for the flowers. I appreciate you thinking of me."

Like an eager puppy, he perks up at her concession. "Do you want to go get coffee?"

She bites her lip and glances at me from the corner of her eye. I shake my head imperceptibly. No fucking way am I letting her go anywhere with Twitch. In fact, after last night, she's not leaving my sight. She'd better get real comfortable living in my back fucking pocket.

My gut twists when she gives him a smile. She swings her hair over her shoulder, blocking my view. Scowling, I focus on my coffee. Her flirting with him is bad enough. She's leading him on, knowing she can't be with a schmuck like him. Add in the insult of doing it right in front of me and she's riding a thin line. I'm about to throw his ass down the fucking stairs.

"I really shouldn't," she says with a sigh and my fingers curl around her ugly counter. "Seriously, Devon. You have to go."

"Come on, Em. One coffee won't hurt anything. Friends go out for coffee all the time."

I'm fucking done. If Twitch has to coerce her to get her alone, that's a red flag. And the fact she seems like she's considering it sends me into a rage. "She said no, Twitch. Better listen or she might gut you."

After a beat, Devon laughs nervously, but Emma's jaw clenches. If she won't shut this shithead down, then I will. Doesn't bother me whether she wants me to step in or not.

"As if Emma knows how to do something like that," Devon murmurs as he smiles at her.

There's an edge in his brown eyes, though. He blinks and it's gone—too fast for me to decipher what it is. Whoever Devon is, he's hiding something. The question is, who is he hiding *from?*

Chapter 7

Emma

Rage. That's all I have bubbling inside of me. One more word out of Titus's mouth and I'm going to throw him out the window. Or gut him and the consequences be damned. It's not like Shane will disown me if I kill Titus. I stomp to the kitchen, throwing the flowers on the counter, and grab the coffee Titus was making for himself. As if he has any right to drink my coffee.

Titus snorts and I press my lips together. "I'd advise you to keep your mouth shut, asshole."

"You going to make me another drink since you stole mine?"

"Go fuck yourself." I sip the hot liquid, burning my mouth, but I refuse to wince. I'm trying to make a point here. I'm not entirely sure what that point is yet, but it'll come to me.

He snorts again and bumps me out of the way with his hip. I close my eyes, pulling in a calming breath. As he makes another cup, I check the cameras to make sure Devon actually left.

"How long?" Titus grunts, spinning around to face me. He crosses his arms and leans against the counter while the machine gurgles behind him.

"I wouldn't know personally, but based on your past, I'd say you don't last long." I take another sip to hide my grin.

"Excuse me?"

I give an exaggerated sigh, setting my cup down. "I'm assuming the only thing you're fucking these days is your hand. And I doubt you last more than a few minutes."

A flush graces his cheeks, and I mentally tick off a point for myself. I'll have to come up with a spectacular prize when I win this little contest I've made up in my head. My eyes drift to the flowers again and my elation deflates. I really do have to figure out what to do with Devon. This is the third time he's randomly stopped by, attempting to butter me up enough to take him back. Add in the number of times he's accidentally bumped into me on campus when that was never a thing before and I'm exhausted.

Titus mutters something under his breath that sounds suspiciously like bitch, but I ignore him. He's not worth my energy. The only reason I'm engaging with him is because I can't get rid of him. Might as well fuck with him in the interim.

"How long did you date Twitch?" he asks, his gaze fixed on the crappy linoleum.

"A while. Does it matter?" I'm not about to have a full-blown conversation about my relationship. He hasn't earned the right for that.

"It does if you plan on bringing Twitch back to Synd." He turns, presenting his back to me and muttering, "And then they'll eat him alive."

I huff, curling my hands into fists. "Why are you calling him Twitch? His name is Devon."

"Don't really give a shit what his name is. And he's a twitchy little guy. Felt appropriate." He opens the fridge, but I don't know what he expects to find in there. I'm pretty sure I only have ketchup and some butter in there.

"He isn't twitchy. He's just...never mind."

"Why the fuck don't you have creamer? Or sugar? Would it kill you to get a little milk?" He slams the door and grabs his cup, spilling practically half the liquid on the counter.

"I eat at the Hub. Or get takeout. Why would I buy milk if I'm not going to drink it? You can go and get your own fucking coffee somewhere else. I'm sure the downstairs neighbor has a cup of sugar you could borrow." I grab my mug, hoping he takes the bait. I just need to get him out of my apartment.

"This place is a shithole. I'm surprised King lets you live here." His gaze bounces around the kitchen as he sips his coffee.

I glance around the room, attempting to see the place through his eyes. The cracked linoleum has stains etched into the scratches. I scrubbed the walls when I got here, not that it did any good. Shitty counters, shitty furniture, shitty appliances, and absolutely no decor. It's a blank box of nothingness. My room has a little more personality, but not much. Most of my stuff is packed away in bags. If I need to make a quick getaway, I'd rather have less to grab.

I bite my cheek, all the fight draining out of me. "The door is sturdy and the windows lock. That's all he cared about."

He shoots me a look, silently calling me out on my lie. Shane hated this apartment. He raged for at least an hour, ripping apart every little thing down to the baseboards. I didn't even know what a fucking baseboard was. Sam calmed him down enough to get him to tacitly agree. She understood why I wanted to stay here. All it took was one look at the bedroom for her to get it. This apartment may be terrible, but it allows me to fly under the radar—blend in with the others. And it's the safest one I found.

"He would have built you a fucking place with armed guards if you'd let him."

I snort, shaking my head. I slam my empty mug on the counter and stomp to my bedroom. Arguing with Titus won't change his mind. I stay in a shitty apartment, he bitches. I have my brother buy me a house, he bitches. I can't win with him. I never could. He's made it perfectly clear I'm never going to live up to his expectations. Actually, I don't think he knows what would make me acceptable in his eyes.

The door busts open, the wood slamming against the wall. Titus leans against the frame, sipping his coffee. "Change of plans."

"Sure. Come on in. Thank you so much for knocking." I spin, mirroring his stance, though I don't have anything to lean on.

"I can't get back to my actual job until I bring you back to Synd. And I can't bring you back to Synd until you tell me what the fuck is going on around here."

"Nothing is going on. You don't need to worry about Devon. He's actually a really good guy, so I'm not worried about him following me or anything." I grab the dirty clothes from the end of my bed and toss them into the hamper.

He snorts, shaking his head. "I'm not here to talk about your fuck buddy. You blew up a fucking gas station. Clearly, there's other shit you're involved with. Tell me what."

"Why should I? You don't give two shits about me, and I don't need you poking around in my business. Let's just go back to Synd so I don't have to put up with your asinine personality anymore."

His nostrils flare, and I brace myself for his verbal lashing. Instead, he spins and marches out of the room. Half the time he doesn't react like I think he will. If I need to go back to Synd for a few days, so be it. Then I can find a way back to Ridgewood and deal with everything. After getting rid of that little gang, it might be the best course. The wolves will be at my heels if they find out it was me, and I refuse to lead them back to Synd. The fucking lectures from my brothers would put me over the edge and I'd go on a rampage around town. I huff, knowing I'd probably just sulk in my room.

I briefly contemplate waltzing through the apartment naked again. He didn't react last night, but it was dark. If I do it during the daytime, I'm sure he'd have some sort of reaction. He plays at being emotionless. He's nowhere near as good as it as I am because I learned from the best.

Titus's face at eighteen flashes through my mind, and I smother a giggle. He certainly didn't have all those muscles when he came to the house. He could barely carry me after I ran home when Sam got taken. Shane plopped me into his arms and he almost dropped me. I had to walk once we got to the stairs.

Exhaustion swamps me and I collapse onto my bed. My phone buzzes and I groan as I snatch it from my bedside table. Daisy's name flashes across the screen and I jump up to slam the door. No reason he needs to overhear our conversation.

"What's up, Daisy? Please tell me no one randomly showed up at your place," I ask, dropping onto my bed again.

"Other than Devon, no. You really need to talk to that boy. He's still smitten with you and if you don't shut him down, he's going to start following you around like a lost puppy." Dishes clatter on her end and I wish I was there. Breakfast would be great right about now.

"He showed up this morning with flowers. Wanted to go for coffee," I mumble. "And Titus was here."

The sudden silence on her end has me grimacing. It stretches until I'm sure she's hung up. Not that she's ever done that.

"Titus. The hot piece that looks like he needs someone to climb him like a tree? Who sat in my car and filled the entire space with his delicious scent that I'm pretty sure was chocolate?"

I snort, staring at my stained ceiling. "He doesn't smell like chocolate. He smells like coffee. And shadows."

"What the hell do shadows smell like?"

"No idea," I laugh, covering my face with my free hand. "When are you going home?"

"Oh, uh, I'm not sure. Soon, probably."

I grit my teeth as I pull the phone from my ear. I refuse to blow up on her. Reminding myself she's my best friend and doesn't understand the danger. When I'm sure I won't cuss her out, I lift the device once more.

"You're not a good liar, Daisy."

She sighs and I brace myself. "Don't be mad. I have to stay in Ridgewood during the holidays. And the summer. My parents decided to move across the country and I can't fly there."

"Oh, that's it? I'll buy your ticket."

"I'm not going to make you pay for my flights, Emma."

"You forget I'm uber rich. Your flights wouldn't even touch the limit on my cards. But if you don't want me using my family's money, then I can just use my personal funds."

"Yes, because I'm totally going to let you use what you earned from working at the library instead of your generational wealth."

"Shit, I suppose it is generational wealth. Wow. I just slipped right back into throwing money around, huh?"

She laughs, a snort slipping out at the end. "It's fine. But I'm still not taking your money. But because I know you're going to insist, I promise I'll go home for break since they won't have moved by then. When summer comes around, though, I'm staying here."

"Fine, but if you need anything, promise me you'll call. When I say I have a shit ton of money, I mean it."

The door swings open and my muscles tense. Titus eyes me, an impassive look on his face. If it weren't for the twitching of his jaw, I wouldn't think he overheard me. My statement doesn't exactly help the image he has of me. I shouldn't care. No, I don't care. Not even a little bit. Titus's opinion means nothing.

"Oh shit. Did he just walk in? What's he wearing?" Daisy whispers as if he can hear her.

He raises an eyebrow, killing any chance he had at me not answering her. My teeth find my lip and I gnaw on the flesh. His nostrils flare, and I expect him to stomp away once more. He surprises me by staying put as I scan him.

"Obnoxious shoes that you can't run in. Dark jeans with a black belt and don't ask me to comment further. Black t-shirt that I'm sure is a size too small with a black hoodie that's terribly nondescript. Oh, and a necklace. A silver one tucked under the shirt." By the time I'm done, he's smirking.

"Does he look good?"

"I fucking hate you right now."

"Spill, bitch."

"Yes. And that's all you're getting."

"Tell him to turn around," she yells, and I yank the phone away, wincing.

Titus huffs out a laugh, then slowly spins. My eyes have a mind of their own as they dip to his ass. I throw my arm over my face, but it's too late. I fear I may have lost this round. A point for each of us now. I wonder who will walk away the winner. It's all fun and games until someone gets hurt. And I'm afraid I'll be the one who forfeits in the end.

"Done ogling me?" Titus asks, jolting me back to reality.

"Get the fuck out of my room. I need to change," I snap.

"Didn't stop you last night," he says, and Daisy gasps.

Thankfully, he steps out, pulling the door shut as he goes. Daisy is hyperventilating on the other end of the line and I want to throw my phone. Or hang up on her. It's not because of her, but more the entire situation. My cheeks heat and I throw a pillow at the closed door. It thumps harmlessly against the wood before dropping to the ground.

"I'm sorry," Daisy whispers.

"Not your fault. But don't ask me about last night."

"Uh, I...what am I supposed to do? Just forget about it? Because we both know that's not going to happen."

"He was here when I came home. I didn't know he was here until I was mostly naked, but I refuse to make him more comfortable when he breaks into my apartment. And now I need to go."

"Oh shit. What are you going to do?"

I smirk even though she can't see me. "I'm going to remind him not to fuck with me."

Chapter 8

Titus

Emma's door squeaks as it opens slowly. I fuss with another cup of coffee, refusing to turn around. I wouldn't put it past her to strip down on her way to the shower. She already pulled that stunt, though. This time, she'd probably video me and edit it in a ridiculous way before putting it on her social media. Not that she has any profiles. My fingers curl into fists as her footsteps come closer.

From the corner of my eye, I track her as she hauls herself onto the counter next to me. Her crossed feet swing back and forth, reminding me of the other times we've been in this position. I feel like I should be handing her a piece of cake and listening to her bitch about the kids at school. Except she's not a kid anymore, which isn't hard to see.

I've tried to ignore her every time she came to visit. Now that she's sitting literally a foot from me, playing on her phone, I can't deny that she's grown up. For fuck's sake, she's twenty-four. She may be an adult, but she still throws her money around, acting like a brat every chance she gets.

"Why'd you blow up that gas station?" I've tried to gather information. This place is a fucking dry zone. No one seems to know anything.

She doesn't bother looking up from her screen. "Fun Friday night activity. Gotta keep my skills up or I'll lose them."

"Like you did your hearing? I'm surprised it came back so fast."

"I had earplugs in, asshole," she sneers, eyes darting to me, then back down.

"Who the fuck are you texting? Figured no one would want to be friends with someone like you." I snap my mouth shut, kicking myself for saying anything. Antagonizing her won't get the answers Ren is insisting on.

"One of my many fuck buddies. Are you planning on staying all day? If you are, you'd better get real cool, real fast. Plus, I require full consent from everyone involved."

I rip the phone from her hands and throw it on the counter. "Tell me what the fuck is going on so I can get the hell out of here."

Shock flits across her face before a mask slips over her features, making my gut turn. She's perfected it down to the dead look in her blue eyes. I hate that I can't read her anymore. I mentally shake myself. If I can get rid of her quickly, I won't need to know what she's thinking. And I don't give two shits about what she feels.

"They were threatening someone I care about, so I dealt with them." She hops down from the counter and snatches her phone. "I'll go finish packing."

She's lying. I'd put all the cash stowed away in my room on it. Maybe she's not as good at hiding her emotions as I thought. Or perhaps I didn't lose my ability to read her. Either way, she's lying about something. She probably took care of them for Devon. Asshat can't take care of his own problems, expecting Emma to do it for him.

"Bullshit," I snarl just as she's about to close her door.

She freezes, then pivots slowly, and I wonder if this is the moment she snaps. "Excuse me?"

"You fucking heard me. Maybe you were doing it for that douchebag, but you sure as hell didn't deal with it. You blew up a goddamn building. Even in the Barrens that shit gets noticed. Tell me what the hell is going on or I'll—"

Her eyes narrow, death dripping from them as they beg me to finish my sentence. "You'll what, Titus? Run to Shane? Or maybe you'll just kill Devon. Threaten to kidnap Daisy? Perhaps you'll lock me up until I spill all my secrets."

I cross my arms, creating a physical barrier between her words and me. Each accusation is worse than the last and I can't dispute any of them. If I needed to, I would call one of the Kings. Killing Devon would be the highlight of my week, but I refuse to examine why. I wouldn't kidnap her friend or lock her up, though. Emma won't believe me if I deny it. I could make all the promises in the world and she'd scoff, roll her eyes, then flip me off.

"You have two choices, Emma. Tell me what's going on so I can get the hell out of here. Or I go poking around myself and possibly fuck up your plans." Which is exactly what I was going to say before. I don't make threats I won't follow through on.

"Get the fuck out of my apartment. You're fucking up the vibe." She slams the door, her anger getting the better of her, and I grin.

Another knock at the front door has me sighing. I wait for her to come out and deal with whoever is here, but she doesn't. She probably didn't even hear them. I grit my teeth, wondering when I got relegated to a butler.

"What?" I growl at the older man standing in the hallway.

He adjusts the cuffs on his light grey suit, then glances at me while raising an eyebrow. When he presses his thin lips together, they disappear into the folds of his face. He clearly hasn't taken care of himself over the years. Between his swollen hands and mottled skin, he's practically knocking on death's door.

"Who are you?" he asks, wheezing slightly. Or maybe it's the restriction from his too-small suit.

"Seeing as how you're knocking on my door, I believe that's my line."

His nostrils flare as he struggles to maintain his composure. "Is Miss Emma here?"

"That's none of your concern. You can tell me who you are or leave. Or I can escort you out."

He tucks his pudgy hands in his pockets and rocks back on his heels. "Perhaps you'd like to inform her I'm here. I believe she'll want to speak with me."

Most people would take my words as a threat and think twice about fucking with me. I know how others see me. I'm the scary guy who puts people on edge. They cross the street when they come across me. They walk on eggshells, choosing their words wisely so they don't offend me. Usually I use it to my advantage. The only ones who don't take notice are the ones who understand the dangerous side of the world.

"Maybe you have the wrong apartment. Might want to try calling her to figure it out."

I go to close the door and his hand shoots out, stopping me. I could force the issue—break his wrist or nose. I'd rather not bring more attention to either of us. If he pushes me, I won't think twice about it. He'll learn the hard way how I take care of shit.

"I apologize, mister..." He lets his words sit between us as I passively blink at him. He clears his throat. "Perhaps I didn't make myself clear. I'm here to speak with Emma whether you like it or not."

I swing the door open a little wider, hoping Emma stays in her room. "Do you see anyone else here?"

He cranes his neck, beady eyes peering around the space. "I suppose not. Perhaps my son told me the wrong apartment number. Unless you've stuffed his girl in a closet."

He chuckles, though nothing he said was funny and there's no mirth in him. No way this man is related to Twitch. Maybe Emma wasn't trying to rile me up talking about fuck buddies. I bite my tongue, forcing myself to focus on the man in front of me. I doubt my initial instincts were wrong, and it's none of my fucking business, anyway.

"Closets aren't big enough for that. If you would." I gesture to his hand still resting on the wood between us.

He nods and slowly removes it, but his fingers twitch by his side. The bulge in his waistband has me tensing and I close the door. As quietly as I can, I flip the lock, then the deadbolt. The keypad on the wall disguised as a thermostat lights up and I put in the code to set the security. We don't need a shootout in this shitty apartment building. I don't know what the police are like in Ridgewood, but I'm not going to find out while I'm getting arrested.

I fish my phone from my pocket and pull up the cameras. All I find is his retreating back ducking around the railing of the stairs. He didn't knock on any of the other doors and I doubt he's trying the ones downstairs. If he checked the other apartments before coming to Emma's, there would be a notification on my phone.

I'm sure Emma doesn't realize Ren linked me to her system and I don't plan on telling her. Once we get back to Synd, I'll delete the app and forget it ever existed. If only I could do that with the woman herself.

"Emma," I call, prowling toward her door. I'm done letting her avoid the conversation. "Get out here, Emma, or I'm coming in."

Silence greets me, and I tip my head back, pulling in a deep breath. I try the handle and it doesn't budge. I swear to fuck I'm going to break this fucking thing down. I barely been here a day and I'm already developing a headache.

I try the knob one more time before I give up and slam my shoulder against the wood. It gives easily—too easily. This entire fucking place is a shitshow. She never should have been allowed to live here in the first place.

"I swear to fuck all, Emma," I growl, then stop short.

An empty room accosts me, and my breath catches in my throat. Was that older man here to distract me so someone could slip in and grab her? Of course my mind goes straight to the worst-case scenario. I scan the space again, noting all the places she could be hiding. No one should have been able to get to her, especially without me hearing. I wasn't so distracted by the douchebag I wouldn't have known someone was taking her.

I toss the piles of clothes, my movements becoming more erratic with each empty pile. I throw open her closet, kicking into the corners. If she is hiding, I'm going to end up hurting her, but I already know she's gone. My body won't accept it quite yet. Flipping the mattress isn't my finest moment. She wouldn't be able to fit under there, anyway.

My body vibrates by the time I approach the window. With the glass intact, I don't think anyone came in this way. Unless she...rage swirls through me and I grit my teeth. Throwing open the sash, I resist the urge to bash my fist through it instead. I curse when my fingers curl around the sill. I glance down at the fabric rope made out of sheets, and it bunches in my grip.

I should have torn down the entire fucking fire escape. Or not let her leave my sight. To be fair, slathering grease around the window and the bricks and the metal railings on the stairs wasn't the wisest thing to do. I didn't think she'd actually try to escape. It was just to piss her off, mostly. I might have assumed she wouldn't want to get her hands dirty.

Grabbing my phone, I realize my hands are trembling. I drop to the round chair in the corner, fumbling when the whole thing slides and my feet fly into the air.

"What the fuck," I mutter, struggling to free myself from this death trap.

At least I'm done trembling by the time I tip to the side and onto the floor. My phone slips from my hand, sliding under her bed. I scramble to my feet and my shin slams into the metal frame.

"For fuck's sake," I yell, gripping the back of my head and yanking on the short strands.

When I finally get ahold of myself, I calmly pick up my phone and pull up her contact. It rings several times before clicking over to her voicemail. I hang up and try again. And again. I blast off a text with more expletives than I'd usually use, then try to call one more time.

When she doesn't answer, I stalk toward the front door. If she wants to ignore me, so be it. I'll track her ass down and make good on my threat to force her back home. And to hell with whatever bullshit she's involved in. She's pushed me too far and I refuse to be sucked into her problems.

Chapter 9

Emma

"Dude, you have to make it stop," Daisy hisses from across the table.

"He won't stop, but I don't want to turn it off." If I turn off my phone, I won't get any texts. If I don't get any texts, I won't know if something's gone wrong. If I don't know if something's wrong, I can't help. My family doesn't deserve me abandoning them.

"You have got to get that boy on a leash. Or put him in a cage and ship him home." Daisy chuckles at her joke, but my muscles tense.

The edges of the room dim, the roaring in my ears drowning out the people busy eating. Frantically, my mind scrambles to remember what Ren told me to snap myself out of this. I can't find the words as shadows obscure the corners of my mind and solidify into a memory from my past. My elbows hit the table, rattling my bones. The sharp pain doesn't help, instead throwing me further into the hallucination.

Logically, I know I'm not in the cage anymore. It's clear I'm sitting in a chair in the middle of the Hub, but it feels like cold concrete seeping into my skin. I can see Daisy's lips moving, oblivious to my panic. Yet all I can hear is the whirling of a chainsaw cutting through the rolling thunder.

I fight to stay conscious. The last thing I need is to pass out on campus. I can't escape this delusion. Closing my eyes will only result in the vision invading every pore, tossing me back to when I was nine years old. I struggle to stay on this side of reality, but I'm quickly losing my grip.

A heavy hand lands on my shoulder, and I cringe.

"It's not real. You're not there anymore." Titus's low voice rumbles through me, warmth filling the holes the flashback has burrowed into my being. "Breathe. In. Out."

My body obeys him, though I'm still stuck in the dark, a red light illuminating the outline of several men. He commands me to breathe again and again.

The roar dissipates along with the shadows. My vision clears until all that remains is a chill. It's engrained in my bones, unwilling to be vanquished. I'm used to it by now. I've been living with an icicle wedged in my chest since the first time I was kidnapped. Most of the time I ignore it.

I shrug off his touch before gazing at him from the corner of my eye. His face is a familiar stony mask as he plops in the chair next to me, his fingers curling into fists in his lap. I didn't make it hard to find me. And I don't have the energy to deal with him or his stalkerish ways. Slipping out the window was supposed to be a fuck you to Titus. It was supposed to be a getaway to see Daisy without having him tail me. Now I just want to go home and sleep.

"Don't worry about her. She'll come back in a bit," Titus mumbles to Daisy.

"I don't know what I said." My best friend's shrill voice cuts through me, adding to the headache building in my base of my neck.

"What'd you say?" His hand slashes through the air when her mouth opens. "Write it down."

She fumbles with her notebook and pen, then slides it over to him. He turns his head slightly, eyeing me before pushing the paper back toward her.

"It was bad, wasn't it?" Daisy bites her lip, worry lining her face. She mouths, *I'm sorry*. I subtly shake my head. At least I try to. It's more of a twitch and I'm not sure she understands I don't blame her.

"She's fine," Titus says, then clears his throat. "Why don't you take off and I'll make sure she gets home. She'll be like this for a bit."

Daisy's eyes meet mine, questions swimming in them. I can't even form the words to tell her it's fine. Unfortunately, Titus has been through this before. I'll probably care later, but I'm numb. Everything he says bounces off me. I wish I could be like this when Titus feels the need to tell me what a spoiled brat I am. Or how I'm too stuck up and snotty.

"Maybe I should take her back to my place. I can put her in the bath—"

"No," he snaps, his face morphing from stoic to alarm. My body shudders and his hand squeezes my thigh, digging his fingers into my flesh. I barely feel either action.

Daisy leans closer to Titus, her eyes never leaving me. "She never did this before. I don't understand."

"You'll have to ask her about it later."

Shock hits me in the gut, and I curl into myself. It's the first full emotion I've felt since she mentioned the cage. I didn't think Titus would keep my secrets. I'm sure he's trained to, but he doesn't know how I've kept Daisy in the dark. For all he knows, I've spilled my whole past to her. Actually, he should expect it since she picked us up the other night. I didn't expect such respect from him and it's throwing me off. Or it would if I wasn't so numb.

"Emma?" Daisy whispers, reaching across the table, and my hand flinches. "I'll call you later. Or you can call me. Just...don't drop off the face of the planet again."

A memory floats from the shadows, dancing just beyond my reach. Titus peeks at me from the corner of his eye. Here's hoping he doesn't ask later about what Daisy is talking about. I won't have an answer, not that he'll believe me. He used to listen to me, but not anymore. Either that or he was very convincing.

Daisy gathers her things, shooting me one last concerned look before the crowd from the Hub swallows her up. I'm lethargic, exhaustion weighing down my bones. This is more than the memories assailing me. It's my whole life. It's falling apart around me and there's no end in sight.

My lids droop, obscuring my vision. Conversations float around me, a low murmur of sound parading through the space. Eventually, I'll wither away in this chair with no one to notice other than the one man I never wanted to see again.

"Emma," Titus murmurs in a soft tone.

I blink, my eyes focusing on his outstretched hand. His shadow spreads over me and a chill runs down my spine. He waits patiently while my hands twitch in my lap. I don't know if I want to touch him. If I do, I might spiral more. Or I might find solace in his embrace. Either one would be disastrous for me.

"Take my hand, Emma."

I gather the strength to raise my head, my gaze meeting his. Silently, I plead with him to make the choice for me. The memory will fade gradually, but it still has a chokehold on me. He'll be waiting here all day for me to make a move and even then I won't be able to. There's a wall between my mind and my body, neither one fully my own.

He sighs, some emotion flashing in his dark eyes too quickly for me to decipher. His warm hand grabs my own and he tugs me to my feet. When he wraps an arm around my waist, warmth seeps into me. I didn't realize how cold I was. I'd kill for a hot shower, though I doubt I'd be able to stand without bashing my head open.

"You got a car here?" he mumbles as we step outside. "I've only got my bike and like hell am I putting you on it."

I have no idea if it's because he thinks I'll fall off the back or he doesn't want me on his motorcycle. I didn't even know he got one. He probably doesn't think I know how to ride. Little does he know Willow gave me one when I went to college. Hawk, her husband, was terrified of the others finding out. As the vice president of a motorcycle club, he still gets worried they'll push him out. Sam and Mac said they'd deal with any fallout.

"Emma, you gotta give me something," he growls, his fingers digging into my hip.

I shake my head, swallowing once, then twice. "Walked," I croak, my voice barely above a whisper.

"Shit."

I don't have a solution other than calling Daisy and I doubt he'll do that. He doesn't seem to like her much. He doesn't like anyone, least of all me. His free hand digs in my pocket and I sway. He curses again before leading me over to a bench. I can't make out what he's muttering. Not that I want to know. It's probably more insults and threats. This would be the perfect opportunity for him to throw me in a trunk and drive me back to Synd. If he only has his bike, he won't be able to stuff me into a vehicle. Thank fuck for small miracles.

I squeeze my hands into fists, hoping the small bit of pain will bring my body back to life. It doesn't help. I dig my nails into my palms harder and harder. My tongue ends up between my teeth and the taste of copper floods my mouth. Still I feel nothing. Sobs well up in my chest, unable to break free. They're blocked by the lump in my throat. I close my eyes and time warps. The flashes of memories slow, a thick haze over the pictures.

"Do not pass out. The last thing I need is security on my ass as I haul around an unconscious woman. We don't own the police around here, Emma. Just stay the fuck awake." He hisses instructions as he tugs me to my feet. It's a steady stream of words I don't really understand.

Under any other circumstance, I'd rip his head off or ignore him. Now I don't have the energy. I'll deal with him later. He deserves to think he's won for at least a little while. My body teeters as we walk, and I suck in a deep breath.

"Do I need to call Sam? Or Ren?"

I shake my head, my feet stumbling over the uneven sidewalk. Titus curses and then I'm floating. The heat from his body seeps into mine, and I realize I'm shivering. I'll yell at him later for carrying me like a damsel in distress. It's not the first time he's tucked me close and saved me from a situation. Tears prick the back of my eyes and I slam them closed. The last thing he deserves is to see me cry. He lost that right years ago.

Apparently, there's a lot of things I'll be bitching at him about later. Maybe I won't even care once this episode is finally over. I'm just so fucking tired.

"I swear to fuck all, if you puke on me..." He lets the threat hang in the small space between our bodies.

"Fuck you," I breathe.

Satisfaction flows through me. Every time I fall into a flashback, I worry I won't find my way out again. The fact that those are some of my first words makes it all the better. Titus can burn in fucking hell for all I care. Even if he's saving me from myself right now.

"In your fucking dreams, darling."

I shiver and I'm not entirely sure it's from the cold still gripping my body. The last thing I want to do is imagine what he's like in bed. I did that enough when I was younger, long before I fully knew what sex was. No use going down that road again. It's riddled with heartache and pain after all the imagined pleasure. It's not worth it. None of it is worth it anymore.

Chapter 10

Titus

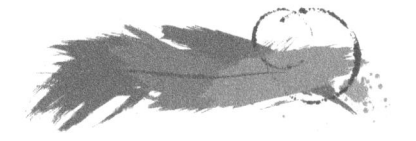

Walking four miles while carrying a practically comatose woman wasn't in my plans for today. We should be halfway to Synd by now. Instead, I'm stuck babysitting again. I could have tried to call a car, but they're few and far between around here. Explaining to the driver why she's almost unconscious wouldn't go over well either.

I've tried to keep a barrier between us, ignoring the closeness we once had. With her shutting down in the middle of campus, my resolve crumbled.

Standing outside of her bedroom, obsessively checking on her, wasn't in my plans for today either. Yet here I am, wringing my hands like a concerned mother hen. It's pathetic and beneath me. Especially since I know she'll be perfectly fucking fine. She just needs to rest, slough off the remnants of the episode, and then I can take her back to Synd.

My phone buzzes and I read the message from Ren. I slip the device back in my pocket before I break the thing. I don't have time to get a new one while I'm here. Peeking into the room, I hold my breath. Emma hasn't moved since I tucked her into bed. She snores softly and I shake my head. It's one of the few things proving she's not as perfect as she pretends to be. I wonder if Twitch knows she snores. Probably, since they probably slept together.

Anger bubbles in my gut. Not that she was with someone else. I don't give a fuck who she dates. Twitch is a fuckwad, though. He doesn't deserve to be within a hundred yards of Emma King. There's something about him I can't put my finger on. He clearly has ulterior motives when it comes to her. He doesn't love her. I'd stake my life on it. Sooner or later, he'll reveal his intentions. They always do.

Another text comes in and I back away from her door before I pull out my phone. Ren's determination to get information on what the hell is going on is relentless. It's not surprising since Emma is avoiding them. I should be there dealing with my men, not being a go-between for them.

A happy jingle, so at odds with my mood, rings through the apartment. I follow the sound until I unearth Emma's phone from a pile of her clothes. Devon's name flashes across the screen and my thumb hovers over the accept button. A few well-placed threats should have him out of her life for good. A man like him won't fight for her. Not that I'm one to talk. The only reason I'd step up for her now is for the King family.

Silence fills the air, and I breathe a sigh of relief. Her phone vibrates and I glance over my shoulder. Another buzz, then a third, and I'm about to toss the thing out the window. When I try to unlock it, a prompt for a fingerprint pops up. Emma would kill me if she found out I was spying on her. She'd want me to respect her privacy. Good thing I don't give a fuck what she wants.

I slip back into her bedroom and gently press her finger to the screen. She doesn't even flinch as the device opens and I retreat to the couch. Collapsing onto the cushion, it practically eats me alive. I'm surprised her family didn't force her to replace this piece of shit.

I swipe through the notifications. Most of them are weather apps. Why the fuck does she need so many places to check the weather? I get rid of them one by one. My eyes skip over the text from Shane. As much as I don't care about spying on her, I draw the line at doing it to my boss. He'd gouge my eyes out before floating me, and I like my job too much to risk it.

Twitch's message flashes on the screen, and I scowl. He's more persistent than I thought. His flowery language might fool someone blinded by love, but Emma would see right through his words. Half his texts consist of him begging her to meet him. Most of the places he suggests are semi-secluded coffee shops or parks. He peppers in the manipulation well for someone who isn't me. I'd assume Emma would pick up on it, too, but with the way she acted this morning, I'm not so sure.

I'm tempted to text him. My thumb shakes with the effort to hold myself back. I glare at his message, crafting the perfect comeback in my mind. Daisy would probably know where he lives. Maybe I could drop by, give him some face-to-face time. Or rather, face-to-fist. He doesn't seem to comprehend the word no. Either he's not great at picking up signals or he's actively ignoring the ones Emma's throwing at him. Some people just learn lessons the hard way, and I don't mind being the one to help him along with this one.

The phone flies from my hand and I grasp for it, whipping my head around. "What the fuck, Emma."

It's been a while since I've seen the full might of her wrath raging in her eyes. It's always annoyed me. So why am I admiring her indignation? I shake my head, gritting my teeth while I get my shit together.

"I swear to fucking hell, if you touch my things again, I'm going to gut you in your sleep." She swipes the screen, searching for whatever I did. "Where the hell are my apps?"

I lean back and drape my arms across the back of the couch, sinking farther into cushions in the process. "Want to explain why you have seventeen weather apps? And why are you avoiding your brother? Oh, and one more thing—"

"Get the fuck out." Her face smooths, emotion emptying from her eyes.

Her anger was slightly adorable. Her calm demand sends a bolt of terror through me. My hands drop to my lap and I thread my fingers together. I can handle when she yells at me, threatens me, fights me. I don't think I can handle her silently seething with a calculating look in her ice-blue eyes. Maybe I pushed her too far, which would mean I'm at fault for this sudden turn of events.

"You know I can't do that, Emma." I lean forward as smoothly as I can and prop my elbows on my knees. "This would go a lot faster if you'd tell me what you were mixed up in and let me deal with it. Then I can take you back home. Sooner you confess, sooner we can wash our hands of each other."

"It's none of your business. I'm a grown-ass woman. I'm done trying to convince you I am. So, you can see yourself out. I will deal with my brother as I see fit. And just for old time's sake, I'll even convince them to let you off the hook. You'll be free to go back to your job without any repercussions." She turns and takes measured steps back to her room. When she shuts her door quietly behind her, I know I'm fucked.

I drop my head in my hands, frustration rolling through me. Regardless of what she said, there's no way the Kings will absolve me from my responsibilities. If she tries, they'll blame me. There's no fucking way they'll think it's her idea. After all this time, she's still fucking with my damn life.

I've spent years distancing myself from who I was at eighteen when I was thrust into the role of her bodyguard. I was young, terrified out of my mind, and had no idea what the hell I was doing. Being responsible for keeping my boss's sister alive came with a lot of pressure. The threats, attempted kidnappings, not to mention the actual kidnappings, kept me on edge for years. At some point, it became more than keeping a mafia daughter alive. She might have been an annoying teenager, but I cared whether or not she was hurt. I wouldn't have called us friends, though.

As I struggle to my feet, a plan forms in my mind. Pressing my ear to her door, I hold my breath. There's no sound and I wonder if she fell asleep again. When she was younger, she would have beelined straight to the shower. I almost wish she would have retreated to the bathroom instead of her room. She's probably gone out the window again.

I exhale heavily as an unfamiliar emotion swirls through my chest. I shove it down and make my way to the front door. If she won't admit to the mess she's made here, I'll just have to figure it out myself. She can wallow or whine or bolt all she wants. Once I have my answers, I'll track her ass down and force her back to Synd. It'll take longer than I wanted, but I can't go back empty-handed.

I pause in the hallway after closing the door, waiting for something. Not her. I don't want her running after me and begging me to stay. She clearly thinks she has everything under control. As I search the area, I realize I'm expecting Twitch to materialize. If he does, he'll be taking the hard way down the stairs. I doubt anyone would notice his absence. Unless his rich-ass parents actually care about him. Doubt it.

When nothing moves, I make my way to the ancient elevator and out of the building. This side of town is rougher than I would have picked for Emma. Not that I wanted a say in the matter. Sam probably thought it would remind Emma of the Barrens. As if she needed more of an incentive to flit around in the shadows.

I may be used to working in the underbelly of polite society, but that doesn't mean I want to keep my bike down here. It's fancy enough to be a prime target for pissants who think thieving is a legit pastime. Thankfully, the chop shop where I stashed my bike isn't too far away to walk. The night is quiet as I make my way down the street.

Buying the building and putting a chop shop in it was a stroke of genius. My contribution was minimal since I didn't have as much capital, but I was able to put my own person in charge. All she required was her own business as a cover.

"Good afternoon, Joy," I say politely as I enter the plant shop. "How's business?"

She rolls her eyes, or rather, the one eye I can see. A flop of hair covers her other one. "You know as well as I do no one buys my plants."

"A damn shame if you ask me." I flash her a smile and she snorts.

"I'm perfectly content with them. The shop had an influx last week, though. Some bikers came through, gave us a tip on some asshats about forty minutes away who weren't guarding their shit enough. We were kind enough to take them off their hands." She smirks as she drums her black nails on the countertop. It's grating, but I like my dick attached to my body so I keep my opinions to myself.

"Glad to hear it." I lean on the glass counter, perusing the random shit she's decided to shove in there.

"Of course you're glad to hear it. You benefit from it." She scoffs, rolling her eyes again. It's annoying since it reminds me of Emma. Half the time I'm worried she'll roll them right out of her head.

I grit my teeth, shoving thoughts of Emma from my mind. "You pick up my bike?"

"Course we did. You left it sitting out in the fucking open on the edge of campus. Not very smart."

I straighten, waving away her concern. "Not like I left it in the *middle* of the fucking campus."

She huffs, shaking her head. "You remember this isn't like Synd, right? No one knows who the fuck you are. And they care even less. Your boss's name isn't going to keep assholes away."

"Maybe not, but they'll learn real fucking quick."

She rolls her eyes one last time and my jaw clenches. She turns away and leads me through a storeroom stuffed with plant equipment. When she pushes open a heavy door in the back, noises from the shop rush through the small space. I worked at a mechanic shop the Kings owned when I was a teenager. The tangy smell wraps around me, throwing me into a flurry of memories. Sometimes I wish I could go back to that time. Shit was simpler then, even if it wasn't typical.

"One of these days you'll figure out not everything can be solved with a bullet or blade, Titus," Joy says quietly.

"And one of these days you'll figure out I don't need your shitty advice, Joy."

She snorts as she weaves through the mess of car parts and shells until we reach my bike tucked in the corner of the warehouse. Hawk helped me pick it out and taught me how to take care of it. I never planned on getting a motorcycle, but I don't regret it. Brushing my hand over the leather seat, I sigh.

"You going to tell me why you got a double?" She stares pointedly at where my palm rests.

"It's called a pillion. And it's clearly for a second rider."

She raises an eyebrow. "I know what a fucking pillion is. The question is, who the hell would want to ride with an asshole like you?"

"Watch it, Sanders. Seems like you forgot who pays your salary."

She snickers as she glances away. "Course I do—Alex fucking King. Want to try again?"

"I'd really rather not." I cross my arms and lean against the wall. "You have any info for me?"

She presses her lips together, shaking her head. Normally, I'd assume she wanted to push the issue, but as I study her, I realize she's keeping shit from me.

"Don't fucking lie to me, Joy. You know how well that goes," I growl.

She sighs, tucking her chin to her chest. "Fine. There's some talk. Not a lot—just whispers, but nothing definitive."

I'm not surprised she tried to keep it from me. Still pisses me off. Unless it has something to do with Emma, though, it's not my problem. I'm more concerned with the shit she's withheld for the last couple years.

"What do you know about Devon Smith?" I dig my nails into my biceps when her gaze darts to mine. "Don't even think about it."

Her chin juts out in defiance. "I wasn't going to lie to you. He's some pricky asshat. Real douchebag, if you ask me. Thinks his shit don't stink because he's got cash to splash around. Problem is, everyone thinks he's an Eagle Scout or something. Always donating to various causes and volunteering at different places. No one's got a bad word to say about him."

Which is exactly what Emma said. He's not a bad guy. If Joy doesn't like him, though, that says something. She's a good judge of character—better than most. She can read people on sight and she's almost always spot on. It's why I gave her this opportunity in the first place. She wanted out of Synd, I needed someone I could trust up here, and she's as loyal as they come. Add in her ability to sniff out a rat and it was a perfect setup.

"You got any evidence?"

She heaves out a sharp breath. "No. Haven't really tried, though. Got enough shit going on, what with your woman sneaking out every other goddamn night."

Pain stabs me in the chest and I rub the spot. "Not mine. Never gonna be. Knock that shit off."

"Sure," she says sarcastically and smirks.

She's been dropping hints since she moved up here five years ago. I've never been able to convince her there's nothing going on between Emma and me. Maybe if she finally sees us together, she'll realize she's barking up the wrong tree. Watching us practically rip each other's heads off should make her understand more than my words will.

"I need all the info you can find on our resident asshat. As well as whatever you can dig up on the whisperings. I'm not about to be blindsided." Again.

Chapter 11

Emma

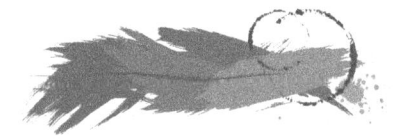

"I'm fine, Daisy. I promise." Even to my own ears, I don't sound convincing.

"I'm not going to force you to talk about it, but I do have another question since you're going to keep telling me you're fine even though I know you're not." She huffs on the other end of the line. I squeeze my eyes shut and wait for her to ask about Titus.

When she doesn't say anything, I mumble, "Go on."

"Is he still there?"

"Seriously? That's your question? I thought you were going to ask if I was dying or something."

I throw some dirty clothes in my hamper. I swear I'd cleaned up in here. Plus, my sheets were skewed and my comforter was put on my bed the wrong way. I freeze in the middle of my room and study the space with a more critical eye. I wouldn't put it past Titus to snoop around. Especially since he had my phone earlier.

Yanking the device away from my ear, I cringe. Daisy's laughter rings through the air and I stare at the screen. Did he put tracking on here? Would he have gone so far as to mirror my phone? I roll my eyes, knowing he'd definitely go that far. He used to have standards, but they haven't applied to me for years.

"Emma," Daisy yells and I wince.

"Sorry. Just weighing my options."

"Options for what?"

"Oh, just which body parts I'll be removing from Titus for going through my things," I mutter, still searching for signs of him being in here.

"He fucking spied on you?"

A smile blooms across my face at her indignation on my behalf. "As much as I appreciate your ire, people have been spying on me for years. I don't know who's ultimately behind it, but it's been happening. I'm not too concerned about it."

She sputters incoherently as she probably works through what I said. I don't blame her. She's just started accepting who my family is and what that means. I'm just happy she hasn't cut me off completely. I'd hate to lose my closest friend because of who I am.

In high school, I never even had the opportunity to find a friend. They all knew where I came from. My classmates might not have always known my brother was the head of a mafia. Didn't stop them from knowing something was off.

"I don't understand how you can be so blasé about this. People following you around, searching your apartment, spying on you. Just seems like a lot to deal with all on your own." She whispers the last few words and my heart aches. I could brush off her concern, but that doesn't seem fair.

I sigh, dropping onto my bed. "Listen, I hated it when I was younger. I barely left the house. I didn't have any friends. The ones who did pay attention to me only wanted to be close to my family or my money. They didn't care about *me*. I had drivers who took me to school, but they were really guards. On the off chance I was invited to a birthday party, someone had to tail me the entire time."

"That sounds like a terrible childhood," she mutters.

"I had an amazing childhood. It just wasn't typical. Sure, there was some traumatic shit, but everyone has shit from their past they have to deal with. When I got to be a teenager, though, I became...well, a teenager. I thought if I could just get out on my own, I'd be able to figure out where I was supposed to belong." I flop back, bouncing on the mattress and staring at the ceiling.

She sniffs and I wonder if she's crying. Her voice is clear when she says, "I think we were all looking for that."

"Probably. Slight difference, though."

"What's that?"

I laugh, but there's no humor in the sound. "When you snuck out of your house to go literally anywhere, where were you going? And what happened when you got caught?"

"One time I went to a party. Mom caught me when I was sneaking back in and I was grounded for a month. It was boring as hell. And I get you probably weren't invited to a party, but—"

"Daisy. Stop." I don't need her sympathy. That's not what this conversation is about. Not truly. "When I snuck out, I went to the Barrens. A dead man's land along the river between the two territories. It's abandoned and dangerous and no one in their right mind goes there unless they live there or are armed. Which I wasn't. When I got caught, it wasn't my mom or dad or even my brother. It was men who wanted to kidnap me and sell me. The only reason I got away was because of Sam."

"Oh," she whispers, then clears her throat. "Not to completely dismiss all that, but I still can't believe that you're practically related to Samantha King. Does she still go by Byrns?"

"No. She's with my brothers. Focus, Daisy," I snap, and she mutters an apology. "After all that, I was sent to my great-aunt's house. And I still didn't learn my lesson. Other shit happened, but the point is, my family went through hell. Most of it was my fault and I've had to live with that. If it makes them feel better to set a tail on me while I'm away at college, so be it. If it puts their minds at ease, I can deal with it."

"I get that. Okay, I don't actually understand what's that like, but it makes sense. Don't you feel like you're constantly looking over your shoulder?"

I roll to my stomach and drop my phone onto my bed, putting it on speaker. "I've been looking over my shoulder since I was three. Plus, I was sent to the mountains for training. Isn't hard for me to slip away when I want."

"I really want to laugh like you're telling me a joke, but I'm afraid you're actually serious. So we'll just leave it." A clattering on her end of the line has me wincing. "Sorry. Listen, if you need a break from Mr. Broodypants, let me know. You can come over and we'll eat ice cream and watch movies or something."

Tears prick the back of my eyes and I slam them shut. I don't need another walk down memory lane. A wave of homesickness washes over me, threatening to pull me under.

"How many nicknames are you going to come up with for him?" I mutter, hoping to pull myself out of the riptide.

"Oh, I've got a fair few brewing in my head." She giggles and the sound fills me up. At least my trauma dumping didn't send her running for the hills.

"Maybe don't use them around him. His head is big enough as it is."

"As if I could. He might be one fine piece of ass, but I'm pretty sure he could pop my head off like a dandelion."

"I...what the fuck does that mean?" I'm trying to imagine it, but it doesn't make sense.

She snorts and I can practically hear her rolling her eyes. "You know, a dandelion. You put your thumb under the top of it and pop it off? There was a rhyme that went with it, but I can't remember now. Didn't you do that?"

"Nope. Next spring you'll have to show me." The ache in my chest is back and the urge to hang up on her rides me hard.

"It's a date. Okay, I gotta go. You sure you don't want to go with us?"

"Nah, I need sleep. And I have to make some calls. I'll see you later."

She pauses and I brace myself for what's coming. "You know I love you, right? And I wouldn't be okay if something happened to you."

There it is. She never pushed when I was vague about my past. I let her assume my family and I weren't that close. To protect me, they rarely came to visit, which meant I always went home for breaks and holidays. Daisy decided I needed to hear how much I was loved at least once a week. Guilt eats away at me every time because, at the root of it all, she thinks I'm by myself.

"I love you, too. Daisy..." I sigh as I gather the courage to confess. "You know I've got an amazing family, right? I'm not unloved."

"Duh. I figured that out years ago when you kept getting care packages." She laughs lightly.

"Then why do you—"

"Because it's never a bad thing to remind someone of how much they mean to you. It's not a bad thing to have feelings. And I know you struggle with things like that," she says, and I scoff. "Girl, you never even told Devon you loved him and you two were together for like ever."

A lead weight drops in my stomach and bounces around. I curl onto my side to ease the nausea bubbling up. I don't know how to explain to her I don't know what romantic love feels like. Did I love Devon? I don't know. Even if I did, I wasn't allowed to. Maybe I knew we didn't have a future, not truly, so I never gave in to what could never be. I suspect it has more to do with Devon not being who I truly wanted. We weren't a good fit. Not really.

"Devon is a great guy."

She snorts again. "Sure he is, in a goody-two-shoes kind of way. In a prissy, *I'm such a good guy I'm going to make everyone else around me feel bad* kind of way. In a—"

"Okay, I get it."

"Listen. One day you'll find someone who knows every piece of you and they'll love you because all your random jagged pieces match the holes inside of them. You'll let them in because you know they're capable of handling all of you. That wasn't Devon and that's okay. I'm sure there will be a delicious morsel waiting right outside your door. Just don't be too scared to take the leap. Gotta go or I'm going to get my ass chewed. Love you!"

She hangs up before I answer, and I whisper *love you* into the empty room. I don't have time to ruminate over everything being dredged up today. With the sun setting, I only have a few hours before I can get going. Hopefully, Titus doesn't catch me. He seems to have a sixth sense when it comes to me. He shouldn't have been able to find me at the gas station. Or the Hub. My gaze darts to my phone. Bastard probably is tracking me. I hate leaving it behind. One of Sam's first pieces of advice was to always keep my phone closer than my weapon.

Backup is always a phone call away.

Her voice weaves through my mind, calming me with its familiar lilt. I have thousands of pieces of advice from her now, some more relevant than others. I've always followed through with my phone, though. Leaving it behind feels like a betrayal. I can't afford Titus catching me—not with where I'm going. I won't be the reason he gets shot. I'll never live it down. If he dies...I shake my head and roll off the bed to my feet.

Before I go off gallivanting into the night, I need food. I would have taken Daisy up on her offer to hang out with our friends, except I'm afraid Titus will show up. Most of the grogginess from earlier has passed, at least. It's been so long since I've had an episode, much less one so public, I forgot how much it drained me.

I slip on my shoes, then glance back at my phone lying on my bed. I stomp back and snatch it up before shoving it under my mattress. It's not the best hiding spot, but it wouldn't matter, anyway. If I'm being tracked, he'll find it right away.

Spinning around, I skip out of my bedroom. I stop by my small bookcase and grab one of my erotic novels. When I flip through it, several twenties flutter to the floor and I snatch them up, then shove the book back. Stuffing the cash into my pocket, I make my way to the door. Titus seems to have listened and stayed away. He probably thinks I didn't hear him leave earlier. Joke's on him.

I flip open a plastic cover by the front door, revealing what seems like a thermostat. Lacey, or rather Nemesis as she likes to be called when doing business, disguised it and somehow put fingerprint recognition on the thing as well. Personally, I thought it was a little much considering it's just an alarm system, but it saved my ass more than once. I set the alarm and it hits me. Lacey must have given him the code and added his prints to the system. I'll have to call her about it. No way am I going to constantly be looking over my shoulder in my own apartment.

I swing open the door and stop dead. There's at least twelve dozen roses scattered in front of my apartment. I'm about to curse Devon to a lifetime of wet socks when my eyes track a couple of ridiculously long legs encased in low-slung jeans to a tight black t-shirt. I'm sure in any other circumstance, I'd be smitten.

Except it's Titus's head attached to this delicious body. He twirls one of the roses between his long fingers. No way he left all these. He is definitely not a flower type of guy.

"What. The. Fuck."

"Hello, darling. Let's go for a walk."

"I told you to leave," I say, attempting to strip my face of all emotion.

"And so I did." He kicks one of the vases, probably on purpose. "What exactly did your brother say?"

I grit my teeth, averting my gaze. He snorts and I realize I gave myself away. I'm better than this, yet every time he's in front of me, I forget everything I was taught. Somehow, he's able to break down all my walls and send me into a tailspin. I'll blame it on our past. The one I never fully dealt with. All my feelings when I was a teenager got shoved under a rug and now I'm constantly tripping over my past mistakes.

The flower he's holding brushes my cheek. I turn my head and glare at him. He raises an eyebrow, silently commanding me to answer.

"Go to hell," I spit out.

He taps my nose with the bloom, and the cloying scent of rose invades my nose. He drops it onto the mess he's created and my breath hitches. I'm trying to hold on to my anger, but the way he's looking at me isn't helping.

"Don't you know we already live in hell? Call your brothers. If you're not going to tell me what happened, then tell one of them. Because I'm done." He turns, kicking over a few more vases along the way.

I gaze at the bouquets, searching until I find a card. Slipping it from the envelope, I huff. Of course they're all from Devon. The note is an apology—not surprising. Devon always knew how to apologize. I wonder how much practice he had to have in order to be this good at saying he's sorry. I shake my head, wondering when I started questioning his motives, and scowl at Titus's back. It might not be his fault, but I'm going to blame him anyway.

"Well, go on then. Be fucking done," I sneer.

I don't know why I'm pissed at him. He's doing exactly what I told him to do. He's doing what he always done—giving up. He gave up on me when I was younger. He gave up on me when I went off to college. And he's giving up on me now. I'm used to it. And I refuse to acknowledge how much it stings.

He turns slowly, shoving his hands in his pockets and rocking back on his heels. It's a move I've seen a thousand times from him when he's avoiding a conversation. I tilt my head, wondering where his bags are. He must have packed something, and I doubt he's keeping everything with his bike.

"Oh, I'm not done with *you*. Unfortunately, I don't have a choice whether I stay or leave. You'll never call them, regardless of your promises to do so. Coming back without you is a death sentence and I quite like my job...and my head attached to my body."

I desperately want to ask what his job is. Last time I checked, he was doing something with the guards, but I did my best to avoid any news of where he was in their ranks. Shane would totally kill him, though. He wanted to when Sam merely hinted at my heartbreak. I wouldn't have even cared about his rejection if he wasn't so fucking cruel about it. I doubt Shane would float him now, though. Enough time has passed and I'm sure they all think I've gotten over it. Shoving all those emotions down deep was a better course of action than reliving it all the time.

"I doubt that would be the case." I shuffle to the side, knocking over yet another glass vase. It shatters when it hits another one, and I cringe. "Unless you're expendable. Which if you ask me—"

"Good thing no one gives a shit what you think." He narrows his eyes, scanning me up and down. "Are you coming?"

"Bet you ask all the ladies that," I mutter, glancing away.

Vases shatter as he plows through them and I gasp, then snap my mouth shut. His hand wraps around my throat and he shoves me until my back hits the door. His gaze bores into me, fury dripping from his dark eyes. My nostrils flare and I dig my nails into my palms. He forces my chin up as he scans my face. I have no idea what he's searching for. My stomach muscles quiver as I ignore the warmth gathering between my legs and I struggle to keep my emotions from my face.

"Careful, darling. Your mouth is going to get you into trouble."

I bite my tongue, desperately trying to stop the deluge of vitriol wanting to spew from me. How fucking dare he manhandle me. How dare he scold me as if he hasn't been goading me the entire time he's been here. How fucking dare he make me feel anything other than disgust for him.

"Fuck you, Titus," I rasp and his fingers flex. "Let. Me. Go."

His head tilts, a dangerous glint entering his eyes. When the corner of his mouth tips up, I know I'm doomed. He's seen something in my face, in my own eyes, in the lines of my form, I really don't want him to notice. My breath hitches as he leans closer and his nose brushes my flaming cheek. Damn my inability to control my body.

"What exactly will you do if I refuse?"

I react without thinking and my foot pops up. Smashing my knee between his legs, my heart skips a beat. He moans as he doubles over, his hand sliding from my throat to my chest. I knock his arm away and he clutches his jewels. Satisfaction flows through me, drowning out my fear. My hand lands on his shoulder and I lean to whisper in his ear.

"Careful, darling. I *am* trouble."

Chapter 12

Titus

I crash to my knees, then to my side. The final vase of roses goes down with me, not that I care. I'm too busy clutching my balls and hoping she didn't pop one. She steps over me, her shoes crunching on the glass. I'm sure some of the shards are embedded in my arm by now. Not that Emma seems to fucking care.

Rolling to my side, nausea bubbles in my stomach and I groan. I peek at her through slitted eyes as she skips down the stairs, humming a jaunty tune. I need to get my shit together and go after her, yet I can't seem to move. Everything below my waist is numb, barring the pain radiating from my crotch. She only hit me once, but I'm pretty sure she has steel kneecaps.

"Emma," I croak before her head disappears. I dissolve into a coughing fit, attempting to catch my breath to call after her again.

The stairs occupy the center of the building, curving around with each floor. It's a strange set-up, but I'm sure it's part of the reason Emma chose the place. Thank fuck only one other apartment is on the third floor and it's unoccupied. The last thing I need is someone wandering to see what all the commotion is about. No one needs to witness a grown ass man writhing on the floor amidst the remnants of Devon's desperate bid for Emma's heart. Fucking bastard.

As the pain recedes, I push to my hands and knees. Blood from my palms oozes into the water, seeping into the yellow petals. It slowly leeches into them, morphing into a garish orange. The red roses from this morning were bad enough. Now he had to add yellow to the mix. As if the color is the reason she won't take him back.

"Are you dying?" Emma snaps.

I lift my head, pain overriding the shock of her reappearance. Her eyes widen and her mouth drops open.

"I might be pissing blood for a week, thanks to you."

She scowls as she crosses her arms. "I'm not driving your ass to the clinic. You'll have to go back to Synd, though I doubt you'll be able to ride in your condition."

"You fucking bitch," I snarl.

My foot slips as I try to stand and another piece of glass embeds itself into my palm. Getting kicked in the balls is never fun, but slicing my hands open will push me over the edge. I didn't want to be here in the first place. Now I'm bleeding and pissed and fucking done. Fuck Ren and his demands. Fuck Shane for giving me this assignment in the first place. And fuck Alex just for good measure. All of them can go to hell.

"My, my, aren't we dramatic." She rolls her eyes as I struggle to my feet. "Maybe next time you'll think before you put your hands on me."

"You'd have to beg me to touch you again. And even then I wouldn't."

I don't have time to inspect my injuries. I need out of here. Being in her presence isn't something I can do anymore. I should have pushed back more against this whole thing. They all knew this was a disaster waiting to happen. They just didn't want to deal with the fallout when it inevitably went sideways. Bastards don't give two shits about how I was supposed to accomplish this impossible task.

Slipping my phone from my pocket, I brush past Emma. If they're so keen on Emma being in Synd, they can come get her themselves. Or let her wander back on her own. Like Sam said, she's fully capable. As long as she doesn't bring her problems to our doorstep, that is.

I pause at the top of the stairs and glare at her. "Whatever shit you're mixed up with, don't bring that fuckery back to Synd. We can't fucking afford to deal with your problems along with everything else."

She blinks at me, alarm and confusion flitting across her face. "What the hell are you talking about?"

"You're a grown-ass woman. Figure it out yourself," I snap before stomping down the stairs. She'll have to call someone if she wants information. I'm not a messenger boy at her beck and call, regardless of what my position in the family is.

Once I step outside, I sneer at the grey sky as my phone connects. "Sam. It's Titus. We've got a problem."

"How'd you get this number?" Sam asks, confusion coloring her tone. "Never mind. Fucking Ren. What's the problem? Is Emma okay?"

"She's fine." *A raging bitch.* "Have you spoken to Ren? He has concerns."

I glance over my shoulder as I walk away from the apartment. Emma doesn't make an appearance, thank fuck. I can't deal with more of her antics. My dick still hurts and the cuts on my hands sting. I need to get the glass out of them before they become infected.

She sighs, and a door shuts on her end. "He's my partner. Of course I've talked to him. If you're calling to get me to change his mind, you'll be sorely disappointed in my response. You can't call Mom just because Dad said no."

"What the fuck," I breathe. I'm not a fucking child, least of all *their* child.

"Sorry. I've been hanging out in Reaper territory with the kids. It's fucking with my brain. Listen, Titus, we've known each other a long time now. You're loyal and we trust you, which isn't easy for us. I know Shane said to do whatever you needed to get Emma back here, but he set you up for failure."

"No shit," I snarl, then bite my tongue. Snapping at Sam is a surefire way to get my ass handed to me. It'll be especially bad if the King men find out.

"Watch it, Titus. I may be on your side, but I won't put up with disrespect." She delivers the threat with no emotion, just like Emma did earlier.

"I apologize." I count to ten, pulling in deep breaths to calm myself. "She won't listen to me. Shane may have said I could throw her over my shoulder, but I like both my kidneys."

Sam's laughter rings over the line, and I grit my teeth. "You'd definitely lose one if you did that. Although, you can live with only one, so really, what are you losing?"

"The ability to walk for a month?"

"Actually, you can walk the next day after you get a kidney removed. Don't ask me how I know that." The line goes quiet and I wonder if she's hung up on me. "You and Emma have some shit to work out. Maybe it's a good thing you're stuck up there while you figure out what she's landed herself in."

I stutter to a stop in the middle of the sidewalk. I've been wandering aimlessly while on the phone and I don't know where I am. It hits me then that I called the wrong person. I don't even know why I picked Sam in the first place. Maybe I thought she could talk some sense into Emma. Or she'd get me out of this assignment. She warned me, though. She's not on my side in this fight. Oh sure, she'll stay out of Emma's and my business like she always has. Doesn't mean she'll pick me when shit goes sideways.

"I apologize for calling you. If something happens, I'll let Mr. King know." My palms itch to hang up on her, though that might be the cuts littering my skin. I won't cut the call, anyway. I'm bound by duty to stay on the line until she deems our conversation complete.

"I won't tell the others the issues you're having with her. Or your current feelings toward their little sister. That's all the help I can give you."

Shaking my free hand out, I try to ease the pain. "Understood."

"One last thing. Emma is stubborn to a fault. She won't admit when she needs help or is in trouble. Do not let her leave Ridgewood without making sure whatever shit she's in the middle of won't follow her back here. Shit is escalating and we can't add another war to the mix."

My spine snaps straight, adrenaline coursing through my body. "Have the threats increased? Who's behind it? The initiates at the new warehouse should be about ready if the timeline hasn't changed. Wright should have more information on it."

I hate not being there. My place is at the Kings' mansion, making sure the family stays safe. If something happens to them on my watch, I'll be to blame. We can't afford to lose any of them. It was hard enough when they went to Rima ten years ago with no guarantee they'd safely return. At this point, there's no one else to take over for them. The city would fall into disarray.

"Settle down," Sam says, pulling me from my thoughts. "These aren't the problems you need to be dealing with right now. We're a lot better prepared than we were when you were eighteen. Your focus is on Emma. Actually, I wouldn't be surprised if Shane tells you to keep her in Ridgewood. She might be safer there, though he's as stubborn as she is."

The need to cuss her out wells up inside me and I shove it down. Once again, I'm being relegated to babysitting their precious little mafia princess. I worked hard to rise in the ranks and be able to lead. It took me a long time to break free of their perception of me. Spending so long being Emma's personal guard and then dealing with the fallout of her confession set me back further than it should have. If she would have kept her feelings to herself, none of this would have happened. Even after growing up in the mafia, she never learned how to keep her emotions in check.

"Anything else?" It's the closest I'll ever come to a dismissal.

"Suppose not. Don't fuck this up, Titus. If she gets hurt, even if it's her own fault, I won't be able to save you from their wrath. And I doubt I'd try." She hangs up before I can respond. Not that I'd know what to say. I always knew this was a doomed mission.

I lean against an abandoned building, the brick digging into shoulder blades. I push harder into the rough surface.

Run, a small voice in the back of my mind whispers. It vaguely sounds like my father's, though I haven't heard it since I was a child. It's more of an echo of a memory I've made up. The advice isn't far off what he'd probably tell me to do. Running was always his way of dealing with things. At least, that's what my mama always said. Not that she was much better.

I shake my head, dislodging the disjointed memories from my mind. No use reliving what I can't even remember. The King mafia has been my life for over two decades—much longer than I ever spent with my biological family. Sam noticing how loyal I am to them was all I've ever wanted. The mafia is all I need. They give me a purpose. After Hep, the previous head of security, died, Shane gave me the option to walk away. He didn't realize I have nowhere else to go. Not that I'd leave even with all the danger surrounding my position. Emma might drive me to the brink, though.

"Titus? What the hell happened to you?" Joy's voice floats around me and I glance up.

I didn't realize I had started walking again, much less all the way to her shop. I swallow hard and tuck my chin to my chest. My balls don't hurt anymore and the nausea has finally subsided. It's not like Joy can help me if I am pissing blood. Gazing at my palms, I realize I might need help with them. I lift them and she sighs.

"Well, shit. Come on in and I'll fix you up." She holds the door open, and I slip inside.

I'll figure out what to do about Emma later when my mind isn't going a million different directions. I've had enough to deal with today. Everything else will wait until tomorrow.

Chapter 13

Emma

As Titus slips past the dark-haired woman, thunder rolls overhead. An ominous omen if I ever heard one. At least now I understand why Titus actually came to Ridgewood. I knew there was something more to it than bringing me back to Synd.

Shane might disagree, but everyone else knows I can take care of myself. Between Sam and my trainers, I have enough skills to travel on my own. I've done it dozens of times over the last five years. Titus's comments from earlier don't have any bearing on whether I can drive. I have no doubt Shane told Titus to come, but my former handler could have refused. He could have told them it wasn't necessary. He's been around long enough they would have listened to him.

The wind kicks up suddenly, whipping around my body as I huddle on the roof of the abandoned storefront. I pull the hood of my sweatshirt tighter over my head and try to peer into the window. Greenery obscures my view, though. Not that I want to spy on him. He's free to do whatever the hell he wants. He's not mine and never will be, thank fuck.

"That poor woman," I whisper.

He's probably much nicer to her than he is to me. They don't have the baggage he and I do. They're probably very happy together. She and I are complete opposites, at least in looks. I'm not usually one to compare myself, but it's hard when Titus's criticisms of me still ring in my ears. After he was no longer my personal guard, I avoided him like the plague. Didn't mean I wasn't aware of the shit he said behind my back. Everything from my height to the color of my hair was fair game for him.

My phone buzzes and I reluctantly pull it out. Sam's name flashes across the screen and I hesitate. I've ignored all of them so far, thinking I can deal with my problems on my own. With Titus tapping out, I realize I truly *am* on my own. I may not want him here, but he was a little slice of home. An extra safety net if I needed one.

I swallow hard before answering. "Hey, Sam."

"Emmie?" It's Alex's voice filtering through the line and a sob catches in my throat.

"Hi, Alex." I try to keep my tone even. I don't want him to think I'm breaking down. Because I'm not. I'm perfectly fucking fine.

"Did you know your brain is constantly eating itself?"

A giggle bursts from me and I shake my head. "Should I be worried?"

"Nah. Helps with grey matter. And even if it was bad, at least you can't feel it. Like it doesn't even exist."

Tears fill my eyes and I slam them shut. This is why I've been avoiding them. I wasn't willing to admit how much I missed my family. My cheeks burn as I swipe the wetness from them. I can't admit to Alex how much trouble I'm in. Even with a plan, I still feel like I'm drowning. Asking for their help would be mortifying. I'm supposed to be an adult and adults deal with their own problems. They don't go running to their siblings and beg them to fix things.

"Did you know there was a chicken who lived a year and a half without its head?" I ask as I attempt to get my shit together.

"Oooh, when was that? I bet it was the 40s, wasn't it? All that weird shit happened in the 40s for some reason."

"It was indeed in the 40s." I clear my throat and brace myself. "So, what's up?"

He sighs and I wonder if he's holding in his emotions as much as I am. "I just wanted to make sure you were safe."

I wait, knowing there's more to the story. Alex loves me, but he doesn't just call to make sure I'm safe. He'd harass me over text or send me an off-the-wall care package. He called for something more and if I wait long enough, he'll crack. He always does. It's why I always asked him if I could go out. He'd hem and haw, but eventually he'd give in. For a guy who grew up in the mafia, he's a big ole softie.

He huffs, and a smile tugs at my lips. "I need a favor. And I don't want no sass from you when you hear it."

"Well, I never," I say with a southern drawl.

"Shut it, Emma, or I'll tell Shane about the time you set the kitchen on fire."

"You wouldn't," I gasp. Fucking snitch.

"Damn straight I will. And he'll make you work off the money he had to put into the repairs. Hope you like chopping wood."

I snort, tilting my head when a shadow filters through the plants blocking the window of the shop. I can't make out who it is, and it only serves to piss me off more. Instead of leaving, like I should, I hunker down in my sweatshirt.

"We don't even own an axe. Or a shed to keep wood. I'm more likely to chop off my leg rather than split a log in half."

"Lucky for you, Blue knows how to do it. I'm sure he'd be willing to teach you. Shit, I got a better idea—babysitting."

I wince, biting my lip. I love my niblings, but they're a fucking handful. Babysitting them is one of the hardest things I've ever done. And I've done some pretty tough things in my twenty-something years.

"Fine. What's the favor?"

He spends the next ten minutes rambling on about some investment he sunk his money into when I went to college. I was a late bloomer, opting to stay home after I graduated, much to Shane's dismay. There was too much going on and I couldn't abandon them. Not that I was able to help much. I spent most of my time in the garage with Alex, learning how to fix up cars.

I check back in when he clears his throat. "You stopped listening, didn't you?"

"Can you blame me? You were prattling on and I'm fucking freezing out here." Instantly, I'm kicking myself. He hasn't asked a single question about where I am or what I'm doing and now I've thrown the door wide open.

"You hanging out on a rooftop or something?"

"Maybe?" I mumble.

He chuckles and I can practically hear him rolling his eyes. "You really are a little too much like Sam for your own good. Alright, so this investment is technically a chop shop. Got some guys up there who run it. Gives them something to do and I get a little cash on the side I can funnel into things I want."

"Like more cars?" I chuckle, but he doesn't join in.

"No," he murmurs, his voice suddenly gentle. "Aelia set up a fund for the people they rescued from the Guild. We've donated what we can, but I wanted to do more."

My heart skips a beat, shame flooding my systems. Apologies crowd my mouth, though I doubt that's what he wants. I help Aelia when I visit Rima. My time is all I have to give them, which doesn't seem like enough. It's never enough. Those victims deserve more than what I can give. I'm not surprised Alex created a whole other source of revenue to aid them.

"Emma," he says, a warning in his tone. "Don't. This isn't a contest on who helps more. Besides, I need you to go check on the shop. I usually get a report, but I haven't heard from them. I just need to make sure it's still there and not in trouble."

"So let me get this straight. I went off to college and you decided to arrange a chop shop in the same city. You sent some guys up here and have been collecting a cut from them for years. And you usually have someone who sends you reports, but they're ghosting you and you need me to check it out?"

"Sounds about right."

"And you expect me to believe you've never come to inspect the place on your own?"

"Uh, what?"

I huff, eyeing the ever-darkening sky. "Just admit that you've been to Ridgewood and didn't even bother to visit."

He chuckles as anger and hurt bubble up inside me. "Oh Emmie. No. I have a guy who does that. It runs on its own. I just put in part of the capital. I'm not coming to town and then slipping away in the dead of the night. Even if your apartment is a piece of shit and I'd never sleep on that godforsaken couch."

"My couch is comfy, thank you very much," I snap, mollified by his explanation.

"I'll text you the address. Just check it out and let me know. And for the love of all that's unholy in this world, do not engage."

"Fine," I mutter, all while making plans to engage as much as I want.

"I'm serious, Emma. They won't know what to do if you walk in there. Plus, you'll be putting yourself and everyone else at risk of exposure. Just leave it be." He waits until I agree before sighing. "One last thing, and you're not going to like it. Titus..."

"I don't want to talk about him. The fact you sent him up here in the first place to collect me like I was some prized hippo statue being shipped home is ridiculous. However, I'll do you a favor and send him back to you alive." I think it's a perfectly fair offer. At this point, I can't send him back completely unscathed.

"We need you to tell him what's going on up there, Emma." He doesn't bother acknowledging my generous offer.

I bite my lip as the lights in the shop window dim and the welcome sign winks out. It's almost dark now, thunder nearly a constant rumble overhead. I'll be lucky to make it back to the apartment before the skies open up on me. I should get going since it's clear Titus isn't coming home tonight.

Not home.

I shake my head, steeling myself against the onslaught of unwelcome emotions. My apartment isn't even *my* home, much less his. Crashing on my couch doesn't entitle him to call it home. Not that he ever would in the first place. I force myself to focus on the conversation instead of worrying about where Titus will sleep tonight.

"You mean Ren wants me to tell Titus all my deep, dark secrets because Ren got an inkling in the pit of his stomach that I'm out sacrificing small animals under the full moon. Or Lacey did some digging and found out there's an underground break-dancing troupe and Shane's worried I'll run off with them. Or Sam—"

"Okay, okay. I get it. You can handle your own shit. And you don't need Titus there. Blah, blah, blah. Just don't lose our head of security. I know shit is weird, but he's loyal."

Alex will refuse to expand no matter how much I push him. It's more than Titus being loyal. It's the reason I never pushed for him to be moved or sent away. I could have asked, given all the reasons he shouldn't be so close to the family. My stubbornness got in the way. I didn't want him to think he'd won. When I got older, I realized how much my brothers relied on Titus—how much they liked him. It's more than his loyalty. And I hate it.

"I'll check on your chop shop and let you know. You going to tell me why I need to come home?" They've piecemealed information out to me in various text messages I've mostly ignored. It's not unusual they keep me out of the loop. It's the first time it's really pissed me off.

"Don't worry about what's happening here. Just get your shit together, check on the shop, then come home. Gotta go. Love you, Emmie."

He hangs up, and I press my lips together. I turn away from the windows I've been fixated on the entire time I've been talking to Alex. A message rings through and I scowl at the address. Turns out I don't have to check out anything since Titus is currently *in* the chop shop. I could warn Titus about Alex wanting an update. Or I could let Titus sink his own ship.

I slip my phone in my pocket before shimmying down the pipe attached to the side of the building. The clang of the metal ringing through the air as I hit the fire escape has me wincing. No one seems to be around, but I'd rather not announce my presence.

Rain splatters slowly on the sidewalk, and I pick up the pace. Two blocks later and I'm drenched as cold droplets slam into me. I don't care anymore. After finding out why Titus really came to Ridgewood and the conversation with Alex, I'm drained. The weather is just the icing on the cake.

None of it matters anymore. Titus showing up threw me off. Now it's time to get my shit together, just like Alex said. Once I get home, I'll let go of all the resentment and pain. For the rest of the walk home, though, I'll let the rain wash my tears away.

Chapter 14

Titus

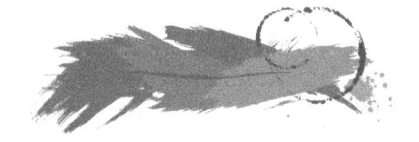

Joy slams a first aid kit on the counter, grumbling under her breath. Her hand swings out, slapping my arm as I lift my finger to my face.

"My eye itches," I complain.

"You touch your eye and I'll punch you in the kidney," she snarls, then flips the cover of the metal box.

I grunt and wander to the window of Joy's shop. I can't see much through the plants, but I doubt anyone is out in this rain, anyway. My gaze darts to the neighboring building's roof. Nothing moves there either.

"What are you staring at?" Joy calls and I turn.

"Nothing." It's the truth, even if she doesn't look like she believes me. Someone may have been there earlier. I can't be sure, though, and I'm not going to admit anything to Joy.

She huffs, pointing to the stool next to her. "You realize you burst a blood vessel in your eye, right? How'd that happen?"

I'm hesitant to tell her about my altercation with Emma. It was hard enough to pretend like I was clumsy and fell onto glass. If I reveal it was because Emma kneed me in the balls, I don't know if I'll recover.

"I'm allergic to roses. Started sneezing and couldn't stop," I mutter.

She rolls her eyes, clearly not believing me. We're not close enough for her to know my allergies. Exhaustion settles over me as Joy snatches my wrist and pushes my arm onto the counter. Leaning over my palm, she grumbles under her breath again. I ignore her while she wields the tweezers, tugging bits of glass from my skin.

"You tell her where you were going?" she asks and my head snaps up.

"Who?" I grit my teeth while she rolls her eyes again. Last thing I'm going to do is talk about Emma with her.

"You know exactly who I'm talking about. Don't play me for a fool."

I glance away as I ignore the buzzing in my pocket. It's probably Ren, demanding an update. I don't have one and I'm not about to be bitched out. The longer I'm away from Synd, the less I'm concerned about their reaction. Probably not the best idea since they hold my life in their hands. I'm a lot less concerned after talking to Sam, though.

"If you think I'm going to have a gossip session with you, then you're definitely a fool."

"God, you're an asshole. No wonder she wants nothing to do with you." She yanks out a particularly deep piece and I wince. "Don't be a baby. You brought this upon yourself."

"It's that fuckwad Twitch's fault. Who the hell delivers over a hundred flowers to someone's doorstep? And then doesn't say a goddamn word about it?"

"A romantic? Some women like flowers. Not *me*, but some of them do." She pins me with a look I can't decipher before returning to her task.

We sit in silence for several minutes before she wiggles her fingers at me for my other hand. This one is worse, and my stomach jumps each time she digs the tweezers into the wounds. Hopefully on the outside I'm not reacting. If she blabs to the men in the back about me wincing, I'll never be able to regain their respect. My mind wanders back to the look in Emma's eyes when I had my hand around her throat.

I shake my head as I mutter, "She doesn't even like roses."

"Were they red roses?" Joy asks, jolting me back to the present.

"No. Yellow. Who the fuck buys a woman roses, much less yellow ones?"

She smirks before tossing the tweezers on the counter and grabs a tube of medicine. "Well, yellow roses usually mean friendship. Did he fuck up? How many were there?"

"Twitch definitely doesn't see her as a friend. Boy is pining hard. I don't know why they broke up, though." Maybe I do want to talk about her. If I get this shit off my chest, maybe my mind will stop focusing so much on her.

"Sometimes..." she murmurs as she wraps gauze around my palms.

"Sometimes what?" I grunt, my lip curling.

She sighs as she straightens and leans against the counter. "Sometimes yellow roses mean forgiveness. Usually between friends, but if he thinks she likes roses, then there ya go. Depending on how many there were, he could be saying a lot."

"What the fuck are you talking about?"

"The number of roses means different things. You said over a hundred, but if it was ninety-nine, he was saying he'll love her as long as he lives," she says hesitantly and I growl. "With that reaction, I really don't want to tell you what a hundred and eight roses means."

My eyes fall closed. "Tell me."

"It's a proposal of marriage. Not that I think he's asking her to marry him with roses. Probably doesn't even know the meanings."

My jaw aches as I grind my teeth together. I don't give a shit what Emma does with her life. Especially her love life. I could give two shits whether she's fucked half the campus. She's free to do whatever the hell she wants. If she brings Twitch to Synd, though, expecting him to survive in our world, she's in for a rude awakening. And I'm not about to save her ass when her brothers tear into her for bringing home such a douchebag.

"Not my problem." I push to my feet, ignoring the twinge in my back from sitting hunched for so long.

"Well, it might become your problem if they actually do get married."

"She's not mine. If she marries him, it has no bearing on me."

She snorts as she packs the supplies away. "And what do you suppose will happen in the future? When the King brothers are gone, who do you suppose will take over? If it's Emma, well, her husband will play a key role in the organization. Granted, that shit probably won't happen for a while, given they've got a pretty good hold on Synd and they're not especially old. Still..."

She disappears into the back room, humming to herself as if she didn't just drop a damn bomb on my world. I usually don't have the luxury of thinking about the future. We deal with problems as they arise. Sure, we anticipate issues that might become disasters, but twenty, thirty years down the road? Not something we typically talk about. At least, the Kings don't bring it up to me.

"In the grand scheme of things, I'm expendable to them," I call after her.

Joy saunters back and leans against the door frame. "Be honest with yourself, Titus. Do the Kings truly treat you like they do the other guards?"

"I'm not having this conversation with you, Joy. Got enough I'm dealing with, without you throwing out ridiculous theories. I'm not about to do a deep dive into my position within the mafia."

"Within the family, but whatever. What are you going to do about her?"

I grab my sweatshirt and tug it over my head. With my hands awkwardly wrapped, it isn't easy. Joy clears her throat when my face finally reappears and I scowl.

"I'm going to do my job. Nothing more. Nothing less. The Kings want her home, so I'll bring her home. Ren wants to know what trouble she's embroiled in, so I'll figure that shit out." I glance at her face and she raises an eyebrow. "Without her. She won't admit anything to me."

"Well, duh. I wouldn't tell you shit either. While I don't support going behind her back, perhaps a different approach to the situation could help."

"If she won't tell me, then I'll *have* to go behind her back," I grumble.

She pushes from the door frame and plops onto the stool. "In that case, be prepared for the consequences."

"I've been dealing with her bratty attitude for years. I'm pretty sure I can handle her reaction."

She'll bitch and moan about me interfering. If she finally calls Sam back, she'll complain about me and how I meddled. Thankfully, I won't have to deal with anything from Sam's end. I might have to start wearing a nut cup, but that's a small price to pay for keeping my junk protected. I doubt she'll go beyond those things.

"You keep saying she's a brat, but you realize she's not a kid anymore, right? She's a woman now."

My stomach tightens and I will my cock not to react. "I'm well aware."

"I'm sure you are," she murmurs.

I snarl at her, then stomp toward the door. I refuse to stand around while Joy alludes to something I'm not ready to face. There's nothing between Emma and me. Even if she wasn't a mafia brat, she's too fucking young. She might be an adult now, but it doesn't change her age. Five years isn't a lot in the grand scheme of things. Either way, I'll cling to that excuse for as long as possible. Emma King is off-limits for so many reasons, least of all her age.

I unlock the door and push it open, battling the wind and rain. I'll be soaked by the time I take two steps. Doubt I'll be doing anything in this weather.

"Titus," Joy calls, and I glance over my shoulder. "Don't be an asshat and ignore shit when a good thing is staring you in the face."

I snort, rolling my eyes. "Emma King is more likely to punch me than stare at me. And I don't blame her one fucking bit."

I step into the freezing rain, droplets pelting my face as I tug the hood over my head. It doesn't do much to protect me from the elements. I'm three blocks away before it hits me how Joy manipulated me. Nothing good ever comes from talking about Emma. I've successfully avoided updates about her for years. All it took was two interactions and Joy had me spilling shit I haven't addressed in years.

She weaseled her way in and set me up just to get me to talk. And I barely even noticed. I'm losing my touch. Being in Ridgewood throws me off. When I come up here to check on the shop, I never stay more than a day. Synd is home and where I belong. I understand the rules there. I understand my place. Blaming the city instead of the woman residing in the shitty apartment I'm currently staring at is easier.

A shadow flits past the window and I grit my teeth. I may have told Emma I was done, but I can't leave her alone. Between Devon and her problems, one of them will catch up with her before long. I refuse to be held responsible if something happens to her. Ren keeps texting me, ordering me to ignore anyone who tells me to bring Emma to Synd. He needs to know what she's involved in. I suspect it has less to do with someone following us back and more to do with his need to know what's going on.

I'm fucking freezing and in pain, so I hurry inside. Hopefully, Emma's shower gets hot enough to chase away the chill settling in my bones. The lights in the hallway flicker as thunder shakes the old windows. Emma better be tucked away in her apartment instead of frolicking around in this weather. It was bad enough the other night, and it was clear then.

Slipping the extra key Shane gave me from my pocket, I hold my breath. The door swings open and I spin to the alarm system. It lights up the dark space, but stays quiet at least. She must have gone to her room while I climbed the stairs. I'm not surprised she's going to bed early. Usually an episode takes her out for a while. With only a few hours' rest, I'm sure she was dragging.

I collapse on the couch and sink into the cushions. For once, I'm thankful for this abhorrent piece of shit. I tip my head back and close my eyes with a sigh.

"What the hell are you doing? Get off!" Emma's shrill voice cuts through the exhaustion.

I launch upright, reaching for my gun. I almost bowl her over in my haste to reach her bedroom. My gaze darts around the space as I grab her wrist and yank her around my body. She curses, digging her nails into my hand when I don't let go. If I could, I'd lock her away in the bathroom while I search her room for whoever she was yelling at.

Her knee slams into my ass, and I growl over my shoulder. She bares her teeth as if it will intimidate me into letting her go. It won't.

"Would you knock it off? Who the fuck was it? Twitch?" I lean into her room and glance around.

"Let me go," she hisses. "I don't know what the fuck you're talking about."

"Who's in here?"

She huffs as I squint at her window. I doubt it's open, but I can't tell if someone was in here without going into the room. If he's hiding in her closet, I'd rather not give him an opportunity to stab me in the back. Then again, Emma is plastered against me, so he'll hit her. Neither scenario is particularly appealing.

"You, asshole. You're here. And sitting on my fucking couch while you're soaking wet. What the hell is wrong with you?" She yanks her arm away and I release her before turning slowly. "You already broke into my apartment. *Again.* The least you could do was have the decency to not track water all over the damn place."

Growling, I stomp to the bathroom and slam the door behind me. As long as she's alive and safe in her apartment, I don't have to deal with her. She can scold me all she wants. She'll be screaming into the void.

Chapter 15

Emma

I'm officially in the shittiest scenario I've ever been in. It's not even the fact I have a fucking shadow. When Titus started following me around campus, it wasn't anything new. He did it for years when I was in high school. It's been a long time and we're both adults now, but the feeling isn't all that different.

I'm different, though. And it's not even because I'm not the person I was before. Here, on this campus and in this city, I'm the complete opposite from when I'm at home. In Synd, an air of uncertainty and risk surrounds me merely because of my last name. Even those who don't know my family is mafia still understand the power we wield. I operated within that sphere, emulating Sam a lot of the time.

Once Sam came to live with us, she pulled away bit by bit from the socialite lifestyle she showed to the world. Watching her shed the weight of being someone she wasn't helped me in a way she'll never understand. I followed in her footsteps, learning how to balance being in the spotlight all while knowing how to kill someone seventeen ways to Sunday.

When I came to college, I shed the scary mafia persona and dove headfirst into an alternate reality. I studied the other women on campus and imitated them until the moves felt natural. After spending so many years making myself as small as possible, it was a strange experience to be outgoing.

"Do you need to follow so closely? You're going to trip me," I hiss through my grin as another girl passes us. Not that she notices me. Her eyes are firmly fixed on the man prowling behind me.

"If I was sure you wouldn't take off at the drop of a hat, I wouldn't have to," he murmurs.

I stop abruptly, the smell of coffee luring me to the cart to my left. Titus's fingers brush my wrist as he tries to grab me, but I slip into the crowd before he can.

Usually, campus empties when there's even a bit of a break in our schedules. Daisy mentioned a lot of people are sticking around for various events, including the new club that just opened in town. Being a small town, it's kind of a big deal.

I wave to someone from one of my classes, and she lifts her hand, smiling. My own smile is forced, but she doesn't notice. None of them will. Some days it's harder than others to pretend I'm this fucking bubbly, especially when I've had a growly man crashing on my couch and putting me on edge.

"Hey, Holden. How's it going?" I ask as I step up to the cart.

Holden glares, hunkering down in his winter coat. I think it's a bit much given it's only cloudy. It's not supposed to snow today, yet he tugs thick gloves on. I wonder how he's going to pour my coffee with them on. Titus's looming presence presses into my back and Holden's eyes widen. Silently, I pray he doesn't comment on my shadow.

Holden's gaze returns to me, annoyance stamped across his face. "It's fucking cold. I shouldn't even be out here. Plenty of places to get coffee inside, but fuck me, I guess. You want the usual?"

"That I do. Unless you want me to go inside instead." I smirk, raising an eyebrow.

"I'm not allowed to refuse service." He rolls his eyes, then glances at Titus. "You want anything?"

A noise from the back of my throat leaves me without warning. "We're not together."

"I'll have what she's having," Titus says.

Shit. I could have convinced people we didn't know each other. Unless they saw him carrying my ass out of the Hub. I could probably gaslight others into believing it wasn't me. With him following me around like a lost puppy, I doubt I can pull it off now.

Holden's nostrils flare as he tugs his gloves off and starts my coffee. Part of me wants to cuss Titus out. The more rational part of me tells me to ignore him. I can still get out of this if I avoid addressing him. Maybe someone will assume he's stalking me and take him out. Then I'll have to deal with him going feral, though.

I peek at him from the corner of my eye as he steps next to me. I wonder if I could take him down. Sure, I'm trained on how to deal with someone so much larger than me, but he grew up in the mafia. Plus, he's the head of security now. I doubt he's letting himself go like the others before him. I've been slacking while he's been training, which doesn't bode well for me.

"Fourteen," Holden grunts.

I dig in my pocket for my money, wavering whether I should pay for his and get this over with or make a stand by refusing to cover his drink. Titus beats me to it. Fucking asshole. From the look on Holden's face, everyone and their mother will be hearing about this. I'm not exactly popular at school, but a lot of people come to this coffee cart.

College isn't like high school when it comes to cliques. Our campus isn't very large, though. Word can spread fast, at least in certain circles. If Holden starts spreading gossip, the image I've presented to everyone around me will be shattered. Titus isn't the type of guy I've surrounded myself with. As I weave my way through the crowd of students, I wonder if Devon was merely part of my cover. I thought I liked him and his easy-going ways. He has an air of innocence to him.

I spot Daisy on a nearby bench and hurry over to her. I crash next to her, almost spilling my coffee as I tug her close.

"Do you think I used Devon as a cover?" I whisper in her ear.

She pulls back, eyeing me before leaning close again. "A cover for what? Who your family is?"

I nod, glancing around to make sure Titus isn't sneaking up on us. "You said yourself, I never told him I loved him. We dated for like three fucking years. And I hesitated every single time he'd say it."

She holds up her hand, narrowing her eyes. "Are you telling me he told you he loved you—multiple times—and you hesitated to say it back, and he never said a goddamn word about it? You never had a conversation about it? He didn't question why you weren't reciprocating?"

"Not exactly."

"Well, what exactly are you saying then? Because it sounds like you strung the poor guy along for fucking years. Talk about unrequited love." Daisy may be my closest friend, but she doesn't hold back when she's calling me out.

I wince, wrinkling my nose. "It sounds bad when you put it like that."

"That's because it is," she hisses. "I may not fully understand your past or what your life is like…Hades knows—"

"Hades? Seriously?"

"Shh. Don't interrupt me. Hades knows you're keeping shit from me." She gives me a pointed look and my cheeks heat. "However, you basically lead the guy on for so long, letting him believe you two would have a future together. I'm surprised he put up with it for that long. Are you sure he never questioned you on it? Even subtly?"

I spot Titus over the heads of a group of woman chatting by the coffee cart. Ducking, I send a silent prayer to Hades he doesn't notice me. At least not yet. He's the last person I need around while I'm having an existential crisis.

"I mean, he never outright said, 'I love you, Emma.' It was more of an alluding type of thing. Like, 'I care about you. You mean so much to me. I don't know what I'd do without you.' Once he told me the sun sparkled from my eyes, which was fucking weird. There was a lot of awkward smiling on my part." The more I confess about my previous relationship, the more I realize I never really stood a chance at convincing Daisy I was in the right here.

Daisy presses her lips together, her gaze darting over my shoulder once, then again. A man clears his throat behind me and I slam my eyes closed. If Devon overheard me, then I'm the asshole. He's not a bad guy and I don't want to hurt him. I don't want to face him and have to explain away what I said. I don't even have an excuse at the ready.

"How you hoodwinked someone into thinking you're anything other than a raging bitch is beyond me." Titus's voice washes over me and rage bubbles in my gut. Daisy's sound of protest doesn't help.

"I'm only a bitch to those who deserve it. Now fuck off."

Daisy tucks her chin to her chest. I'm not surprised she doesn't have a retort for him like I do. She's much too kind for something like that. She's better than I'll ever be. Often I've wondered if I should push her away. I don't want the shadows I was raised in to touch her light. She deserves more than what I can give her with my friendship.

"Can't do that, darling. Time to go." He has the good sense not to attempt to force me. He's going to have to if he wants me to go anywhere with him.

Daisy sucks in a sharp breath and I wonder if she's laughing or afraid of our back and forth. I'm sure most people would be put off by the way we talk to each other. I'd be perfectly fine not engaging with him at all. Unfortunately after the last few days, I doubt I'll get rid of him anytime soon. He literally snarled at me when I suggested he go fuck a duck this morning.

"So for lunch I was thinking Monsoon. Or maybe Tricky's? Did the others say anything? I haven't checked the group chat in a minute." I dig my phone from my pocket.

"You're not going," Titus growls.

Pulling up the chat, I find over two hundred unread messages. I sigh, slipping it back into my pocket without reading anything. Daisy keeps up with it better than me. I'll just let her catch me up instead.

"Tricky's has breakfast all day." I can practically hear Titus seething in anger behind me. It flows from him in waves, threatening to burn me up.

"Um, yeah. I don't know if we should go there," Daisy mumbles.

I cock my head, willing her to look me in the eye. She peeks at me through the curtain of hair blocking most of her face. As soon as she glances over my shoulder, she ducks her head again. I sigh, reining in the urge to punch Titus in the dick, then plaster on a smile.

"What's wrong with Tricky's?"

"Don't know why you're talking about this," Titus hisses. "You're not going."

Bold of him to assume he has any say in the matter. Daisy should know I don't want to go to Tricky's. It's too early for the good buffet there. The cook this morning isn't as good as the one on Monday afternoons. Anything to rile Titus up, though.

"I'm not feeling breakfast. And I'm slightly concerned about the company there." She straightens and presses her lips together. "Monsoon's food is terrible. If we're going to do this, I'm not putting up with shitty food."

As much as I want to fuck with Titus, I'd rather not put up with shitty food, either. We reserve Monsoon for drinking. Tricky's would make Titus the most uncomfortable, what with the half-naked dancing going on in the background, but we usually only go when one of our friends is working.

"No one is going anywhere regardless of the quality of food." Titus's mutterings are getting louder. If he keeps it up, others will take notice and I'll have to deal with him directly.

I snap my fingers, an actual grin blooming on my face. "The Hungry Beaver. Quick, simple, and good food."

"Yeah, I could get down with the Beaver," Daisy says, and I bust out laughing.

"I'm sure you could." I wiggle my eyebrows at her and she giggles.

"If I was going for *that*, I'd have voted for Tricky's. Haley's working today. Oh, and she invited us on Saturday. Apparently, we'll get in for half off the cover." She focuses on the phone in her hand and a few seconds later, my own buzzes. It doesn't let up for at least a minute as the others respond.

"Alright, we've got six going, so eight all together." Daisy glances up and clears her throat. "Maybe nine."

I stand, tugging her with me. When I loop our arms together, I dig my fingers into her sweatshirt. She keeps trying to glance over her shoulder and it's frustrating. Logically, I understand she's not used to us, but annoyance still weaves its way through me.

"One of these days we need to check out the Tower. I heard they have a secret entrance to the basement," I say, trying to pull her attention back to me.

"I heard they put a net around the rooftop you can crawl around on...and do other things." She giggles again as we make our way through the crowd of thinning students.

Her words send a flurry of images through my head as I imagine what it would be like to be so exposed while doing something so intimate. My gaze skips around, barely registering anything while my mind throws fantasies at me. I'm ignoring that the man in those fantasies looks suspiciously like Titus. He's not the only tall drink of water around here. Sure, he has an edge to him, but it's merely a cover for his asshole-ishness. I snort to myself and Daisy gives me a questioning look. I shake my head, not wanting to explain I'm amused at my own made-up words.

My laughter dies in my throat as I jerk Daisy to a stop. Titus's hard body slams into mine and I stumble. His arm circles my waist, pulling me tight against his chest. My eyes meet Devon's across the square. His gaze darts down and Titus fingers dig into my hip. As much as I don't like the very fucking public display Titus is asserting, I'm grateful. Because by the expression on Devon's face, I'm in deeper shit than I realized.

Chapter 16

Titus

Devon's face keeps flashing through my mind, and it's distracting as hell. Emma doesn't seem to be fazed anymore since she's laughing with her friends. I didn't want Emma flouncing around town without a care in the world by herself in the first place. And I sure as hell didn't want to be at the fucking Hungry Beaver. Who the fuck names a sandwich shop after a euphemism? I half expect Willow to pop from the back with her pink-streaked hair streaming behind her.

"You did not just say you'd crack your kneecaps," one of her friends shrieks. I think her name is Haley, and she apparently works at Tricky's.

"Well, when you're presented with such an impressive specimen..." another woman says, and I roll my eyes.

Thankfully, there was an open table by the door so I didn't have to sit with them. Every once in a while one of them will glance over at me, but I've been studiously ignoring them. I hate having to tail Emma around. It reminds me too much of when we were younger. At least this time, she actually has friends. It was pretty pathetic watching her eat alone for years. Eating with her wasn't an option then and now I don't want to.

"Can a dick ever truly be impressive? I mean, sure, the girth could be spectacular and the length magnificent, but in the end it's still just a dick. And they're *not* pretty at all." Emma's voice rolls over the other patrons. I expect someone to tell them off, but no one bats an eye.

"Depends on the dick, I'd think," Daisy chimes to the chorus of giggles.

"There's certainly a few of them I'd like to inspect. For scientific purposes, of course," Haley says.

I make the mistake of glancing at them right then and find most of their eyes on me. Glaring merely sends them into more peals of laughter. Emma avoids my gaze, clearly pissed about the turn in their conversation. It's her own damn fault. She knew exactly what would happen when she insisted on coming here. And again when she chimed in her lovely observations about dicks.

Emma slowly turns her head until her eyes bore into mine. "I'm sure you can find prettier ones that aren't attached to a raging asshole."

Haley doesn't seem to notice Emma isn't really speaking to her as she snorts. "Oh honey. They can't be assholes when they're moaning."

Emma averts her gaze, finally realizing I'm not going to back down or retaliate. She can make all the accusations she wants. She's not imparting some vast wisdom I wasn't aware of. I am a raging asshole. And I do have a pretty cock. Not that she'd know that. I'm not going to inform her or her friends either.

"You just haven't been dicked down by the *right* asshole, Emma. I'm sure you could find someone who'd be willing," another friend, Jenny I'm pretty sure, says after the tittering dies down.

Emma smirks, and I narrow my eyes as I track her profile. "I'm perfectly content with the dicking downs I've received. No need to fix what isn't broken, ladies."

I grit my teeth, pushing to my feet. I stomp toward the small back hallway to the bathroom. If Emma isn't able to keep herself out of trouble for the five minutes it takes me to piss, she doesn't deserve to live. Especially with all her extensive training. Prickles of annoyance batter my skin as I do my business.

After I wash my hands, I brace them on the sink and suck in a deep breath. I don't give a fuck who Emma's been letting dick her down, as she so crassly put it. She can fuck whoever she wants and clearly she doesn't have complaints. Alluding to her friends that *I'm* the one fucking her? Therein lies the problem.

Right now, it might be just with her girlfriends. If it somehow gets back to the Kings, though...

Then I'll be dead.

I like my head attached to my body. I'm also quite fond of my limbs. Plus, I can't handle the squelching sound when an eyeball is removed. It's not standard practice in Synd, but I'm not taking the chance. Confronting her in a cafe called the Hungry Beaver in front of those women would only solidify their assumptions. I doubt she'll listen to me either way, but I'd rather get my ass chewed out in private.

A knock at the door has me gritting my teeth. I splash some water on my face, letting the droplets slide down my neck and cool my flushed skin. If I'm this worked up here, I can't imagine what it would be like at a nightclub or a sex club, which is exactly what Tricky's and the Tower sound like, respectively. She ignored me every single time I told her we weren't going here. Like hell am I going to let her go out at night where a shit ton of horny frat boys grind on unsuspecting women. I'll lose her in the crowd, and she'll end up blowing up another building.

When there's another knock, I resist the urge to fling open the door and bury my fist in their face. Clearly, there's someone in here and their patience is in the gutter. Common courtesy dictates they wait for him to be done, but apparently that's lost on some people.

When I finally have my shit together, I tug open the door to an empty hallway. I lean forward, scanning the small area. Whoever needed to use the bathroom so fucking badly must have given up. I saunter out, letting the wood swing shut behind me. I make it all of three steps before I realize I can't hear the girls anymore. They had no problem filling the shop with their laughter before. Why stop now?

"Fuck," I breathe as I step into the main area.

They left. Emma was probably just waiting for me to go to the bathroom so she could slip away. I send her a text with more than a few expletives and slip my phone back in my pocket. I doubt she'll text me back.

"Sir?" a woman asks from behind me, and I turn. "I'm supposed to give you this."

She hands me a napkin and hurries away. A growl sticks in my throat when I read Emma's scrawl. It's nothing mind-blowing—mostly her gloating about pulling one over on me. They couldn't have gone far. I crumple the note in my fist and glance around the space, searching for clues to where she's gone. The farther she runs, the greater my annoyance will grow. Once I catch up to her, she'll learn how far she can truly push me before I snap.

I stomp back to the hallway and shove the back door open. A grungy alley meets me, the dumpster blocking my view. I doubt she came back here, but I'm not really searching for her. The only reason I've insisted on staying close to her is because of the feeling rolling in my gut. Emma doesn't know how to keep herself out of trouble.

When I got out of the shower last night, she'd already gone to bed. I spent the next few hours peering out the window, expecting to spot her form flitting about the shadows. Instead, it felt like someone was watching me. I never actually saw them, but the sensation stayed with me until I fell asleep. If someone is tracking Emma, I need to find them before they get to her.

The end of the alleyway opens up to another street lined with shops selling apparel from the college and a bookstore. I make a beeline for the books. When I was her bodyguard, she'd insist on slipping into every one we saw. It was annoying as hell since I couldn't just sit back and let her wander the aisles. She'd slip out of sight and I'd panic until I found her. Usually, she'd be sitting on the floor, her head buried in a novel she couldn't put down. If she's anything like she was back then, she definitely insisted on going inside the store.

The bell above the door announces my arrival with a joyful ring, and I scowl. It's so at odds with the emotions thrumming through me. I peer into each aisle, failing to find her. The longer I search for her, the less convinced I am about her being here. This right here is why I think she's still a brat. She's too fucking confident in her skills, thinking she can deal with everything on her own.

When I reach the back of the store, I let out a frustrated growl. I check my phone all while knowing she didn't respond. I text her again with more threats and f-bombs. As I stare at the screen, my chest tightens. My stomach flips and my shoulders curl as a thread of unease coils through me. There's no reason to imagine she's in trouble. This isn't the first time she's run and it probably won't be the last.

I stalk back through the aisles, head whipping from side to side as if she'll pop out of the stacks. My agitation grows when I reach the front and glance out the large window and spot none other than Twitch himself. He's not doing anything suspicious per se, but there's something about his gait. I've spent years perfecting my ability to spot when someone's hiding something. I'd love to say his involvement with Emma has nothing to do with it. I shake my head and shove into the sunlight as Devon slips into the alley.

"What the fuck are you up to, Twitch?" I whisper as I follow him.

He glances over his shoulder, and I duck behind the corner. I count to ten before peeking around the brick. He's continued on, almost to the dumpster now. I slip into the shadows and track him as he stalks along. He's searching for something—or someone. He'll have a rude awakening if it's Emma he's hunting. He obviously doesn't know Emma could kill him before he even hit the ground. I'd be less subtle with my actions, though I doubt I'll have to actually kill him. As long as he stays away from her, we'll be fine. At least that's what I tell myself.

His soft chuckle echoes through the cold air. The nefarious sound sends a chill down my spine. Whatever the hell he's up to, it's not good.

"Oh." Emma's voice bounces off the walls, and I quicken my pace. "What are you doing here, Devon?"

"I could ask you the same thing, Emma. Hanging out in a dirty alley? Not exactly like you," Twitch says with a forced laugh.

I duck behind the dumpster and wait for her to answer. Eavesdropping might backfire on me, but I'd really like to know what the hell Devon wants with Emma. He doesn't seem to like me much, so he's less likely to speak plainly in front of me. Which is the only reason I'm hiding right now. It has nothing to do with curiosity. I grit my teeth and lean against the wall.

"I was thinking about getting a job here. Good to know where they throw the trash."

Devon snorts, his foot scuffling on the concrete. "Hope that wasn't a dig about me."

Emma sighs and I know she's going to placate him. "Of course not."

"Are you going to tell me why you're really out here?"

"I was thinking of taking up smoking. Then I thought better of it. What are you doing here, Devon?" Annoyance weaves through her tone, though I'm sure he'll ignore it.

"Ah well, I was at the bookstore. Thought I saw your new shadow and figured you were around. Did you get my apology?"

She sighs and I imagine she's plastered on a strained smile. "I told you to stop doing things like that. I know you don't understand why we broke up, but you're not going to change my mind with over a hundred yellow roses."

"Ninety-nine," he murmurs so softly I almost miss it.

"What?"

He clears his throat. "There were ninety-nine yellow roses. I realize red might have been too much. It's just what I always bought you before, so it was habit."

I make a mental note to ask Joy what that all means again. With him being so specific, I imagine he knows exactly what the meaning behind it all is. At least he wasn't proposing to Emma.

"I think we need space, Devon. I don't want to hurt you any more than I already have, but we can't keep doing this."

I don't know why she's still placating him. Regardless of what happened between them, he's clearly not getting the message that they're over. Handling him with kid gloves isn't working, yet she keeps trying and I don't understand why. This isn't the girl I once knew. Nor is it the woman I've watched from afar the last few years. Emma King is anything but timid. She wasn't raised to be meek, giving into a man's whims. Even if she doesn't want to hurt his feelings, she needs to grow a goddamn backbone.

"If you'd just listen and stop putting up walls, maybe we wouldn't have to tiptoe around the inevitable, Emma." An edge creeps into Devon's voice and my hands curl into fists at my sides. If he fucks with her, I won't hesitate to step in.

She scoffs, and some of the tension leaves me. "And what, pray tell, is the inevitable?"

"Us together. You know we're perfect for each other, baby doll. We were meant to be together. I don't understand why you're pushing me away."

"Devon, stop."

I can't see whether he's crowding her or if she's responding to his words. I'd rather not reveal my presence unless absolutely necessary. The moment I do, I'll have to deal with him as well as Emma's wrath for interfering with her business. I'm too fucking tired to keep going round for round with her.

"Don't tell me to stop when you know I'm right. When you know you want this."

I step around the dumpster, struggling to keep my steps measured and unassuming. Their forms come into view and I bite back a growl. Devon's fingers are wrapped around her wrists and he's backed her against the wall. She doesn't look worried, but that's not saying a lot since her mask is firmly in place.

"I suggest you let her go before you lose your hands, Twitch."

Chapter 17

Emma

Devon's hands tighten around me and anxiety flashes through me. It's gone before I can fully comprehend it. This is Devon. I was with him for years. It might not have been the most exciting relationship, but I always felt safe. Maybe a bit too safe. He'd never survive in my world, and I can't leave my family behind. He's too docile, too honorable, too weak. Add in the fact I never loved him and I doubt our relationship would have survived.

"Tick. Tock. Twitch. You have five seconds and that's me being generous, which Emma here can attest to." Titus's voice has dropped to a deadly level. We can't afford a body around here. I've piled them up enough for the police to start being suspicious.

Devon's eyes bore into mine as he tugs me away from the wall, but doesn't drop his hold. "Emma doesn't need you to stand up for her, buddy. She knows I'd never hurt her."

I can't tell whether I'm reading too much into Devon's behavior or if Titus's presence is eclipsing my judgement. I have no reason to be scared of either of them. The wrath from my family would rain hellfire upon Titus if he hurt me. If Devon did, well, he'd have a very long period of not walking. And then my family would probably retaliate afterward. I've never had to think about those scenarios before.

"Apparently, you really don't enjoy having hands," Titus murmurs as he slides around Devon and settles behind me. The heat from his body seeps into mine, forcing me to acknowledge how cold I was.

A chill rolls down my spine as I wait for one of them to back the fuck off. I could easily get out of Devon's grasp. His grip isn't harsh, yet I don't want to hurt him. It's the way I've handled everything between Devon and me. If he doesn't let go of me soon, though, I'll have to break free. Otherwise, Titus really will remove his limbs. And I doubt he'll be quick about it.

"Devon," I say, and his eyes snap to mine. "Let go."

He clenches his jaw, brows pulling low. "You can't honestly be choosing him, Em."

"I'm not choosing anyone. We're not together anymore. And Titus is—"

"She's not interested in you anymore, asshole. Take a hint and fuck off," Titus interrupts, and I struggle to keep my face the same calm facade I've held since Devon ambushed me.

I wish he wouldn't have opened his fucking mouth. If I had one of my hands, I'd elbow him in the gut. I might do it anyway later when he's least expecting it. He deserves it even if he has no idea why I'm assaulting him. I could've played Titus off as a family friend. I might have alluded to everyone in Ridgewood that I wasn't in contact with anyone in Synd. Actually, no one knows I'm *from* Synd. Calling him a friend is even more of a stretch.

Messy. This whole fucking thing is messy as fuck. I should have gone back with Titus when he first showed up. My foresight was clouded by his arrival. I might have to cut my losses and hope no one follows me to Synd. And get Daisy out of here. And probably Devon, no matter how much of a shithead he's been lately. Not to mention my other friends. If anyone figured out my identity and is watching me, they'll definitely go after everyone around me. I can't be the reason any of them get hurt.

"Okay," Devon whispers, releasing my arms. "Okay, Em. I understand. I'll...I'll see you later."

Dejection weaves through his tone, and his shoulders slump as he turns. His shuffling steps echo through the alley as he hangs his head. I'd think it was an act with anyone else, but I know Devon. In my quest to not hurt him, I've done twice the damage. He doesn't deserve any of this. I fucked him over every day I was with him. I might not have realized how deeply I used him, but it doesn't negate the result.

"Devon," I call, stepping away from Titus. I wait until Devon turns. "I'll text you later."

He gives me a small smile, then turns and disappears around the corner. I swing around and bring my knee up. By the time I get done with Titus, he definitely won't pee straight for another week. Apparently, I wasn't subtle enough in my movements and he grabs my leg. Our gazes collide, rage dripping from his dark eyes.

"Think wisely on your next move, Emma."

I scoff, throwing my head back to get the hair out of my face. "Or you'll what? Put me down like a rabid dog?"

His fingers flex, digging into my skin. "Make no mistake, darling, the only thing keeping me from taking you out is your last name."

His words cut deep, slicing through the hard shell I've constructed around my heart. It's a flash of pain—a stinging wound I'll ignore like all the others he's inflicted. And when the ache becomes too much, I'll allow it to consume me, hopefully taking him out with me in the process.

I shove the anguish aside, seizing the opportunity to put him on his ass. Slamming my forearm into the side of his neck, I twist my knee out of his hold and use the momentum to spin. He doubles over, meeting my elbow as he does. Blood gushes from his nose and I wonder if I broke it. I pulled back at the end, but sometimes I forget how strong I am now. I still remember a time when I was too uncoordinated to throw a punch, much less take down a man a foot taller than me.

For the second time since he got here, I lean down as he languishes in his own blood. "Go to hell, Titus Prince."

I walk away, his curses ringing in my ears.

I flip my phone onto my bed, then pick it up and do it again. Daisy's supposed to be calling soon, but I can't seem to sit still. I roll my shoulder, trying to ease the tension in the muscle. It would be cool if I had a reason for the ache embedded in my arm. It could be from slamming my elbow into Titus's nose. Sadly, I think I merely slept on it wrong. And it wasn't because I was tossing and turning all night. Or because I was wondering where Titus was sleeping.

Tossing my phone down, I flop onto my back. After our altercation at the Hungry Beaver, I wasn't surprised he avoided me. He probably ran to the lady at the plant shop to fix him up again. Which is entirely none of my business. I avoided my apartment, using my shadow-free time to make sure the small-time gang I had a run-in with a few months ago was still where I left them. They're not particularly organized or smart, which means I found them in the same rundown building they were in before.

I thought Titus would be waiting when I came home. When he wasn't, I didn't think much of it. He is clearly pissed I hit him. Maybe next time he'll think twice about threatening me. I didn't put much stock in his words. Even if he does hate me enough to kill me, he'd never act on it. Plus, he was talking out of his ass. If he hated me that much, he wouldn't care about my relationship with Devon.

Yesterday, I thought he would finally come back, barging into my place like he has been the last week. When morning turned to afternoon and then to night, a shot of worry hit me. I'm ashamed to say I went searching for him. I kept wandering around, waiting for him to magically appear. Even contemplated texting him. Thankfully, I didn't since that would have been embarrassing as hell.

Daisy's muffled ringtone sounds from beside me and I blindly reach for my phone. "What's up?"

"Please tell me you picked the sexy black dress you've refused to wear ever since you bought it." Daisy's panting voice comes through the line.

"Are you running or fucking?"

She chuckles breathlessly. "I just walked up like fourteen flights of stairs."

I surge upright, clutching my phone. "Not my stairs, right? We said we were going to meet at the Tower."

I don't want Daisy here. I shouldn't even be seen with her—not with the people out for my blood. Every time I step outside with any of my friends I put them in danger. At this point, I'm a selfish bitch. I should've cut them all off months, maybe years, ago. Being on campus should help. Most of the people I pissed off stay as far away from the school as possible. Which means going to the Tower probably won't end well. I'm hoping the sheer number of club goers will hide my presence.

"Of course I'm not. I had to run to Claire's to drop off a pair of shoes. She had like seven people there so I couldn't just slip away. Which, of course, means I'm not dressed. Thought I'd give you a heads-up. We can meet at my place instead, if you're ready."

I wince, plucking at a loose thread hanging from my comforter. "No. Just tell me when and I'll be there."

"You sure? I don't like the idea of you being all alone."

"I'll be fine. I'm used to being alone. How long will you be?" I swing my legs off the bed and slip on my heels. I probably should wear flats, but I need the confidence the extra height will give me.

"Ten minutes. Wait for me, though. I might need your help getting in." Daisy huffs and I roll my eyes.

"I'll grab a spot in line. I'm sure I won't get in before you get there. Is anyone else coming?"

"I'll text you," she mutters and we say our goodbyes.

Setting the alarm, I close the door softly. I peer around the space before hurrying down the stairs. With Titus still in the wind, I'd rather not be ambushed as I come out of my apartment. No way I'd be able to climb out the window in this dress. I tug down the hem when I get to the ground level. The last thing I want to do is call a car since it'll take longer for them to get here. In such a small city, there aren't a lot of options.

My thoughts scatter on the pavement in front of me as I make my way to the club. Wading through them gets harder with each step. Between berating myself for my own mistakes and wondering if Titus ran back to rat me out to my family, I'm too distracted to be walking alone in the dark. Somehow I make it to the club without issue.

As the thump of music fills the air, I send a text to the group chat before slipping my phone into my bra. With the various knives I've stuffed under just a little piece of fabric, there's barely any room left. I join the end of the line and cross my arms, wishing I would have brought a coat. I'd have a regretted it once I was inside, though. The group of men in front of me laughs wildly, drawing more than a few stares. If the rumor Daisy heard is true, I doubt they're here for the dancing.

"Baker," a man yells from by the front door, and I look up out of habit. "Get your ass up here, pumpkin."

I glance around, then shuffle out of line and toward the bouncer grinning at me. The others groan as I walk by and my cheeks heat. I'm used to fading into the shadows. When I was younger, I wanted to be the center of something—anything, really. Shane never made me go to the galas in Synd, and Sam didn't want the media following me more than they already were. In Ridgewood, it was easy to blend into the crowd of college kids and I never got used to living any other way.

"Well, lookey here. Pumpkin got all dressed up for us," Dylan says, scanning me up and down.

"Bold of you to assume all this is for you." I smirk, planting a fist on my hip.

He crosses his arms over his beefy chest and grins. "Wouldn't want it even if you were offering, Baker."

"I'd be offended if your boyfriend wasn't glaring at me over your shoulder."

Dylan spins around, his hand dropping to his sides. I can't contain my giggles, and he turns back and scowls.

"That wasn't very nice, pumpkin. I thought you just got me in trouble," Dylan hisses, a sparkle in blue eyes.

"You did that all yourself, buddy."

The hair on the back of my neck stands up, and I peer at the barely moving line. Steve, Dylan's boyfriend, waves another group forward to scrutinize their IDs. He doesn't care who's standing in front of him as long as they're of age and can afford the cover. Subtly, I peek over my shoulder, yet the darkness remains unchanged. I wouldn't put it past Titus to be lurking in the shadows and spying on me.

"Emma," Dylan says, his voice suddenly serious. "Let's get you inside. You're probably freezing. Next time bring a jacket and we'll keep it in the back."

"I get the feeling this'll be the first and last time I'm here," I mumble as Dylan leads me inside.

Two days ago, I was excited to check this place out. Fucking with Titus was an added bonus. Now, I just want to go home. Not my apartment, since I never felt like I truly belonged there. No, I want to go back to Synd. I miss my family and the familiarity of the streets. There I understand my place in the world. It may not be perfect, but it's home.

The urge to turn around and run all the way back to Synd overtakes me until Dylan's arm wraps around my shoulders. He leads me around the corner and through an employee door. He shoos away the few people in what looks like a mini breakroom, and they scatter.

"Alright, tell me what's going on with you and that fine piece of ass." He plops onto one of the two chairs.

I could pretend I have no idea who he's talking about. Or make the assumption he's alluding to Devon. From the look on his face, though, he won't let me get away with either of those things. I'm too tired for the game. Somehow, Dylan always has the inside scoop. He knows who's coming and going or who's hooked up with who. I'm surprised he hasn't found out who I am. Especially since I've known him since freshman year.

"Absolutely nothing. He's from my past and needs to stay there."

He smirks, glancing away. "Alrighty then. Suppose there's nothing else to talk about. Let's get you out on the floor so you can break some more hearts."

Chapter 18

Titus

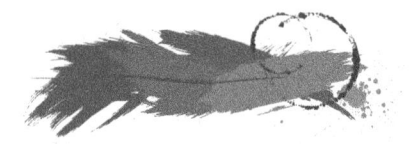

I lift the glass to my mouth and swallow, the liquor burning its way down my throat. I'm sure it's perfectly good scotch, yet the taste is lost on me. Scanning the club, I wish Emma would hurry the fuck up. If she changed her plans at the last minute, I'm going to be pissed. Daisy assured me they'd be at the Tower tonight. She even texted me that she'd be late, but Emma was on her way. Best decision I made to befriend Daisy.

At least they built the round booths lining the walls on a platform. I have a clear view of the front of the club and I keep waiting to spot her blonde head flouncing through the crowd. Despite the early hour, hundreds of bodies curl around each other, surging to the beat of the music. My chest thuds with each drop of the bass. I'm not used to coming to places like this and I find I don't particularly like it.

"Another one, honey?" a young server asks as she sidles up to my table.

I swirl the remaining scotch around the glass, then knock it back. Sliding it toward her, I nod. Two is usually my limit, but tonight I might need to double it. As long as I'm not stumbling around the city, I'll be fine. She smiles as she grabs the empty drink and spins to disappear into the crowd. A small group of women at the next booth burst into laughter. I can't see them with the walls of the booths extending to the ceiling and wrapping around. When they took their seats, though, I noticed how young they were. It'd be a miracle if they were truly of age to be in a place like this.

A man approaches me, and I raise an eyebrow when he crosses his arms.

"You really going to take up the whole fucking table yourself? Or are you actually waiting for someone?"

"Fuck off," I say, then smile my thanks to the server as she slides my new drink to me.

"I don't think you want to fuck with me. You're clearly not from around here," he hollers over the music as several other men post up behind him. "Do you know who I am?"

"No, and I don't particularly care, either. Now, kindly fuck off." I shoo him away lazily and take another drink of my scotch.

If I wasn't in such a mood, I'd entertain his little temper tantrum. However, I'd rather not be thrown out for putting this asshat in his place. He doesn't have much meat on him and he's wearing a fucking polo. I still associate those shirts with rich douchebags. He and his friends look like the kind of guys who think they're a gift from the universe, and if a woman doesn't fall at their feet, they're clearly slutty bitches. The sentiment never made sense to me. If the woman is slutty by their definition, wouldn't she *want* to sleep with them?

"Calvin," one of his friends says, a warning in his tone. The man nods toward me, his gaze fixed on my waist.

"Big man thinks he can walk around with a goddamn firearm," Calvin growls, and I raise an eyebrow.

I rest my hand on my upper thigh, close to my gun. "Perhaps you'd like to move along now."

Calvin rolls his eyes, lifting his shirt to show his own. Apparently, he's more prepared for a fight than I assumed. I'm sure he thinks he's intimidating me, but I'm just annoyed now. If Emma has shown up while I've been dealing with them, I'll be more pissed.

"Seems to me we've got more power here than you, dickhead. So why don't *you* move along?" His buddies laugh along with him while I stare impassively.

"Does that usually work? The whole tough act you've got going on? Because I'm surprised someone hasn't floated you yet."

Confusion swirls on his face, and I realize he has no idea what I'm talking about. Being gone from Synd for so long is fucking with my brain. I need to go back home. No more fucking around. No more attempting to get information out of Emma. No more dealing with this shitty town. Or the shitty men who think they run the fucking place.

Calvin's face distorts into one of rage, and I glance away. It takes everything in me not to react when I spot Emma through a gap in the crowd. She's glaring at someone, but I can't see who. She throws up her hands and makes her way toward the bar. I couldn't get to her if I wanted to. Not unless I want to shoot my way through these men.

"Problem?" The bouncer who let me in an hour ago steps between my table and Calvin.

"Yeah. This piece of trash took our booth."

The bouncer might actually be security. In Synd they usually don't mix the two jobs, but this city is smaller so it makes sense. He makes a show of examining the top of the table, then the pats his hands along the sides blocking the other booths. When he goes to lift the seat next to me, Calvin slams his fists beside my glass. I snatch up my scotch, not wanting to lose it if he decides to chuck it at my head.

The bouncer doesn't flinch, just straightens and cocks his head. "Doesn't look like it's labeled. You sure you haven't had a few too many? Seems to me it'd be pretty fucking clear if you actually had claim to any of this area. You want to try again?"

Calvin gets in his face and his finger digs into the bouncer's chest. "Get this asshole out of my booth or I'll—"

"You'll what? Call your daddy? Because I can call mine over if you want, too. He's a bit of a hothead, though."

Calvin's face turns a dangerous red. As much as I'd love to see the bouncer pound Calvin into the floor, I don't want to draw any more attention than we already are. It'll only delay me in finding where Emma slipped off to. The scene unfolding in front of me is blocking my view of the bar. If the beefy bouncer could just throw these fuckers out already, I'd be able to keep an eye on her.

"Fuck this shit. I'll take my money elsewhere," Calvin spits out before spinning around and shoving his way through the crowd. His friends follow, though with less fanfare.

"You good?" the bouncer asks, seemingly unfazed.

"I'm fine. How does one engage in the activities upstairs?" I tip my head toward the hallway hidden around the corner.

His brows pull low, though the corner of his lips twitch. "Gotta have a partner for that, sir. Are you waiting for someone?"

I stare at him, wondering if he's fishing or just doing his job. "Maybe."

"Can't just pick up someone off the dance floor. The attendants will know if you're strangers."

"That won't be a problem." As long as Devon doesn't show up, Emma won't be able to wander up there.

"If douchebag comes back, let one of us know. Can't kick his ass out since he didn't put his hands on anyone." He lifts his hand before weaving his way to the entrance.

I lean forward, searching the bar area for Emma. It takes a minute, but I finally spot her by the end of the bar closest to me, a drink in her hand. She's chatting with the bartender as she wears a false smile. My gaze travels over her body, taking in the tight black dress. The neckline dips almost to her navel and my chest tightens. I swallow hard when I notice how short the skirt is, showing off an ungodly amount of skin. My mouth waters and my hands curl into fists.

When I spot her heels, my face twists into a scowl. No fucking way she'd be able to run in those monstrosities. Shaking my head, I scold myself for having any type of reaction to her. Just because she wears a sexy dress doesn't mean she's not Emma. It doesn't change my feelings toward her, no matter how hard my cock is.

The other bouncer from the door, I think his name is Steve, sidles up behind Emma. His hand comes up to squeeze her side and I dig my nails into my leg. It didn't occur to me she had other men lined up to take Devon's place. Maybe that's why she's so hesitant to tell the asshole off properly. If Devon has been a dick to her, scared her in some way, she wouldn't want to piss him off more. It only brings attention to her, and since she hasn't told anyone who she really is, it makes sense. Doesn't mean she should go to a club and flirt with every person who moves.

Emma glances over her shoulder, a genuine grin taking over the falseness from before. She spins and smacks his chest. I glance away, taking in the dancers while I ignore the annoyance bubbling within me. The Kings never told me to police what she was doing or who she was sleeping with. It's not my job. I doubt she'll bring someone back to the apartment with me crashing on the couch, though.

My heart skips a beat when I turn to find her again. Both of them have disappeared and I lean forward, searching the bodies weaving together. I catch a glimpse of her blonde hair right before she slips around the corner and my booth blocks her from view. I grab my drink and down it, then slide from my seat to follow her. That way over there only leads upstairs. Like hell I'm letting her get to the rooftop. She wants to put on a display for others, she can do it on her own time. After she's given me the answers I need and I know for sure she isn't going to be followed back to Synd.

As I round the corner, I slam into Steve. He steadies me with a chuckle and I scowl.

"Easy there. No need to rush. Plenty of time for activities and we wouldn't want to kick you out for not watching where you're going," he says. His tone may be mild, but the glint in his eyes tells a different story.

"Just wasn't watching where I was going. If you'll excuse me."

I slide around him, expecting him to stop me at any point. He doesn't, thank fuck. The more I have to deal with others, the less I want to be here. I didn't bother trying to get upstairs before since I doubted Emma would be going up there. Now I'm kicking myself since I have no idea where she went.

The dark hallway swallows me up as I push past the thick velvet curtain, cutting off the music from the club. The silence soothes my brain and I slow my steps to soak in the quiet. I let it seep into me and ease the tension from my muscles. It takes the edge off, though the deep-seated anxiety that's been riding me since I got here still turns in my gut.

Another heavy curtain blocks the end of the hallway and I wonder if I'm headed the right way. I glance over my shoulder, searching the dark space for doors and find none. Sighing, I turn back and continue onward. If Emma is already up there, I'm going to lose it.

I shove aside the fabric and stomp through. All the tranquility I gained vanishes as the muted light hits me. Several men loiter around, blocking the elevator I'm facing. I scan the area, both to find Emma and get the lay of the land. Two doors and another hallway to the right are the only other things.

A short man in a black suit clears his throat. "You need a partner, sir. If you're waiting for someone—" He tilts his head and presses his finger to his ear, obviously listening to someone through an earbud.

His gaze focuses on me. "Sorry, sir. You can go up."

He presses the button and the elevator dings before the door slides open. Part of me wonders if Ren pulled some strings. I wouldn't put it past him to track my phone and know I'm here. I nod to him as I step into the box. My breath stalls in my lungs when I'm closed within and I close my eyes, counting to thirteen, then starting again. After the third run through, I'm finally freed from the temporary prison and I step out into the dark cool night.

The music isn't as loud up here, barely covering the moans of others. Shadows curl around one another, creating a lustful scene rarely seen out in the open. Daisy was right about the nets. They're spread out along the border of the roof parallel to the ground, then curving skyward. Bodies meld together over the ropes tightly woven to create a sense of solid ground beneath them. It can't possibly be safe. Inspections must have been a fucking nightmare.

"Shit." Emma's voice filters from beside me, and I turn.

"Well, hello, darling. Looking for a little risqué action?" I raise my eyebrow as she emerges from the dark.

She huffs, spinning to walk away. I don't have much of a choice but to follow her. I'm sick of running after her like a lost puppy, waiting for a scrap of her attention. She heads toward the bar set up along one of the perimeters. Between one step and the next, she freezes and I stumble into her, forcing a yelp from her.

I wrap my arm around her waist, attempting to steady us both, and tug her back to my chest. Her body curls and she tucks her chin down, letting her hair cover her face. The small group of men by the bar turn and I let out a curse. How the fuck Calvin got up here, I have no idea. His eyes narrow when he recognizes me and I spin us around. I force Emma forward until we're against the wall built up along the backside of the building.

She thrashes silently, nails digging into my bare arms, and I release her. No use getting bloodier. My nose is still tender from the other day. If she hits me again, it'll break for sure. Her hands land on the wall as her breaths heave from her body. I step away, wondering if she's having another episode. I don't want to have to haul her out of here practically catatonic. Someone's bound to call the cops then.

When she faces me, though, a different kind of panic lines her eyes. She leans to the side and peeks around me. Her gaze darts to me, then to whatever is happening behind me, but I'm loath to look. I'm about to demand an explanation when true fear flashes across her face. Her fingers curl into my shirt and she yanks me toward her.

My hands land on the wall on either side of her head, and I glance over my shoulder. She grips my neck, forcing my head back to face her.

I scowl, ready to scold her, and she slams her mouth to mine. My mind shuts down, zeroing in on her soft lips and her body melting into me. It could be five seconds or five minutes, but I eventually gather my wits about me and wrench away from her grasp.

"What the fuck was that?"

Chapter 19

Emma

I'm not going to be able to ignore Titus for long. He's the least of my worries, though. I duck my head under his arm to peek around his body. I'm hoping Calvin didn't recognize me. Maybe he'll just assume I'm some bimbo blonde who definitely didn't blow up his gas station. I wish he wasn't such a stuck-up prick throwing around false rumors of coming from a rich family. It's all an act, anyway. Calvin is nothing more than a glorified gang boss with too much money. Actually, maybe he is living off a trust fund. He certainly didn't make a lot slanging weed and running guns. I don't even think he has any connections outside of Ridgewood.

Calvin's gaze is fixated on Titus's back, and I hide again. Thank fuck Titus isn't a skinny thing anymore. I suck in a deep breath, trying to calm my pounding heart. Whether it's from kissing Titus or the possibility of being caught, I don't know. And I'm not ready to find out. If the seething man in front of me can keep his shit together, maybe we'll get out of this alive.

Titus seizes my chin and forces me to meet his gaze. When he bares his teeth, rage warring with something else in his dark eyes, I realize how much I fucked up. It was the only distraction I could come up with, though. I don't have time to explain every little fucking thing to him. If he's going to keep following me around, he's going to have to get used to just going with the shit I come up with.

"You have ten seconds to explain or we're going to have problems, Emma."

I rip my face away from his grip and sneer, "Going to run to my brother?"

He leans closer, and the back of my head hits the brick. "Most men have an issue with stabbing a woman. I have no such compunction."

"Big word for such a—"

"I suggest you stop assessing my intelligence and start telling me why you...did that."

The hesitation in his voice gives away how rattled he is. I could chalk it up to him being nervous that I'd tell my family. Or I could believe it's because I've frazzled his brain with my amazing kissing skills. Maybe he should have thought about how awesome I am before he dismissed me so quickly. Not years ago, but now—in the present. Maybe I'm not an empty-headed brat like he thought. Is my mind going haywire trying to justify myself? Yes. Am I completely off-base? Also yes. But it makes me feel better and I'm going to call this a win in our little battle.

"While I'd love to mess with that pretty little head of yours a little more," I say, smirking, and he growls. "There's a man over there who might not exactly want me alive."

"What did you do?"

"Why do you assume I did something? Maybe *they're* the ones who messed with me?"

I shouldn't be surprised he blames me without knowing all the facts. Sure, I fucked up. Really, really badly fucked up. But he doesn't know that. He just assumes I'm the root of everyone's problems. I never could figure out why. It's not like I derailed his promising career. He's still the head of the King's security. It's not like I broke his heart. It was never mine to begin with. Even if I would have been of age, it wouldn't have mattered. He always hated me. He was just better at hiding it than others.

"Because much to my dismay, I know you. I know how you operate, how you think, how you make shitty decisions. Calvin may be a pompous ass, but you..." His lip curls, disdain dripping from him. "*You* are always the problem. And I'm done cleaning up your messes. Find your own way back to Synd. Or not. I don't fucking care."

He pushes from the wall, then pivots and walks away, leaving me completely exposed. Less than a week and he's already eviscerated me at least three times. I thought I was winning, but I'm not. I'll never win in a fight against him.

He disappears around the corner, headed toward the elevator. For all his threats, I didn't think he'd actually leave me here. My phone buzzes in my dress, sending pulses through my already vibrating body. I search for Calvin as I ease farther into the shadows. I thought he'd be making a beeline right for me, but instead he's changed directions, following Titus. What the hell happened between them? Unless they're in cahoots with each other. I snort, not knowing where *that* fucking word came from.

I tug my phone out and check my messages. Daisy's apology pops up with three crying emojis. I'm not surprised she bailed. She kept talking about one of her friends with benefits maybe sticking around for the weekend. I'm sure she assumes the other girls showed up to keep me company. It's the only explanation for why she abandoned me.

Waving at one of the security guards, I gesture him over. I'd rather not expose myself, even in the dim light, in case Calvin is waiting to ambush me. The older man saunters over, a gruff expression stamped on his face.

"Miss?"

"Are there stairs?"

He raises an eyebrow, then glances over his shoulder. "Is someone bothering you?"

"No, not really." I slip my lip between my teeth and soften my face while I ring my hands together. "My ex is taking the elevator—didn't know he'd be here. I'd rather not run into him if I have a choice."

He shakes his head, concern stamped across his features. "They're for emergencies only, miss. Why don't I check up here and with the guards downstairs and make sure he's cleared out first? Then we can send you down."

I nod, giving him a strained smile. I'm used to playing the damsel in distress even if it makes my skin crawl. Pretending to be someone I'm not is frustrating.

I've hidden so many parts of myself, I'm sick of it. I need one person I can be myself with. Not a little sister. Not an insignificant member of the mafia. Not a vapid blonde. The list goes on. I need someone to see me. Someone who knows every part of who I am and loves me anyway.

I swallow the tears, attempting to focus on the present. I can't afford to lose myself in the pain of something that will never be. If Devon wasn't enough for me to fall in love, I doubt I'll ever truly find someone. Which is fine. There are plenty of other things to live for other than a partner. And with Daisy knowing who my family is now, I'll be able to open up more. I'll probably still hide parts of my life in Synd, striving to protect her from the darker aspects of it. Once I go back home, I'll be relegated to whatever status my brother feels like I can handle, which will be woefully inadequate compared to my skills.

"Miss? Are you ready?" the security guard calls, and I make my way toward him.

"I really appreciate this," I say as I step into the elevator.

He nods, opening his mouth, but the door slides closed before he can get a word out. My hand twitches toward the button to open it again just to find out what he wanted to tell me. The box jolts and my stomach ends up in my throat. An electrifying shock runs through my limbs, and I smooth my dress down nervously. I'm not claustrophobic like Titus, yet the thought of plummeting thirty stories with nothing to look forward to other than a sudden stop doesn't make this trip any easier.

I'm about ready to spiral when the elevator halts its descent and a ding echoes through the small space. I bounce on the balls of my feet, both to relieve the ache in my ankles and expend the excess energy built up within me. My breath whooshes out of me as the door slides open, revealing another security guard's kind face.

"Miss Baker, are you okay?"

I search for his name as I step forward gingerly. "I'm fine, Cory. You know how it is."

He huffs, waving away a younger guy. "I'm going to walk you out the back. No reason you should have to deal with an asshole. You tell Dylan, and we'll make sure he's on the ban list."

"That's not necessary," I murmur.

Maybe I took this too far. Calvin will pitch a fit if he's banned from the Tower, which will only cause problems for them. And I'd rather my name, even if it's half fake, not be tied to an action like that. I don't know how much pull Calvin has in this city. I should, seeing as how I've been tailing him for over a year. It wasn't until recently I entertained the thought of him having someone above him in the food chain other than his daddy. He's too cocky to organize a drug ring, though. He has to have a backer at the very least.

"You going to come back? I know a lot of us wouldn't mind seeing a familiar face around here."

It's a strange statement since this is the first time I've been to the Tower. Except a lot of the people who work here came from other clubs. Some of them are from the college, too. I've seen more familiar faces tonight than I have in the last week. I've tried to cultivate relationships here, just like Sam did in Synd. She always seems to know someone, finding connections in the most unlikely of places. I took that attribute and morphed it to fit my time here.

"We'll see. Probably will stay off the roof for a bit either way." I smirk, trying to lighten the mood. I don't think it works.

He leads me down the back hallway, away from the heavy curtains leading to the nightclub. My muscles tighten, the nausea coming back full force. I hold my breath as the light from behind us fades away. Thankfully, Cory pulls out his phone to light the way.

"Sorry. I forgot they haven't fixed the sensors back here." He stops in front of an emergency door and turns. "This'll lead you to the back alley. Kind of dirty, but it's the best I can do. The employee entrance is across the club, so I figured you wouldn't wanna go through all that."

"I appreciate it. As long as I don't have to run away from any rats, I'll be fine. Thanks, Cory."

He smiles, but it doesn't quite reach his eyes. "Do we need to ban the guy you've been hanging out with?"

I close my eyes, pulling in a calming breath. I don't know which ones he's talking about. Between Calvin, Devon, and Titus, I'm over it. Calvin and I don't hang out, so I doubt Cory's referencing him. Devon should be a moot point by now. We broke up and we're never getting back together. Titus, though...the petty part of me wants to ban him, regardless of whether he comes back. It would soothe the bitchy areas of my soul.

Unfortunately, the rational side takes over, and I shake my head. "Don't worry about it. Are there cameras back here?"

He winces. "They're on the same grid as the sensors. I'm not an electrician, so I don't understand it. Just turn left and you'll come out on the main street."

He shoves on the handle, and I take that as my cue. Once in the alley, I take two steps to the left, focusing on my feet. The bang of the door behind me sends me wobbling on my heels and I instantly regret wearing them. I catch myself on the grimy wall and grimace. Muted thuds from the music within the club echo through the alley, adding to my slowly growing headache. The lights ahead of me are too bright. The crowds loitering there are too thick. The music is too loud. And my plan won't work if I'm surrounded by others.

I pivot on the ball of my foot and click my way toward the shadows. I'm not entirely sure if this will work. Calvin might have gone home. He might be in the club still. Or he went somewhere else to close out the night. Hell, if he was actually following Titus, I might stumble over Calvin's body any second now.

Either way, I don't care. I've made enough mistakes in the last couple months—one more won't matter. Or it will and I'll die and it still won't matter. At least to me it won't. My brothers will probably burn Ridgewood to the ground. Sam might kill Titus for letting it happen. And yet, I'll never know.

A foot scuffles on the concrete ahead of me and I smirk. Maybe my luck will turn around. I could be walking straight into my death, but just like Titus, I don't fucking care.

Chapter 20

Titus

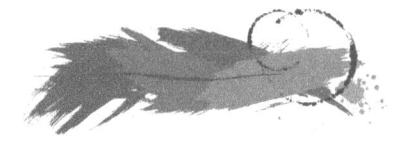

Joy flips the lock on the door behind me with a scowl. "You realize if I keep closing every time you run away from her, I'll never make any money, right?"

I snort, shoving through the curtain to her back room. "As if there's a shit ton of people stampeding through here."

"If you're going to be an asshole, I suggest you go back to Emma. She's much more patient than I am when it comes to your shitty attitude," she snaps as she follows me.

I'm halfway across the empty chop shop before the ache in my chest eases enough for me to pull in a full breath. She's right, though I won't admit it to her. It's not the first time she's taken the brunt of my ire. And it's always because of Emma fucking King. Joy would understand if she ever met Emma. Those two will never cross paths if I have any say in it. Emma has a way of sucking people in and bamboozling them with her charm. She can't fool me as easily.

Joy leans against the wall next to the locker I've been using to store my things. "Where the hell are you going?"

"Back to Synd. If the town burns down, call Alex. He'll take care of the fallout." I ignore her shocked expression. Whatever arguments she's going to throw at me won't change my decision.

"Should I come to your funeral?"

"Doubt they'll give me one," I mutter, then slam the locker shut before throwing my backpack over my shoulder.

She hurries after me as I make my way to my bike, her boots thudding against the smooth floor. I'm hoping I'll be able to convince Shane I had no choice. He should know what his sister is like. And if he doesn't, I'm clinging to the hope that Sam will back me up. She knew this was a terrible fucking idea. It's not my fault the others didn't listen to her.

"What could she possibly have done to actually push you over the edge? For fuck's sake, the woman kneed you in the balls *and* almost broke your nose. I can't imagine there's much more unless she—" She steps between my bike and me, blocking my way. "Did she stab you?"

I roll my eyes, slipping around her to stuff my pack in the saddlebag. "She didn't stab me. I'm just done. She made the mess and she can clean it up."

"Bullshit," she snarls and shoves me against the wall.

"I'm not fighting with you, Joy. And I don't owe you a fucking thing."

It takes a minute for me to decipher the look on her face—disappointment. I've never had someone care enough about me to be disappointed in me. It doesn't change my mind about revealing anything to her, though.

"You might not owe me anything, but you do owe the Kings. They've given you a task and from where *I'm* standing, it seems like you're failing. Miserably. Better think long and hard about your future. Because if you come back without that woman, they won't just float you. They'll torture the shit out of you. They'll strip every piece of humanity left in that black heart of yours, and you'll have no one to blame but yourself."

"She's capable of taking care of herself," I snarl.

"Until she isn't. Until she gets herself in so far over her head, she doesn't know which way is up. And if something happens to her, it'll be on your head. I hope you can live with the guilt filling the hole she leaves behind."

We glare at each other, neither one willing to back down. The thought of something actually happening to Emma has a vise squeezing my heart. I spent so long protecting her I forgot she's not invincible. She told me someone wanted her dead, and I walked away. I left her vulnerable, even if it was in the middle of a club.

Shaking my head, I shove the regret away. Joy played right into my weakness. Not Emma. Never her. She hurt my pride. My loyalty lies with the Kings, and if I fail at protecting her, I've failed them. They took me in when no one else would. They gave me a home—a family. It's an unconventional one, yet just as legitimate as one built on flesh and blood. I grit my teeth, slamming my eyes closed.

"Would you like me to unpack?" Joy asks sweetly, and my hands curl into fists by my sides.

"I need a place to stay," I mutter. No fucking way I'm staying on that fucking couch another night. And the cot in the shop isn't much better.

"Either you stay at her place or you take the cot like you have the last two nights. I'm not housing your ass just because you're too chickenshit to face her after what you did."

I explode from the wall, hands flying up and a growl rolling from my throat. "I didn't do a goddamn thing. She thinks she can do whatever the fuck she wants without any consequences. She waltzed into shitty situations without a care for who it fucking hurts. Because she doesn't give a damn about anyone but herself. She's a fucking witch."

"Watch it," Joy snaps, and I sober, my breaths heaving from me. "Stop dancing around with vague bullshit. Either tell me what she did or suck it the fuck up."

"Suck it up? That fucking wench kissed me. How the fuck am I supposed to—" My teeth clack together as I clamp my mouth shut. Joy's face reddens as she tries not to react. I stomp away from her, though I have nowhere to go.

"So you two—"

I swing around and glare at her. "Shut the fuck up, Sanders. I'm not talking about it with you. Or anyone. She needed the cover. It wasn't some declaration of love, and no one had a goddamn epiphany. She crossed the fucking line."

She presses her lips together, eyes bouncing around before finally settling on me. "While I don't condone her kissing you without permission..."

"Don't try to justify what she did."

Joy holds up her hand, and my nostrils flare as I attempt to get my emotions under control. "I just have one question. What did you feel?"

"Huh?"

"You were at the club. Dancing."

"We were on the roof against a wall next to the elevator. Not dancing. I don't fucking dance."

She snorts, hiding her grin behind her hand. "Okay, so what did you feel when you were locking lips?"

"I'm not having this conversation with you." I pivot on my heel and stomp back toward her shop. Her footsteps race after me, and I quicken my pace. She won't give it up until she's satisfied with my answer. And she'll never accept that I felt nothing.

"You can run away all you want, just like you do every time she makes you feel something other than guilt."

I freeze, then spin around to confront her. She stumbles back, pursing her lips. If she keeps this up much longer, I'm liable to do something drastic. I don't think I'd hit her, but I'm holding on by a thread. She doesn't want to admit she doesn't know what she's talking about.

"The only feelings I have for Emma King are the ones that make me want to strangle her."

She smirks as if she's won something and crosses her arms. "And you think that doesn't mean anything?"

"Other than the fact I hate her? No."

She rolls her eyes and waves me toward the door. "Go, then. If you truly don't care even a little bit for her, then fine. Go back to Synd and explain your reasonings to the Kings and leave her to her own devices. I'm sure she'll be fine, just like you said."

"I plan on it."

The tapping of her toe sends a metallic taste through my mouth. I shove all the emotions bubbling within me down and nausea bubbles in my gut. Blaming the guilt over not protecting a member of the King family would be perfect. Yet

I can't bring myself to use it. Joy won't accept my excuse anyway. And she refuses to think I truly hate Emma. My jaw aches the longer we glare at each other.

She leans forward, a glint in her eyes. "Why aren't you moving?"

"Excuse me?"

"You said you were leaving, yet you're nowhere by your bike. *And* you said you didn't want to talk about it, but you keep bringing shit up."

I throw my hands up. "I didn't bring shit up. You did. And I've been trying to leave for the last goddamn hour."

"Oh, so it's because you respect me so you can't walk away unless I allow you to?"

I fucking hate when she calls me out on shit. This might be the first time she's pushed this hard. I wish I could walk away. When I left the club, I had every intention of leaving Ridgewood. To hell with Emma and all her fucking baggage. I was prepared to deal with the fallout. Leave it to Joy to muddy the waters enough for me to second-guess myself.

"I don't need your permission, Joy. If I choose to leave, I will. You're not—"

She holds up her hand, closing her eyes. "Don't say something you're going to regret. You may get away with that shit when it comes to her, but I'm not her. Thank fuck."

I rear back, my spine snapping as I tense. "What the hell does that mean?"

She sighs, giving me a pained look. "You're not ready for the truth. Frankly, I don't know if you ever will be. But Emma King has been through more shit than anyone else I've met. And that's saying something. I wouldn't trade places with her if you paid me. Not to mention the other shit."

I know better than most the struggles Emma's been through. I watched as she was shunned by her peers. Her family had bigger issues when she was a teenager and more often than not, she was shipped off to her great-aunt. Being kidnapped would be too much for a person. Add in all the other shit and it's a cocktail of trauma no one seems to understand.

I don't like thinking about those things. Every time I do, I'm liable to forget how she derailed my life. I'll forget she's a spoiled brat who only cares about herself. I'll soften toward her, and I don't know what will happen. Nothing good can come from the unknown, from being anything other than Emma's enemy. But I can't ignore Joy's words.

"What other shit?"

She rolls her eyes, and my chest tightens. "As if you care. You're too busy holding on to the ridiculous notion she's to blame for all your troubles. Of which there are very few, mind you." She rolls her eyes, and I open my mouth to remind her of everything Emma's done to me. "Yeah, yeah, yeah. She fucked up your relationship with the Kings and railroaded your trajectory within the organization. Except she didn't really railroad anything. You still got what you wanted and you're now the head of security."

"She could have gotten me killed," I snarl.

"Still a shit reason. And since you're not willing to admit there's anything else to it, then we're done here. If I find you on the cot, I'm burning it. Whether you're sleeping on it or not."

She pushes past me and stomps through her back room. I'm still determined to go back to Synd, regardless of Joy's opinion. It's hard enough to deal with Emma on a good day. With what she pulled tonight, I'm done. She pushed me too fucking far.

I'm halfway to my bike when my phone buzzes, and I answer it without thinking. "What?"

"Do you know where she is?" Daisy's frantic voice rings in my ear.

"She's at the Tower."

She lets out a choked sob and my feet stutter to a stop. "She's not. D-do you know wh-where she is?"

"Calm down, Daisy," I growl.

Her voice takes on a shrill quality. "When has telling a woman to calm down every fucking worked, you worthless sack of shit?"

I wince, pulling the phone away from my ear. "I'm sure she's fine."

"She's not fucking fine. She's not at the Tower and she's not answering her phone."

I check the time, then hang up on her. I never thought I'd need Emma's number, but I'm thankful for it now. With each ring, my chest tightens more.

When her voicemail picks up, I redial. I'm not surprised she isn't picking up my call. We didn't exactly end on the best of terms. It doesn't ring this time, just an automated voice telling me to leave a message.

Daisy picks up on the first ring, her gasps echoing down the line. "No-no one's h-heard from h-h-her. Sh-she's not...She's not answering."

"I don't have time to listen to you cry, Daisy. When was the last time someone heard from her?" I snarl as I stomp toward my bike. If Emma truly is missing, I won't have time to walk around this blasted town.

"I don't know. Two hours? Maybe? Her phone goes straight to voicemail. I just—" She sniffs, dread weaving through her voice. "She's never not answered except once. And when she showed back up, she was covered in blood."

"Blood?" From what I understand, Daisy didn't know about Emma's family or who she truly is until recently.

"Okay, it wasn't, like, soaking her, but it was more than you think. And she had a swollen nose and two black eyes. She said she ran into a wall. What the fuck. Who cares what happened? Just fucking find her."

I climb on my bike and roll it around to the large garage door. "Assume if I'm asking, it matters. When was this?"

"I don't know," she cries.

I drum my thumb against the handlebar, sick of waiting for her to get me the information I need. "Get your shit together, Daisy."

"God, Emma was right. You're an asshole. It was like six months ago. What can I do?"

"Nothing. Stay in your apartment. Keep in touch with your friends. Don't fucking leave your apartment."

"You already said that," she sneers. "Are you going to—"

I hang up and kick the door, the sound ringing through the empty space. I call Emma once more, cursing when it goes straight to voicemail.

"Joy," I yell.

"No need to scream at me," she mutters, then slams her hand on the button. "Have fun saving the damsel in distress."

I pretend not to hear her over the rumble of my engine and take off into the cold night. As determined as I was to leave, I have to make sure she's not in actual trouble. She probably just hooked up with a guy and turned her phone off. My hands flex at the thought and I shove away the emotions I won't name. Wherever she is, I'm going to rip her a new one when I find her. Then I'll go back to Synd and she can truly be on her own.

Chapter 21

Emma

I force tears from my eyes, letting them silently drip down my face. As the door shuts, I peek from behind my curtain of hair, searching the space for cameras. I'm not surprised when I don't find any, seeing as how this place is nothing more than a shack in the woods. I'm impressed they found a chair to tie me to, even if it is wooden. They're clearly not used to taking people.

I tug at the rope securing my wrists to the arms, the roughness itching against my bare skin. It's almost as if they watched a shitty horror movie and attempted to replicate it. I have at least an inch of give and could easily slip my hands free. Not that I intend to anytime soon. I need information, and I'd rather not take on the burden of kidnapping one of them.

Is this one of my better ideas? Probably not. Which is exactly what happens when I get sick of waiting. I refuse to give Titus any credit for my rash decisions. If I do, I'll have to admit he affects me, and he doesn't. Not one bit. He's an asshole who works for my brothers and that's it. I'm determined to enter my "I don't feel a goddamn thing" phase. He's probably halfway back to Synd, anyway. If I'm lucky, we'll never have to interact again.

Too bad my luck is shit.

Kicking my feet back and forth, I tip my head back. Calvin should probably be here soon. He was there in the alley when they grabbed me. I fought, losing one of my heels in the process. I had to make it look authentic, though I'm pissed I lost a potential weapon. The sequins from the hem of my dress dig into the back of my thighs. If Calvin doesn't hurry the fuck up, I'm going to go searching for him.

An argument outside the small window has me rolling my head toward the waning moonlight filtering through the glass. I can't make out what they're saying, but I doubt it's important. Sometimes people will let things slip when they're upset, yet I've found it's the things left unsaid that are more useful.

"She's just some dumb bitch, Cal. Why the fuck did we take her?" a man shouts above the group.

Calvin's response is lost among the mumblings of the others. I'd like to know the answer myself, though I doubt he'd tell me the truth. Hell, he's probably lying to his men right now. I'm loath to call them friends. More like cronies. They follow Calvin around like a feral dog pack, content to lap up the scraps he leaves behind.

"Well, if her family comes after us, we're fucked," the man hollers.

"The whore doesn't have one, so shut the fuck up and let me handle this," Calvin growls.

The voices move away from the window, and I breathe a sigh of relief. The fact he doesn't know my true identity helps. I thought Calvin recognized me when I broke into his little operation two months ago. From the way they're behaving, I'm starting to doubt he knows for sure it was me. I wonder if he's been scooping up all the blondes with my figure since then. Shaking my head, I huff out a laugh. If he was kidnapping unsuspecting women, I doubt he'd be able to keep it under wraps. The police might be shit at their jobs, but the gossip chain at the college works wonderfully. I'd definitely have heard something. Or one of my friends would have said something.

Footsteps echo under the crack around the door, and seconds later the worn knob jiggles. I drop my chin to my chest, plastering on a helpless expression. I'd kick the leg of the chair and hope the pain would bring tears to my eyes, but I doubt the wood would hold up to the onslaught. By the time the soft light from the kerosene lamp filters into the room, I've relaxed my muscles, giving off a defeated aura.

Calvin's wing-tipped shoes come into view right before he grabs my chin and forces me to lift my head. His fingers dig into the soft flesh of my neck and I wince. My reaction isn't entirely faked.

"Why were you stumbling down the alley earlier?" he asks as the door shuts softly behind him.

I expected him to come in guns blazing, demanding answers. Instead, his calm voice washes over me and my eyes dart around the room to buy myself time. Feigning ignorance seems the only plausible way out of this. If I pretend we've never crossed paths, he might assume he has the wrong girl. It's a good thing we've never interacted on campus or in town.

"Wh-where am I? What do you w-want?" I stutter out, a single tear escaping as I focus on his face.

He releases my chin and straightens, then tucks his hands in the pockets of his slacks. He looks wildly out of place. His fancy clothes are a stark contrast to the crumbling wooden walls and dirt floor. I'd love to think he didn't plan this little sojourn, but he was dressed similarly the night I broke into his makeshift business. I'm used to dealers or lower gangs clothed in dark colors, sweatshirts and jeans being the most common attire. For fuck's sake, his polo is cream. He'll never get blood out of the cashmere.

"If you answer my questions, we'll let you go. No harm, no foul."

I swallow down the snort, wondering if that line is supposed to ease my anxiety. "I didn't do anything. I was just going home. I want to go home."

I let out a sob, pressing my lips together to give it a muffled quality. I always wished I was a pretty crier instead of having to deal with the blotchy redness and swollen eyes. I never thought it would come in handy, but I'm grateful for it now.

"Stop crying. It's...distasteful." His lip curls and he shuffles back to lean against the wall. "Now, why were you with that man?"

I pull my brows low, hoping my eyes haven't dilated enough that he can tell. "What man?"

Honestly, he could be talking about a plethora of men. He's probably asking about Titus since he likely saw us together, but I was around Dylan and Steven, too. Not to mention Cory, though I think Calvin had left by then. I dig my nails into the wood of the chair as he stares at me.

"The one on the roof. Looked like you two were pretty fucking cozy. Who is he?"

I bite my lip, wishing I would have taken the time while I was alone to come up with an excuse. I can't very well tell him Titus used to be my bodyguard. Calling him my boyfriend would be ridiculous. No one would ever believe we were dating. And usually people aren't allowed up top without a partner. The only reason they let me onto the roof was because of Steve. I wonder how Calvin was able to accomplish it without someone on his arm. Unless he paired off with one of his homeboys or paid off one of the bouncers.

"He's an ex. It wasn't a good break up," I murmur, ducking my head again.

"Then why were you kissing him?"

I shrug, sniffing. "Because it's hard to let go."

I'm banking on Calvin not knowing about Devon and me. I wouldn't put it past Calvin to call me a whore or assume I'll give it up to anyone if he thinks I was in two serious relationships back-to-back. It hasn't been that long since Devon and I broke up. For some reason, it feels like a lifetime has passed.

"You women are so fucking emotional. Who is he?"

I peek at him, and he smirks as if he thinks I'm checking him out. While tied to a goddamn chair. He licks his bottom lip and raises an eyebrow. The fucking audacity.

"Nick. Nick Barton. He's not from around here. Can I go home now?"

He pushes from the wall and saunters around my chair. I whip my head around, trying to track his movements. When he disappears from view, my muscles tense. When his fingers trail along my shoulder, I jerk away from his touch. I lean as far away from him as the ties will allow, but it's not enough. From the commotion on the other side of the door, I'm sure there are at least six people waiting for Calvin to reappear. If I attack him now, I'll have a hard time getting out of here without injuries.

He crouches in front of me and tilts his head. Thank fuck he hangs his hands between his legs. If he starts touching me again, my foot will end up buried in his nuts. He's definitely a man who doesn't deserve to procreate. A loud bang from outside has me jumping, and I glance to the side, trying to keep Calvin in my line of sight all the while. He smirks again, and I face him once more.

"Jumpy little thing, aren't you? Are you scared, baby doll?" His oily voice coats my skin, leaving a bitter taste in my mouth, and I nod. "No need. I told you we wouldn't hurt you if you were honest. Are you being honest?"

I nod again, swallowing hard as his eyes dip, tracing my body. If I ever admit to Daisy where I ended up tonight, I'm going to fucking kill her. She's the only reason I wore this blasted thing. It's too tight, too revealing, too inviting of his lascivious gaze.

His hand shoots out and grips my ankle. I resist the urge to rip away from his grasp. He lifts my leg, running a finger along my arch and goosebumps erupt along my skin. My toes curl as my limb begins to shake, and I can't seem to tear my eyes away from the scene.

He drops my foot abruptly and clears his throat. "Answer the question, baby doll."

"Yes. I'm telling the truth." I breathe, hoping he doesn't hear the tremor in my voice. Maybe I should have let it out. Then again, I'd probably end up snarling at him or something.

"Well, then. I haven't seen you at the clubs before. What do you do at night?"

"S-study. Hang out with f-friends. One of them is waiting for me. Sh-she wasn't f-feeling g-g-good. I shouldn't have gone out alone."

He shakes his head, an expression of sympathy flashing across his face. "No. You really shouldn't have. Although, you never would have met me if you'd stayed home. And while this—" He nods his head toward my bonds. "—may seem extreme, they can be fun as well."

He reaches for my foot again and I lash out, kicking him in the knee with my heel. He falls back on his ass with a grunt. I scream, infusing my tone with as much fear as I can. Struggling against the rope hurts, but eventually I slide my wrists free. I'd go through the window if I thought I could make it. It's too small, too high for me to escape easily. Calvin struggles to his feet while I round the chair, keeping it between us. He blocks the door, fists curling at his sides, and I cower behind the flimsy piece of wood. I open my mouth to scream again, but only a sob escapes.

Adrenaline pumps through my veins, and I fight to keep my shit together. I could still get out of this without giving myself away. All my plans to get information from him have fled. He didn't grab me because he thought I was the one who attempted to burn down his operation.

It all stems from fucking Titus. Of course, this shitshow leads to him. Because why the fuck not? I probably would have figured it out if he didn't infiltrate my mind so goddamn much. And I can't even take my anger out on him since he left. I have half a mind to go back to Synd just to kick him in the balls again.

"You stupid fucking bitch. You're going to pay for that." He heaves to his feet, teetering like a newborn colt. He didn't hit his head, so I'm not sure what's actually going on with him. Unless he's drunk, but he's not exhibiting any of the typical signs. I should have done more research before I came here.

"I'm sorry. Please don't hurt me," I cry, forcing myself to cower lower.

His nostrils flare, and the door behind him pops open. A scrawny guy who looks more boy than man awkwardly takes in the scene. He clears his throat, and a flush splashes across his cheeks.

"Someone's coming," he mutters, his eyes fixed on me.

"Grab her. We're not letting her go until I get my answers." Calvin sneers before pivoting on his heel and prowling from the room. He's probably on the warpath to find his next victim to torment.

The boy glances between Calvin's retreating back and me, and I shake my head, allowing some of the rage I've been holding back to show through. He blanches, then hustles from the room. I straighten and peer into the equally dilapidated outer space. The rest of Calvin's entourage follow him into the night, the boy slipping out last. I wonder how long it'll take Calvin to notice his orders weren't followed.

My shoulders slump, my muscles aching. As the rumble of engines fills the previously silent air, I sigh. I'm about to make my way around the chair when a large form steps into view, filling the doorframe. He's at least a foot and a half taller than me and built like a goddamn tank. When he slams his fist into his palm, I suppress the urge to roll my eyes. I didn't think people did that in real life.

"Ready, princess?" he coos, and I wrinkle my nose.

I didn't like being called baby doll by Calvin. Hell, I don't like it when Devon does it, either. But I especially don't enjoy hearing my brother's nickname for his wife on someone else's lips. It feels dirty and disrespectful coming from this asshole.

I weigh my options as he leers at me. I could distract him, then run. Or I could wait for whoever is coming to "rescue" me, though I don't need it. At least that would preserve my reputation of a damsel in distress. If I kill this behemoth of a man, Calvin might think it was whoever is coming. I doubt he'd assume I could take on someone almost three times my size.

I'm sick of sitting back and waiting. I'm sick of playing it safe. I'm sick of making mistakes and having to clean them up. Most of all, I'm sick of no one realizing how capable I am. They all think I'm still a kid sneaking around the Barrens without a clue. Shane sure as hell thought I needed protection. It's why he sent Titus in the first place.

"You have two options here," I murmur, slipping my fingers under the hem of my dress. "You can walk away and tell your leader whatever the hell you want. Or I can kill you. Either option is fine with me, but I'd rather not get your blood on my dress. I've only worn it once."

He tips his head back and guffaws. It's obnoxious, but I take the opportunity to slip the knife from the strap on my thigh. I could stick him in the throat with it right now. I hate the gurgling noise they make, though.

"Come on. I don't have all night." He lumbers forward, and I skip toward the back wall.

He kicks the chair out of the way, and it shatters into several pieces under the window. I kick off my heel and grab it before brandishing it in my left hand, my right gripping the knife. Neither weapon seems large enough to do him much damage. It'll be like stabbing him with a toothpick. Exhaustion weighs down my bones even as I dance toward the corner.

He grins, several teeth missing from his smile. "We don't have time to play tag, princess. Put those down before you cut yourself."

"Still time to walk away." I glance over his shoulder, and my heart clenches until he takes the bait.

Dropping the heel while his gaze is elsewhere, I search the remnants of the chair for a better weapon. One of the legs catches my eye, the splintered edge exactly what I need. I snatch it up as he turns back. My arm swings out before he has a chance to react, and I catch him in the jaw.

His roar of pain mixed with rage rings in my ears. I don't wait for him to recover. This isn't like the movies where an opponent lets the other shake off a blow. Dashing forward, my bare foot hits a sharp rock and I yelp. I can't stop my forward motion and I wildly thrust my knife into his exposed side.

His fist comes out of nowhere, and I duck on instinct. My head explodes with pain as his punch connects with the side above my ear. He missed my temple by inches and while my vision blurs, tears springing to my eyes, he wasn't able to knock me out. I can't take another blow like that. Hell, even with half the force I doubt I'll stay upright if he gets another one in.

Lifting the chair leg once more, I stumble back a step, brushing the wall. He lumbers toward me, his movements slow. I grin, my training coming back, and I crouch. He reaches for the knife still clutched in my hand, or maybe for my wrist. Either way, it doesn't matter. I jab my makeshift weapon into his Adam's apple as hard as I can. He stumbles away, choking, and trips on the other pieces of the chair.

His arms pinwheel, shock splashing across his face as he falls in slow motion. I rush forward, intent on slashing his neck. I swear I can see the artery pulsing, calling to me to spill his blood. Instead, I stutter to a stop when his head cracks against the dirt and his eyes fall closed. I inch around him, then poke him in the side with the chair leg. He doesn't move—not a twitch, flinch, or jiggle. I lean down and wince. Blood seeps into his light hair, the edges of a rock barely visible under the strands.

If he's not dead yet, he will be soon. I throw the leg across the room and take off for the door. No reason to stick around. As I step into the cold night, gravel biting into the soles of my feet, I realize how fucked I truly am. Calvin might have dismissed me as a weak, scared female before, but I'm on his radar now. I have no idea where the hell I'm going to go from here. And it's entirely Titus's fault.

Chapter 22

Titus

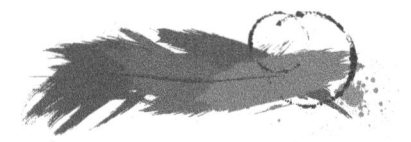

Emma emerges from the rundown shack, and I crane my neck as I hide around the corner of the building. The window I found was too high to peer into. No one follows her, but that doesn't mean they're not waiting just behind her. She takes two steps, sweeping her gaze around the forest. Only the sounds from the night encroach upon the heavy silence from the small shed.

Adrenaline rushes through my veins, and my body vibrates with the need to grab her and run. I'd rather not get shot in the back, though. I'm not fucking dying for her. One of the perks of no longer being her bodyguard. The instinct to protect her is buried deep, rearing its head at the worst time. Every time I think I've broken free of her, I'm reeled back in. The fact I'm standing here saving her ass once again…One of these days I'll learn my lesson, but apparently not tonight.

I have to act now before any others join her. I slip behind her and wrap one arm around her waist, the other covering her mouth. She struggles, just like I knew she would, and I grip her tighter.

"Shh," I whisper harshly.

She doesn't stop squirming, and I realize my mistake a second too late. Before I've registered I'm flying over her shoulder, I'm already on my back. My breath whooshes from my lungs and I gasp for air. I groan, my vision blurring. I curl to my side, pulling my knees to my chest. It does nothing to help. Only wringing Emma's neck will truly heal me.

"What the fuck were you thinking?" Emma hisses, her face swimming above me.

"That you weren't completely—"

"Don't finish that sentence. You've sparred with me before. You should have known better." Her lip curls and she rolls her eyes. "Stop rolling around in the dirt. It's unbecoming of a mafia man."

I heave to my feet, ignoring the warmth spreading through my chest. It's probably the side effects of getting knocked on my ass. Emma hasn't exactly been good for my health as of late. Then again, she's never called me a mafia man. No one has. I'll take the compliment, even if it did come from her.

"What the fuck happened? Where are they?" I peer into the shack, the lamp barely illuminating the interior. I'm surprised there's two rooms. It doesn't seem large enough to hold that many.

"They left. Except for the one who was supposed to bring me somewhere else. His body is in the back."

"You killed him?" I snarl, rounding on her.

I don't have time to clean up her messes. Even after I was removed as her bodyguard, I was sent to deal with her mistakes. Whatever she left behind was for me to handle, according to Shane. I'm fucking tired of having to pick up the pieces while she flits away like her decisions don't affect the rest of us.

She tucks her hand under her other arm and inspects her nails. She may want to appear disinterested, but I know her better than that. Her muscles bunch, the lines of her body a harsh contrast to the lazy expression on her face.

"Technically, he killed himself. Perfect placement of a rock." She drops her arms, narrowing her eyes. "Why are you here?"

A rumble rolls through my chest and I stomp into the shed, not bothering to answer. I'm only here so I keep my head. My heel crashes through a broken board and I stumble while pulling it free. If I end up face first in the dirt, I'm going to lose my shit.

"You took out this guy?" I shout as I scan the large man's body. I doubt I'd be able to take his motherfucker on.

When she doesn't answer, I stomp back outside. Of course, she's not where I left her, opting to start her trek back to town, apparently. Cursing, I take off after her. I wasted most of my night tracking her here. I could have been well on my way home by now. Yet here she is, rejecting my help once more. I don't know why I bothered in the first place.

"Where the fuck do you think you're going? You don't even know where the hell you are," I holler at her back.

She lifts a hand over her head, flipping me off. A yelp floats along the air as she hops a little and I realize she's not wearing any shoes. I'm going to end up carrying her ass back to my bike.

"Every fucking mistake," I mutter as she disappears between the trunks.

She pivots and plants her fists on her hips. "What was that?"

I crowd into her space, forcing her back against a thick tree. "I'm sick and tired of cleaning up your fuckups."

Her lip curls and she scoffs. "I didn't ask you to come. I didn't beg you for anything. And I certainly didn't expect you to clean up my messes."

Her words flow over me, planting sordid images in my head of her begging on her knees and my cock hardens. I shove the intrusive fantasy away, focusing on my anger. She's not someone I want. She's certainly not someone I want begging me for anything. I refuse to delve any deeper, especially with my physical reaction to being this close to her. I press my body closer, all while my mind screams at me to back up.

"If I wouldn't have come—"

"Then I would have been perfectly fucking fine," she retorts. "He was already dead when you got there, if you'll remember."

"We don't exactly have a goddamn river to—"

My head snaps to the side, the rustling in the underbrush catching my attention. Branches crack as a repetitive thumping echoes through the forest.

"We don't have to get rid of the body," Emma cries and stomps her foot.

I roll my eyes, even as I shush her. She sputters, indistinct noises erupting from her. Whoever is stalking through the woods isn't attempting to stay hidden. If it's an animal, it might just pass us by. If it's one of the men who took Emma, we might be fucked. I only brought one gun since I was in a hurry to get to her.

"You complete ass—"

I slam my hand over her mouth, whipping my head around to glare at her. Does she really not hear what I do? For someone who's so fucking quick to remind me how much she's trained, she's doing a shit job at keeping quiet. Her blue eyes, almost black in the moonlight filtering through the branches, bore into mine.

We stare at each other for ten seconds before a glint enters her pupils and she bites me. I rip my hand away, a snarl exploding from me. She shoots me a smug smile, and I grab her waist, intent on shaking her. As soon as my fingers dig into her sides, she gasps. She attempts to smother her reaction, but it's too late.

When she opens her mouth to cuss me out, I'm sure, I do the only thing I can think of. My lips crash onto hers, our teeth clashing in our quest for domination. My mind blanks, all the reasons this is a bad idea fleeing in the wake of tasting her. The sequins from her dress dig into my palms as our tongues duel. It isn't until she moans, a guttural sound I've never heard from her before, that I break the kiss.

Our panting fills the air, our breaths mingling as my stomach flips. Her eyes, still closed, flutter behind her lids. Part of me wishes she'd say something—anything. The other part desperately hopes she doesn't say a goddamn word. The minute she does, it'll shatter whatever resolve I'm clinging to.

"Do it," she says, the edge in her voice daring me to step into the shadows swirling around her.

"You're not fucking worth it," I growl, though I can't let her go. My fingers flex, and a shudder runs through her.

She licks her swollen lips, drawing my gaze to them. I did that. Once again, she led me straight into the flames, riled me up to the point where I broke. She's always tested my resolve, peppering the wall I've built around me as if one day she'd be able to tear them down. I'm done being controlled by her whims.

"Fucking coward. Always running away in fear."

My nostrils flare and I push my knee between her thighs, pinning her to the tree. "Call me a coward again."

"Aw, did I hurt your precious feelings?" she sneers.

"Someone needs to fuck the attitude out of you."

"Why? You volunteering? I doubt you know how to satisfy yourself, much less a woman."

I shouldn't play into her game. Neither of us will win if I engage. I can't help it, though. It's instinctual to meet her head-on, never back down. She's a viper, infecting me with her venom. I lean closer and her breath hitches as my lips brush her ear.

"Is that a challenge?" I growl.

I slide one hand to the hem of her dress, playing with the fabric. My other hand slips to the nape of her neck and her head tilts.

"You could try. I doubt you'd get me there. Men like you—"

A vise wraps around my heart, squeezing until I'm suffocating under the weight of her insults. Each one burrows into my soul, begging me to show her exactly who she's dealing with. My hand dives between her legs, and I shove her panties aside. She whimpers when I slide my fingers through the wetness gathered there. Little fucking liar.

"If I'm so fucking inept, then why are you so wet?" I growl into her neck, and she shivers.

I thrust two fingers into her, and she yelps. This isn't gentle or loving. This is a quest for domination—for control. She thinks she can spout off whatever the fuck she wants and there'll be no consequences. Her desire coats my palm as I surge into her again and again. She moans, rocking her hips as she rides my hand.

"Is this what you wanted? To come all over my hand? If you beg, I might just fuck you against this tree," I whisper, earning myself another whimper.

She grips my wrist, and I squeeze her throat, expecting her to push me away. Instead, she holds me there, and I sink my teeth into the soft skin of her neck. My fingers slow, wringing a frustrated cry from her. I slide my other hand down to her neckline, yanking it down, and her tits spill out. I swoop down, capturing her nipple between my teeth.

She hisses and I switch to the other one, flicking it with my tongue. Her head dips and I grab her throat once more, then force her head against the rough bark. Images flash through my mind of sinking into her heat, fucking her hard and fast. My cock twitches and I grit my teeth.

"Beg for me to let you come."

"P-please," she whines, and my cock strains against my jeans at her sudden obedience.

My thumb finds her clit, and she shudders out her release. I curl my fingers, stroking as she sags in my hold. Possessiveness punches me in the gut, demanding my attention. I tear my hand away from her cunt, and her scent washes over me. Her gasps fill the night air and my resolve disappears. I slip my finger into my mouth, and her taste explodes across my tongue.

Our eyes meet in the darkness, hers still heavy with desire. "Next time I won't be so generous."

I pivot and stalk away from her. If I don't leave now, I'll end up fucking her. She'll end up becoming irresistible—a drug I can't quit. She'll invade my senses more than she already has. I can't afford to fall under her spell. Not only is she a King and therefore off-limits, she'll also leave me a shell of myself. Nothing good would come from giving into my desires.

Yet no matter how far I walk, I can't get the image of her coming out of my head. Knowing she was shuddering because of me doesn't help. By the time I'm halfway to my bike, I know I'm completely fucked. Before long, she'll be screaming my name while her cunt clings to my cock. And I'm running out of reasons to deny myself.

Chapter 23

Emma

I didn't expect Titus to leave me here. In the woods. Completely alone.

To be fair, I didn't expect him to finger fuck me either. Pretending it never happened would be the best course of action. Hard with the evidence of my orgasm running down my thighs. I wish I wouldn't have worn a thong. Or this dress. I'm throwing them both away as soon as I get home. I grit my teeth, wondering if I should just take my underwear off to mop up the mess he left behind.

I swallow down the tears threatening to overwhelm me. I don't have time for a breakdown. He's not worth any of my tears. It doesn't stop them from falling. I should have learned my lesson all those years ago. Titus never gave a shit about me. I don't know why I thought it would be any different after I orgasmed.

I swipe angrily at the wetness on my face. Tugging on the neckline of my dress, I try to tuck my tits back under the fabric. After struggling with it for a minute, I proclaim it good enough to get me home. I run my fingers through my hair, yet the snarls don't give easily. Huffing, I give up and glance around.

Trekking through the woods without shoes wasn't at the top of my list. It's even less appealing now. I didn't think about it when I walked away from Titus earlier. I slip my phone from my dress, cursing when I realize there's no service out here. It's probably the reason they didn't search for it. Daisy would pick me up. She'd come get me in a second. She wouldn't leave me in the woods to fend for myself. She wouldn't make me come, then walk away without a backward glance.

"Fucking bastard," I whisper as I pick my way through the forest.

The moonlight I used to guide my way before has disappeared behind a cloud casting more shadows across the barren landscape. This wouldn't be so terrible if it wasn't so fucking cold out. Goosebumps erupt along my arms and legs, reminding me of his fingers skimming along my skin. I doubt I'll be able to push him out of my head anytime soon.

I didn't think we'd ever be in this position. I thought I'd moved past any fantasies involving him, yet I jumped him at the first opportunity. For fuck's sake, I goaded him into it. This is as much my fault as it is his. I'm not surprised he left. He's probably regretting every decision he's made tonight. I didn't expect him to come after me, though. That was all him.

I wander through the trees for five minutes, checking my phone every thirty seconds. My foot hits a twig and I wince as it pierces the tender flesh. Tears fill my eyes again and I drop onto a fallen branch. It doesn't hurt enough to push me to tears. All the shitty things from tonight have finally piled up, overwhelming me beyond my abilities to cope. Thank fuck Titus isn't here to mock me. Exhaustion settles in my bones and my body curls into itself.

Sniffing, I push to my feet. A brisk walk through the woods in the dead of night will wash away the pain radiating from me. Between learning nothing from Calvin and my encounter with Titus, I'm done. I can't take any more tonight. If a bear comes to eat me, so be it. At least I won't have to face my mistakes. I won't have to scurry home and admit to Shane I fucked up. I won't have to confess I failed while Titus looks on. I won't have to confirm everyone's suspicions—that I was never as good as them and I never will be.

I'm too busy wiping the tears from my eyes to notice the tree looming in front of me. My shoulder slams into it, the bark cutting into my skin. I yelp, swallowing the sound a second too late. Crouching, I lean against my current nemesis. Hopefully there aren't any bloodsucking vampires in the forest. Then again, I wouldn't mind being bled dry right about now. It would get me out of slinking back home with my tail tucked between my legs.

"What the fuck are you doing?" Titus's voice rings through the air.

I let out a choked sob before slapping my hand over my mouth. I didn't expect him to come back. Despair crashes over me as I brace myself for his insults. He'll walk away again before eviscerating me. He'll break me down more than I already am. I don't know how to pick up the shattered pieces of myself, much less put them back together.

"Fuck off," I gasp, hiding my face in the crook of my arm.

His heavy sigh washes over me, and I hold my breath. I can't cry if I can't breathe. It's the only way left to protect myself. I've used the tactic with him before, yet it never works. But nothing seems to work the first few times, so I just keep trying.

My breath whooshes out of me as he hauls me into his arms. My heart flips, my stomach in my throat. The shock to my system dries up my tears. A little voice inside my head screams at me to push him away. He left and I don't need his help. I can't resist the warmth seeping from his body, though. I crave his presence even while I lock my heart away once more.

"Why the hell are you crying?" he mumbles. It's as if he's trying to be upset and failing miserably.

I don't want to answer. I want to soak in his heat and leave the rest behind. I want him to shut the fuck up. I want to pretend it's someone else holding me—someone who wants me, someone who cares for me, someone who loves me. Titus doesn't fit any of that. I tried before to shove him into the role, and I quickly found out he would never be my person. He'd never become my person.

"I'm not." I close my eyes, my head resting against his chest as he lumbers through the trees.

"You were. Don't tell me Twitch never gave you—"

"Stop talking," I snap. He'll keep pushing if I don't tell him. "I stepped on a stick and fell into a tree."

"For fuck's sake."

I tuck my chin to my chest, digging my nails into my arms, and wait for him to insult my training. Instead, he keeps quiet, only the sounds of the forest and his heavy footsteps filling the night. I didn't realize how far out we were. Calvin dropped a dirty pillowcase over my head before we left the alley. At the thought, my face itches and I scrub my hands across my cheeks.

Titus huffs as he steps over a fallen log. "Stop wiggling or you'll end up on the ground again."

"You could just put me down."

"No," he growls, his arms tensing around me. "You'll probably hurt yourself again. Then you'll end up crying again, and I'm not fucking dealing with your shit."

"Yeah, yeah, yeah. Always cleaning up my messes and fixing my mistakes. Heaven for-fucking-bid you show an ounce of empathy for another human being." Even with my sudden burst of energy, I burrow farther into his hold. I love being warm more than I hate him.

"Keep talking shit and I'll make you call a car," he grumbles before stepping from the tree line and onto a dirt road.

I bite my cheek to keep my retort in check. The urge to bite back at him sits beneath my skin, filling my pores with the need to continue the dance we've been engaged in for years. Ignore, insult, ignite. One after another in perfect sequence. Then we start again. Eventually, one of us is going to erupt into rage, and we'll begin once more by pretending the other doesn't exist for another year. We've been doing this so long I don't know how else to perform.

"Well, well, well. I never thought I'd see the day where the infamous Emma King was rendered speechless."

"I'm not infamous. No one knows who I am."

He snorts and his fingers dig into my thigh. "And the people who do wish they didn't."

I stiffen, no longer concerned with the cold. "Put me down."

"Not on your fucking life."

His foot hits a rock and it skitters into the ditch. The soles of his boots crunching on the gravel grates on my already frayed nerves. I lean as far away from him as possible without tumbling out of his arms, and he growls. If he drops me now, I'll have to contend with stones digging into my already beat-up feet. This isn't the lowest I've ever been, but it's been a while since I've wallowed. And to think, less than an hour ago I was feeling pretty damn good. I suppose an orgasm, regardless of who provides them, does wonders.

I yelp when he drops my legs, and I cling to him. His low chuckle rolls over me and I wonder if I can throat punch him from this angle. My feet brush the grass on the side of the road, and I set them down gently before releasing him from my death grip.

Smoothing down my dress, I wince. My shoulder burns, my foot aches, and my eyes itch. Not to mention I'm sticky. I fucking hate being sticky. I could live with the rest if my thighs weren't glued together. Another wave of exhaustion hits me, and I contemplate if I should sit down. I might not be able to get back up, though.

Titus rolls his bike next to me and I glance around, wondering where he stashed it. I still don't know where we are. The roads out here twist and turn, and I tend to avoid them. I assume we're west of Ridgewood since there's more open space out there. The next town is a good forty-minute drive on the best of days. Calvin having a random shed in the middle of nowhere makes sense considering what he's involved in.

"Get on," Titus calls over the rumble of his engine, and my head jerks up.

I bite my lip, wondering how the fuck I'm supposed to ride with this dress and no shoes. I barely make out Titus rolling his eyes before rolling closer to me and holds out his arm. It's the bare minimum, but I'll take it. He ends up tucking my legs under his shins and my hands flutter at his sides. He growls out a sigh and seizes my wrists and yanks me forward. My fingers end up gripping his belt, and I bury my face into his back.

The ride back to my apartment is terrifying, and my muscles are quivering by the time we get there. He ends up plucking me from the back and tossing me over his shoulder. Apparently, I've run out of tokens for the princess treatment. I contemplate stabbing him in the kidney. He has two, so it wouldn't be that big of a deal. Then I remember I left my knife on the dirt floor next to a dead body.

"Don't hit my head," I snap as he swings open the door.

"No promises."

Maybe I should have left two bodies behind.

It's not surprising when he takes the stairs. I expect him to slow at some point, but he doesn't. I bet he'd be struggling if he had an extra hole in his body. My mind wanders to all the ways I could make it happen as we reach my floor. He hasn't bled nearly enough for my liking. Not after all he put me through. If I could go back, I'd swallow all the words I said to him when I was too fucking young. Then maybe I wouldn't be here now, flopping around on his shoulder after practically begging him to fuck me. I may not have said it in so many words, but we both know what I wanted.

"Put me down," I murmur as my door swings open, and he steps into the apartment.

He ignores me, kicking the door closed before punching in the code for the alarm. I still need to change it, though I suspect it's too late for that. He'd just end up breaking in without a care. Tonight has been too much—a rollercoaster I never wanted to ride. I doubt it'll end anytime soon, not with all the weight of my mistakes sitting on my shoulders.

My back hits my bed, and my breath leaves me with a whimper. My shoulder protests as I roll onto my side. I don't have it in me to change, even though the sequins jab at my skin. His footsteps fade and I groan. Bastard didn't close the door. And he left the light on in the living room. He probably did it on purpose just to piss me off.

I close my eyes, attempting to empty my mind. He's taking up too much space. There are plenty of other things I need to work out without him interfering. Like what the fuck I'm going to do. Because I have no fucking clue.

Chapter 24

Titus

I slam Emma's apartment door behind me, my bag slung over my shoulder. Setting the alarm, I realize my hands are trembling. It's been a long time since I've seen her cry. Her default in situations is to shut down, cut off all her emotions, and pretend they don't exist. Even all those years ago when I gutted her, she kept her tears to herself. I never saw them and I convinced myself she was fine.

And then tonight happened. I never should have touched her. My plan was to get her ass back to safety, then leave. She pushed me, knowing exactly which buttons to press. We've always known how to rile the other up. She used to do it when she'd come back for holidays. I never could prove it was her, but we both knew. The smirk on her face after I'd find grease smeared on the seat of my bike told me everything.

"Fucking bitch," I mutter as I kick off my boots.

By the time I've made it to her bedroom again, she's sleeping on top of the covers, still in her ridiculous dress. It's a good thing I wasn't here when she picked it. I would have told her all the reasons it was a shitty choice, all of which have nothing to do with the length. She always hated sequins. Not to mention the heels. Part of me is glad she lost them.

I desperately cling to my anger as I reach out and gently move her arm. I'm not in the mood to get into a sparring match with her again. Undressing her might not be my brightest idea, but my cock is certainly on board. The zipper on the side gives easily, exposing her skin inch by inch. At least I won't have to pull it over her head.

As I tug the fabric, trying to get it over her hips. No matter how much I yank on it, the dress doesn't give. I let out a curse, then grit my teeth as she rolls onto her back. My gaze snap to her shoulder and I narrow my eyes. She mentioned she ran into a tree, but it looks more like she was attacked by a badger. I shake my head and fix my gaze on the dress once more. I'm not about to ogle her while she's basically unconscious.

The fabric falls away and I'm reminded of the wound on her foot. I swipe away the dirt and her leg jerks. She sighs, though her eyes stay closed, thank fuck. I grab a shirt from my bag and carefully slip it over her head. Her nose scrunches up as I tuck her arm into the sleeve.

I haven't put this much care into someone in a long time. I'm studiously ignoring that fact by telling myself I just don't want to deal with her defiance. It didn't go like I expected the last time I dealt with her attitude. Having her splayed out on the bed is enough of a distraction. Not wanting her to suffer has nothing to do with how I feel about her. It's because of her family. I can't hand her over broken. My taking care of her has nothing to do with the ache in my chest or the hardening of my cock.

Digging through my bag, I search for the first aid I stashed in here before I left Synd. I should have packed the bigger one. She hasn't gotten any better at not hurting herself. It's as if she thinks she's invincible, barreling into any situation with no regard for her safety. I huff as I find the ointment and bandages.

As I smear the cream on her shoulder, she mumbles what suspiciously sounds like my name. If she keeps it up, I'm going to wake her ass up just to get her to stop and damn the consequences. Once I've tucked her other arm in the sleeve, I breathe a sigh of relief. At least she's clothed now.

I end up in the kitchen, wetting a washcloth to wash her foot. As the water soaks into the fabric, my phone buzzes. Dropping the cloth, I shut off the water and dry my hands on my jeans before I yank it from my pocket. My brows pull low when the sound echoes around me again, yet the device stays black. I tip my head back before I reach for Emma's phone in my other pocket. It's probably Daisy, begging Emma to respond. I already told Daisy she was fine, but I'm sure the woman won't calm down until she hears from Emma herself.

I scowl as Devon's name pops up in the notifications with a preview of the message. Bastard. I can't decipher what his true intent is with so few words, and I don't have time to deal with him right now. I wring out the washcloth after I've dropped her phone on the counter next to my own. If he keeps up his shenanigans, I'll have to pay him a visit.

It takes me another fifteen minutes of carefully washing her foot, then wrapping it before I'm finally done. I roll her to one side of the bed, hoping she doesn't fall off the edge of the mattress. I should have just picked her up, but I don't trust myself not to crawl in with her. Not because I want to make sure she's okay throughout the night. I'm merely sick of sleeping on her fucked-up couch. My back twinges from the thought alone. If we're stuck in Ridgewood for a while, I might force her to sleep on it instead. She's the one who bought the fucking thing.

I end up spending too long on the chair in the corner of her room, watching her sleep. By the time the sun rises, my lids droop and I let myself sink into the darkness.

I shake out my hands for the fifth time while I pace the small space in her apartment. I should've left after she woke up like I planned all along. Yet I can't seem to get myself to walk out the door. I open the fridge again and immediately shut it. The contents haven't changed in the five minutes since I last looked.

Finally, I give up and stalk to her bedroom. Moonlight streams through her window, casting shadows on her face. I've been patiently waiting for her to fall asleep so I can get on with my night. Her arm twitches and her hand slides from underneath her pillow, revealing a knife tucked in a sheath. Thank fuck I made the right choice last night to sleep in the chair. I ease the handle from her fingers and her lip pops out in a pout.

Setting the weapon on her nightstand, I resist the urge to wake her. She doesn't need to come with me for this mission. It's a side quest at best, not important to the main storyline of our game. She'll likely never know I've left or what I've done.

As I slip from the apartment, I flex my fingers. Today was a shitshow of a different variety. We ate in silence, messed around on our phones in silence, and danced around each other in silence. She was determined to ignore me, and I had no problem obliging her. I was pissed enough when I woke up and her bed was empty. She'd only retreated to the bathroom, but it was enough to send me into a panic. Which only pissed me off more.

While she showered, I took the opportunity to break into her phone and read the messages from Devon. The subtle digs at her character sent my mood into a dark space. What really pushed me over the edge was when an unlisted number texted her, alluding to the events of the previous night. It wasn't hard to figure out it was Calvin threatening her. Should I have told her about it instead of deleting the evidence? Probably. But I'll deal with the consequences later. If I can find him tonight, he won't be a problem. Hopefully then I can finally bring her ass back to Synd.

Joy leans against the apartment building with a raised eyebrow as I exit. She didn't question why I was still around when I texted her earlier. I hold out my hand for the keys dangling from her fingers, and she yanks them back.

"Couple questions before I lend you this car," she says, and I gesture her farther into the shadows of the building.

I cross my arms, glancing around to make sure no one is watching us. "Ask them quickly. I have a lot to do and I'd like to actually get some sleep tonight."

"Can I expect this car to return to me? And in the same condition?"

"Probably not. But since I technically own it, that shouldn't be a problem." I smirk and she rolls her eyes.

She taps her booted toe against the concrete, the noise grating on my nerves. I'm wound tight enough as it is, and she's not fucking helping. I still have to find Calvin before I can deal with him, and I have no idea where he'll be. I don't have the connections in Ridgewood like I do in Synd. The bouncers at the Tower might help me, but I can't count on them. Plus, I have no idea if Calvin will be there tonight.

"Is this mission for her?" she finally asks, fixing her gaze on me.

"Does it matter?"

"Of course it does. Do you need me to keep an eye on things while you're gone?"

I'm shaking my head before she finishes her question. "That won't be necessary. You're more likely to get stabbed if she finds you in her apartment."

She rolls her eyes again, and I wonder if she'd mind if I plucked them out. I wait for her next question, checking the area again.

She clears her throat and I glance her way. "You wanna think about my offer for more than five seconds? Whatever you're about to do probably requires your full attention. Can you do that if you're worried about her being alone?"

"Is this a ploy to meet her?" I ask, and she smirks.

"Two birds and all that jazz. That's all the questions I have tonight, folks, don't forget to tip your servers, and have a good night."

She flounces off and disappears through the front door. I have half a mind to let her get all the way up there and realize there's an alarm. The noise would wake Emma, though, so I pull out my phone to put in the code. I wait until she texts me she's inside before setting it once more. Hopefully, she doesn't try to leave before I'm back or she'll fuck up everything.

It's a strange sensation driving a car after riding my bike for so long, and I'm still not used to it by the time I reach the Tower. The bouncer from last night lifts his hand as I approach, a few men groaning when the bouncer leads me inside. I thought I'd have to convince him to talk to me. I'm not about to question it when I'm getting what I want.

He leads me to a small room that looks like it doubles as a shitty breakroom for them. I didn't realize he could see the disgust on my face until he chuckles.

"It's not much, but it's better than the last club I worked at. Bigger one in the back," he says, collapsing into one of the chairs. "Dylan, by the way."

I take the other, my lip curling when my hand hits something sticky. "Titus. What exactly is between here and the roof?"

"Offices, mostly. I think they're going to make some of them apartments, but the club is the real draw. Gotta drive a few hours to find a place even close to somewhere like this." Dylan drums his fingers on the table. "What did you need?"

"I'm looking for the man I had an encounter with last night."

He nods, glancing away. "Calvin Astor. Pretentious douchebag, if you ask me. I tried to get him banned after you left. Manager doesn't want to ruffle any feathers. Apparently his father doesn't live around here, but daddy's reach is further than expected."

"You know where he lives? His friends? Anything you can tell me would be helpful."

He sits back in his chair, crossing his arms over his chest. "I'd ask if I'm about to become an accomplice, but that would probably solidify my accomplice status."

I struggle to not respond or check the time. It's never good to piss off the person I need information from. My skin itches, bitterness at having to do this in the first place filling my pores. It has nothing to do with the guilt boiling in my gut. If I focus on the contempt I feel for Emma instead of the obligation, it'll make this night go smoother.

Dylan clears his throat, and my gaze flicks to him. "You know we all talk, right? We're literally paid to pay attention."

"I fail to see how that applies to my questions."

"She's my friend," he murmurs, a glint entering his eye. "From what we've seen, you're protecting her. Don't know why. Don't really care, either. But if you turn..."

What the fuck did you stumble into, Emma?

"Is that a threat?"

He rubs his chin as he eyes me. "I suppose it is."

"Good. Now tell me what you know."

Ten minutes later, he leads me out the back to the same alley Calvin grabbed Emma from. We don't bother shaking hands as we part ways. I doubt we'll meet again. Unless Emma decides to sneak off to the Tower again. Dylan gave me a list of places Calvin was known to frequent. He even texted some friends at other clubs, asking if Calvin had been spotted. We finally narrowed it down to a house his dad bought for him on the outskirts of town.

I guide the car around a curve, searching the tree line for animals. They like to jump in front of the headlights, and while it may be easier to take a hit in a car than a bike, I'd still rather not deal with it tonight. I thought I'd be there by now and I grind my teeth. When Dylan said the outskirts, I thought he meant the edge of Ridgewood. I've been driving at least ten minutes farther than I expected.

My phone buzzes and I pull to the edge of the road as my headlights sweep across a modest house. The two-story building isn't what I thought Calvin would be living in. With the way he blusters around, I'd assume he'd live like a fucking douchebag as well.

I read Joy's text, scowling at the screen. I trust Joy not to snoop through Emma's things, but I wouldn't put it past Joy to wake Emma up on purpose. She's been dying to meet Emma since the move to Ridgewood. Every time I talk to her, she brings it up. I never should have left them alone. Hell, I shouldn't be here in the first place.

I shove open the door, wondering if I should hide the car better. Calvin had a couple friends with him the other night. I'm hoping I can sneak in and take him out before they notice. I might not even have to break into the house. Maybe I can just shoot him through a window or something. It'd make my life easier.

Skirting around the lawn, I stick to the trees and loop around to the back. Most of the lights are off and I'm worried I miscalculated. He clearly isn't the type to lounge around on a Saturday. I can't fathom why he'd want Emma dead. Every time I tried to talk to her about it, she'd brush me off. At one point, she tried to climb out the window just to get away from the conversation. I fucking hate that she won't just admit she's in over her head.

There are several windows overlooking the backyard and I sidle up to one. It's dark inside, but I can make out the outline of a kitchen. I'm about to go to the next one when a shadow stumbles into the room. He weaves around the table, then slams his hip into the oven. He rips on the fridge handle, practically taking it off, and his feet shuffle as he digs inside. I snort when he swings around, leaving the door wide open, and guzzles down a beer. I wonder how many he's had. Not enough to change my mind about killing him.

I stroll around to the front of the house, brushing my hand against the gun at my side. It's something I picked up from Emma, actually.

Always check your weapon. Last thing you want is to need it and it's no longer there.

It didn't make sense. It still doesn't. But her words stuck, and I found myself pressing my palm to my gun every time I walked into a situation. I made peace with it long ago. I kick down the front door, the lock giving easily under my boot. I step into the dark interior and glance around, waiting for someone else to pop out. At this point, I don't care if he's got friends here. I'll kill them all.

"Honey, I'm home," I yell, giddiness rolling through my veins.

This isn't how I do things. I've never been the one to bust into a situation, shouting cliches like I'm in a movie. Usually, I don't need to. If I walk in and start shooting, it leads to issues—mistakes I need to clean up. I do that enough for Emma. No need to add to my load.

Yet here I am, excitement thrumming through my body at the thought of fucking with Calvin. I skirt around the furniture in the living room and practically skip down the hallway. I doubt Calvin has moved from his spot in the kitchen. He doesn't seem to have strayed far from his fridge, though I'm surprised he's sunken so low as to drink beer. He seems more like a guy who drinks top shelf and nothing else—spend thousands of dollars on a bottle of scotch just to deem it unworthy.

My feet stutter to a stop when I come upon a door on my right. I spin the knob and kick at the wood. My mouth drops open as I take in what's probably meant to be a bedroom. The entire space is filled with board games and puzzles. Boxes fill the shelves, stacked on top of one another to the ceiling. A large table takes up the center of the room, a half-finished nature scene on top. Slowly, I inch the door closed. I'm not one to judge someone's hobbies, but I sure as hell didn't expect that.

A chuckle leaves me as I imagine Calvin hunched over, fitting pieces into place. Too bad he won't be able to finish the puzzle he started. The hallway opens up, revealing the small kitchen. Calvin sways in the chair next to the table, a bottle dangling from his fingers. I kick out the other chair across from him and plop down.

Resting my hand on my gun, I fix my gaze on him. His bloodshot eyes meet mine, not a flicker of recognition in their depths. The bastard tips the bottle toward me, offering me a drink. I shake my head, a manic grin taking over my face.

"He send you?" he croaks, blinking slowly.

"Nope." I pop the *p*, tilting my head at him. I didn't plan on chitchatting with him, but if he reveals something, so be it.

Confusion overtakes his features. It's like watching a lemming approaching a raging river and assuming it can make it across.

"You're not here to drink. You're not here to kill me. So why are you here?"

"Bold of you to assume I'm not here to kill you," I murmur and place my gun on the table.

He nods, then tenses. He's not very subtle in his intentions, though in his drunken state, I'm not surprised. I smirk as he tumbles to the floor in his quest to reach the knife block on the counter behind him. Nudging him with the toe of my boot, he groans. I've met some incompetent assholes in my day, but Calvin might take the cake.

"Do it, then. Do his fucking dirty work," he moans, writhing around on the floor.

"Who exactly do you think I'm killing you for?" Clearly, he doesn't think I'm here for Emma.

He pushes to his feet, a frenzied giggle erupting from him. "If you don't know, I won't tell you. It's my little secret."

"As fun as this has been, I fear our interaction has come to an end." I run my finger along the barrel of my weapon. "Would you prefer to sit or stand?"

Calvin drops to his knees, and I expect him to beg, but he just tips his chin up. I lean forward, and he bursts into tears. His hands drop to the floor and he becomes a blubbering mess, wailing words I can't make out.

"Fucking pathetic," I growl and shove to my feet.

"I-I-I can fix it," he wails. "J-just give me a chance."

I tip his chin up with the barrel of my gun, my lip curling. "How?"

He hiccups, his breath shuddering out of his body. "I'll get her again. I know where she l-l-lives."

"Do you." The giddiness I had before flees. It's a statement, but he nods vigorously. I half expect his head to pop off.

His chin quivers, tears filling his eyes again. I shouldn't have engaged him. I already knew he wasn't acting alone. Calvin may have a shit ton of money, but he isn't smart enough to pull off Emma's kidnapping alone. I don't know why he took her. He probably doesn't either. He probably doesn't even know who he's actually working for. So often they keep their identities hidden for just this reason. Mid-level men are easy to break.

"I can get her. I swear," he gasps.

"Therein lies the problem."

His brows pull low and he shakes his head. "I d-don't...I don't understand."

I lean in, the scent of liquor seeping from his pores and swirling around me. "You touched what was mine."

As I ease back, recognition flares in his watery eyes. His mouth parts, but I don't wait for him to connect all the dots. I smash the butt of the gun into his nose. Satisfaction rolls through me as he doubles over, clutching his injured face. As much as I want to draw this out, I need to get back to Emma. I've been gone long enough.

Still, I step around him and ease a butcher knife from the block. Hopefully, he kept them sharp enough to cut through tendons. I'd hate to have to get the bread knife out.

Gripping his hair, I wrinkle my nose at the amount of product coating my hand. I yank his head up, euphoria sending my heart rate soaring. He drops his hands, attempting to reach my legs as if he could knock me over.

I swipe the blade across his throat, blood coating my fingers. I drop my hold as he claws at the gash I've left behind. He won't last long, thank fuck. I must have hit an artery with the amount of red dripping down his skin. Stepping around him, I tilt my head, wondering if I should bury him. That seems like a lot of work.

His mouth gapes as he struggles to breathe, wide gaze finding mine. I smirk once more before dropping the knife in front of him.

"In case you want to finish the job."

I pivot, heading back the way I came, my mind already focusing on the next step to keeping Emma safe.

Chapter 25

Emma

There's someone in my apartment.

I've spent the last ten minutes staring at my bedroom door, waiting for it to open. At first I thought it was Titus, but the footfalls were different—lighter. Daisy was my next guess. She wouldn't come without calling, though. Whoever they are, they haven't bothered to check the bedroom, and it doesn't sound like they're stealing anything.

My muscles bunch as I ease myself upright and swing my legs over the side of my bed. Reaching behind my nightstand, I hold my breath until I feel the extra gun I have stashed there. I'd rather not shoot someone in my apartment. Like Titus so helpfully reminded me, there's no river to dispose of the bodies. I might not have a choice, though.

I ease the door open, hiding behind the wood, and a woman curses. My heart pounds and I bite my cheek. Maybe it's the training I went through or the way I was raised. Either way, I'm more terrified of taking on a woman than a man. If they're femme, they're more capable of taking me out, and I'm not messing with fate.

"You can come out now. And please don't shoot me. I've got enough holes in my body."

I swing open the door and peek around, finding a woman planted on my couch. She flips on the light and grins at me. Annoyance worms its way through my gut, and I lean against the frame. She gestures to the chair under the window, and I shake my head.

She sighs, playing with the hoop through her lip. "You going to shoot me?"

"Not yet. Why are you in my apartment?" I wish I could tuck the gun in my waistband, but I'm not wearing any pants. I don't know why I pulled on Titus's shirt again before I crawled into bed. And now isn't the time to unpack my choices.

"I'm afraid you'll shoot me if I tell you." She smirks as if this is all a big joke.

"Let me guess. Titus told you to keep an eye on me while he went off to fuck knows where. Strange, since I assumed he'd be with you."

Her eyebrows rise, and I struggle to keep my mask in place. She doesn't need to know about the emotions weaving their way through me. Hell, I can't even identify half of them. Whatever she discovers will end up whispered in Titus's ear. The less he knows, the better. He'll just use the information against me. He'll throw it back in my face the next time I piss him off, which is never long enough.

She purses her lips. "You're exactly how I thought you'd be. Next time you plan on carving someone up, can I watch?"

"Excuse me?" I'm not surprised she knows who I am. I assume Titus told her all about me and my family. I didn't expect her to be so bold about it, though.

She waves her hand, dismissing my tone. "Listen, I'm not here to get in your way or out you or something. I just wanted to meet you."

"Why?"

"To see who could capture Titus's...attention so thoroughly."

My chest tightens and I glance away. I hate this whole thing. I hate standing here while wrapped in Titus's shirt. I hate feeling like I'm in a competition with this woman. Especially since it's a game I know I can't win. Titus isn't mine and he never will be. He'd rather I never existed. His life would be so much easier if I just disappeared.

"I'm a job for him. Nothing more." I swallow down the bile inching up my throat. "You don't have to worry about me interfering."

I want to say more, but all my words will be a thinly veiled exploration into their relationship. I don't want to know, nor am I entitled to that information. It's why I left the other night. I could have spied on them longer, followed them to wherever they ended up. Yet I didn't. I'm loath to admit it, but it would have hurt. Not that I want Titus. That ship sailed long ago. No burning torches for him or pining for a life of could-have-beens. He's not worth fighting for. At least that's what I tell myself.

"Don't know what you'd be interfering in, but sure. I'm assuming he didn't tell you, then?"

"Tell me what?"

"That's enough, Joy," Titus growls from the kitchen.

I jolt, then curse myself for not paying attention. I was so focused on Joy and whatever secrets she holds I didn't even notice he came in. He's trained to be silent, but still. I'm better than that.

"Welp, that's my cue. Nice to meet you, Emma." Joy slaps her thighs and struggles to stand. Her nose wrinkles as she glances at the couch.

"It's a piece of shit. Don't try to understand it," Titus says, still loitering in the shadows.

"Dickhead. My couch is comfortable," I grumble. I reach around the door frame and set my gun on the single bookshelf.

"My back begs to differ."

I roll my eyes, refusing to engage with him. Glancing at my feet, I wince. I didn't think of what it would look like to Joy. I should reassure her that regardless of whether I'm wearing Titus's shirt, we're definitely not sleeping together. Who knows what their relationship is? But I'm not about to get between them, no matter what feelings it stirs up. For all his faults, Titus isn't the type to cheat, though, so I assume whatever they have is casual.

Joy stops next to Titus, and I fix my gaze on the couch. I don't want to eavesdrop. Then again, this is my apartment. If they want to have a private moment, they can go outside. I sure as hell am not going to hide in my own space. It might be an asshole move, but I'm kind of a bitch and I refuse to apologize for it.

"You should tell her we're not sleeping together. And never will," Joy whispers loudly.

My breath stalls in my lungs. She didn't need to say that. Even if she's telling the truth, it has no bearing on me. Or my relationship with Titus. I almost snort. The door clicks loudly and I peek from the corner of my eye. Titus sets the alarm, his shoulders drooping for a second before he straightens and faces me.

"Go back to bed, Emma."

He grabs something from the fridge. Hopefully, it isn't the water Devon left outside my door yesterday. Titus was in the shower and Devon didn't knock. Just left the package filled with a muffin and a couple bottles and disappeared. I tossed the muffin into the crisper since it was pistachio. I've never met a person in my twenty-something years who likes that shit. Devon seems to think they're my favorite. I never had the heart to tell him otherwise.

"I'm not particularly tired. You going to tell me where you were?" I finally turn my head, taking him in fully. "And why you're covered in blood?"

His eyes tighten as if he's holding back a wince. My heart skips a beat and I push from the door. I scan his frame, searching for injuries. For once, he doesn't have a snarky reply, just stares at me with a blank expression.

I dig my nails into my arms, praying my voice doesn't waver. "Are you hurt?"

"Would you care if I was?" He raises an eyebrow, and I open my mouth. "The only injuries I've sustained while here have been inflicted by you, darling. It'll take more than a drunk man to take me out."

He empties his pockets and wrinkles his nose when he spies his hands covered in crimson. His phone clatters onto the small island before he stomps toward the bathroom.

"You didn't answer the question," I call after him and he flips me off over his shoulder.

I slump against the wall as he slams the door behind him. The sight of him covered in blood shouldn't turn me on. When I've taken someone out, the adrenaline sends me into a tailspin sometimes, but I've never gotten horny. I close my eyes and press my thighs together. It takes everything in me to stay where I am instead of following him into the shower.

I'm so absorbed in thinking of every non-sexy thing I can think of, I don't hear him approach until his hands land on my hips. I squeeze my eyes shut harder, my mouth parting as I try not to gasp. His fingers flex, digging into my skin through the fabric. When his breath ghosts across my ear, I suppress a shiver.

"As much as I enjoy fucking with you..." He pauses dramatically, and I press my lips together. "Give me my shirt."

His hands drop, and the heat from his body recedes. I gaze at him through narrow slits as he smirks. At least he washed his fucking hands. I grab the edge of the fabric and rip it over my head, then drop it at his feet. His nostrils flare as his gaze tracks down my body. I don't know what he expected, but apparently it wasn't for me to be completely fucking naked. I didn't even bother with underwear.

I duck my head until his gaze snaps to mine. "My eyes are up here, asshole."

I spin before he can respond. Or maybe I've rendered him speechless. It's not often, but I'm taking the point in our imaginary game he knows nothing about. I saunter into my room, not bothering to shut the door behind me. If he wants to watch me walk away, so be it. I'm not ashamed of my body.

"What the fuck is that?" he growls, violence lacing his words.

It's so unexpected—so different—from his usual tone that I turn. "Huh?"

"Turn the fuck around," he snaps, stomping toward me.

My eyes widen seconds before he grabs my arm and forces me around. I hold still as his finger traces a scar running from my shoulder to my hip. It's long and puckered, though I can't see it. I've spent hours with a mirror, studying it as it slowly healed. I wince when his hand tightens, and his breath stutters as he traces the tattoo along my side. Thank fuck the wound didn't mess it up. He switches back to the scar and a low growl leaves him.

"Who the fuck did this to you?"

Usually I'd snap back, tell him it's none of his fucking business. Or I'd make up some story he'd see through just to piss him off. The barely suppressed rage lacing his voice tells me those wouldn't be the best options. Anger flows from him, the heat of it washing over me as I drop my head and curl my shoulders.

"It was an accident. It's not a big deal," I whisper, hoping he doesn't push further.

I don't have it in me to tell the story, and he wouldn't care by the time I got it all out. As soon as he hears Devon's name, he'll make all sorts of assumptions, and it'll be my fault. No reason for him to tell me what I already know. Titus may complain about cleaning up my messes, but I've dealt with more than he'll ever know over the last five years.

"This scar suggests otherwise," he snarls.

I rip my arm away and spin around. Having this fight, because it will definitely end in a fight, while I'm naked isn't an option. I swipe another one of his shirts from the floor and tug it over my head. He must have dropped it while he was focused on uncovering my past. I'm not going to question it as long as it covers my important bits.

"Listen, it was a foolish mistake and this is my souvenir. It's not the first one and it probably won't be the last."

"Mistake or souvenir?"

"Both. Surprised you didn't jump at the chance to point out the mistakes I've made since you got here."

"I didn't think it was necessary. Plus, your kidnapping was mediocre at best," he says with a huff.

I snort, shaking my head. "I wasn't fucking kidnapped. I set that shit up. Which is also not a big deal. Drop it. Go take a shower before you drip blood all over my floor. I'd like to get my deposit back."

I cross my arms and the hem rides up my thighs, so I drop my hands to my sides. It's not as intimidating, but telling him to wait while I put on pants might be pushing it, and he already looks like he's about to lose it.

"Like I give a fuck about your deposit." He steps into my space, his hands landing on my waist, and he pushes me until my back hits the wall. "Tell me who did it to you. It was Twitch, wasn't it?"

"No, it wasn't."

His eyes narrow as his jaw clenches. Apparently, I'm not the only one unable to keep my emotions in check. Every twitch tells me exactly what he's thinking. And he is definitely not happy. I'm not lying, per se. From the look on his face, he doesn't believe me. He pushes his hips into me, holding me against the wall, and a bolt of need hits me.

"I've got all night, darling."

"Then maybe we should grab some snacks," I sneer.

"Why would we do that when I have one right here?"

My tongue darts out, pulling his gaze to my mouth. We shouldn't do this. Not again. The first time was a mistake. The second would be inexcusable. Yet I can't stop the butterflies erupting in my stomach. Or ignore the wetness gathering between my legs.

His hand skims down my leg until he brushes the hem of my shirt. He leans close, making my breath hitch. I'm aware of the consequences of taking this any further, yet I can't stop my eyes from closing.

His lips brush the shell of my ear. "Too bad I'm not very hungry."

Chapter 26

Titus

Emma's eyes fly open, her pupils blown wide. I can practically smell the desire pouring off her. It takes a few seconds for my words to filter through her pleasure-addled brain. I smirk as she scowls, then drop my hold on her. I can't help but graze my fingertips along her thigh, making her muscles clench.

I pivot, keeping my steps even as I walk away from her. It wasn't my best comeback, but I couldn't think of anything else. Between her very naked display and the heat radiating from her, I couldn't think straight. Add in that she fucking set up her own kidnapping and I'm not on my game. I'm no longer riding the high of my little hunting trip. I wish I could have taken my time with him.

Emma yells something I can't hear over the closing of the door. I strip off my clothes before flipping the handle in the shower. Water sputters out of the head, taking forever to create a steady stream. I fucking hate her shower. I hate her couch. I hate her kitchen. I hate every single part of being here.

As I step under the cold spray of water, goosebumps sprout along my skin. If I hate being here so much—hate *her* so much—why did I claim her? Why the hell did I touch her? I shouldn't have done either. Yet all I can imagine is how it would feel to sink into her wet cunt. I close my eyes and she's there, a flush spreading across her tits to her throat. An image of her coming, ecstasy stamped across her face, and it replays over and over.

I duck my head under the freezing water, practically waterboarding myself. It's enough to shock my system and erase the images from my mind. Or at least push them into the deep recesses. It's not enough to make my erection go away. Nothing is enough these days. Not reminding myself I hate her. Not remembering how she kneed me in the balls and tried to break my nose. Not the warning I give myself about her family. Not a goddamn thing.

I give up, wrapping my fingers around my cock. A groan leaves me as I stroke myself. The shower wouldn't be my first choice to relieve the tension riding me, but I refuse to fuck my hand on that goddamn couch. I turn and brace my fist on the wall, the water finally warming. Or maybe it's the heat from my body.

Emma's image pops back into my head, spurring me on. I can't help but picture her sprawled across the bed, writhing underneath me, coming all over the cock in my hand. Tightening my grip, I groan as my release hits the wall in front of me. My breath heaves out of me, ragged and heavy. I expect shame to wash over me like the water dripping down my body. It doesn't. Instead, my cock hardens again as my mind conjures more visions of her in compromising positions.

I wash away the evidence of my time and move on to cleaning my body. When I reach for my shampoo, I realize I left my bag in the living room. Grumbling, I use Emma's, the scent that's distinctly *her* filling the small space. I hesitate before reaching for the conditioner. Usually, I just use whatever is in the showers in the King's basement. I stuck to the west wing where the old training rooms were. Fewer people over there compared to the east end. The water pressure is shit and the soap is cheap, but it's quiet.

A sharp knock at the door has me jolting, and I swipe the water from my face. I'm surprised Emma didn't bust in here without a care. Then again, I left her pretty hot and bothered. She's probably been licking her wounds. Maybe she's been using one of the toys I found in her nightstand. The thought has my cock standing at attention.

She knocks again, and I grunt as I flip the water back to cold. "What the hell do you want, Emma?"

"Don't use all the hot water. I need a shower."

"You're not fucking showering. Go back to bed," I yell, then dunk my head under the spray.

Her muffled reply sounds like it's coming from underwater. "Fuck you."

I roll my eyes as I wash the soap from my body. I'd love to take my time just to piss her off. Except I don't have anything else to do in here and I'm actually getting cold. Exhaustion ripples over me and my hand slips from the handle, the water dribbling to a stop.

By the time I'm finished drying, chills wrack my body and I shudder. I swear to fuck if I get sick, I'm going to blame Calvin. Or better yet, Emma. If I was in Synd, I'd be healthy and not running around at all hours of the night. Not with my new job title within the family.

I tug on some sweats and toss the shirt I took from Emma into my bag. I never planned on wearing it but seeing her in my clothes had my chest aching. My plan didn't work since she found another one on her floor. I don't know how it got there. All my clothes probably smell like her now. I wonder where the hell Emma does her laundry. There's certainly no hookups in this small-ass apartment.

Once I know I'm not about to push her against a wall again, I rip open the bathroom door and stomp through the dark space. Another wave of shivers hits me, and I almost stumble into the wall. No fucking way am I sleeping on the couch tonight. The waning moonlight filtering through her window illuminates her face and her dark eyes find mine.

She opens her mouth as I step to the side of her bed. A squeal leaves her when I seize her and stalk into the living room again.

"What the hell, Titus? Put me down," she cries, bucking in my arms.

"Gladly," I snarl and drop her onto the couch.

I leave her cussing behind as I collapse onto her bed. Closing my eyes, I suck in a deep breath and my muscles relax. It's the bed, not the smell of her wafting off the sheets. Not only is this better than the couch but it beats the cot at the chop shop too. I won't give this up if I can help it. I'll fucking fight Emma just to stay on this cloud.

My mind slowly sinks into sleep. When I'm on the cusp of dreamland, Emma's small hands shove on my shoulder and hip. Thankfully, she's not strong enough to move my deadweight and she snarls.

"Back to the couch, darling. I refuse to sleep on that shit again," I mutter, peeking at her from under my lashes.

She huffs. "At least move the hell over, fucker."

"Couch. Now," I growl, closing my eyes again.

She mumbles under her breath and seconds later, the door slams. I sigh, flipping the comforter over my legs, then fold my hands over my stomach. At least I won't have to fight her for the covers.

The mattress sinks as Emma crawls in next to me. Her side presses to mine from thigh to shoulder, her warmth sinking into my chilled skin. The logical side of my brain screams at me to push her off the bed. I give into the illogical side and scoot closer to the edge. If I can at least put some distance between us, I might be able to get some sleep tonight.

"Do I need to put a pillow between us?" she snarls.

"Stop talking."

"If you end up on the floor, don't blame me."

"If I end up on the floor, I'm taking you with me."

She huffs, flipping on her side to face away from me. My lids droop and I finally give in to sleep's seductive hold.

An alarm wailing around me sends me hurtling from sleep. My arms tighten around a soft body sprawled across my chest. Emma grumbles, burrowing into me more.

"Shut it off," she whines.

"Get the fuck off me and do it yourself."

"Phone, asshole."

"On the kitchen counter, bitch."

My eyes fly open, finally registering the sound shrieking around us. I shove Emma away from me and throw the covers off. My shoulder slams into the door frame and I curse. Whether it's directed toward Emma or the wall, I have no idea. I grab the gun Emma left on the bookshelf and flip the safety off as I race through the apartment. No one seems to have broken in, but someone definitely tried to. They might have merely tried to open the door, though.

I snatch up my phone and pull up the alarm app. I'm greeted by Devon's retreating back. Gritting my teeth, I track him until he disappears behind the elevator doors. The fact he waited so long while the alarms blared around him says something. My sleep-addled brain can't come up with the answer.

I turn off the alarm, then toss my phone on the counter. My shoulders slump as I brace my fists on the cracked surface. Emma shuffles behind me, her footsteps barely registering over the pounding of my heart. She swipes at her screen and groans.

"Who the fuck was at the door at five in the morning?" she whines.

My head aches and I crack my neck, the muscles pulling awkwardly. "I'll give you one guess."

"You've got to be fucking kidding me," she breathes. "I'm going back to bed. And so help me if you dump me on the couch again, I'll fucking stab you in the kidney."

I smirk and a chuckle escapes me. "Good to know I'm growing on you, darling."

Any other day she would have gone for a vital organ, but I can live with one kidney. Her threat doesn't piss me off as much as it would have yesterday. I'm not about to examine the change. I'll blame the too little sleep and the ache in my bones.

I push away from the counter and my head swims. My vision blurs as my body sways, and I reach out to steady myself. The counter warps and my hips jams into the corner of the island.

"Fuck me," Emma grumbles. At least I think she's grumbling. She may be yelling and I just can't tell over the roaring in my ears.

Her skin brushes against mine, leaving fire in its wake, and I stagger away from her.

"Go away," I say. My words slur and my stomach churns.

"Stop pushing me away," she snarls, wrapping her arm around my waist. "For once in your life, can you just fucking listen?"

It feels like it takes us an hour to get back to the bedroom. The world spins around me and I can't seem to direct my body. She moans as she lowers me onto the bed, a guttural sound that rips at my heart.

"Goddammit, Titus. Stop making that noise. And let go of me." Emma shoves at my chest and I loosen my grip. My mind spins, grasping at some semblance of reality.

I grit my teeth and my jaw pops as I roll to my side. Curling into a ball, I swallow down the nausea and another moan. My gut might be eating the rest of my organs. I can't go out like this. I can't die from some random fucking sickness. I just fucking can't.

"It'll be okay," Emma whispers. It's the last thing I hear.

Chapter 27

Emma

I wonder if Titus felt like this when he was watching me sleep. He probably sat with his arms crossed, mumbling under his breath about how bratty I am and how he didn't want to take care of me. He probably didn't have anxiety curling in his gut. Or a hole in his cheek from biting it. Or half-moon indents in his skin from his nails.

He probably didn't feel helpless. Nothing I do seems to fix him. I've given him extra blankets, a trash can, and pain meds. I tried to get him back in the shower, hoping the steam and heat would help, but he could barely sit up, much less make it across the apartment. No way I'd be able to carry him.

My head snaps up when he groans. He burrows farther under the covers, hiding most of his face from my view. I shouldn't be this worried about him. It's only been…I have no idea how long it's been. I glance at my phone and wince. Five hours. That's nothing in the grand scheme of things. Still, I don't think I can wait another five hours for him to deteriorate.

I shove from the chair and slip out of the bedroom, easing the door closed as I do. I pull in a deep breath before pulling up Ink's contact. He's not the Kings' usual doctor, but he's helped me out in a pinch. As long as he can keep his mouth shut and not tell anyone in the Reapers, we'll be fine.

"Emma? Who's dead?" Ink's gravelly voice echoes in my ear, and I instantly regret calling him.

"No one. I'm just wondering if I'm overreacting." I wince, waiting for the plethora of questions he's about to throw at me.

"If you're calling me, probably not. Where's the wound?"

"Uh, everywhere?"

I don't know how to describe what's going on with Titus. I could just search for his symptoms, but I'm pretty sure Ren monitors my phone. Which means he'll know I called Ink. Pulling the phone away from my ear, I consider hanging up right now.

"If it's everywhere, then you're fucked. Want to be more specific?"

A cacophony of sounds from his end has a wave of nostalgia crashing into me. The Reapers headquarters may not be home, but it's close enough. I've spent so much time within the club, it's hard not to think of it as a refuge. Dozens of voices fill the line, and Ink grunts. I wait until everything dies out and there's a click.

"Shivers, dry heaving, slight fever. I think lightheadedness or whatever. He's confused and slurring. At one point, he looked like he was going to faint. Oh, and he's curled into a ball on my bed, and for a man over six feet, that's a feat. I did everything I know how, but I'm scared he's going to die."

"Dramatic much? Get your shit together, little King. He's not going to die from a little food poisoning. Which is exactly what this sounds like. When he starts shitting his brains out, maybe don't make fun of him until he's on the mend."

Relief floods me, but I still can't relax my muscles. "Poisoning?"

"Food poisoning, Em. Don't get ahead of yourself." Ink's voice softens, taking on a quality I've rarely heard before. "If he's not better after a day or two or starts looking like he's actually dying, call me. I'll come up and check him out."

"You don't have to. I can take him…" I can't take him to the hospital. The closest one is too far away, and I'd never get him into a car if he gets worse. Not only that, but they'll ask questions I don't have answers to. This place isn't like Synd with connections and ties everywhere I turn.

"Just accept the offer, Emma," Ink growls softly.

"I should come back," I mutter, more to myself than to him.

He sighs and I close my eyes. "You can't right now. Everything's locked down. No one in or out."

"What? No one told me—"

"And I'm not going to either. Just call Shane. Or hell, Alex or Ren or Sam. I don't give a fuck, but stop fucking avoiding them."

He hangs up before I can respond, and tears fill my eyes. I wish I could go home. If I was in Synd, I'd have people I could turn to. Sam would know what to do. Shane would step in and fix everything. There'd be a fair amount of yelling, but I wouldn't have to deal with it on my own. Titus doesn't count, since he's an asshole. An asshole who might have been poisoned.

"Emma," Titus calls, pain lacing his tone.

I send Ink a quick text begging him not to say anything about my call. He sends a thumbs up in response, and I roll my eyes. Wiping the wetness on my face with my sleeve, I hope Titus isn't awake enough to notice. Even with him knocking on death's door, he'd make fun of me for crying. No amount of explaining it's homesickness will matter. Not that I'd admit to him I'm homesick. We don't have that type of relationship. Which is why it's so ridiculous of me to care whether he lives or dies.

A loud thump from the other side of the door has me swinging it open. "What the fuck are you doing? Get back into bed."

He blinks at me slowly, then shakes his head. "Where…"

It's like he lost the question halfway through and confusion takes over. A heavy sigh leaves me as I try to help him back into bed. It takes more effort than it should. His legs hang off the side, and I swear he starts snoring before I get them under the covers. I grab the thermometer and swipe it across his forehead.

"At least your fever isn't bad."

I don't know why I'm talking out loud. He's sunk back into dreamland and can't hear me anyway. I'm not used to having someone in my space. Now that he's here, the need to fill the silence overrides anything else. The other day when we were ignoring each other was torture for me. I kept opening my mouth to say something, and then I'd catch myself. Maybe it's just him, though. I never get this way with Daisy.

"I called Ink. He thinks you have food poisoning. Would help if you told me where you went the other night. Joy said she didn't know either. And don't even start on me about texting her. It's your fault she was here in the apartment in the first place. I'd appreciate a heads-up next time. I almost put a bullet in her."

I gather my dirty clothes from the floor and throw them in the basket. Cleaning isn't my first choice of things to do, but it keeps my hands busy.

Snapping my fingers, I glance over at him. "Speaking of your fuck buddy who won't admit she's your fuck buddy. Where does she get her hair done? I was thinking about going dark. No way am I having a box dye moment in my tiny ass bathroom at three in the morning."

"No."

I spin away from the window and stare at him. "Are you awake?"

"No."

I roll my eyes as I think back on the mindless drivel I was just spouting. I don't think I said anything I wouldn't tell him when he was conscious. It may have been in a nicer tone than I usually use, but nothing damaging.

"Well, in that case, I'll just keep talking. I'm thinking red, though Daisy thinks it'll wash me out. Then again, I don't have the freckles to pull it off. Maybe black. I've never dyed my hair before. Shane never let me when I was younger."

"You're not dyeing your hair," he mumbles, and I narrow my gaze on him. His eyes are closed, breathing not as labored, but even. His shivering has died down as well. Maybe I jumped the gun by calling Ink instead of waiting.

"Bold of you to assume you have a say in anything."

He coughs and the fit ends with a groan as he curls into himself. My body sways, wanting to take action. There's nothing I can do other than feed him more meds. I've already done that and it's not time for more.

"Don't puke on my bed," I snap.

Am I hiding my worry behind angst? Probably. It's something I'll fret about later when he's out of my life once more. Because that's the only way this whole thing ends. We'll go our separate ways and go back to pretending the other one doesn't exist.

When he told me before how much he hated me, I wasn't prepared for it. This time I am. He's made no qualms about how he feels, regardless of the things he's done recently, the least of which is giving into the attraction I'm studiously ignoring. I haven't had enough time to process how I feel about what happened in the woods. I doubt I ever will. If I pretend it didn't happen, maybe I'll be okay.

Titus rolls onto his back and I turn back to my closet to hang up more clothes. I need to organize everything. Actually, I need to pack more than my go bag. I have enough in Synd to sustain me for a few weeks, but once winter break starts, I'll need to be mostly out of here. My lease doesn't end until May and I still haven't decided whether or not I should stay here.

"Not a fuck buddy."

I jolt and make my way to the side of the bed. "What was that?"

"Joy. No fuck buddy. You."

I wait for him to finish, but he's back to pretending he's sleeping. I'm assuming he's saying Joy isn't his fuck buddy. Is he propositioning me for the role instead? I'll blame his illness for whatever the hell is going on with him.

"Don't say shit you don't mean," I say under my breath as I leave the room.

"Matter."

I have no idea what the fuck he's trying to say, and I'm not about to wake him up to find out. I grab a water from the fridge and twist off the cap when there's a knock at the door. My shoulders slump and I set the bottle down. My phone trembles in my hands as I pull up the camera. I'm running off too few hours of sleep to deal with more bullshit. Devon's concerned face fills the feed, and I swallow down a curse. I don't have the energy to deal with him.

He knocks again as I pray he'll walk away. When he reaches for the knob, I jump toward the door. If the alarm goes off, it'll add to the headache building behind my ears and wake Titus up. I rip open the door and force myself to smile, yet it's more like a grimace, I'm sure.

"What do you want, Devon?" I don't have it in me to be more than passably polite to him.

Something flashes in his eyes, too quick for me to decipher, before his lips pull into a smile. Maybe Titus was right and I need to be more forceful with Devon.

"Hey, Emma. I know you said you'd call, but I haven't heard from you. I got worried when you didn't answer my text and thought I'd come check on you." He flashes me another smile, then his brows pull low. "Are you okay?"

"I-I'm fine. Just tired. It's been a crazy couple of days." I'm not about to tell him I haven't gotten any of his texts. Titus probably blocked Devon's number just to piss me off. Or piss Devon off. Probably both, actually.

"Are you sure? You don't look so good," he murmurs as he leans forward and brushes a strand of hair from my face.

I resist the urge to jerk away. He's just trying to be nice. I'm not sick often, but the one time I was and he found out, he was sweet. He sent me chicken soup and some tea. I know he was trying to help even if it didn't. The soup was watery, and I don't like tea. I never told him since I didn't want to hurt his feelings. Maybe it's time to stop worrying about how it'll affect him and concentrate on myself instead.

"Why are you really here, Devon?" I ask wearily.

His eyebrow raises and he leans back. "I'm just concerned for you, Emma. You broke up with me out of the blue, no explanation. And I took it. I didn't push you or demand anything. I didn't turn into a dick who called you a whore. I didn't do shit to you, yet you avoid me like I cheated or something. I thought with time—"

"What? That we'd get back together? We're not. I made that clear. Our lives are going in two different directions, Devon. Which I also told you. I don't know what else you want from me." I shake my head, wishing he would go away.

"I want us to get back together," he cries, throwing up his hands. "But you keep pushing me away. I'm going in whatever direction you are. I'll follow you to the ends of the earth. We're soulmates—meant to be. Why do you keep denying fate?"

My muscles tense, the last of my fatigue disappearing. I grip the edge of the door, ready to slam it in his face if he grabs me. I never used to have the urge to get away from him. Ever since the incident in the alley, though, I'm wondering if maybe I don't know who Devon really is.

"Devon, I'm sorry. I really am. But we're not meant to be together. You can't go where I'm going. I promise you'll find someone who loves you the way you deserve." I pull in a deep breath as his face falls. "But it won't be me."

I close the door and lock the deadbolt. He pounds on the door, yelling at me to open up and finish the conversation. My forehead hits the wood as he calms down, his shouts turning to pleading. I should have done this weeks ago, but I didn't want to hurt him. I wasn't lying when I said he was a good guy. He was the perfect boyfriend. Everything should have been perfect.

Eventually, I watch through my phone as he walks away, promising to return when I'm feeling better. I can't keep doing this. I just fucking can't.

Chapter 28

Titus

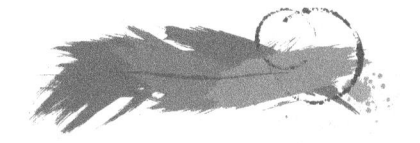

Fucking finally. I didn't think Emma would ever have the balls to put Twitch in his place. I'm sure it'll take more than her words to get him to leave her alone, but at least she finally stood up for herself. With her shoulders slumped and her forehead resting against the door, I wonder if she'll start crying. Hopefully, she doesn't want a fucking hug. I'm not a hugger and even if I was, I might end up puking on her if she squeezed the slightest bit.

She turns, then freezes, wide eyes finding mine. A blush creeps up her cheeks and she glances away. I don't know why she's embarrassed about telling Twitch off. Although, it may just be me.

"Why are you out of bed? And easedropping is a sin, you know."

"First of all, it's *eavesdropping*. And second, I have to pee. Thought about taking a shower." I don't move from the door frame. I'm slightly terrified I'll end up on the floor if I do.

"Then why aren't you moving?" She crosses her arms over her chest, her tits practically falling out of her tank top.

"I will when I'm good and ready. Go put some fucking clothes on," I snarl as I push off the wall.

My head swims and my body lurches to the side, seeking a firm surface to save itself. My hand shoots out and smacks into the bookcase, almost toppling it over. Emma rushes toward me like she'll actually be able to catch me. I'll end up flattening her and while I might be sick, my cock is not. He's already waking up, straining toward her as if she's a fucking lifeline. I haven't even fucked her yet. Ignoring the issue isn't helping. I might just need to get her out of my system. First, I need to deal with whatever illness is plaguing me.

"There's nothing wrong with what I'm wearing," she snaps as she slides her arm around my waist.

I don't want to lean on her, but I don't have another choice. We labor toward the bathroom, painstakingly slow. She slips around me, her front pressing into my back. I can't hold back the shudder when her skin hits mine as she attempts to help me through the doorway.

"Do you need me to hold your dick for you?" She has entirely too much snark for the situation. She may think she's hiding her feelings, but I can see right through her.

"Don't be a bitch, Emma. I don't have the energy to deal with your brattiness."

She snorts, her breath coasting across my skin. "At least you're speaking in full sentences now."

The shower looms in front of me, mocking the idea I could actually stand long enough to turn on the water, much less enjoy a full shower. I shuffle to the toilet instead. Emma flips the lid up and I stare at my feet as my vision darkens. Nausea bubbles in my gut and I wonder if I'll make it to my knees in time.

"Get out," I growl.

"For someone dependent on my good graces, you'd think you'd try to not be an asshole." She slams the door behind her, then shouts through the barrier, "Let me know when you're done, and I'll help you into the shower."

After what feels like an eternity, I'm finally able to do my business. I don't want her help in the shower. I don't want her help at all. It wasn't in my plans to get sick while here. Relying on Emma to nurse me back to health is the last thing I want. I'm supposed to protect her, not the other way around. If Devon would have attacked her, I doubt I would have been able to save her. He could have snatched her from right in front of me, and I would've been on the floor before they left the building. I'm no good to anyone like this.

"Are you decent, or did you fall in?" She inches the door open, and I scowl.

"Call Joy," I grunt, pressing my fingers into my temples as she glares at me.

"Why?"

"Just fucking call her," I bellow. It does nothing except add to the pain building in my head.

"No. If you want to call her, be my guest. But you're not going to boss me around just because you're staying here. If you're so fucking pissed about me being a brat, maybe you should stop treating me like one. You're so fucking insufferable," she cries, throwing up her hands.

Against my better judgement, I spin and grab her wrists. "I can't protect you right now."

The admission takes more out of me than I thought it would. Whether it's our past or our present, I have no idea. It doesn't matter either way. She needs someone else here who can do the job.

"I'm capable of—"

"He was working for someone," I say through gritted teeth.

"Calvin? Of course he's working for someone else. And I've managed to keep myself alive this long without your help, Titus. I don't need Joy hanging around."

My burst of energy drains away, and I drop my hands to my sides. I don't have it in me to fight her anymore. Silently, she leads me back to bed. If the bathroom was big enough, I'd crash in there. It wouldn't be the first time I slept on the floor next to a toilet. Those days are long gone, though. I'm not a kid bouncing from one gang to the next, searching for a home.

"Would it make you feel better if I promised to call her if I need help?" she murmurs as she throws the covers over me.

"No. Because you'll be lying." I grab her wrist as she tries to walk away. "Twitch isn't done."

She sighs, indecision stamped across her features. "I know."

"He's hiding something. I don't want you around him." I should keep my mouth shut, but I can't stop the words from tumbling out.

"You don't know what you're talking about," she whispers, and her chin quivers. Whether it's from heartache or fear, I don't know.

"I know guys like him, darling. He's not what he seems."

No matter what I say, she'll do whatever the hell she wants. Emma never did let anyone tell her what to do, least of all me. If she doesn't take action against Devon, he'll end up hurting her. I'm convinced of it.

She glances away, hiding her face as she sniffs. "He's a goo—"

"Stop. Stop defending him," I snarl, shaking her arm.

She drops to her knees and buries her face into the comforter. Thank fuck she's not crying. Still, I bury my fingers into her hair. We spend so much time at odds with each other. In this moment, I don't want to hate her. I don't want to do anything other than know she's safe. For now, she's not to blame.

"Did you sleep?" I ask, and she shakes her head, confirming what I already knew. "Get in the bed, Emma."

For once, she doesn't argue and climbs over me. There's no snappy comeback or sarcasm. No talk of pillows between us. It's as if we've come to a silent agreement to live in this bubble where we'll pretend we're not each other's downfall. She curls against my side and I loop an arm around her back. I close my eyes as my muscles relax one by one.

She mutters something as darkness licks at the corner of my mind. I can't be certain, but it sounded like "I'm sorry."

The fog lifts from my body slowly as Emma twitches in my arms. However long we've been asleep was clearly not enough. If she keeps moving, I'll wake up completely and I'm not ready to leave this slice of peace we've found between us.

"Stop wiggling." My gravelly voice sounds harsh to my ears.

"Then let go," Emma snaps, and I sigh, loosening my hold on her.

I expect her to run like she always does. She's not used to being vulnerable. She locks her true self away, waiting for someone to notice. The only time I've seen her drop her mask is when I've pushed her to the edge and thoroughly pissed her off. Even then I'm not sure it's truly her.

Instead of dashing from the room, she flips to her side and scoots her ass into my hip. Rolling over, I tuck my arm around her. Her tank top rode up while we were sleeping and my fingers skim along her soft skin. I should regret what I'm doing, but I can't find it in me.

"Don't fucking try anything," she snarls.

My eyes close and I bury my nose in her hair. "What exactly would I be trying?"

"Don't be obtuse."

"I have no idea what you're talking about." I smirk, though she can't see.

"Go back to sleep. And watch that hand."

With my cock nestled in her ass, I doubt I'm going to slip into slumber once more. Based on her breathing, she won't either. We've already flirted with the line we shouldn't cross. I'd give anything to watch her fall over the edge again. Getting her on board with fucking the sexual tension out of our systems might be the hard part.

"You're the one who crawled into bed with me."

"It's my bed, motherfucker." Her actions contradict her words as she burrows into me.

I wrap my body around hers, and she slides her leg between mine. My thumb traces circles on her hip as her warmth settles into me. Minutes pass, the sound of her soft breaths the only thing filling the room. It's like the illness stripped away all the arguments I had for staying away from her. Tomorrow we can go back to being at each other's throats.

"For someone who hates me so much..." I murmur, letting my sentence trail off, hoping she'll take the bait.

"Don't flatter yourself, Prince. I'd cuddle with Daisy if she were here."

"Would you fuck her, too?"

Her body tenses, then relaxes. "We're not fucking."

I lean down, whispering in her ear, "Then why are you so wet?"

I slide my finger along the waistband of her shorts, and she shudders. She tries to hide it, but with my body wrapped around her, she fails.

"For someone who claims to hate me so much, you'd think you'd stay as far away from my pussy as possible," she says breathlessly.

"I can hate you and still want to fuck you." The words slip out before I can stop them and I swallow hard. "Tomorrow we can go back to our normal."

She tugs her leg from between mine, and my hand stalls on her stomach. I won't keep her here, but if she leaves now, I'm going to need another shower. When her foot brushes along my shin, I expect her to shove me out of the bed. I wouldn't blame her. I've told her often enough how much I loathe her. My fingers flex as she hooks her knee over my hip, leaving her wide open for me.

"Tomorrow we pretend this didn't happen," she whispers.

"We'll see," I murmur as I skim my hand to her inner thigh.

Her breath catches and her leg trembles under my touch. When I dip under the hem of her shorts, I'm met with more skin.

"Have you been naked this entire fucking time?" I growl.

"No underwear doesn't mean naked."

A groan rumbles from me when I slide my finger along her cunt, finding her completely fucking soaked. Whatever reservations were left flee as I stroke her. They're chased away by the whimpers pouring from her. Her hips push into my hand as she strains for more. If this is the only time I get to touch her, though, I'm taking my time.

She cries out when I pull my hand away. I resisted the urge before, but I can't this time. The taste of her explodes across my tongue as I pop them in my mouth.

"Fucker," she breathes, and I chuckle.

I lift her leg off me and she tenses. I'm sure she thinks I'm about to leave her. Instead, I hook my thumb in her waistband and shove the fabric down.

"Off," I command when she doesn't move.

She rolls away from me and practically rips her shorts off. My retort sits on the tip of my tongue until her shirt goes over her head. Every other time I've seen her naked, we've been in the middle of a battle of wills. I can't seem to pull my gaze away and my mouth waters. I'm not recovered enough to do everything I'd like to. Doesn't mean I'm not willing to try.

I lean over and seize her waist, then haul her on top of me. She gasps, her hands landing on either side of my head as I grip her hips to keep her in place. Her tits hang over my face, and I pull one nipple into my mouth. A strangled cry leaves her, and she grinds her cunt into my stomach, searching for the friction she craves.

I release the sensitive bud with a graze of my teeth, then move to the other one and give it the same treatment. I could spend an hour right here. Instead, I dig my fingers into her hips and yank her up more. Her eyes meet mine, desire swimming in the light pools.

"Up."

Confusion swirls with her pleasure. "What?"

"On my face. Now."

I don't wait for a response before picking her up and sliding her knees over my shoulders. Her hands hit the wall as her cunt hovers over me. I lick my lips, the memory of her taste dancing along my tongue. She suspends above me, her legs trembling. If she thinks I'm going to lift my head the entire time, she's sorely mistaken.

Wrapping my arms around her thighs, I wait for her to give in. When she doesn't, I dig my fingers into her skin. She tips her head back, hiding her face from me while she resists.

"I swear to fuck, Emma."

Her head snaps down and she glares at me. "Keep being a prick and see how far it gets you."

I lift my head and lick her from core to clit and she shudders. She drops, and I groan as her scent overwhelms my senses. I don't know why I resisted her for so long. She rocks her hips, and I run my tongue along her cunt, losing myself in the moment. I suck her clit between my lips, then flick the already sensitive bud. A moan leaves her, the intoxicating sound rolling around us. I'd love to work her into a frenzy, but my cock can't wait.

Sliding my hands to her waist, I relish the feel of her skin beneath my palms. When I latch onto her waist, she grinds her cunt on my face and I grin, then shove her off me and onto her back. She yelps, her body bouncing and limbs flailing.

"You absolute ass," she shouts.

I ignore her cursing me out and shimmy out of my pants and underwear. They bunch at the bottom of the bed. Her foot shoots out, slamming into my hip, and I growl, glaring at her. She props herself up on her elbows and raises an eyebrow before pulling back her leg again. Seconds pass, tension and a challenge hanging between us. She kicks out again, and I grab her ankle before she can connect.

A squeal leaves her as I yank her toward me. She rolls, attempting to wrench from my hold. I push upright as she scrambles to her hands and knees after I release her. The more she struggles to get away, the faster the blood rushes through my veins. I don't have enough strength to chase her ass around the apartment. If she makes it off the bed, I doubt I'll be able to follow.

I swing my legs around and rise to my knees. My arm loops around her waist and she straightens, her back pressing into my chest. Our panting fills the room, and I wonder if she'll tell me to stop. Fuck, I hope not. I need to get her out of my system. As soon as I do, we'll be able to move on. I'll be able to protect her, deal with the mess she's fallen into, and we can go home. I won't be haunted by the what-ifs of being with her.

"Let me go," she gasps, her hands curled into fists by her sides.

"Why would I do that?" I murmur as I trail my fingers across her stomach, making her muscles quiver under my caress.

"You're clearly not capable of making me come, so I'm going to take care of it myself." Her haughty tone is ruined when she gasps as I dip my fingers between her legs.

I duck my head into the crook of her neck and graze my teeth across her rapidly beating pulse. "I've already made you come."

"Must have been a fluke." Contrary to her words, she tilts her head, giving me more access.

"Hmm. How do you explain how fucking wet you are, then?"

I stroke her slowly, then dip my fingers inside her. She rides my hand, trying to force me deeper, and a low chuckle leaves me. Nibbling on her earlobe, I drink in her whimpers.

"Stop fucking teasing me," she cries.

I keep my fingers buried in her cunt as I slide my other hand to her throat and force her head back. I wish there was a mirror in here. Then I could watch the pretty flush splashing across her chest.

"Such a fucking brat even now. Let's see if you can be a good girl. Get on your hands and knees."

I drop my hand and pull my fingers from her. I can't help myself and pop them in my mouth. I lick them clean, wondering if I'll be able to stop myself from tasting her after today. The thought sends an ache through my chest and my nostrils flare. I force myself to concentrate on the here and now. Thinking about the future won't get me anywhere.

A surge of desire hits me when I focus on her again. For once she's listened, her ass on display as she waits for me to do something. If I wait much longer, she won't be the only one bitching about it. My cock twitches, and I stroke my length once to ease the torment I've put it through.

She flips her hair over her shoulder and narrows her eyes at me. I smirk, tilting my head as I run my tip along her weeping cunt. I'm torturing both of us at this point. When she opens her mouth, probably to snap at me again, I thrust into her hard. I bottom out, groaning as she spasms around me.

Her forehead drops to the mattress, forcing me deeper and I grunt. Seizing her hips, I stop her from moving. If she starts wiggling, I'll come before I'm ready. I'm already teetering on the edge of oblivion.

"Move," she whines, and I pull out of her slowly, then slam back into her.

I repeat the move twice more, then instinct takes over. She writhes in my hold as I plunge into her over and over. Her pussy clings to me, then spasms around me as she screams into the mattress. I never slow, digging my fingers into her flesh. Desperation flows through me as I bury my cock in her.

She grips the comforter, bunching the fabric as needy noises fall from her lips. She pushes back in time with my thrusts, urging me onward. I wish I could savor this moment, but I'm so close to exploding. I've never wanted anything more than to watch her come again. With her face buried, I won't be able to, though.

I grit my teeth and pull out of her. A choked sob leaves her, but I don't give her time to cuss me out. I slide my hand between her legs and grab her inner thigh. She yelps as I flip her onto her back. Shoving her knees apart, I lick my lips when I spy her cunt glistening with need.

A growl rips through me when she tries to touch herself. I grab her wrists and trap them above her head before thrusting into her once more. Her legs wind around my waist. The instant our eyes meet, I know I've fucked up. This is intimate, familiar. I tuck my chin to my chest just to get away from the emotions rolling through me. I focus on the intoxicating view of my cock disappearing into her cunt.

Her back arches as she sails over the edge, and my gaze snaps up. Ecstasy washes over her face and the sight overtakes me. I empty into her with a groan. Our movements slow and I duck my head as our heavy breathing fills the silence left behind.

This was a mistake. I never should have fucked her. Now, I'll never be able to get away. She'll fill my thoughts more than she already does. I'll relive the memory of this moment. I was a fool to think once would ever be enough.

Chapter 29

Emma

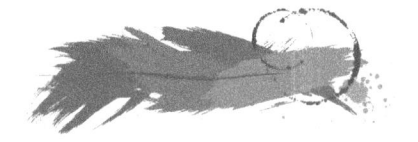

One of these days I'll learn from my mistakes. But today is not that day.

Titus grunts as he rolls off me and stomps from the room. As the evidence of what we've done seeps out of me, wetting my thighs, I close my eyes and my legs. I don't know why I expected anything else from him. He walked away in the woods, too. Sure, he came back eventually, but it wasn't for a cuddle and whispered words of love.

I scramble off the bed, searching for something to clean myself. It's a good thing I'm on the shot or I'd have a whole other set of things to deal with, and I don't think I can handle him right now. Swallowing down the anxiety creeping up my throat, I pinch my arm. The pain in my chest is greater than what I've inflicted on skin and therefore doesn't do shit.

My eyes catch on Titus's white shirt sticking out of his bag in the corner of the room. My lips curl into a smirk and I tiptoe over to it. I'm halfway through cleaning up when his footsteps echo through the apartment. I toss the shirt back and dive onto the bed. Holding my breath, I flip the covers over my body and pretend I'm sleeping. I exhale slowly, trying not to make it obvious.

He flings the comforter from my body and my eyes fly open. I'm about to yell at him, but he shoves my knees apart. My nose wrinkles while he swipes a warm, wet washcloth along my thighs. I snap my legs closed when he gets close to my pussy. It's still overly sensitive down there, and the last thing I need is for him to work me up again. I'm sure he won't be down for a round two.

His jaw ticks, and he climbs on the bed on his knees and grabs my own, then pushes them apart once more. He glares at me while I fight to close them again. I don't need him doing this, not only because I already got rid of the evidence, but because it's awkward enough as it is.

"Titus," I snarl, trying to push myself up.

"Don't even fucking think about it."

"What are you doing?"

"Cleaning up your mess," he says, a tinge of laughter in his voice.

With the look on his face, I'm afraid he'll scrape me to shit. Instead, his touch is gentle, and I ease onto my back. At least it's dark in here. If he turned on the light, he'd be able to see the blush on my cheeks. I stare at the ceiling as he finishes the job. I grind my teeth together, both to keep my retorts inside and to just get this over with.

When he's done, he walks out the door again and I close my legs, the chill sending a shiver through me. I pull the covers back over my naked body, wondering if I should get dressed. I doubt he'll come back, at least not without showering first. If I'm lucky, I'll be sleeping by the time he wanders back in. I crowd to the edge of the bed just in case.

My muscles relax the more time passes, and my breathing evens out. My stomach grumbles, and I curl onto my side. I don't regret sleeping with him. I *want* to feel guilty or embarrassed. It would probably kill the longing worming its way through me. I don't know if I can pretend we didn't fuck. Especially since I already want to do it again.

The mattress dips, and I pretend to be sleeping yet again. He sighs, the heat from his body seeping into my back. His hand slides along my stomach, and I tense. When he tugs me against his chest, I really wish I would have put clothes on. Then again, his cock is nestled between my ass cheeks, so he didn't put on clothes either.

He runs his palm along my body before he cups my tit and buries his nose into my hair. I didn't take Titus for a cuddler. I should say something, anything.

Yet I keep my mouth shut. I'm slightly terrified I'll say something to ruin things. Tomorrow we'll end up at each other's throats again. I try to quiet my mind enough to sleep, but after ten minutes, I figure it's not meant to be. When I try to slip from Titus's embrace, he tightens his hold.

"Where are you going?" he murmurs.

"I can't sleep. I'm going to take a shower."

He props himself on his elbow and peers down at me. "Would you like to try that again?"

"Uh, no?" I turn to stare at my closet instead of dealing with his intensity.

I didn't have a plan. Trying to figure out where Calvin went would be smart. I don't want to wait around for him to retaliate. Next time I might not be prepared and I'll end up leaving more bodies in my wake. Then I'll be stuck at a dead end with nowhere else to turn. And I refuse to ask Titus for help. Us fucking doesn't change his opinions on cleaning up my messes. If I don't figure things out soon, I'll end up going back to Synd and run the risk of someone following me.

"You're going to leave, aren't you? Run the fuck away again." He leans in close and brushes his nose along my jaw.

"Wasn't planning on it."

His fingers flex, and he skims his thumb across my nipple. I didn't think this would happen. If anything, I expected him to run away. Everything in me screams to stop him, snap back that I'm not the one skipping out as soon as something goes off the rails. I can't seem to drum up the righteous anger I had several hours ago. He's broken down all my walls, decimating them in the blink of an eye. I thought I had built them up high enough—thick enough. Yet here I am, falling once more.

It's the worst kind of risk I've ever taken. I can't let him in. I have to remember we're not friends. We're not fuck buddies. We're not lovers. We're nothing more than two people who hate each other and happened to sleep together. There's nothing in our future except heartbreak. At least for me. He'll probably ride off into the sunset, none the wiser to the misery he's left behind.

"Tell me what happened," he murmurs, breaking into my thoughts.

A chill runs up my spine, and I roll toward the edge of the bed. He lets me go this time, and I drop to my hands and knees. Thank fuck I didn't fall on my face. I gather some random clothes and tug them on before I face him. I shouldn't have. If I was smart, I would have walked right out the fucking door without glancing at him at all.

Because of course he's sprawled out with his hands behind his head and the sheet riding low on his hips. Of course he has a fucking six-pack and the moon peeking through the slit in the curtain catches every single one of them. Of course I want him even while I want to wallop him.

"Fly away, little bird." He grins, an edge of something in his eyes. It's too dark to decipher what it is.

"I'm not running away. *You're* the one who walked away. *You're* the one who left me long before I met you. So, grin at me all you want, but we both know who's the asshole here." I cross my arms, wishing I could shove the words back in.

"That's a conversation for later," he growls, finally breaking eye contact. I don't blame him. Shit was getting too real. "Start talking."

I don't want to tell him. Especially right now. Maybe it'll distract both of us from the sexual tension still swirling around us. Admitting to him how I fucked up isn't going to be a pleasant experience. I bite my lip, wondering how long I can put him off.

"What exactly am I supposed to be talking about?"

His eyes close and he pulls in a deep breath. "I'm trying here, Emma. But if you keep pushing me..."

"You'll what? Go back to Synd?" I glare at him, though he can't see.

"Can we not fucking do this? You're at the end of the line. It's time to face the music, darling. You can't do this yourself." He levels me with a stare, and I glance away.

"Why do you fucking care so much? It's not like I begged for your help."

He pushes up and rolls off the bed. I swallow hard, keeping my gaze fixed on his face instead of his very naked body. A bolt of desire zings through me, and I bite my tongue to keep myself in check. It doesn't work.

"Maybe because you're putting yourself in danger." He holds up his hand when I open my mouth to snap back. "And don't tell me you had it all sorted. Because I was the one who had to take care of him."

My spine straightens and my eyes widen. Shock floods his face before he scowls and turns away. He paws around the bottom of the bed until he finds his sweatpants and yanks them on. I have no idea what the hell he's talking about. The only person he knows about is Devon, who had no part of my mistakes. Unless you count the entire relationship. Still doesn't have anything to do with the shit I stepped into. When he faces me again, he's fixed his features into some semblance of normalcy. At least for him.

"Listen, Emma. No matter what you've gotten yourself into, you can't handle it alone. So spill," he says, and I let out a choked laugh.

"Oh no, no, no. You're not going to sweep that shit under the rug. Who exactly did you 'take care of'?" And then it hits me. Bastard came home covered in blood. I completely forgot about it once he got sick. "Where the fuck did you go the other night?"

He rolls his eyes, and I have the irrational urge to giggle. It bubbles up my throat and I press my lips together. I doubt he'd appreciate the gesture. I've never seen him roll his eyes and it's throwing me off. Joy seemed to do it a lot. Maybe he picked it up from her.

"It doesn't matter where I went. Or what I did. Stop avoiding the question, Emma."

I grumble under my breath as I try to slip by him. He latches onto my upper arm and swings me around until my back melds to his bare chest. One hand grips my hip and the other goes around my throat. My breath stalls in my lungs, and I press my thighs together. My eyes flutter closed as I completely forget what the hell we were talking about.

He leans close to my ear and whispers, "I thought I'd fucked the brat out of you, but apparently I didn't do a good enough job."

Like hell is he going to manipulate me again. I can't believe I fell for his scheme to get me to talk. I let him fuck me. For fuck's sake, I sat on his goddamn face. And all the while he was just buttering me up so I'd tell him what's going on. Then he'll be able to clean up my mess and take me back to Synd before going on with his life. I'll be left in the dust, just like every other time. Doesn't matter who it is, I'm always the burden. The kid who can't get her shit together. The one who constantly fucks up. The one none of them actually wants around. I may be older, but I'm not any more valuable than I was at thirteen.

"Let me go," I say, my voice devoid of emotion. He must hear the lack of inflection since he releases me. I steadily take two steps forward before slowly turning to face him.

His brows pull low as he scans my face. He won't find what he's looking for. I finally found my emotionless mask. He's always been able to throw me off just enough that I allow my feelings to dictate how I act with him. I'll be thankful later that I've discovered the key to shutting him out.

"There's a low-level gang operation sprouting up in Ridgewood. At first it was just some dealers slanging weed. I assumed it was some frat boys who were a tad more organized than normal. Then they got a bit bigger. So, I decided to fuck with them."

"You decided to fuck with them." It's not a question yet his nostrils flare like he's waiting for an answer.

"I've been doing it for years. Messing with the supplies mostly. When they ramped up their enterprise, I decided to intercept messages and...sabotage their efforts. It worked and kept me busy."

"Kept you busy."

I grit my teeth, struggling to keep my mask in place. "I needed to keep my skills up. Eventually, it looked like they were trying to move to the next level. They set up a gun supplier. Don't ask me why since this town is so fucking small it's not like they'd be able to actually establish any type of control here. Especially in the summer when most of the college clears out. Still, I couldn't sit by and let them."

He rolls his neck before settling his gaze on me again. "Couldn't let them."

"No. Because they were going after *our* suppliers. They started diverting shit from Synd and then Rima. It might have been small-time, but chipping away at our base would only weaken us in the long run. I decided to nip it in the nub."

When he pinches the bridge of his nose, I brace myself. "It's nip it in the bud. Not nub. Where the fuck did you learn this shit?"

"Whatever. You knew what I meant, didn't you?" If he keeps interrupting me to teach me about cliches, I might punch him in the throat again. "Anyways. I got a tip there was a drop happening. So, I went to one of their shops and was going to follow them. Instead, I found Calvin and his posse dappling—"

"Dabbling," he mutters, and I roll my eyes.

"*Dappling* in Oracle."

His head snaps up at that. "Oracle? We got rid of that shit."

I let out a sharp laugh and shake my head. "It's a drug. One the Guild distributed much farther than just Synd and Rima. Of course you didn't get rid of all of it. It's out there, hanging around like a particularly nasty case of pink eye."

He rubs his forehead, clearly getting lost in his thoughts. Maybe it'll distract him from the bombshell I'm going to drop. Weed is one thing, but Oracle is on a whole other level. I don't even know what's in it, but I've seen the effects of it floating around the Barrens. Shane tried to shield me from a lot of it when I was younger. He couldn't hide it completely once it got into the schools. It took a long time to push the last vestiges of it from Synd.

Rima had a harder time since the Guild took up residence there for a time. Sam described the shit as radioactive and I'm inclined to agree. I snort when I remember Alex joking about it turning people into zombies. We have a whole contingency plan if there's an undead apocalypse. None of the others thought it was very funny.

"You think this is funny?" Titus growls.

"Would you like to hear the rest? Or would you rather scold me like a toddler?" I reign in my emotions once more as he waves me on. "Calvin isn't blessed with common sense, but he's got money. I assume that's how he got involved in whoever's operation it truly is. I snuck into the building to get a closer look and—"

"For fuck's sake," he breathes. "Let me guess, you got into an altercation and came away with a brand-new scar to mar your beautiful skin."

He says it with a sneer, but all I can focus on is the beautiful part. Besides, I don't think scars are blights. They're badges of honor, if anything. He's got plenty, so he can go fuck himself.

"No. The scar on my back was from an accident. I did, however, get spotted. They took some pockshots at me—"

"Potshots. Not pockshots."

"None of them hit, but I wasn't wearing a mask. I assumed that's why Calvin was waiting for me. And why I was worried about him seeing me at the Tower. Turns out he wasn't after me. He was after *you*. Care to explain your role in all this?"

His mouth drops open, and a surge of satisfaction hits me. For once I've rendered him speechless. Another point to me. I've lost count of how many I have now, but I'm going to assume I'm winning. It's the only thing I have going for me at the moment, because he looks like he's going to wring my neck. And I hate to admit it, but I probably deserve it.

Chapter 30

Titus

I should wipe the gloating smirk off Emma's face. She clearly thinks I'm more involved than I am. Every tie I have to Calvin leads directly back to her. I'm sure she thinks she's caught me and I'd love to laugh in her face. I don't have it in me.

"My involvement is nothing more than a product of *your* involvement. Calvin didn't like that I took his booth at the Tower. I assume he had no idea you and I were connected at all. The bullshit you pulled is much worse than anything I did." I cross my arms, wondering how the hell I'm going to find Calvin's boss.

"Well, then you can just stay here and rest up while I go have a chat with him." She spins around and pulls a sweatshirt from her closet.

"Hard to talk to dead men," I mutter, running a hand through my hair.

She freezes halfway through zipping up her sweatshirt. "Excuse me?"

I plop onto the bed again and lean back on my hands. "Calvin is dead."

She clears her throat and stares at me. "How do you know that?"

She obviously knows I killed him. Apparently, she needs the confirmation. She probably thinks I got sick because I fought him or something. Little does she know he was fucking drunk. And I don't plan to reveal that tidbit.

"I may have dripped some of his blood on your precious floors."

Her eyes take on a faraway look as she gazes over my shoulder. Fatigue drags me down, but I doubt she'll drop this long enough for me to take a nap. I shouldn't have pushed myself. Couldn't turn down what she was offering. I would have regretted it more in the long run. I doubt she's out of my system. I've been half-mast the entire time we've been talking.

"Why?"

Her question throws me off, and I scramble for an explanation. I can't very well tell her it's because he hurt her—because he kidnapped her. Or rather, thought he was kidnapping her. Just the thought of admitting what I said to Calvin before I slit his throat sends a shiver of anxiety through me. She'll never let me live it down.

"He was a threat."

"To me. You took care of him because he was a threat *to me*."

I grit my teeth and prop my elbows on my knees. "That's my job, Emma. I'm supposed to protect you."

"Uh, no. You're supposed to escort me back to Synd. Protecting me while we're traveling, okay. Why are you still here? Why stick around and deal with any of this? You could have knocked my ass out and borrowed a car from that chop shop you think you're hiding."

"Giving me ideas isn't really going to help your case here." A disgruntled noise leaves her, and I fight a smirk. "Besides, Ren told me to figure out what the hell you're up against."

"Ren? Shit. What does he know? And what the fuck is happening in Synd? Ink said the whole place is in lockdown. No one in or out."

As thankful as I am she's finally talking to me, I don't think I'll last much longer. My head feels heavy, my eye is twitching, and my stomach rebels every time I move. It's the middle of the night and we both should be sleeping. I'll deal with all the feelings bleeding into my soul tomorrow.

I tip to the side and throw my legs onto the bed. I can't keep my eyes open, not with my head on a pillow and her scent floating around me. Groaning, I flip to my stomach, hoping the move doesn't upset it more. If she insists on talking, she'll be having a one-sided conversation. She seems to be used to that, though.

"You can't get out of this by pretending to sleep, Titus. I swear to fuck if you're faking—"

"You'll what? Stab me? Go ahead. It'll give me something to focus on other than the pounding in my head," I mutter.

"So fucking dramatic."

She slides in next to me, and I throw an arm over her waist. I may be pissed at her, but I forgot how nice it is to have someone beside me. I'm used to being alone. Emma wouldn't be my first choice. Actually, I don't have any other prospects. Which I will never tell her. I told myself I'd take tonight. Tomorrow night she's sleeping on the couch. And when I get her back to Synd, I'll wash my hands of her.

The next several hours I don't exactly sleep. Emma's light snores fill the air as I drift in the grey space between waking and dreaming. At one point, Emma woke up and forced me to take some meds. It barely made a dent in the pain building in my head. I thought about getting up and showering, but it was more work than it was worth.

As the sun peeks through the slit in the curtains, I bury my face in the pillow. I tug Emma closer to my side, soaking up the last bit of warmth from her body. My attention wanders, my mind conjuring up images of what it would be like if we didn't hate each other. If she wasn't five years younger than me. If she wasn't a fucking brat who keeps putting herself in danger.

Yet I can't stop the fantasies from invading my psyche. Every night she'd be next to me—under me. Every morning I'd bitch about the coffee she made since it'd be bitter like she always makes it. Every afternoon she'd complain about my dirty clothes on the floor. The domesticity would drown me slowly, like quicksand. I'd be dead before I realized I was in danger. That type of life isn't for me. So why in the hell is my brain summoning up a life I've never experienced? I don't know, but I sure as hell don't like it.

"Would you shut the fuck up?" Emma mutters, her voice thick with sleep.

I don't think I was talking out loud, but I may have been mumbling. I roll onto my back, releasing her from the temporary prison I've caged her in. She grumbles some more before sighing. If she cuddles up to me again, I'll never leave this bed. Plus, I can smell myself. Between the sickness and fucking her, I need a damn shower. She scoots closer, and I swing my legs over the side before making my way to the bathroom. She mumbles something as I leave, but I don't bother trying to decipher her words.

This time, I wait until the water is hot before stepping under the spray. My aching muscles relax bit by bit. I thought I'd be worse off after food poisoning, but I'm just run down still. Most of my other symptoms have eased into the back of my mind, only evident when I focus on them. I run my hands through my wet hair. It'll take more than ten minutes to fully get my shit together.

I wish I could stay under the hot water for longer. It'll turn cold soon, though. I need the extra time to work through the shit Emma told me. I'm not surprised she kept everything to herself. The Kings don't exactly confide in me, at least until recently. Doesn't mean I didn't hear shit. Once I was removed as Emma's bodyguard, she made a point of making her new shadow's life a living hell. He wasn't very observant. Emma would slip away and get into all sorts of trouble. Even after I was moved, I cleaned up her messes.

Flipping off the water, I slump against the wall. Calvin isn't a problem anymore, but whoever he works for might be. I'm surprised Emma wasn't able to find out more. Ridgewood isn't exactly large, and if she's been trailing them for a while, she should have the information. The fact she doesn't just shows how inexperienced she is.

I dry off and dress quickly, then sneak out of the bathroom. The middle of the day isn't the best time for a recon mission. I need to check on the aftermath of Calvin's death, anyway. Dylan didn't know anything about his friends, but someone out there does. It's merely finding the right person to press for intel.

I snatch up my phone from the kitchen counter and send a text to Joy. Hopefully she'll have something for me. I'm sure she'll drill me about what happened with Emma. Too bad I won't be spreading the gossip she so desperately wants. The three dots blink across the screen as she crafts a response. They disappear, then reappear, and I roll my eyes. Absently, I pick up the bottle of water Emma must have left out. I'd rather have it cold, but beggars can't be choosers.

As I lift it to my mouth, Emma comes screeching through the apartment and knocks it from my hand. Water splashes across the counter, the bottle tumbling into the sink. She stares at the mess, panting, then races to the fridge and rips open the door. The rest of the water ends up in the sink. She lifts the half-eaten pistachio muffin, a horrified expression on her face.

"Did you eat this?" she wails, and I rear back.

I close my eyes and heave out a sigh. "Listen, I get you don't like pistachio muffins—"

"You don't either! No one likes pistachio muffins. It's a wonder they're still making them. But that's besides the point. Did you eat this?"

I wave a hand at her before grabbing a towel to mop up the water. "I probably did it in the middle of the night. I don't remember. Why exactly does it matter? And why the fuck did you throw perfectly good water away?"

"Because, you absolute asshole, we don't know what made you sick. Unless you decided to share a late-night snack with Calvin," she snarls.

I open one of the cupboards, then another before I find a roll of paper towels. "He didn't offer me any. Where are their hideouts?"

"Oh, you're not going to get out of this discussion."

"For fuck's sake, Emma. It's a pistachio muffin. I doubt it made me sick. Or the water."

She throws up her hands and spins to toss the muffin in the trash. "You can't be sure. Pistachios can have salmonella. And while you might not care about getting sick again, I'm not going to take care of you next time."

"Why the fuck do you have it, anyways since you hate pistachios?" I mutter, and her head whips around. I pretend not to notice her glare. Revealing how much I know about her isn't the smartest idea. She'll read more into it than need be.

She stomps away from me and into the bathroom without answering. Which is an answer in and of itself. Devon must have dropped them off with the water. I don't know how he dated her for so long without learning a goddamn thing about her. First the roses, now the muffin. What else has he given to her that she hates? Why the hell didn't she say anything?

I follow her down the short hallway and lean against the wall across from the bathroom. When she opens the door, her feet stutter back and she grips the frame.

"How long did you two date?" I ask, crossing my arms.

"Who?"

I tilt my head and study her face. Usually, I'd assume she was being deliberately obtuse and avoiding the question. From the confusion on her face, she truly doesn't know who I'm talking about. Which only has more questions bubbling to the surface.

"Twitch. You dated for like three years, right?" I raise an eyebrow and she nods. "So how is it he doesn't know a damn thing about you?"

"I, uh...what? He knows me. Why do you care anyway?"

"When did you break up?"

She rolls her eyes and sighs. "Like a month ago. Again, why do you care?"

"Did you cry?" I don't know why I'm pushing this. It doesn't really matter either way. I lie to myself, convincing myself it'll be an insight into Twitch's motives.

"Seriously, Titus. We're not having this conversation." She tries to push past me, and I step in front of her. "What the fuck."

Apparently, I'm not entirely beyond the sickness since a wave of heat washes over me. "Were you in love with him?"

Her mouth falls open, but nothing comes out. Indecision hangs in her eyes, and I have my answer.

"So you broke up with him because you didn't love him. And you didn't cry over it. Which tells me you feel guilty and that's why you haven't told him to fuck off. He doesn't know anything about you or what you like."

Her shoulders slump, and she ends up against the wall. If Devon doesn't know anything about her, it stands to reason she doesn't know anything about him, either. He always set me on edge. It's not a leap to suspect he was working with Calvin. Emma will deny it, which only makes shit harder for me. I don't have time to convince her of the possibility.

"Not that it's any of your business, but I did break up with him. It had nothing to do with how I felt and everything to do with him not fitting into *my world*. We both know this life isn't safe. I hope I don't have to explain what I mean," she snaps, and I shake my head. "Contrary to what you've seen, he's a good guy. He was...attentive. So what if he didn't do everything perfect? He tried. Which is more than a lot of men do."

"Bare minimum." I crowd into her space when she tries to slip away.

"It's not bare minimum to drop off breakfast or flowers. Or have someone send you soup when you're sick."

I lean close, whispering in her ear, "Except you did more for me when I was sick than he ever did for you. And we're not supposedly in love."

I should drop this—walk away and pretend this conversation never happened. Yet I can't seem to pull myself away from her. She's sucked me into her world and into her drama. I'm committed, and I don't even know if I care anymore.

Chapter 31

Emma

I don't know how we got so wildly off track. My love life is none of his fucking business. Sleeping together doesn't give him the right to psychoanalyze my life. He hasn't given two shits up until now. Why now? The only thing that's changed is the fact he's been all up in my lady bits. Which doesn't change anything. Fucking him was a mistake. I knew that as soon as it was over. I just didn't think he'd get so fucking...involved. If I hadn't slept with him, I wouldn't be in this position.

I jerk back, my head knocking into the wall. My mind is stuck in a loop and I need to stop. Nothing good can come from this line of thinking. My obsessive, useless line of thinking. I focus on Titus's face, attempting to read his emotions. My lips curl into a grin and he narrows his gaze.

"You're jealous." The words slip out before I can rework them in my mind.

His mouth pulls into a frown. "No, I'm not."

I snort, glancing away. "And I'm a fucking unicorn."

"What do I possibly have to be jealous of? Your extravagant apartment? Your deep, personal friendships? Or perhaps your extremely healthy relationship?"

"Perhaps you're just bitter since I've lived a whole fucking life while you've been stuck in Synd."

It's not true. Nothing could be further from the truth, actually. Being in Synd is all he's ever wanted. At least, that's what he told me. He never wanted to leave. He just wanted a place to belong. All I ever wanted was to get away. I needed to find myself somewhere else. And I thought I had. I didn't expect to miss Synd so fucking much. As hard as it will be to go back, I need to go home. I just don't know how to live there as the person I am here.

And none of that is Titus's fault. I wish it was. I wish I could hate him with the passion I had for so many years. It's fled in the wake of him showing up here. He still pisses me off, but I don't have the urge to stab him as much as I once did.

"I'd be a lot further along if it wasn't for you," he snarls, then stomps away.

I'm so flabbergasted I don't run after him. The bedroom door slams and the wall behind me rattles. They're too thin to be able to truly get away from another person. It's part of the reason I rented this place. If someone was able to get past my security system, I'd be able to hear the squeaking from the floorboards and their footsteps through the walls.

Right now, I'm regretting the choice. I can hear him lumbering back and forth while a string of muffled curses ring out. After a minute, there's thudding and I grit my teeth. I don't know what the hell he's throwing around, but I'm not going to sit here and listen to him destroy my space. Then again, I'm not going to interrupt him.

I tiptoe into the kitchen and grab my phone. There are a dozen messages from Daisy, plus more from Devon. I don't even bother reading his, skipping right to Daisy's. Mostly, she's progressively spiraling into hysteria. She's not used to me dropping off the face of the planet. I glance behind me, making sure Titus hasn't snuck up on me. All the loose floorboards in the world don't apply to him, apparently.

Slipping on my flip-flops, I key in the alarm code and slip out the front door. I probably should let him know I'm leaving. I remind myself that I don't owe him anything. My shoulder aches as I grab the railing and hurry down the stairs. Once I stumble outside, I rush around the corner between two buildings. My bike is only a few blocks away, but the wind bites into me. I should have grabbed my jacket. I wasn't about to go into my room and find it while Titus was bumbling around.

I pull up Daisy's number and she picks up on the first ring. "Where the hell have you been, young lady? I've been worried sick."

"Sorry. Shit has hitteth the faneth, so to speak," I grumble as I glance behind me.

"Is anyone dead?"

"Don't ask questions you don't want the answers to. Can I come over?" I slide through the small opening in a fence and uncover my bike. It'll be fucking freezing. Maybe Daisy will let me shower at her place.

"Of course you can. Are you going to have a shadow? Because I don't have a ton of food right now. We could always order." The line clicks as she switches over to loudspeaker. "What are you craving?"

"The usual. I need tacos in my life. I haven't eaten in like three days." My stomach grumbles and I realize I've only eaten granola bars since Titus got sick. And I don't even like them.

"Well, get out here and I'll have tacos. And a quesadilla. The one from that one place that makes them with a lot of cheese."

She hangs up without saying goodbye, and I climb on my bike. It takes me ten minutes to get there, and I was right. I'm totally fucked. Chills roll through my body and my fingers feel like icicles. Thankfully, Daisy's apartment is on the second floor. If I had to climb up ten flights of stairs, I doubt I'd make it. She'd have to roll me into a comforter and drag me up.

I kick her door and there's a jingle of a chain before it swings open, revealing Daisy's smiling face. Her mouth drops into a frown as she takes in my frozen form.

"Alright, in the shower. Now. Did you walk here?" She tugs me inside her warm apartment.

"Rode my bike," I say through gritted teeth.

"Who the hell rides a bicycle in this weather?"

I let out a sharp laugh as she leads me to the bathroom. "Motorcycle. I don't know how to ride a bike."

She pulls up short and swings around to face me. "What do you mean you don't know how to ride a bike? I thought everyone did."

"Kind of a popsicle here." My teeth chatter and I rub my hands up and down my arms. "Could we maybe talk about my lackluster childhood after I shower?"

She huffs but leads me onward. Her bathroom is ten times better than mine in every way. I quickly shower, then stand under the hot spray for another ten minutes. Once I get bored, I step out and dry myself off, spotting the sweatpants Daisy tossed in here for me. I don't deserve her or her friendship. I'd like to think I'm a good friend, but I always feel like I'm falling short. She goes out of her way to be there for me, above and beyond what I ever could.

"Stop sulking and get out here. I want to eat and hear the tea," she shouts from outside the door, and I smile.

Settling on the couch, my mouth waters as she hands me a paper plate. She plops next to me and we spend the next ten minutes inhaling the food. Thank fuck she got the big box. I'm tucking into one of the quesadillas when she abandons her plate and levels me with a look.

"Spill. I want to know everything that's happened. Starting with why you fucking disappeared. I was so worried I called Titus."

My head snaps up, the food turning to a lead ball in my stomach. "You called Titus? Why?"

"Uh, duh. Because you were fucking ghosting everyone. No one had heard from you and I bailed on you. I felt so fucking guilty. I know you always say to take advantage of an opportunity, but then you vanished, and I felt like it wouldn't have happened if I had been there." She refuses to meet my gaze and I flick her knee, forcing her eyes to mine.

"Yes, you bailed, but you're not to blame. And if you would have been there, we both would have missed the opportunities presented to us."

I don't know how much to tell her. If she was Sam or hell, any of the women in Synd, I wouldn't hesitate. She wasn't raised in the shadows like I was. This is Daisy, though. I feel like I'm corrupting her—pulling her inch by inch into my shadowed world. It may be selfish, but I need a friend.

"Titus wouldn't tell me shit. Just said you were fine. So, give me the rundown. Please," she whines.

Daisy might be separate from my mafia life, yet she's a helluva good listener. She gasps, glares, and giggles at all the right moments. I swear she's more invested in my life than I am. She even kicked her feet when I confessed Titus and I slept together.

"Was he good?" she whispers, and I shake my head.

"I'm not going to kiss and tell. I'm sure you can read between the rinds." I wave my hand lazily before grabbing my drink.

She shakes her head, a rueful smile on her face. "Read between the lines. *Lines*, dear."

"Shit. That makes a lot more sense."

She chuckles as she tucks her legs underneath her. "How the hell did you get through life saying all this shit wrong?"

I shrug as I survey the destruction of our dinner to avoid her eyes. "I wasn't really into watching shows. Movies, yeah, but that was with my brothers, and Alex always talks through the whole damn thing. I read mostly fantasy novels. Not a lot of cliches in them, now that I think about it."

"Okay, but you had to have heard it in school. You know, with your friends and shit?"

My cheeks heat and I bite my lip. "I was more of a loner. Titus always pointed shit out when I got it wrong. By the time I was almost sixteen, though, he wasn't around anymore. Guess I just didn't pay enough attention."

"Wait. Back up." She holds up a hand. "How the hell does 'between the rinds' even make sense?"

"Uh, like, you have to peel the rind back in order to get to the fruit? I didn't really think too hard on it."

"Okay, back to the important bits. What happened after you bagged the baddy?"

I choke on my drink, dissolving into a coughing fit. Thank fuck she didn't call him daddy. He's more of a sir than a daddy, anyway. The thought sends me hacking again. From the giddy look on Daisy's face, I won't be telling her that either. I need to get my shit together. Talking about Titus only makes the ache in my chest and the flutters in my stomach worse.

"I told you. He kind of passed out—"

"Because you're such a good—"

"Don't finish that sentence," I say, barely keeping my laughter in check. "He got pissy, asked me a bunch of questions about Devon, of all people, then stomped away. So, I left." I slump against the couch, wondering if I should have told him.

"Well, that explains a lot," she mutters as she stares at her phone.

I lean closer, trying to peek at her screen. "What the hell does that mean?"

She tucks her phone between her legs and shakes her head. "He just asked if I knew where you were. Don't worry about it. Tell me what you plan to do now that Calvin is...gone."

I narrow my eyes, trying to figure out if she ratted me out without knowing she was. He probably doesn't know where Daisy lives. I pull out my phone and check it for notifications, but there's nothing. I turned off the group chat, not wanting to implicate any of them. No one from Synd has reached out and my palms tingle, making a note to ask Titus about it.

Daisy snaps her fingers and I glance up. "You okay?"

"Sorry. Yeah. I'm going to go around to the different warehouses they have and see if I can gather some information. I can't go back to Synd until I make sure nothing bad will happen here." I slide to the side, a puddle on the couch.

"I thought you were only staying to make sure no one would follow you? That's why I needed to turn tail and run home, right?"

I sigh, wishing I could pretend to go to sleep. "Originally, that was the reason. Now, I'd rather not leave the town I've been living in for the last four fucking years to the dogs. They'll poison Ridgewood, slowly and thoroughly until it's nothing but ashes. And then they'll move on. It may have started as a small-time drug thing, but it's grown into...something sinister. And I can't live with that."

"You know, if you let him—"

"Absolutely not. I'm not asking him for help. He probably won't give me a choice either way. I refuse to allow him to clean up my messes. And don't tell me it's not my mess, because I may not have been the one to light the match, but I sure as hell fanned the flames. And that's on me."

She opens her mouth, yet her response is cut off by Titus busting through the front door. The chain lock scatters, pinging across the tiles, and Daisy screams, throwing a taco in the air. Lettuce rains down on her head before she flips over the arm of the couch. I haven't moved. In fact, I barely flinched.

I roll my head toward him and take in his seething face. "You could have just knocked."

Chapter 32

Titus

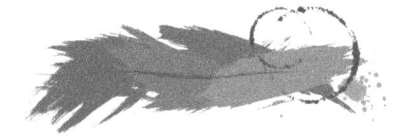

"Whatcha got there?" Emma asks, nodding to the bag in my hand.

I scowl, tossing it at her head. She smacks it away, her gaze never leaving mine. She didn't even flinch when I busted through the door. I'll have to at least replace the lock for Daisy. I glance at Emma's friend, who's still wallowing between the couch and the wall, lettuce and salsa scattered on her hair.

"I'm sorry about your door, Daisy," I say through gritted teeth, and her eyes widen.

"Don't worry about it. I'm just glad I didn't set the deadbolt," she mutters.

"Me too." I run my hand through my hair. "Get dressed, Emma. Now."

She purses her lips, then straightens before reaching for another taco. "No thanks."

"That wasn't a question. Go now or we're going to have problems."

She narrows her eyes at me, and I glare right back. She knows exactly what I'll do if she doesn't comply. I'd leave her here with Daisy if I thought she was safe. The fact I was able to break down the door with one solid kick proved that she's not. I'm furious she slipped out without a goddamn word, but we have other shit to deal with. I grit my teeth as she contemplates my threat.

"Fine." She pushes up and grabs the bag before skirting around the coffee table. "But this doesn't mean you can order me around."

"You weren't saying that earlier when I ordered you to sit on my face," I murmur as she passes.

Her footsteps falter, tripping over the oval rug. My hand flies out and I grab her waist, keeping her upright. Daisy smothers a giggle behind her hand. Emma snarls, shoving my arm away from her, then stomps into what I assume is Daisy's bedroom. She slams the door behind her, and I roll my eyes.

"So, what's on the agenda for tonight?" Daisy asks as she stands, brushing various pieces of taco off her.

"Do you really want to know, or are you just making small talk?" I ask, immediately regretting snapping at her. It's not her fault Emma came running to her. It's not her fault she doesn't understand how fucking dangerous it is for Emma to be out without someone to protect her.

"Not one for small talk. Got it." She slips around me and grabs a broom to clean up the mess. "You know she's capable of taking care of herself, right? She's been doing it for four years."

I should help her. I cross my arms instead. "She tell you the absolute shitshow she got herself into?"

"I'm sure I didn't get the full story. Then again, you probably didn't either. She likes to sugarcoat most things."

I nod, though I don't know what she's talking about. Emma King isn't knowing for holding back. At least not with me. She keeps shit from me, but she doesn't try to make it all sunshine and roses. She stopped confiding in me years ago. Even with her confessions this afternoon, I'm no closer to knowing what truly went on with her. I don't know whether to be grateful for the lack of details or pissed she doesn't trust me enough.

The more time we spend together, the less resolute I am in my convictions. When she came to me all those years ago, we both knew she was too young. I didn't have to eviscerate her. Yet I couldn't let her harbor some schoolgirl crush for me. If I let her down gently, she would've ended up secretly pining for something we'd never have. Then she turned around and made my life a living hell—sabotaged me at every turn. It's hard to blame her when I truly think about it.

"She doesn't do that with you, does she?" Daisy whispers, and I glance toward the bedroom.

"No. She doesn't. Then again, she's not very forthcoming with information." She lets out a humorless laugh. "I've known Emma for four years, yet sometimes I feel like I'm still trying to worm my way into her life. I know she cares for me. I know we're friends, but she's always held herself...separate. You, though...you really know her, don't you?"

"Maybe," I hedge, then swallow down the lie. "She was the closest I ever had to a friend. I know her like the back of my hand. Probably the only thing I've ever felt completely sure about."

Daisy's eyes soften, and I scowl. I'm sure she has some fanciful idea flitting around her brain, convinced Emma and I will fall in love. She probably thinks I've already fallen for the woman who's taking for-fucking-ever to get dressed. I haven't and that's not about to change. I may see Emma in a different light now, but it doesn't absolve her from the shit she's put me through. Falling in love with her would be the cruelest thing fate could ever inflict upon me.

"You know she's lonely, right?"

"Not my problem. Don't take what I said to heart, Daisy. Emma is a fucking menace who makes my life harder."

"Gee, that was almost devoid of any vitriol, Titus. You losing your touch?" Emma says, and I close my eyes.

When I finally open them again, Emma's in front of Daisy, whispering too low for me to hear. I suck in a sharp breath, the ache pounding in my chest again. Or maybe I'm having a heart attack. Explaining the medical emergency I might be having to a paramedic would be ridiculous. Especially because I'd have to tell them it was brought on by seeing her in my sweatshirt. The tight black leggings aren't helping either.

"You need a taco for the road?" Daisy asks, and it breaks whatever spell Emma cast over me.

"She doesn't." I stalk forward to grab her.

I miss her wrist, and our fingers tangle together. I'm already committed, though, and I tug her toward the door.

"I was actually asking if *you* wanted a taco, but sure. Text me when you get home, Emma." Daisy's voice fades into a fit of giggles as I pull Emma out the door.

"You know you're going to have to pay her for the door, right?" Emma asks, our hands still linked.

"Joy will take care of it." She'll bitch about it, but she'll deal.

We step outside and I breathe a sigh of relief. The wind has died down since we were in the building. Riding on a bike when it smells like snow isn't fun. Even Emma tucked behind me won't make that much of a difference. We'd both end up shivering by the time we got to our destination. We reach my bike hidden behind Daisy's apartment, and I finally drop her hand.

"Don't run off," I snap as I grab the helmet from my seat.

"Wasn't going to. You going to tell me where we're going?" She crosses her arms, hip jutted out, and taps her toe on the concrete.

"Got a tip." I shove the helmet over her head, then grab the front and yank her toward me. "Do not make me regret bringing you along."

She rolls her eyes, her blonde hair sticking to her lashes. "Not like I requested an invitation."

"Just don't get us killed," I snarl, releasing my grip on her helmet and climb onto my bike.

She settles behind me, her arms wrapping around my waist. "There a reason I'm wearing a helmet?"

"Use your brain, Emma." I reach back and slam the visor down, cutting off her response.

The rumble of my engine drowns out her response. I wind my way through the quiet streets, Emma's helmet knocking into me at every stop. She's probably doing it on purpose just to piss me off. I'm not entirely sure where we're going, but I know the general area. Asking Emma requires I talk to her, and I'm not ready to do that. I'm barely holding my rage at bay as it is. The second she opens her mouth, my anger will flare again, threatening to send me spiraling.

The streetlights thin, casting longer shadows as we reach the outskirts of town. Joy wasn't much help when I asked her where the warehouses were. Her only advice was to ask Emma. The men at the chop shop refuse to talk to me, afraid I'll shoot them or something. Apparently, I have a reputation thanks to Alex. Emma taps on my arm, and I pull over before cutting the engine. I don't bother turning around as she slides up the visor.

"Are you out of your mind? We can't just go rocking up to their base without weapons," she snaps.

"Give me some credit, darling." I grit my teeth, then turn my head. "How close are we?"

A frustrated noise erupts from her, and she slides off the seat. Ripping the helmet off, she stomps onto the shoulder, mumbling to herself. I lean back, waiting until she's done with her little temper tantrum.

"You about done? I don't want to be out all night," I call when she doesn't seem to be losing steam.

"Oh. Oh *you* don't want to be out alllll night? Well, then by all means we'd better hurry the hell up and bust into a place you know nothing about without any goddamn guns." She pants, hands flexing by her sides, the helmet forgotten at her feet.

I raise an eyebrow, running my gaze down her body. Her tension is palpable, exuding off her in waves of fury. I'd probably be worried about her rollercoaster of emotions if I cared. Which I don't. I glance away, hoping she doesn't read the lie of thoughts she'll never hear. Shaking my head, I focus on the problem in front of me.

"Get on the fucking bike, Emma, or I'll leave your ass here."

Her eyes narrow. "You wouldn't."

"Fucking try me."

She throws up her hands, then snatches the helmet. When she shoves it on her head, I start the bike. Her body slides behind me and I take off. I grin as she shrieks, fingers clawing at my shirt. It's not until she punches me in the kidney I realize I've been driving in circles. The last thing I need is to have Emma taking over all my thoughts.

I pull between two abandoned buildings and cut the engine. "Get off. We're walking from here."

Her hands skim across my stomach and I grit my teeth. When one slips lower, I grip the handles tighter. She snickers under her breath before finally obeying me. She's playing with fire. And she's doing it just to fuck with me. Doesn't mean my cock understands. Once I've calmed down, I climb off the bike and pull the weapons I grabbed from Emma's closet. She had an impressive collection hidden behind a false wall in her apartment. She's definitely not getting her deposit back. I wonder who helped her install it.

"Thank fuck you're not a complete waste of space," Emma mutters as I hand her a gun and a familiar-looking dagger. "You going to tell me what the plan is, or are we flying by the seat of our pants?"

"This is fact gathering. Nothing more. I don't care what the hell they're doing, we're not getting involved. We'll deal with it later."

I link our hands again to keep her close. At this point, I don't know why I keep doing it, so I'll hide under the guise of making sure she doesn't slip away. We creep through the shadows silently, taking back alleys as much as possible. She tugs me to the side when headlights illuminate the road. I spin her around and press my chest to hers. Ducking my head, I breathe in her scent while we wait for the car to pass.

"I think they're gone," she whispers.

"Don't get in my way," I mutter, and she snorts, the sound echoing in the small space between us. "Stay behind me, Emma."

"Planning on taking a bullet for me, Titus? Interesting."

"You get shot and I get blamed," I say gruffly, shoving away from her and lace our fingers together again.

She huffs, tugging my hand every time we come to a corner, directing me on where to go. I don't like relying on her. Actually, I don't like not knowing where the hell I am. I didn't realize there were so many abandoned places here. This whole thing could go south just because I didn't recon the area first.

Emma freezes, hiding in the darkness. Across the street I spot a run-down one-story building. It doesn't look any more occupied than any other, and I wonder if we have the right place. I'm about to question Emma's judgement when a shadow slips from the front door and proceeds to teeter down the sidewalk. He's clearly on something, and I hope to fuck it's not Oracle. It was hard enough dealing with that shit in Synd.

"Are we following him or waiting?" Emma asks as she pulls her hand from mine and checks her gun.

My palms itch, the urge to touch my own weapons riding me hard. I give in and make sure they're loaded and still on my hips. My head snaps up when another person exits the building. He looks familiar, and I'm pretty sure he's one of Calvin's minions. He takes off the opposite way as the previous guy, and I track him until he's gone.

"I'm going around the back. See if there's any windows. You go up top and keep an eye on shit for me," I whisper.

I step from the alley just as the streetlight sputters out, and I thank whatever gods are on our side tonight. As I skirt around the side of the abandoned barber shop, I glance back. Emma's gone and I hope, for once, she fucking listens to me. But I'm not holding my breath.

Chapter 33

Emma

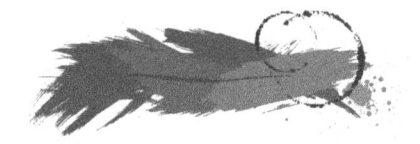

I lean against the brick building and count to sixty. If Titus thinks I'm going to be a glorified lookout, he probably should have thought about who he was talking to. This is my town—my mess—and I plan on cleaning it up myself. I won't be able to stop him from tagging along, but that doesn't mean I have to take orders from him.

I wipe my hands down the warm leggings Titus made me change into, attempting to dry my palms. I slip my gun from my waistband and take off for the opposite corner. Titus is probably at the back by now and won't see me until it's too late to send me back.

My mind scrambles as I try to focus on the task in front of me instead of the memory of his hand in mine. The more time we spend together, the more the lines between us blur. One of these days, the thread tying us together will unravel and it scares the shit out of me. I knew where I stood before. I stayed firmly on my side of life and he kept to his. Our worlds didn't collide unless I allowed it. The loss of control has messed with my head and thrown me off course. I may not have known where I'd end up, but my future certainly didn't include him in any version I envisioned.

I glance around the darkness, realizing I completely froze while I spiraled. Fucking Titus. He's wormed his way into my mind, poisoning it with his sorcery. I refuse to call it charm since he's never turned his charisma on me. In fact, it's been absent the entire time he's been in Ridgewood. Unless he's saving it all for when he sees Joy. He's not able to turn off the magnetism exuding from him. He's able to dial up the charisma and women fall at his feet. Men too, actually. I fucking hate it.

Sneaking around the corner of the building, I even out my breathing. I spot Titus's large frame pressed up against the back door as he peers through the window at the top. I tiptoe closer, then crouch under a shattered window with boards covering the opening. Thirty seconds pass and I grab my dagger to pick at my nails. They're getting too long and if I need to climb something, I don't want to deal with the pain. Not that I'll use my knife to pare them down, but the tip is good for getting dirt out from under them.

"What the fuck?" Titus whispers harshly, and I peer up at him. "I told you to watch the front."

"No, you told me to keep an eye on shit. You're the biggest piece of shit I've seen, so here I am. Keeping an eye on you." I smile sweetly, then continue on my nails.

"I said, 'go up top.' This is clearly *not* up top," he grits out.

"You're not very good at being on a stakeout, are you?"

"What the hell is that supposed to mean?" he snarls, his voice carrying through the night.

I tap the tip of the knife against my lips, wondering if I should allow him to keep making an ass of himself. When the vein in his forehead pops out, I decide I'd rather not get shot because he couldn't keep his shit together.

"You're a bit too loud for the typical intel gathering mission. Plus, the other person on your team should probably know the plan. Oh, and you should *have* a plan. Which by the Peeping Tom routine you're pulling, I'm guessing you don't." I smirk as his hands flex by his sides.

When he scowls, I know I've won. I tick another point for me and slide my dagger back into the sheath I attached to my thigh. It's awkward since it's the wrong one, but at least he grabbed me one. I'm trained enough not to poke myself in the leg. Easier to avoid when there's a place to put a blade.

"Fine. If you're so fucking smart, then why don't you figure out what they're doing?"

Titus leans against the wall and crosses his arms as I heave to my feet. I strain to peek into the window and huff when his soft snickers float around me.

"Need a boost?"

"Fuck you," I snap.

I drag a plastic carton riddled with holes in front of the door and gently step on it. It bows under my weight and my hand ends up on Titus's shoulder. I expect him to shrug me off, but he doesn't. I hold my breath, narrowing my eyes as I gaze into the darkness within. There's not even a sliver of light. I don't want to strain my eyes. That'll give me a headache, and I doubt Titus will take care of me. He may have patched me up after the whole kidnapping debacle, but I'd be silly to suspect that type of treatment a second time.

"Come to the same conclusion I did?" he asks, piercing the silence once more.

"That you're—"

"Don't finish that sentence," he growls, the sound reverberating through me.

As much as I try to ignore him, I can't. My body won't let me. I swear I didn't even need the fleece leggings he got me, just a minute next to him and my bottom half warms right up. Hell, a mere chuckle from him and my pussy is turning against me. She'll fucking riot soon now that she's been awoken.

He pushes from the wall and steps next to me. I stare down at him as he gazes into the window. My mouth parts as I scan his body.

"What the fuck are you staring at?" His eyes dart to me, then away.

"I'm taller than you. I don't know if I've ever seen the top of your head from this angle. Do you really not have to look up people's noses constantly? You can see the top of it? Your nose doesn't look nearly as big as I thought it did." My entire view has changed—literally and figuratively. I never thought about it before and now it's messing with my head.

"This isn't exactly the time for an existential crisis about how fucking short you are, Emma. Get your shit together." He points at the building. "There's no one inside. Those last two guys were it, so we missed them."

He turns away and stalks to one side of the building to peer around the corner. When he goes to the other side, I realize he's clearing the way. Titus will insist we go back to the apartment where we'll bicker again. We'll end up in bed together and I won't be able to stop myself. He's too warm and the lines of his body fit against mine. Against all odds, I'll end up draped over him and I don't know where it will go from there. We said one night, but if we keep skipping along this path without a plan to divert, we'll end up in another compromising position.

"We should check it out. They probably left some damning evidence laying out on a side table or something," I say, not bothering to whisper.

"Abso-fucking-lutely not."

He stalks back to me, hands reaching out to snatch me from my perch. I hop backward, the carton tipping, and my arms pinwheel as I tumble toward the ground. Titus lets out a low curse as he lunges for me. He won't reach me in time, and I'll crack my skull open. We can't afford to waste time. We've already lost so much.

Miraculously, his arms wrap around me, one hand cradling my head and the other gripping my waist. My breath leaves me as I land on his chest, and he buries his face in my neck. Somehow he grabbed me and twisted, all before hitting the ground.

"How the hell did you do that?" My cry is muffled by his sweatshirt, and he refuses to loosen his hold. In fact, I think he's trembling. Then again, that might be me.

"Stop moving," he says through gritted teeth.

My brain says freeze, but my body doesn't listen. I wiggle against him and he groans. His arms tighten around me before letting go. I scramble off him and dust myself off. He groans again, curling on his side.

"Are you hurt?" I probably shouldn't be so flippant, but he brought it upon himself. He didn't *have* to save me.

"I'm fine," he gasps.

"Probably knocked the wind out of yourself. Take your time. I'm just going to slip inside and peek around while you..." My nose wrinkles and I gesture at his prone body. "Deal with all this."

I spin and he grabs my ankle, keeping me in place. Huffing, I drop my heel and wait while I keep my gaze on the back door. He'll probably use this as another excuse to leave. Now that I've made up my mind, he won't be able to deter me. It would be weak to change course. At least, that's what Shane taught me. I shake my head, realizing he never actually told me that. I just internalized it from his behavior when I was young. He hasn't acted like asking for help or changing opinions is wrong for years—since Sam came into the picture.

"They'll have a guard," Titus wheezes as he pushes to his feet.

"Except the entire place is dark and those two who left were definitely high. Feels like they weren't doing anything tonight. What was the tip you got?"

I don't want to do this anymore. I don't want to go inside. I don't want to think. The last couple weeks have been nothing but a whirlwind of emotions and shit hitting the fan. As soon as Titus stepped foot in Ridgewood, my world was blasted upside down. It would have been better if he'd left town long before I kissed him at the Tower. He never should have come in the first place. I could've dealt with everything and been back home already.

Running away won't help now. We're too far into the storm. The only options we have are either riding it out or getting swept away. I shiver and cross my arms. Someone's going to get hurt if we don't end this quickly. I can handle it if it's me, but what if it's Daisy? Or one of my friends? Or hell, even Devon? None of them deserve to be pulled into this. Titus signed up for this at least. He knows what the risks are. None of them do. They'll pay for the mistakes I've made, never understanding the reasons why.

"Just that this place existed," he says, interrupting my thoughts. He seems to be doing that a lot lately.

"I could have told you about the other places, ya know. Except that would have required you to actually talk to me. And that's just too fucking hard, isn't it?"

"Don't pick a fight with me, Emma. I'm still riding the edge of being pissed off at you for disappearing earlier," he growls, approaching the door.

I roll my eyes, wanting to snap back, but I don't have it in me. He's busy trying to pry off the wood nailed to the windows, and I sigh. I jump as high as I can to see inside just to make sure there's still blackness within. Then I waltz up to the back door and turn the knob. It gives easily—no rattle or stickiness. I poke Titus in the side and present the way to him as the thin metal swings open.

He scowls at my sweet smile before pulling out his phone. I press my lips together, keeping my comments to myself. If he turns on the flashlight, I might just smash it against the wall. There's probably not a guard inside since their operation is so fucking terrible. Doesn't mean someone couldn't walk by and spot the light. Instead, he starts texting. Or searching for something.

I slip inside, leaving him to follow if he notices. The back area looks like it used to be an office, though the entire place is stripped except for a desk. The door separating the back room from the next area is long gone. The back of my hand brushes the frame and comes away with soot. My nose wrinkles, and I wipe it off on my leg.

Empty shelves greet me, and I hurry through the short hallway to the main area. Long counters line the space, though the barber chairs are long gone. The streetlight outside barely illuminates the room, but it's enough to make out the haphazard setup they have. I slowly turn, taking in the scales, half-filled bags, and large buckets. I'd put cash money on those buckets having Oracle in them.

Shane kept me away from a lot of the drug operations in Synd. Alex snuck me into a few places, though. He figured it was better for me to be informed so I knew what I needed to stay away from. It worked, though I never fully understood why we were involved in that side of the business in the first place.

"Would you stop wandering away?" Titus hisses, then sucks in a sharp breath. "Holy shit. They actually did it."

"Looks like they only have the powder form. Wonder where they got it from."

"Not from Synd, that's for fucking sure. Ghost, the president of the Phantoms—"

"I know who Ghost is," I huff.

"He said they're still dealing with remnants of it in Harris, though that was a couple months ago."

I run my hands through my hair, then gather it into a ponytail. I'd rather not get any of this shit on my skin, but I've heard it can stick to your hair. Once it brushes against your neck, it can cause rashes. It might just be the liquid form of the drug, but I'm not taking any chances.

"You ran one of these when you were younger, didn't you?" It comes out more like an accusation rather than a question.

"For your brothers, yes. Problem?"

I wave my hand, dismissing him as I step closer to one of the stations. I don't want to get into his past. If he keeps talking, he'll eventually blame me for something I never had a hand in. And this isn't the time for that conversation. It'll probably never be time for it, to be fair. Once we deal with this, we'll go back to Synd and pretend the other doesn't exist. Like it should be.

"What's your issue with drug running?" he asks gruffly as he inspects the other side of the room.

"I don't care about weed. But the other shit? I just never understood why we got involved in it."

"Same could be said with any of the other enterprises your family is involved with. However, if the Kings, the Byrns, and the Reapers control the supply, they'll be able to control where shit goes. Won't go to the schools or kids. Same with guns. It'll be available anyway, so why not make sure it doesn't get out of control? You saw what happened when the Guild brought Oracle in. It'd be like that with everything."

I turn to study him. This might be the most civil conversation we've had in years. He's not ridiculing me because I didn't understand. He's not telling me how naive I am. He's not making me feel smaller because I questioned my family. I'm not used to it. This might be what it would be like had I not confessed my ridiculous feelings for him when I was fifteen. I wish I could go back and slap my teenage self. She was so sure of her emotions, thinking Titus was her future and nothing else mattered. She was wrong. Even if shit hadn't gone sideways, there's so much more to life than a boy. I just didn't know it at the time.

Instead of answering, I amble my way to the back to check the desk drawers. As I pass through the storage area, a shadow detaches from the wall and a flash of silver catches my eye. He's too fast for me and the space too small to avoid him as he punches me in the side. He rears back and punches me again in the same spot. I stagger back, a whimper escaping me. The man rushes forward, a crazed look in his eyes as he brandishes a wicked-looking knife in one hand. A hand doused in red.

Shock spreads through my body, all those years of training fleeing. He's nearly on me again when a sharp report rings out and a hole appears on his head between one blink and the next. He's dead before he hits the ground. A dull ache spreads from my side and I sway, knowing I'm about to pass out. The edges of my vision go black and Titus roaring my name rings in my ears as the darkness overtakes me.

Chapter 34

Titus

Cradling Emma's body to my chest, I rock back and forth, muttering for Daisy to hurry. We're not nearly far enough away from the building, but I needed to make sure her bleeding stopped. It hasn't, and it's starting to freak me out. She moans when I press my shirt harder to her side, wondering if the bastard hit any organs. At least she's making sounds.

Headlights cut across the night as Daisy's beat-up car careens around the corner. I struggle to my feet, trying to hold Emma while still keeping my shirt in place. Her tires screech as she slams on her brakes next to us. She flies from the driver's seat. Racing around the trunk, she flings open the back door. Somehow I make it inside and she's behind the wheel, taking off once again. Time warps, skipping from one moment to the next with no way for my mind to keep up.

"Where?" Daisy snaps as if she's asked more than once.

I blank, the reality of the situation crashing into me with the force of a thousand bricks. I shake my head, trying to pull myself away from the dark thoughts swirling in my brain. Acknowledging them will only make them a possibility, and I refuse to let that happen.

"Emma's," I grunt, glancing down.

She's pale, sprawled on my lap. Awkwardly, I slip my phone from my pocket, intent on calling Joy only to find I've already texted her. I don't remember doing that. I barely remember calling Daisy. At least she's not freaking out. One of us needs to stay calm, and I'd prefer it to be the person behind the wheel.

"Talk to me," Daisy says as she whips around one corner after another. I have no idea where we are, but I'll have to trust she knows the fastest way back.

"No." I can't tell her what happened. I'm not entirely sure what occurred and reliving what I do know will only send me into a panic.

"Just...anything. Tell me about literally anything because I am two seconds away from bursting into tears, and I need to be able to see so we don't crash into a fucking building because then we'd be in a whole other shitshow. So speak now."

"When Emma came home from college last Christmas, she was giddy. She's usually happy to be home, but this was different. We don't interact. I don't know what she's told you, but we haven't exactly been on speaking terms for a long time. I thought she'd met someone or had news. Turns out it was none of those things. She told one of her brothers she'd gotten a job offer. No one was particularly happy about it, but they hid it well. We all thought she was going to disappear—forget where she came from."

"We?" Daisy whispers as if she's not entirely sure she wants to ask.

I clear my throat, staring at Emma's face. "They hid it well. They weren't so great at hiding their enthusiasm when she said she obviously wasn't taking it. She was just happy to be offered something. No one cared what I thought. I'm just a guy who works for them. My opinion doesn't matter."

"Bet it would matter to her." The streetlights become more frequent and my breathing evens out slightly.

"It wouldn't." I swallow hard. "When Sam mentioned she thought Emma might be in love...I was jealous."

I've never admitted it. Not out loud. I've kept memories of Emma firmly locked away in the deepest parts of my mind where they can't hurt me. My reactions didn't make sense to me, anyway. I don't have any claim on her and I'd convinced myself I didn't want one. She's firmly off-limits, even if our past didn't exist.

"So you were jealous of a hypothetical man she may or may not have fallen in love with?"

"I don't know. Maybe I was just jealous she had the option to love someone."

Daisy's eyes meet mine in the rearview mirror before darting back to the quiet street. "I don't understand."

"Can't bring just anyone into the life. It's dangerous and some enemies will go after our loved ones. Takes a certain type of person to slip into that role and survive."

I lift the shirt away from her wound and breathe a sigh of relief. Only a little bit of blood seeps from the wound. I suspect she was stabbed twice, but he must have hit close enough to the first injury to only lengthen the gash. I press the fabric to her side once more and she flinches. Small fucking miracles.

"I imagine you can't just download a dating app and ask for someone who's cool with the mafia. Better to find one on the inside already."

"Probably," I murmur as I glance out the window.

She's slowed down now that we're closer to the college. I didn't think there were any police, but I'll have to trust Daisy. She knows this place better than I do. My palms itch and nerves bubble in my stomach, the need to shout at her to go faster creeping up my throat.

It feels like a thousand years have passed by the time we pull in front of Emma's apartment. Once again, Daisy opens the door for me, and I struggle to get us both out of the car without doing more damage to Emma. Daisy's already in the building, mashing on the elevator button. I grit my teeth as I kick the door shut and hurry inside.

The ancient metal box takes for-fucking-ever, and I'm sweating by the time we get to the third floor. I push past Daisy, almost knocking her to the ground. I rush to Emma's apartment and kick aside a neatly wrapped present sitting outside her door. Daisy slides around me and pulls out her keys.

"The alarm," I mumble, trying not to jostle Emma as I step inside. "The thermostat."

"Holy fuck. Wait, it's beeping at me. What the hell? Is it going to blow up? Shit. What's the code? I don't know the code. I feel like I'm defusing a bomb. Shit." Daisy flaps her hands, staring at the keypad as if it's going to catch on fire.

I settle Emma on the couch and stride back to Daisy. She bounces on the balls of her feet and I reach around her to punch in the code. Emma groans and I hurry back to her. I slip my phone from my pocket and make the call. As it rings, I hold my breath, hoping he won't rat me out when the time comes.

"Should I lock it again? Is the alarm set? What if they come after us?" Now that Daisy is no longer driving, it's as if all her anxiety has nowhere to go. I don't have time to comfort her.

"Shut the fuck up and leave the door alone. Someone will be here soon," I bark.

"Maybe we should take her to the hospital."

The call connects, Ink's growly voice filling the line. "What the hell do you want, Prince? Don't tell me she caught whatever you had. I'll tell you the same thing—"

"Shut the fuck up. Stab wound. Short blade. About an inch below the bottom rib."

"Still bleeding?" he asks, the background noise I didn't notice before cutting off.

I peel back the layers of fabric and eye the wound. "Doesn't look like it. But I can't tell."

"How long is the hole?"

I swallow down the nausea his words induce. "About an inch. Maybe two."

"Probably needs to be stitched up, but I don't trust you to do that. I'm coming. Be there in—"

"You're not coming here. I've got someone who can wield a needle."

Joy opens the door just then and hurries to my side. She shoves me away and examines the wound. I have the irrational urge to throw her out the window. I don't like Joy's hands on her. The need to grab her and run overwhelms me, and my hands tremble as I clutch my phone tighter. Beeping echoes through the space as Daisy punches in the code again. Ink's still muttering, more to himself than me.

He clears his throat. "How long ago did this happen?"

"I...I don't know."

Daisy leans closer. "They called me twenty minutes ago. I don't know how long before that it took place."

"Who the fuck was that?" Ink snarls, and Daisy skips back, tears filling her eyes.

"It's been about a half hour. What else do we do? Do I need to take her in?" I say, hoping he doesn't ask again. I'm not about to out Daisy to anyone in Synd. They'll insist on vetting her, making sure she's not aligned with their enemies.

"Fucking hell, Titus. You know what the hell to do. You know she's not bleeding out. You know how to clean the wound. Why the hell are you calling me?" Ink growls, his tone a contradiction to his words.

I pull in a deep breath, focusing on Emma's face. Her blue eyes glisten with unshed tears and I hang up on Ink while I rush to her. Dropping to my knees, I ignore the vibrating of my phone. I swear to fuck if he tells the Kings...

Joy has already cleaned the wound, a bowl filled with red water at her feet. She threads a needle and I wince. I doubt she has anything to numb the area. Her gaze meets mine and she nods.

"Maybe we should have locked the back door," Emma whispers, and my eyes snap to hers.

"I told you it was a possibility. But sure as shit, you didn't listen. You just waltzed in there without a fucking care."

I shouldn't be scolding her, but I can't seem to turn it off. She fucked up. And she put herself in danger, not caring about the consequences. It could have been so much worse. He could have hit an artery or an organ. I could be hauling her dead body back to her family right now. For all the training she's had, she should have been able to dodge his attack. This might not be the best time, but she needs someone to call her on her bullshit.

"Titus," Joy murmurs, a warning in her voice. "Why don't you go check on the other one? I believe she's throwing up in the bathroom."

I shove to my feet, careful not to jostle Emma. Her whimper turns into a groan as Joy starts stitching her up. I slow, the nerves turning to rage with nowhere to go. Taking my anger out on Emma isn't fair. I don't know Daisy well enough. If I blasted Joy, I'd have a hole matching Emma's. There's no one else unless I leave.

My feet stutter to a stop outside the bathroom door, Daisy's quiet sobs coming from the other side of the wood. I glance at my phone, Ink's notification a glaring reminder of what I've done. He'll know I was talking about Emma. He'll tell the others. They might have sent me to get her instead of themselves, but if they know she's hurt, they'll come. It's my fault she was stabbed.

I pivot, heading for the front door. In seconds, the knob is in my hand and I freeze, Joy's words ringing in my ears. *You can run away all you want, just like you do every time she makes you feel something other than guilt.*

I pivot once more and stomp back to Emma's side. If they come for me, so be it. I'll accept the consequences of my negligence. She's braver than I am. The last time someone was stabbing me with a needle, I howled like a fucking baby. Emma hasn't reacted after the first stitch. My hand slides into her hair and I rest my forehead on hers.

"I hate you," she murmurs, exhaustion lining her voice.

"Keep telling yourself that, darling. One of these days you'll mean it."

Chapter 35

Emma

The stitches in my side pull as I sit up in bed, the comforter pooling at my waist. I don't remember moving to the bed, so I have to assume Titus carried me here. I'm strangely wide awake, though I should probably be sleeping like he is. His neck is at a wonky angle as he snores lightly in the chair.

I thought he'd leave. I watched the emotions dance across his face, one after another. Each one was worse than the last. The instant Joy scolded him, I knew he'd run. I wanted to be pissed at him. He has every right to rage at me. I fucked up—too enamored with proving him wrong. And while I may have a lot of sway over my brothers, they're still his bosses. He answers to them. Shane doesn't give two shits if I'm at fault. He'll need somewhere for the anger to go. He won't lay the blame at my feet. He'll come straight for Titus.

When the decision cemented on Titus's face to run, I wasn't surprised. I would have done the same damn thing. I *did* do the same thing. Five years ago, I had no plans to go to college. It was my brother's dream, not mine. I was able to fend him off, saying I wanted a gap year before I went. When the time came to actually make a decision, though, I froze. There was no right path, no perfect choice. But if I made the wrong one, I'd fail myself and my family. I was going to ride the limbo as long as I could. Until I overheard Shane and Sam talking about moving Titus up in the ranks. He would be in the house all the time. He'd be in meetings and skulking around. I couldn't handle seeing him all the time—not after what he said to me. I thought I'd gotten over it, and for the most part I had. Yet when it came down to it, I ran. I went off to college and tried to pretend that part of my life didn't exist.

"Emma," Joy hisses from the doorway. She gestures me to follow her and I throw the covers off.

The last thing I want to do is have a conversation with her. She'll lecture me or question what the hell I was thinking. I'm sure she thinks she was hiding her disapproving looks last night while she stitched me up. Or maybe she didn't give a shit whether or not I saw. Joy clearly has deep ties to Titus and most likely thinks I'm a bad influence on him or some bullshit.

Still, I wander into the living room and spot Daisy snoring on the couch. Guilt swamps me, and I wrap my arms around my middle. This is why I didn't tell her years ago about my family. It's as if I invited in the demons, allowing my life to blow the fuck up merely because I exposed who I really was. It was selfish and unfair to her. I should have just left. If I would have gone home when Titus showed up, or hell, when Sam first called, none of this would have happened.

Joy waves me over to the kitchen, a coffee mug already in her hand. She nudges the other mug across the island toward me and I pick it up. The bitter taste slides down my throat, electrifying my nerves. I settle next to her, both of us leaning on the counter as I stare at Daisy's sleeping form.

"We need to check your stitches. Make sure you didn't pull them too much while you were flopping around in bed," she murmurs, then takes another sip.

"I don't flop. Usually, I slowly migrate to the edge until I'm about to fall off, then wake up."

"How many times do you wake up in the middle of the night?"

"A couple. It's fine. I'm used to not sleeping through the night. Half the time my schedule is fucked, anyways."

Her gaze rakes over me, curious and probing. I'm sure she knows more about me than I could ever know about her. I wonder how long she's been in Ridgewood and whether she's been watching me—keeping track of my whereabouts. Does she have ties to the King mafia? Or maybe she's aligned with the Byrns.

They're practically the same thing now since we're all friends. We're more of a unit than we were in my younger years. Apparently, our families worked together before the fallout, but that was twenty years ago.

Joy sighs, tucking her chin to her chest. "Anything you want to ask me?"

"Uh, no?" I sure as shit am not going to ask her anything.

"Except I can practically hear the cogs turning in your mind. You want to know whether Titus stayed at my place. You want to know what he's told me about you. You want to know if he's been in town without telling you. So ask away."

I snort, but my side aches at the move and I curl into the injury. "Actually, I wasn't thinking any of that. I was wondering if you worked for my brother. And whether you were his spy."

She steps to the island and leans against the chipped counter, facing me. "Seriously? You weren't thinking of Titus?"

"Contrary to popular belief, there are other things going on in my life that have nothing to do with Titus," I mutter.

"Clearly. Or you wouldn't have an extra hole in your body." Her gaze flits to my side as if she can see through the t-shirt someone stuffed me into before tucking me in bed. Probably Titus, but I'm ignoring that fact.

"Might as well get this over with," I say, plopping my coffee down.

She raises an eyebrow. "What exactly are we getting over with?"

"The lecture. Have at it. I've been through a fair few so I'm prepared." I cross my arms and settle in.

She fights a smile as she plays with her lip ring. The small light over the oven catches the silver.

"Did that hurt?" I ask, tipping my chin at her piercing.

She drops her hand, tilting her head. "Nope. Want one? I've got a guy who does a good job. Unless you're looking for a tattoo. My artist works at the same shop."

I open my mouth to tell her no, then snap it shut. "Do they cover scars?"

Her eyebrows crawl up her forehead, and I wish I wouldn't have asked.

"She does. As long as it's...fully healed and ideal."

"Ideal?"

"Some scars don't hold the ink as well. I don't know a lot about it, to be honest."

Silence descends between us, and she glances away. Thank fuck, because I'd feel the need to fill it with babble, regardless of whether I want to tell her what happened. I told Titus the scar on my back was an accident. Walking that back would take more courage than I have. And I wouldn't put it past Joy to mention it in passing. At least I told the truth when I said it wasn't Devon's fault.

"You're not going to ask?" I wince, hating myself just a little.

"Not really any of my business. Seems like you want to tell me, though."

I bite the inside of my lip, worrying the flesh while I weigh the pros and cons. "I was in a car accident. Sort of. It was an accident. Riding my bike, but it was an accident."

"I didn't quite catch that. Was it an accident?" Her lips pull in a smirk, and I roll my eyes. "What happened?"

"I was riding. While upset. Doesn't matter why." I swallow hard. "My ex was worried and followed me in his car. I don't really know how, but I must have hit something on the road and I skid. I made the poor decision to not wear anything other than a thin shirt so I didn't have anything to protect my back."

"Were you wearing a helmet?" she asks, her nostrils flaring.

I nod, glancing away from the anger in her eyes. "Still knocked my ass out. When I came to, I was at the hospital. I'd been out of it for a while. Lost three days and had a fancy new scar to show for it all. I'd rather you not tell Titus."

"Why not?"

"He's not exactly Devon's biggest fan." I grab my coffee again, wrinkling my nose when I find it cold.

I spin around and stick the mug in the microwave and hope the beeping doesn't wake up Daisy. Rapid footsteps have me turning as Titus grabs his keys from the hook by the door. I didn't even notice he was hanging them there. I shake my head, forcing the random thought away as anxiety takes over. Shit. He probably heard what happened.

He's busy punching in the code on the alarm, not bothering to even glance at me. I slide between him and the door, blocking his way.

"Move, Emma," he growls.

"I'd rather not be responsible for another death. So, why don't you just go back to bed."

Joy snickers, and Titus's head turns to bare his teeth at her. She holds her hands up in surrender, a smile still firmly on her face. When he faces me again, a shiver runs through me.

"Move or I'll do it for you," he snaps.

"Shh. You're going to wake up Daisy. Also, I'm wounded. You probably shouldn't be manhandling an injured person."

His nostrils flare as he battles with the demons in his mind. It hits me how our relationship has morphed. Before, I never would have thought he'd hold himself back for my sake. Sure, he'd keep me safe—protect me from the evils in our world—for his own self-preservation. It made sense with the way I was raised and with our past. I'd let go of a lot of the heartache. I used it as an excuse to continue the feud between us. Didn't help when he kept being an asshole to me. I was merely matching energy.

Now things have shifted in a way I don't fully understand. I can't help but wonder what changed. Maybe he's coming around to the fact that I'm not the bratty bitch he accused me of. Maybe he's seeing I'm more than I was. Because no matter what I thought of myself when I was fifteen, I was a brat. I was self-centered. I was spoiled. Hell, I still am, no matter how much I try to make it on my own. My brother still funds my lifestyle regardless of how much I've cut back.

Some things never change, though. I'm a liability to my family and I always will be. No matter how much I train or fight or run. I'll always be the weak link because it's just me. I could disappear—go anywhere in the world I want—just not home. Not without sinking back into my assigned role. And that's something I can't change.

"So, as much as I'd love to watch this stand-off. I need to check her stitches and then leave. Not to mention, Emma seems like she's having an existential crisis," Joy says as she grabs my wrist and tugs.

She pulls me toward the bathroom, and it's not until I hear a thump from behind me that I glance over my shoulder. Titus's hand gripping the knob, his forehead resting on the wood. If I go with Joy, there's no guarantee he'll be here when I get back. Joy forces me onward and she shoves me into the tiny space, then squeezes herself in as well.

"How are you going to check my stitches if there's like a foot of space in here?" I ask, and she opens the shower door. I step inside, chuckling ruefully as she sits on the closed toilet.

"He won't leave," she says softly as she lifts my shirt. I probably should have put on some pants.

"I'm not his keeper. He can do whatever the fuck he wants. As long as he doesn't try to kill an innocent man, I don't really give a fuck." The words are hollow even to my own ears.

"Sure you don't." She rips off the bandage and I yelp. "If you say it enough, you might actually believe yourself. I don't think he's going to kill Devon."

"He's been waiting for a reason," I mutter, then suck in a sharp breath as she prods at the tender flesh.

Joy glances up at me. "And why do you think that is? Based on the shit he's said about you two, he shouldn't give two shits about your love life. And yet..."

"My family? I don't fucking know. And I don't particularly care," I snap as she smears ointment on my wound, then tapes on another bandage.

Her head tilts when she's done, staring at my skin. Her finger brushes against the tattoo crawling up my side.

"Morning glories," she murmurs.

"They're my favorite."

She hums. "Not roses?"

I narrow my gaze, but she keeps hers on my skin. I wonder what Titus told her. Maybe she already knows about the roses. He went to her after I kneed him in the balls, his hands cut up from all the broken vases. I wonder how many times he's bitched to her about me. For some reason, it doesn't bother me like I thought it would. I've bitched plenty of times to Daisy about him over the last couple weeks.

"Does Titus know you have this?"

I lean back and her hand falls away as the hem of my shirt drops to brush against my thigh. "Wouldn't know. We don't exactly talk about shit like that. Why?"

She shakes her head, a rueful smile on her lips. "No reason. Just interesting."

She's moving before I can question her further. We've only been gone about ten minutes, but it feels like much longer. I run through our conversation in my head, wondering if I gave her too much. Too much information. Too much fuel. Too much emotion. Until I know otherwise, I have to assume she'll tell Titus everything. They're obviously close. My stomach flips when I realize why my mind can't settle on how I feel about Joy. Jealousy curls its way around my heart, and I suck in a deep breath. I wish I was as important to him as she is. I wish he'd talk to me.

I shake my head, dismissing my emotions. Getting sucked in by him again would be disastrous. I can't handle another heartbreak. Besides, I have more important things to deal with than my fickle heart.

Chapter 36

Titus

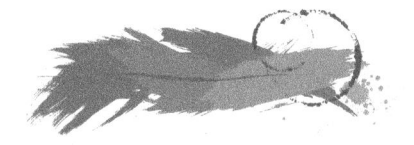

Emma has been avoiding me for the last two hours. Joy left before Emma even came out of the bathroom. Daisy followed shortly after, whispering to Emma as she went. Emma retreated into the bathroom again, yet the shower didn't start up. She was fucking hiding from me.

I don't know what the fuck was going through her head as we stared at each other while I tried to leave, a wordless battle I wasn't sure I could win. The emotions flashed through her eyes too quickly for me to decipher. I don't think she even realized the mask she'd slipped over her features.

Something's changed between us. When I overheard her telling Joy about how she got her scar, I was prepared to kill Devon. Except it wasn't for the reasons I went after Calvin. He posed a threat to her, and I eliminated him. It's part of my job, no matter how I claimed her before I slit his throat. Devon, though...he allowed her to get hurt. I don't know if I believe Emma's version of events, anyway. I wouldn't put it past him to make up some story she probably swallowed because he's such a good fucking guy.

I glance toward the front door, wondering when Devon will drop by again. Joy took care of his latest present. I didn't ask what she did, but I assume she threw it away. He hasn't bothered texting Emma yet. It's just a matter of time. I've been waiting for her to realize her phone is missing. She hasn't, which is surprising in and of itself since she's been wandering around the apartment in a daze.

"Would you knock it off?" I grunt as she opens the fridge for the seventeenth time in ten minutes.

"I'm hungry. Fuck off," she snaps.

"I ordered food. Just find something to do that isn't going to annoy the fuck out of me," I say from the couch as I bury my face in my phone.

She huffs, and I track her from the corner of my eye as she shuffles from the kitchen to her bookshelf. I glance away when she bends over to examine the titles. The last thing I need is to get hard while staring at her ass. Seconds later, she plops herself next to me, her body sinking toward mine as the cushion defies the laws of gravity. Her arm brushes mine and a flicker of electricity streaks its way to my hand.

She huffs again and I grit my teeth, refusing to engage. I'm still pissed I'm stuck in this goddamn apartment on this shitty couch, waiting until the next catastrophe hits us. I need more information about the organization here, but I'm loath to ask Emma, and Joy can only do so much. She doesn't work for me, at least not in this capacity. She's supposed to run the chop shop and keep an eye on shit in Ridgewood. Not bring down a drug ring.

Emma swings her legs up and tucks her feet under my thigh. She flips open her book and settles it on her knees as if she'll be here for a while. I scroll mindlessly, never fully seeing anything on my screen while trying to ignore the warmth rolling through my body. I close my eyes, a flash of déjà vu hitting me. Yet it's different from before. I don't know what else to call it, though. We never would have sat on the same couch. She never would have touched me. I never would have allowed her. It wasn't appropriate and we both knew that. The silence between us isn't wrought with tension now. At least, not the kind I'm used to.

"When is the food coming?" she asks, interrupting my thoughts.

I pull up the app and see the driver is on their way. "Couple minutes."

"Here," she says, and I glance at her for the first time.

She holds out a book, and I scowl. "What the hell am I going to do with that?"

"Uh, read? I know you can. Plus, this is a good book."

I take the small paperback slowly, my lip curling at the cartoon cover. "What's it about?"

"Oh, it's alien porn. But it's really cute. And quick. Plus, you might find a few pointers in there to help your game." She taps her finger on her chin, staring off into space. "Then again, you don't have a sucker, so maybe not."

"What the fuck," I breathe as my phone dings, indicating the food has arrived. Thank fuck.

I toss the book next to me and push up from the couch. It takes me two tries to free myself from the prison, and I vow to burn the fucker the first chance I get. I rush from the apartment, wondering if I need to check the food before Emma eats it. I should have gone myself, made sure the takeout was safe. Now I have to be a fucking taste tester, too.

The driver left the paper bags by the mailboxes, just like I instructed. I snap a picture of the college kid climbing back into his car. He doesn't look suspicious, and he never looks back as he takes off down the road into the setting sun. By the time I make it back upstairs, I've already tried some of the fries. The bottles of soda haven't been tampered with.

Once I'm back in the apartment, I set the alarm before making my way to Emma, who hasn't moved an inch. She barely glances up as I collapse back onto the couch.

"Did you get the right sauce?" she mumbles, eyes fixed on the page.

"Don't insult me." I hand her some fries, and she hums.

It's not until we're halfway through our meal I realize how easy this is. Every once in a while she wiggles, joy radiating from her. It's the nuggets. And the sweet and sour sauce. She winces, and I almost spill my drink as I swing around. She waves me off, focusing on her food again.

"I'm missing one," she snaps, narrowing her eyes on the nuggets.

Rolling my eyes, I snatch one of mine and plop it in her lap. "Quit bitching and eat the rest of your food."

"You ate one, didn't you?" she accuses, glaring at me.

"You've already been stabbed. You wanna be poisoned, too?" I shove a handful of fries in my mouth.

"So your solution was to eat one yourself ten seconds before you handed me the rest of the food? What if you keel over in like ten minutes? I'm not dragging your ass to the hospital. And I don't have any antidotes here." She gives me a snarky look before popping the nugget I gave her into her mouth.

"Sure you do, darling. They're hidden behind the dozens of knives you stashed in your closet."

"You went through my closet?" she shrieks, and her heel connects with my thigh.

I rub the spot, then grab her foot when she tries to kick me again. "Knock it off. You're going to upset my fries and then I'll be pissed. And where the fuck you think I got your dagger from?"

She sniffs, refusing to meet my gaze. "I assumed I left it out."

"No, you didn't. You don't question a goddamn thing when I'm with you, do you?"

"I trust you'll take care of...shit." A stunned expression slides across her face, probably mirroring my own. She ducks her head, her hair hiding her from view. "Shane wouldn't have made you head of security if you sucked at your job. I assumed you'd know what the hell you were doing."

"Liar," I breathe, and her gaze snaps to mine.

"Eat," she says, but she's breathless.

I don't think, just react. If I think too much, I'll talk myself out of it, and later I'll regret it. I have every single fucking time. I shove the remnants of my meal to the floor, stray fries scattering at my feet. She yelps when I grab her ankles and slide her closer to me.

"What the fuck, Titus? What are you doing?"

"Eating. Now shut the fuck up."

I hook my thumbs in her underwear and yank them down her legs. She doesn't resist as I shove one foot on the back of the couch and push the other to the floor, opening her up for me. Her book tumbles to the ground along with the rest of her food. Thank fuck she's done with her nuggets or I'd never hear the end of it.

Leaning down, my mouth waters the closer I get. She bucks when I bury my nose in her cunt, her scent overwhelming me. I lick her slowly, and she moans as her fingers grip my hair. She twists the strands until my scalp burns, and I groan before pulling her clit between my lips. Wetness coats my face as I flick the sensitive bud over and over. Her legs shake, and I wrap my hands around her thighs, keeping her right where I want her. I swear I've been dreaming of her cunt. If I'm not careful, I'll become addicted. I don't even care anymore. As long as I get to taste her, I'll take whatever consequences come later.

"Titus," she whimpers, and I release her leg before sliding two fingers into her core and pumping them slowly.

I glance up just in time to watch the ecstasy wash across her face as her back arches. A grin bursts across my face as I lap up her orgasm, relishing the sounds coming from her. Her leg slides from the back of the couch and onto my shoulder. Her grip on my hair tightens as she rocks against my face. She doesn't seem to know whether to push me away or pull me closer.

I press a kiss to her clit before pulling my fingers from her, and she whines. As I straighten, her leg slips between me and the cushion and I trap her there as I strip my pants and boxers off. They pool on the floor next to her panties. My cock aches with need and I refuse to deny myself any longer.

Her lips part, a dazed expression on her face, and I swallow a chuckle. I haven't even gotten started with her yet. Grasping her waist, I haul her onto my lap, mindful of her stitches, and her gaze flies to me. It's not the smoothest transition, but I wrap my arm around her waist and grip my cock as I guide the tip into her dripping cunt. She sinks onto me slowly, throwing her head back as she moans. I can't stop my own groan from mingling with hers. Once she's taken all of me, I hold her in place, savoring how her cunt spasms around my length.

"Move," she whines, trying to roll her hips.

I grab the hem of her shirt and whip it over her head. Her arms get stuck, and an image of her tied to my bed back in Synd flashes through my mind. I shake my head, dropping the fabric on top of the rest of our clothes.

I run my gaze down her skin, making note of every nick and faded scar. Her morning glory tattoo crawls up her side and I skim my fingers along the faded blues before gripping her waist again. I've tried to ignore the ink, thinking I'll forget when she got it. My plan didn't work since we've been sleeping together. Every time I see it, I remember the dead look in her eyes after she got it, explaining to Sam it was a fresh start after the latest kidnapping.

I shake my head, dismissing the memory as she quivers around my length.

"I c-can't..." she stutters.

She pushes my shirt up. The move gives me a clear view of where we're connected, and I can't pull my eyes away. I lift her slowly until only the tip remains, then slam her down until we're molded together again. The couch doesn't help in the slightest as her knees sink into the cushions. For once, I don't mind since it gives me full control. Holding her still, I plunge into her, mesmerized by the sight of my cock disappearing into her cunt over and over. Her nails dig into my chest, leaving half-moon indents in the flesh over my heart.

My eyes catch on the bandage, glaringly white against her skin. I freeze, gaze snapping up to search her face for any pain. I grit my teeth as her cunt flutters around me and she lets out a choked sob, grinding into me. I slide my hand to the back of her neck and tug her closer. Her forehead rests against mine, our breath mingling.

"Touch yourself," I rasp, then release her.

Her hand slips between us without hesitation, and I thrust into her. My movements aren't as frantic as before, but it doesn't matter. My stomach tightens while her fingers circle her clit. I'm captivated, my attention split between where we're joined and her face. I don't want to miss the moment she falls over the edge.

Her cunt quivers around me, a ragged moan leaving her as she comes all over my cock. Her cunt isn't the only thing I'm addicted to, apparently. She throws her head back, shuddering out her release, and I grit my teeth as I follow her into oblivion. I slide my fingers into her hair and yank her toward me. Our mouths crash together as she clings to me. She gasps, breaking the kiss, and her body melts into mine.

I close my eyes, holding her to me, and wonder what the hell I've gotten myself into. This wasn't a bid for domination like in the woods. And it wasn't a quest to fuck her out of my system. We've fallen into something more. Something I'm not entirely sure either of us will survive.

Chapter 37

Emma

I groan before I even open my eyes, the ache in my side driving me from sleep. Or maybe it's the ache between my legs. Honestly, it's a toss-up on which one is worse. I can't do much about my stitches. They'll itch and annoy me to no end, but I can't stop it. My horniness, on the other hand...I could definitely take care of that little problem.

Cracking my lids, I try to keep my breathing even. I don't want to wake Titus. He's gotten a lot less sleep than I have since I was stabbed five days ago. We've essentially holed up in my apartment, careening between bickering and fucking. He wants to plan our next steps, but we can't do anything until I'm healed. I've got at least another two days before I'll be doing anything moderately strenuous, and that's only if I can convince Titus I'm fine.

Every position we've fucked in has been done with care for my injury and it's starting to piss me off. I'm not made of glass. It barely hurts anymore. Then again, I've been popping pills the entire time, so I might not be the best judge of my pain.

I brush my hand down his side, smirking when his cheek twitches. Gently, I roll away from him and reach into my nightstand. Masturbating with my toy in the shower isn't my first choice, but Titus really does need to sleep. My fingers close over my small vibrator when Titus presses his chest to my back and grips my wrist.

"Going somewhere, darling?" he murmurs, his voice still laced with sleep.

"Shower," I gasp as his hand dips between my legs, and he groans.

"So fucking wet for me."

I snort even as I shudder as he strokes me. "Maybe it's for me."

He buries his face into the crook of my neck, chuckling. "We both know this cunt belongs to me. She gets wet for me. Begs for my cock. Just like she's doing right now."

My knee slides up, opening me further for him as he slips two fingers inside. A yelp leaves me when he adds a third, pumping slow and steady. He's not exactly helping since he's teasing me so fucking much. He tugs them out, replacing them with his cock, and I sigh. No matter how much we've fucked over the last couple days, I'm still enraptured every time he sinks into me.

A buzzing fills the air and my eyes fly open. He pulls my leg over his, slipping deeper. I jolt when the vibrator hits my clit. Wheezing, I push against his body, trying to get away from the pleasure pulsing through me. Usually it takes a bit to get me going, but I was already primed before he'd touched me.

"Come for me," he growls in my ear, and my body responds.

I bite my lip as euphoria washes over me. He doesn't move the vibrator and pinpricks of pain mix with the pleasure. My hand wraps around his wrist, trying to pull him away. He snickers, keeping up his steady pace. Finally, he lifts the toy from my clit and I whimper.

"Such a good girl. Do you see how much you belong to me?"

He rolls us before I can answer and my face ends up smashed into the pillow, my arm trapped underneath me. His knees settle on either side of my hips and his fingers dig into my ass as he pounds into me, each thrust harder than the last. Another orgasm crashes over me without warning, and I moan into the sheets.

He mutters something I can't hear over the roaring in my ears, and his movements become erratic. It doesn't matter. My pussy spasms around his cock, though I can't tell if I'm coming again or if this is the same as before. Stars explode behind my lids, and he groans out my name as he erupts, grinding his hips into me. His body collapses on mine, the smell of our escapades floating around us.

My limbs are like Jello. I couldn't move even if I wanted to, which I don't. Even when he pulls off of me and flops onto his back, I can't summon the strength to do anything other than turn my head. His hooded gaze finds me, and I smile lazily.

"Well, that's one way to wake up," I mutter.

He hums and my eyes flutter closed. I could lie here all day, but my skin is sticky and I need to clean up the mess he made. He smacks my ass as I trip out of bed, and I glare at him over my shoulder. He grins, his eyes fluttering closed. I press my lips together as I make my way from the room. He'll be asleep before I step into the shower. It feels as if we're trapped in a bubble. If we leave the apartment, it'll pop, and I don't know what the world will look like then. We'll probably fall back into the same roles we've taken up for the last ten years. I don't know if I can handle that.

As the water washes over me, I contemplate the future. I've been studiously ignoring what's to come. Eventually we'll have to leave, deal with the shitshow swirling around us, and face the music with my family. I'm impressed they haven't descended on us yet, though Ink promised to keep his mouth shut as long as we kept him informed of my recovery. Titus has been texting with him. I don't have the energy. Eventually, we'll have to tell them what's happened. Once we do, everything will change, and I don't know how to process my world shifting. I swallow hard as I swipe the droplets from my face.

By the time I'm conditioning my hair, I've settled on dealing with things as they come. We'll have the next two days, maybe three, where I can pretend the outside world doesn't exist. I won't even have to discuss things with Titus. He clearly isn't thinking about the future. I snort and water trickles into my nose. It burns and I lean out of the spray, almost hitting my head on the door. Flapping my hands in front of my face, I wait until the sensation eases.

"Unlock the door, Emma." Titus's deep growl filters through the wood and I pop open the shower.

"I'm almost done and you're not fucking peeing while I'm showering," I call. I probably don't have to yell since everything in this place is thin—the walls, the floors, the doors—everything.

"Unlock it or I break it down."

I roll my eyes, wondering if he's holding a needle to pop the bubble prematurely. Or maybe he just doesn't care. The thought brings me up short. Of course he doesn't care. Not in the way I thought. Not in the way I want. Because as much as I tried to protect my heart, I failed. I should have known in the woods. I should have known the first time we slept together. I should have known...I just should have known.

I reach over and flip the lock before slamming the shower shut behind me, making the glass rattle in its cheap metal frame. I duck under the lukewarm spray, hoping he does his business and leaves. Lady luck has apparently abandoned me. He swings open the shower and the spray hits his bare chest, soaking his grey boxers.

"Can I help you?"

"Are you crying in here? I can't tell with the"—he waves his hand around—"water."

"While crying in the shower is an excellent way to hide the tears, I wasn't. I snorted some water accidentally." I thought I'd kept my sputtering to a minimum, but apparently not.

He narrows his gaze at me, then runs it down my body. I have the irrational urge to cover myself. He's seen me completely naked. Several times, in fact. With the places my thoughts have been taking me over the last ten minutes, my mind can't settle on how to deal with him.

"Are you going to get out and let me finish my shower?" I ask when he doesn't move.

He shuts the door without a word and stomps from the bathroom. I don't know why he's so pissed. Maybe he thinks I'm lying. Huffing, I shut off the water and dry off quickly, taking care not to hit my stitches. Joy must have a lot more experience than I thought. The row is even and clean. I probably won't even have a scar after a few years. Part of me wishes she would've made it jagged. I like having the reminders of my exploits displayed on my skin. Then again, most of my injuries were because of my mistakes. They're good reminders to not do shit like that a second time.

By the time I'm done dressing the wound, my head is clearer. Whatever Titus decides to do is no concern of mine. I'll go on with my plans, carrying out the ones I had before he busted into my life. I didn't have any grand visions of us falling in love and living happily ever after. My world isn't primed for devotion of that kind. It's why I broke up with Devon. Among other things. My world isn't safe, least of all for outsiders. A relationship with Titus brings its own problems, ones I doubt we'd be able to overcome even if he wanted to.

"Pastries are on the counter," he grunts as he passes me in the kitchen on his way to the bathroom. He'll be taking a cold shower, though I doubt he cares.

I dress quickly, for once pulling on my own clothing. I've taken to wearing his shirt, but I can't bring myself to put it on. After grabbing a chocolate croissant, I search for my phone. After five minutes, my mood sours. It really goes downhill when I find it nestled among Titus's clothes. Normally, I'd accuse him of taking it. It's not worth the fight. He's clearly in a shitty mood now. You'd think an orgasm would have mellowed him out. Maybe his dick is raw. The thought makes me giggle as I flop back on my bed.

"Please tell me you've been holed up in your apartment for happy reasons and not because you caught an infection and are actively dying," Daisy says before I can even say hello.

I chuckle, then listen for the noise from the shower to make sure Titus isn't about to sneak up on me. He has a habit of doing that, and it's annoying. Especially when I want to talk about him.

"I am perfectly fine. No dying this time around." I run my fingers across the comforter, realizing Titus made my bed.

"That suggests this isn't the first time you've been stabbed, and while the nosy part of me wants to hear all the stories, I legit don't think I can handle it. I puked in your bathroom, by the way. Which you should be proud of me for."

"Why would I be proud of you hurling up your guts?" I ask with a laugh.

A cupboard slams on her end of the line, and I wince. "Because I didn't do it while you were bleeding to death in the back of my car. I've gotta say, I'm impressed Titus didn't get any blood on my seats. At least I won't have to explain that to Dad when I get home."

"Oh, that's easy. Just say it was your period. He won't question it." It's how I got out of many a lecture when one of my brothers found a stain.

She snorts, and I can practically hear her rolling her eyes. "Except periods don't freak Dad out. He's one of the good ones."

I sober, the smile dropping from my face. "You're really lucky. You know that, right?"

"I am. Plus, I have an amazing best friend who would be there for me in a second."

I sit up, my stitches pulling, but I have other shit to worry about. "What do you need?"

"What? Nothing. I'm good. What do *you* need?" Her tone is off, and I close my eyes.

"You whore. You're lying. Tell me what's wrong."

She sighs, some rustling on her end swallowing up the sound. "I may have gotten a call from someone you know. They were...intense."

"Who?" I swing my legs to the side and rush to my closet, tucking my phone against my shoulder. "Did they give you a name?"

"No, but they said they knew you and you were in a shitload of trouble. They advised me to go home. Thank fuck we're on break or I'd have to worry about classes. So, I'm packing, but I wanted to ask you who would be able to get my number and if you actually think I should leave."

"Fuck," I breathe as I kick aside the mess Titus made when he was raiding my closet for weapons. I can't find my fucking shoes and I'll need them.

"So, you know who it was?"

"No. I have my suspicions, but it could be a couple people. Was it a man or woman? What exactly did they say?"

"Man. Kind of gruff, like they were trying to distort their voice." She stumbles through their conversation, trying to give me as many quotes as she can.

She's not trained to pay attention and I'm sure they caught her off guard. I wish she would have recorded it.

"Okay, I'm going to send you an address. I want you to go there and stay two nights. Then you'll meet your family at the airport in Rennick. There will be tickets for you at the service desk."

"Wait, what? Why?"

"Because I don't know who the fuck called you, but I'm assuming they knew where you live. They probably know where your family lives. If they're going to use you to get to me, we're going to make it fucking hard. Don't answer anyone's call other than Titus's or mine." I lean my forehead against the closet door, mentally rolling through the list of people I trust.

"Do you have Joy's number?"

"Yes," she breathes, panic lacing her voice.

"Then add her to the list. I'll deal with your family. Go now and I'll send you the address." Tears fill my eyes and I bite my cheek to keep them at bay, at least until I'm off the phone. "I'm sorry."

"It's fine," she murmurs. "I knew what I signed up for. You told me to leave and I chose to stay. My choices aren't on you, Emma. I'll call you when I'm on the road."

"Good. Don't stop for anyone, even the police."

She sniffs, then whispers, "You really don't know who it was?"

"No. But I intend to find out."

Chapter 38

Titus

"Where the hell do you think you're going?" I snarl as Emma stomps toward the front door. I'm in no condition to race after her since I'm in a goddamn towel.

"Don't worry about it," she snaps, punching in the code.

I lunge forward and grab her wrist before she can finish. She spins, tugging away, but I refuse to let go. I'm not surprised she's trying to run. I probably would too if she'd fucked me, then treated me like shit afterward. One of these days I'll learn how to keep my emotions in check when things happen. Emma probably doesn't even know why my mood changed so quickly.

"Don't fucking run away, Emma. Just answer the fucking question."

She twists her arm, breaking my hold. She could just dash out the door without putting in the code. I could deal with the aftermath of the alarm blaring through the apartment. To my surprise, she crosses her arms over her chest and raises an eyebrow.

"I wasn't running away. I have shit to deal with and you were—" Her gaze dips, then settles on mine. "Indisposed."

"Bullshit. You were running because you got spooked."

She throws up her hands. "What the hell would I get spooked by? It's not like you got down on one knee and proposed."

I rear back and scowl. "Why the fuck would I do that?"

"You wouldn't. Which is the fucking point. Did you think perhaps my life doesn't revolve around you? That just maybe I have other shit to deal with instead of coddling your fragile fucking ego?"

"I expect after everything we've been through, you'll fucking talk to me before running off into the night," I growl, running my hands through my damp hair.

"It's daytime, asshole." She glares at me, and I realize we're never going to get anywhere if we keep bickering.

I pull in a deep breath to calm my pounding heart. "What happened?"

She huffs and for a second, I think she'll refuse to say anything just to spite me. We've never been good at communicating and today is no different. Sleeping together hasn't changed who we fundamentally are. Setting our bickering aside would take a goddamn miracle. She eyes me, indecision weighing heavily on her face.

"Talked to Daisy. Someone called her up and told her to get out of town. That it wasn't safe being around me. I don't know who it is, and they conveniently didn't leave a name." She glances at her phone, then swipes a few times, and I resist the urge to snatch it from her.

"Could be Ren. Or Nemesis."

"You want to call them and ask? Because I sure as hell don't. And while Ren would be cagey like that, Lacey wouldn't be. I don't care if she's in her alter ego mode or not. But Daisy told me some specifics and it doesn't seem like Ren." She sighs, tipping her head back.

"What's your plan, then?"

She rolls her head from one side to the other, cracking her neck, and I shudder. "Send her ass to a hotel for a couple days. Then send her entire family to Cabo or some shit until I figure everything out. It's not ideal, but it's all I got."

I tuck my chin to my chest, running through the various ways her plan could go to shit. I don't know Daisy that well, but she seems utterly devoted to her friend. Emma probably told her to go home, and Daisy refused. For all of Emma's faults, she protects those she loves.

"Go ahead," she says, exhaustion lining her voice. "Tell me it's a foolish plan. Tell me I'm throwing my family's money at a problem I created. Not like you haven't said it all before."

I don't blame her for thinking that way. I've harped on her enough, calling her a spoiled brat in every way I can think of. Glancing around her dingy apartment, I realize I might have been wrong. At least partly.

"I wasn't thinking that. This is for your friend. I'd be pissed if you didn't help her. Why two days in a hotel?"

Her lips part, confusion building in her eyes. "In case they caught up to her. Then she wouldn't lead them home, but she'd be close enough for me to get to her quickly."

"And Cabo?"

She shrugs, glancing away. "Always wanted to go on vacation. Never got the chance. Cabo seems like as good a place as any."

"So where the hell were you off to if you've got her all set up?"

"I—I don't know. I guess I just needed to do something. I can't sit here and do nothing."

I'm not surprised. It's what's gotten Emma in trouble more than once. She never could sit still. Not to mention how she has the need to save everyone by herself. I blame Sam since she has the same issues. Both of them blaze into situations, assuming shit will just work itself out. Doesn't help Sam when the King brothers step in to clean up the mess.

My gaze snaps to Emma. "For fuck's sake."

"What? Was it Ren?" She peers at her phone, narrowing her eyes as if she can force a notification to appear.

"You learned it from *her*. That's why you never fucking ask for help and assume someone will come along to fix shit. Because they do it for her. Now, you're in this shitshow and you kept expecting someone to show up, but all you got was me. How fucking disappointing for you."

I'm not even pissed anymore. It's how she was raised. The Kings spoiled her. Sam passed on all her horrible traits to her. Emma's a product of her environment. I wonder what she would have become had her father lived through the attempted coup twenty years ago. To be fair, she'd probably be dead. Or he would have sold her off to the highest bidder to become a mafia wife.

I snort as I make my way around the island, leaving Emma to mull over my words. We'll need to continue the conversation, but I refuse to do it in a towel. The minute she licks her lips or exposes the long column of her neck, my cock will announce its presence. It's not something I'll be able to hide as well with a thin piece of fabric between us. I'll end up throwing her onto the counter and fucking her, and we'll never finish talking.

"I wasn't disappointed to see you," she murmurs as I'm pulling on my underwear, and I glance over my shoulder. She leans against the door frame, her unfocused gaze fixed on the wall.

"Why don't we agree to stop lying to each other, Emma? Doesn't seem like there's a point now."

"Was there ever a point?"

I shake my head, yanking my pants over my hips. "Sometimes it was the only way to keep you safe."

"You remember when the Guild took me?"

"Yeah. What about it?" I search for a shirt among the mass of clothes scattered across the floor.

"Did you ever wonder how I got home?" she whispers.

I freeze, then slowly straighten. I don't like remembering the times she was kidnapped. When the Guild swept through Synd, she was thirteen and thought she was invincible. I was barely eighteen and had just been moved to the Kings' residence. I was terrified of fucking up and getting dismissed. I wasn't even worried about them floating me. Death would have been preferable to being told I wasn't good enough.

I almost threw up when Shane King handed me Emma's sobbing form while they went to take down the Guild. He'd handed me someone who was the most important thing in his life. And I was supposed to keep her safe. The responsibility almost broke me. I didn't know how to help her or the guilt she felt at getting caught sneaking back into Synd when she was supposed to be safe at her great-aunt's house. It wasn't the worst thing we've been through, but it's up there.

"I didn't. I was more concerned with making sure you were never taken again."

"And you succeeded where no one else could." She lets out a humorless laugh. "Until we went our separate ways, that is."

I don't like to think about that time either. It's never fun to be woken in the middle of the night with an emergency. It's even less fun when it's a frantic mafia boss begging me to find her. It's the closest I've ever seen Alex King in tears. I glance at Emma, then tug my shirt on. I wonder if she knows it was me who found her that night. Probably not. She was unconscious by the time I got to her. And I was gone by the time she woke up. I wasn't her handler at that point and wasn't needed after I rescued her.

"How did you get home after Sam got you out?" I ask when I stop in front of her.

She glances up, blinking to dispel the shadows from her eyes. "There was a guy hanging outside the Depot. Didn't look like he belonged with the Guild. I ran from him, obviously. I may have been naive, but I wasn't *that* naive. He chased after me, pinned me to a wall—"

"Who?" I growl as my hands curl into fists.

"Oh. No." She holds her hands up, a nervous chuckle leaving her. "No, not like that. He just needed me to listen, but I wasn't capable of it. Everyone was a threat. Hell, Helms or Byrns could have walked up and I would have lost it. But he said he was your friend."

"I don't have friends."

She snorts, crossing her arms again. "Sure you don't. He might not have said friend. It was ten fucking years ago, so I don't remember. But he *did* know you. Said he'd help me if I'd stop screaming."

"Tell me you didn't listen to him," I groan, scrubbing my hands down my face.

"Course I didn't. Except I wasn't trained, and I had like no meat on my bones. So it wasn't very hard for him to pick me up and toss me in the back seat of his car parked a few blocks away. He kept talking, telling me about you two being in the same section of the city. Told me some of your escapades. He couldn't go too deep into King territory, but he brought me across the river, dropped me outside the Barrens and told me to run. So I did." Her gaze lifts, searching for something I doubt she'll find.

"What does that have to do with Daisy?" Because that's where this all started. We've skipped from topic to topic, never fully finishing anything.

"Nothing. You accused me of starting shit I can't finish and expecting someone else to come along and save the day. And I do. You're right. I probably am spoiled and a brat and used to other people helping me. But that's because I grew up in a family who did that. Especially now. If I wanted to, I could call up a dozen people and they'd drop everything to help me. Because that's what family does. We help each other. I guess I just don't understand why you thought you weren't a part of that equation." She shakes her head gently as she turns away.

"Because I'm not," I wheeze as my chest tightens. "I've only ever been dispensable. I know my place, Emma, and it isn't a part of your family."

"Are you sure about that? Because from where I'm standing, all I see is you. Out of all the people they could send to help me, they sent *you*. Do you really think Shane, asshole extraordinaire, would really have let you off the hook all those years ago if he didn't trust you?"

Frustration builds inside me the more she refuses to listen. She has this sunshine and roses outlook on life. At least for a mafia life. The fact she can't see what's right in front of her is infuriating.

I have never been a part of her world. Her family is a million miles from mine. She never gets it through her head that I'll never be accepted. Not like her. And I don't begrudge her for that. I just wanted a seat at the table. Hell, I just wanted to be in the room. Even if I was guarding the door, at least I was in the room. I've finally gotten there and I'll do everything in my power to stay there.

"I don't doubt he trusts me. Even when I was younger, he trusted me to take care of you." I swallow hard, running my hand through my hair. "It's my job,

Emma. Not just before. This has always been my job—to take care of the King family. Protect the Kings. I take that seriously. Doesn't mean the sentiment flows both ways. If I die, they'll replace me without a thought. Which is fine. I don't expect to be anything other than an employee to them. Don't make this more than it is." I can't think of anything else to say—any other way to get through to her. If she doesn't understand now, she probably never will.

Tears fill her eyes and my hand twitches by my side. She glances away, angrily swiping at the wetness on her cheeks. I don't know why she cares so fucking much. I didn't make her any promises. We agreed whatever happened between us was temporary. I should have known sleeping with her would bring up the tangled emotions of the past. I should have run as far away as possible from her.

"Good to know," she whispers before turning around and walking away.

I let her go.

Chapter 39

Emma

Pretending nothing happened between Titus and me isn't easy. It eats away at me, bit by bit, crumbling my resolve to accept the role he's shoved me into. It's not as painful as it was all those years ago. Eventually, it'll burst from me, though. Hopefully, I'll have someone to take my rage out on.

"Don't worry, Daisy. I talked to your mom, and while she's incredibly disappointed in me, she understands the urgency. You're leaving tomorrow morning in case someone is watching you," I say for the third time.

"Why is she disappointed in you? She loves you. You're like her favorite person." Daisy's voice echoes, and I realize she's in the bathroom again. She's taken to locking herself in there while she stays at the hotel. I told her she didn't need to, but if it makes her feel safer, so be it.

I chuckle, shaking my head. "Maybe because I lied to her? Or put her only daughter in danger? Oh, or it could be because my family is a bunch of glorified criminals. Just a guess, though."

The front door opens and Titus walks in with food. I track his movements as he sets the alarm, then starts unloading the bags. He insisted on going to the restaurant to pick it up since salads are disgusting and he wasn't about to taste test mine. I stopped arguing with him about potentially poisoning himself. Actually, I stopped arguing with him about everything. We've been tiptoeing around each other. The tension that once sat in the air has shifted into an uneasy silence between us, and I hate it.

Not that I'll do shit to change it. Once we deal with Calvin's boss, whoever he is, maybe we'll clear the air. Or we'll go our separate ways like I thought before. I focus on Daisy again, realizing she's been babbling this entire time.

"You weren't listening, were you?"

I wince, shoving from the couch to slip into the bedroom. "Sorry. Start over."

"Nah, it was mostly me just complaining about my mom blaming you. It wasn't important." She pauses and I brace myself. "Is he there?"

"Yup."

"Is he looking fine as hell still?"

"Yup." I plop onto the bed. "No, we haven't talked. No one has stabbed anyone. And no, we still haven't figured out a plan."

"I suppose we have had the same conversation every day, huh?"

"That we have," I murmur as Titus fills the door frame. "I have to go eat, but I want you to text me before you go to bed and again when you wake up. Every time you—"

"Get naked?" Her giggles fill the line, easing some of the tension in my shoulders. I'm going to need a week-long massage after this is over.

"Yes, Daisy. Every time you get naked, please text me. Pictures aren't required. My imagination is enough to fulfill my deepest desires."

Titus smirks before spinning around and collapsing on the couch. A twinge of pain settles near my heart, and I glance away.

"Whatever you wish, I shall provide," Daisy says, snapping me out of the sudden morose mood.

I bite my lip, knowing she'll hang up soon. "Stay safe. I'm sorry, Daisy."

"Fuck you and stop apologizing. I'm fine. I'll talk to you tomorrow. Love you."

The line goes dead, and I swallow down the tears threatening to overwhelm me. I don't have the energy to break down. I hate feeling like this—like I'm not doing enough. Like I've fucked everything up. Like I can't fix anything. Guilt and shame are my constant companions. With Titus constantly watching me when he thinks I'm not looking, I'm about to snap. I don't have it in me to wallow. If I spiral, I might not pull myself out again.

I grab my salad from the coffee table and find dressing already on it. I shake the container as I pace around the living room, wishing I would have bought a stool or something. No one ever comes to my apartment, so I never needed more seating. Eating next to him on the couch is a lesson in patience and awkward as hell.

"Sit down, Emma. I'm getting nauseous just watching you." Titus stuffs a forkful of pasta in his mouth.

I shake the container aggressively once more, then collapse on the couch. We eat in silence just as we have every other meal. I tried to talk to him after he convinced me not to go after Daisy. After I attempted to tell him how important he was to the Kings. After he told me not to make more of *this* than what it is. I got the memo, yet I still tried, and he shut me out.

So I gave up. I stopped trying because what's the point? He doesn't want to talk about anything. We slept in the same bed last night. I woke up with his arm over my waist, holding me close to his hard body. I soaked in the feel of him for as long as I could. Too soon he woke up and immediately rolled away, straight off the bed. I might sleep on the couch tonight just to avoid a repeat.

"I'm meeting Joy later. You can come if you want," he says, then shoves more food in his mouth.

"Okay," I mumble, focusing on my salad. With that rousing invitation, how could I possibly resist?

I'm only halfway through my food when Titus's phone buzzes and he checks it. He tosses the rest of his garlic bread into his empty container and pushes to his feet. He disappears into the bathroom and seconds later, the shower starts up. My appetite plummets, and I toss the rest of the salad in the trash.

Even though I want to be petty and refuse to go, I can't. Whatever Joy has to say will be important. I'm not going to rely on someone who isn't really speaking to me to convey vital information. I could call Joy myself, but I'm not about to come between her and Titus. She stitched me up, and I spilled some random story. That doesn't make us friends. Clearly, since she didn't bother to text me about this meeting.

I wander into my bedroom and change. I don't know what we're walking into, so I add my dagger to my thigh. Wincing, I press a hand to my side when my wound throbs. Titus cut out the stitches last night. He didn't want to, insisting they needed to stay for another couple days. It wasn't until I threatened to do it myself he gave in. It was the longest conversation we've had in three days.

My head hits the closet door and I close my eyes. Everything is unraveling around me, yet the more I try to catch the stray threads, the more they slip through my fingers. Nothing I do fixes things. My actions merely make things worse.

Maybe it would be best for everyone if I just stepped back. I'm terrified someone will get hurt. Daisy is already running for her life. Next time someone might die. And regardless of what Titus says, my brothers would disown me if I got him killed.

Still, I can't handle staying home alone. I didn't use to care about those types of things. Loneliness didn't plague me like it does others. I enjoyed the quiet. No mindless small talk, no worrying about waking anyone, no cleaning up after someone else. It was perfect. Until Titus came and burst my bubble of silence. Now, I hate being by myself. It's probably why I want to go with him. It's not Titus, it's just the crushing vacuum of emptiness.

"Titus?" I call as I make my way into the living room.

The bathroom door hangs open and he's nowhere to be found. Rage boils within me, fueling my rampage through the apartment. The fucking bastard left me. It's not like I told him to go without me. I said okay, for fuck's sake. Goddamn asshole. Just when I thought we might be getting somewhere, he pulls a bitch-ass move like this.

I'm practically snarling while I dial his number. Of course he doesn't pick up. He's too fucking scared to face me after his cowardly retreat. And to think I tried to convince him he was part of the family. That he meant more than just another body to protect the Kings. Family doesn't sneak off in the dead of night after inviting someone along for the ride.

"I'm going to fucking stab him," I growl as I pull up Joy's number.

A frustrated groan leaves me when her phone goes to voicemail after too many rings. I'm so pissed off as I leave the apartment, I almost forget to set the alarm. After I set it, I trip down the stairs, hoping I don't break my neck. I don't blame Joy for not answering, but Titus? If he didn't want me to go, then he should have just said so. It's not the first time he's gone off by himself and left me behind. But that was years ago, and I was a teenager—impulsive, brash, and untrained. I'm none of those things now. Well, mostly none of those things.

The cold autumn air hits me as soon as I step outside, and I pull up the hood of my sweatshirt. Stuffing my hands in the front pocket, I grip my gun. I don't like to use them as much as my dagger, and I wonder what that says about me. I used to flinch at the sharp report, though I grew out of that reaction. Still don't like them much.

I assume Titus won't be expecting me to pop up at Joy's plant store. If they're not there, I'll be fucked. No way am I wandering around Ridgewood to find them. Giving up isn't usually in my nature, but it's fucking cold out. I value warmth over most things. Every alleyway I pass has another burst of wind hitting me, sending a chill across my body. This was a terrible idea. He's still an asshole, but I could have just waited to yell at him when he got back.

"Shit." A man's voice floats from the alley ahead when I'm only a few blocks from Joy's store.

I freeze, scanning the area for a hiding spot or a way up. Most people rarely look up when they're doing something shitty. The brick buildings aren't equipped with fire escapes and most of the pipes are broken. I sidle closer to the wall and shuffle toward the opening. He's muttering under his breath, then groans.

When I make it to the corner, I peek into the alley and suck in a sharp breath. Devon's head snaps up, but it's too dark to make out his features.

"Emma?" he calls. "Emma, I need help. She's hurt."

My nerves ease, and I step into the opening. He cradles a woman's body, stepping toward me slowly. My breath rushes out of me when the streetlight washes over her face.

"Joy. What the hell happened?" I cry, rushing to meet him.

"I don't know. I was walking to your place to check on you and I heard footsteps down the alley." He gestures behind him with his shoulder. "I went to investigate and found her passed out. I think whoever did this ran when they heard me."

I peer over his shoulder at the quiet street beyond. Not a single soul moves through the shadows. Whoever hurt Joy is long gone. I glance back at Devon's distraught face.

"We should get her to the hospital. My phone is dead. Can you call the police?" He walks around me as Joy's head lolls against his arm.

I hurry after him, then skid in front of him, blocking the way. "No. She wouldn't want that. Just...let me see her."

"This isn't something we should mess with, Emma. I'm taking her to the hospital," he snarls, and my stomach tightens. I don't think I've ever heard him so insistent.

"Put her down, Devon. I need to see her injuries." I point at his feet, and he gives me a peculiar look before lowering her to the ground.

He whips off his sweatshirt and tucks it under her head. I brush Joy's hair away from her face and find flecks of blood. It doesn't look like it's coming from her ear, though. Thank fuck for that. Gently, I run my fingers over her head, searching for a lump. Leaning down, I breathe deeply and a bitter smell emanates from her. It's stolen away by the wind before I can figure out what it is.

I pat her down, hunting for some type of injury. Her body curls when I reach her ribs and I figure she's bruised, if not broken, at least one of them. Joy groans, rolling onto her side, yet her eyes stay firmly closed.

"Why were you coming to my place so late?" I ask, and his spine straightens.

"I haven't heard from you. I was worried when you didn't answer my texts. You might be able to turn off all your feelings, but I can't, Emma. Do you think we should have this conversation later?"

We probably should, but there's not much I can do for Joy. She doesn't have any physical injuries I can see. I can't help her if I don't know what's wrong. I pull my phone from my pocket and send a text to Titus, since I doubt he'll answer my call. Hopefully, he didn't block me. Wouldn't put it past him, though.

"I'm sorry. It's just..." I sigh, contemplating whether I'll be able to carry her.

"It's just what? You don't think *I* did this, do you?" he snaps, hurt filtering through his tone.

"No. Of course not. It's just a strange coincidence." I press my lips together, not willing to say more. Ren always said there's no such thing as coincidences. I can't connect things together like he can. He'd be able to see the pattern—the pieces I'm missing. A pang of homesickness hits me, and I focus on Joy. She's the one who needs help.

I glance at Devon, who still looks offended. "Can you carry her to my apartment?"

I don't want him in my space. I don't want Titus to come back and find Devon there. I don't want to open the door to him and give him hope. There's no other choice. With my wound barely healed, I'll end up dropping her. He nods and I push to my feet. As Devon follows me through the night, I hope I'm not making yet another mistake.

Chapter 40

Titus

By the time I reach Emma's apartment, my patience has unraveled. Joy never showed at our meeting point. Everything was dark and quiet when I went by the shop. I didn't have any other leads on where she might be. I've focused so much on Emma I haven't done my due diligence when it comes to the area. We haven't discussed in depth the structure of the organization trying to take over Ridgewood, either.

I've been woefully lax. Just another example of why getting involved with Emma is a terrible idea. We're no good for each other in any capacity despite the chemistry still building between us. I've neglected everything else in favor of her. Ren told me to take care of whatever is going on here. Clearly, a gang is trying to take over. Normally, I wouldn't care. With the threat to Emma and them possibly following her back to Synd, it's something we need to squash before it grows.

Annoyance bubbles within me as I climb the stairs. She's going to be pissed. I left her behind on purpose. I couldn't stand the silence from the last few days, and I didn't need to worry about her. The last time she was out, she got stabbed. I'm not willing to put her at risk again. It might not have been the best idea to not say anything, but I'll just have to deal with her temper tantrum.

I slide the key into the lock, then freeze. Pressing my ear to the door, I try to decipher the mumbled words coming through the door. I wouldn't put it past Joy to come here if something went down. Why she wouldn't text me to give me a heads-up is beyond me. My annoyance bleeds into full-on irritation as I swing the door open.

"She should have woken up by now," Twitch mumbles, and my gaze zeroes in on his hand resting on Emma's shoulder. She's crouching next to the couch, Joy's motionless body hidden by them.

Emma pushes his hand off her as I stalk across the room. My hand latches onto the back of Devon's neck. Ignoring his cries, I force his head down. When he attempts to break free, I squeeze, putting pressure on his arteries. It's not enough for him to pass out, but he stops trying to break free.

"What the hell, Titus? What are you doing?" Emma yells. I expect her to jump up and stop me from hauling his ass to the door. Instead, she stays by the couch as she wipes a wet washcloth over Joy's face.

"Taking the trash out."

When we reach the kitchen, Twitch spins out of my hold and faces me. I almost laugh when he attempts to square up, his red face and flaring nostrils creating a delightful picture of ineptitude.

"Seriously, Devon? Stop this," Emma says, exasperation in her voice.

"Stay out of it, Emma. This has been coming for a long fucking time," Devon snarls as he holds his fists in front of his face.

A frustrated groan leaves her. "He's six inches taller than you and outweighs you by at least fifty pounds. He'll pulverize you. Just go."

I didn't think it was possible, but Devon's face reddens even more. He drops his fists to his sides and leans around to glare at her. I swear to fuck if he says one goddamn word, I'm going to knock his ass out. I may just fucking kill him for the hell of it.

"Why the fuck are you taking his side?"

"I'm not taking his side," she cries. "There are no sides."

I bite my tongue, letting him dig the hole a little deeper. If he crosses the line, it'll be a race between Emma and me of who gets to him first. Unless she chickens out yet again. I won't have any issues, though.

"Are you fucking him? Is that what's going on here?"

I step into his space, and his gaze snaps back to me. "Watch it, Twitch. You're on thin fucking ice."

His lip curls, darkness swirling in his eyes as he whispers, "She's mine."

"Go, Devon. Before you say something you'll regret," Emma calls, unaware of what Twitch said. I wonder if she'd agree after everything he's done—after everything between us.

He tips his chin up and steps back. Usually, I'd mock him for backing down so easily. It's a lesson in patience, but I need to let Emma handle this. If I keep stepping in to save her, she'll never learn how to do it herself. I coddled her just like everyone else. Fully walking away isn't an option, but I can force her to deal with this fucking douchebag.

"When you're done being his whore, let me know," he sneers.

My fist is flying before he's even finished. I connect with his face and blood flies from his nose. Emma, to her credit, doesn't shriek like I imagined she would. She huffs behind me while Twitch twitches on the floor, holding the injury. I snort, smirking as Emma steps next to me. She tilts her head, scowling down at him.

"What the hell are you giggling about? Did you have to fucking hit him?" she snaps.

"Twitch is twitching. And yes, I did."

She sighs, crouching down. "Stop it, Devon. It's not that bad. And you brought it upon yourself. I told you to go and you didn't. I'll get you an ice pack and then you'll go."

She straightens and makes her way to the kitchen. As she searches through the freezer, I bury the toe of my boot in his stomach. He groans, curling his arms around his waist.

"Knock it off, Titus." She's scolding me, yet the corner of her lip twitches as if she's holding back a smile.

She hands Twitch the ice pack. "Up. He didn't even break your nose. We need to take care of Joy."

I swing around, torn between helping my friend and making sure Emma's taken care of. Devon mumbles something as Emma crouches in front of him. If she doesn't end this soon, I will. She stands, her body closer than I expected.

I lean down, whispering in her ear, "Want me to kill him? I'll drop his body in the same woods I—"

"That's enough," she hisses.

Devon scrambles to his feet, hurt warring with betrayal sitting in his light brown eyes. "Emma, you're clearly in danger here. Come with me."

Emma's shoulders slump. "I can't. Just go, Devon."

Devon's gaze meets mine over Emma's head. "Don't worry, Emma. He can't threaten you forever. I'll be back. And next time, I'm taking you with me."

"Is that a threat?" I growl, itching to hit him again. This time I will break his face. He'll have more to deal with than a bit of blood and two black eyes.

"A promise."

He pivots and marches out the door, slamming it behind him. Emma puffs out a breath and wraps her arms around her waist. I'm not about to comfort her. It's her fault she has shitty choice in men. The more I see from Twitch, the more I realize he's a complete non-threat. He's all talk and nothing else. I make my way to Joy and drop to my knees. My hands hover over her, not sure where to start.

"What happened to her?" I ask, glancing over my shoulder at Emma, still frozen where I left her.

"I don't know. She woke up for a minute, then fell asleep. I think she was drugged or something. I don't think she's in danger. Her breathing isn't labored. Heart rate is fine. No blood. Probably a couple bruised ribs, but not much more. She had some flecks of blood on her face, by her left ear. I couldn't find a source, so it might have been her attacker's." She lists everything off like she's reciting a grocery list. I'd take offense at her lack of emotion if we hadn't been here before.

We may not share much, but we did grow up in the same world. There isn't a lot of room for emotions. People get hurt. People die. It's an unalterable part of our lives we'll never get away from. I'm surprised Emma isn't freaking out like she was when I was sick, though. Then again, she doesn't have a connection to Joy. They're not friends by design. I needed someone here to keep an eye on shit. If they would have met, I would have lost my eyes and ears in Ridgewood.

"How did Twitch end up here?"

"You really should stop calling him that," she sighs. "He found her in an alley a couple blocks from her shop. Said he was on his way to check on me."

I didn't realize she knew where the chop shop was. Or that Joy's plant store was the front for it. I shouldn't be surprised, but I wonder if she followed me whenever I went there.

I shove to my feet and face her. "You're telling me you just stumbled upon him, crouched in an alleyway with an unconscious woman, and your first thought was to fucking believe him?"

She spins around, glaring at me. "Yes. Because I dated him for almost three fucking years. Go ahead and think I'm a poor judge of character. Or a vapid, bratty girl without a thought in her head. I don't fucking care. Maybe you could put your goddamn jealousy aside for one fucking second and think maybe I know him better than you."

"He called you a fucking whore," I roar, and she flinches as if I've slapped her.

"I'm aware. I'm also aware of the fact he thinks you're blackmailing me. He doesn't know the full story, so I'm sure it would look that way from his point of view."

"Stop fucking defending him. What the fuck is wrong with you? What in the hell did he do to you? This isn't you, Emma. For fuck's sake. You're not a spineless fool taken in by shitty men with their ridiculous excuses. Get your fucking shit together or I'm dealing with the rest of this shit alone."

"Seems as if you've already made up your mind about that," she says softly, a familiar mask slipping over her features, and I know I've lost her.

I run a hand through my hair. The only way I've been able to crack through her mask is to piss her off more. I push her right to the edge, hoping she'll fight back. I can't bring myself to do it now. Too much has happened between us.

Too much has changed. I can't keep hurting her and expecting her not to break. One of these days, I'll shove her over the cliff with no way to save her if I do.

"What do we do about Joy?" I ask.

"She's your friend. I think she'll be fine, but I'm not a doctor." Her voice is still emotionless, grating on my nerves.

"She found a drop point. Some men were hanging around. They took off, and I tried to follow them, but they just went to a strip club. I don't know what else Joy wanted to tell me."

"I'm leaving tomorrow. I'm going to check on Daisy before she leaves."

"The hell you are," I snarl as she makes her way to her bedroom.

Joy coughs. "Would you two knock it the fuck off? I'm trying to sleep here."

Our bickering forgotten, Emma rushes to Joy's side and shoves me out of the way. She drops to her knees and grips her thighs as if she wants to grab the other woman yet is holding herself back.

"How do you feel? Does anything hurt? Did you see anything? Where exactly were you going?" Emma's questions pile on top of one another, barely a breath in between them.

"Let the woman breathe for fuck's sake," I mutter, although I'm hovering too.

Joy waves us away. "I'm fine. Woozy. A little lightheaded. I didn't see who it was. Cloth over the mouth like a fucking thriller movie. He wasn't much taller than me, but definitely male."

I open my mouth, but Emma beats me to it. "What did the cloth smell like?"

"That's the question you're asking?" I close my eyes, tipping my head back.

"Like nuts and something floral? You thinking cyanide?" Joy says.

"Maybe. I'd assume you'd be sicker, though. That shit can put your ass in a coma," Emma says, her brows pulling low.

Joy grunts as she pulls her shoulders to her ears. "Probably mixed it with something so that wouldn't happen. The question is—why?"

Emma glances at me, then back at Joy. "I have some ideas."

Chapter 41

Emma

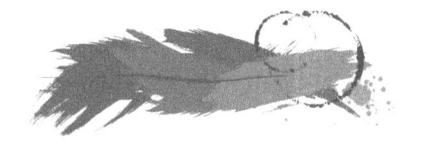

"You can't go by yourself, Joy," Titus growls, posting up in front of the door.

I snort, meeting her gaze. "As if that's going to stop her from leaving. She could just go out the fire escape."

Joy smirks, crossing her arms. "I'm perfectly capable of walking in the middle of the day by myself. No one is going to attack me. And if they do, I'll be able to fight them off."

He rolls his eyes. "Like you did before?"

"Don't be a dick, Titus." I glare at him, mirroring Joy's stance.

I understand his need to keep her safe. It's in his nature, hammered into him from his years of service to the King family. He doesn't know how to turn it off. Doesn't mean he has to treat her like she's not capable of taking care of herself. Last night's circumstances were much different. And it doesn't give him a right to snap at her like he does me.

"I'm going to the shop. Without you," Joy says.

"At least take Emma with you."

I barely contain my surprise at him offering me up in his stead. I study his face, then burst into laughter. He scowls at me, and Joy shoots me a questioning look.

"Uh, are you okay?" Joy asks hesitantly.

I hiccup, fanning my face. "Yup. I can totally take you home. Just two women taking a stroll during the day. Totally not going to have a shadow lurking behind us just out of sight to make sure we make it safely."

Joy's chin juts out as she glares at Titus. If he keeps grinding his teeth, he's going to have problems later. I doubt he'd appreciate the advice, though. He seems a bit put out, seeing as how I figured out his plan.

"I wasn't going to—"

"Oh, you totally were. Like hell you'd let me walk back by myself." I turn around and plop onto the couch. "Just move, Titus. She'll be fine. And she's going to message us when she gets there. And she's not going to go out alone until we can figure out how everything is connected."

"Pretty fucking clear. Calvin's boss is after you, saw Joy coming here the other night, attacked Joy to get to you," he snaps, and I try to not take it personally.

He's so used to blaming me for every little thing, this won't be any different. At least he's no longer giving me the silent treatment. I wish we were still sleeping together. I could just fuck his shitty attitude away. As I eye him, I doubt he'd be down for it. We've moved past the point of falling into bed together to deal with the sexual tension. He probably has different reasons for shutting me out. I'm sure his heart doesn't fit into the equation at all.

"They could be going after *you*," Joy says when I don't respond. "You did kill Calvin. And you were at the drug lab when Emma was stabbed. Who knows what else you've gotten yourself into that's put you on their radar."

Titus throws up his hands and stalks to the bedroom. Joy snorts when he slams the door. I stretch out on the couch, burrowing into the sunken cushions. I might as well get comfortable since he'll be sulking in there for a while.

"I'm going then. Try to not get stabbed and let me know if you go out later." Joy's boots clomp across the floorboards.

My eyes flutter closed. "Try not to get drugged again."

The door closes behind her, cutting off her chuckle. I should set the alarms, but I can't move my arms. I'm used to running off little to no sleep. Being stabbed and spending most of my nights running off mostly adrenaline hasn't helped, though. A nap will do me good. I teeter on the edge of sleep when I groan and reach for my phone to secure the apartment. The last thing I want is Devon busting in here to scold me again.

I wish I could just cut him off. I'm still banking on him eventually giving up. He can't seriously expect me to come crawling back to him after calling me a whore. I have more self respect than that. Then again, Devon doesn't really know me. Not truly. Guilt eats away at me when I start adding up all the things I kept from him.

It was more than just who my family is. He doesn't even know my real last name. He doesn't know I can kill a man with my bare hands. Hell, he doesn't know my personality. I kept it all hidden, worried I'd blow my cover. I became what was expected of me. Forcing myself into the role of docile creature he expected me to be became too normal. The only way I survived was by going out at night. I kept my sense of self by flitting through the shadows. Explaining it to Titus wouldn't help. He doesn't fucking care *why* I was sneaking around, just that I was. It was supposed to be fun—something to keep my identity and keep up my skills.

"Burning it," Titus whispers as he slips my phone from my hand.

"Alarm," I murmur, and he grunts.

I don't know what that means, but I can't be bothered to ask. His arms slide under me and I groan, wishing he'd leave me be. He lifts me, and I can't help but snuggle closer. We're in a weird limbo. Doesn't mean I want to push him away. I wish we could be something more.

As he cradles me against his body, I finally admit to myself I want more. I want the future I once dreamed of. It wasn't even him specifically. I want someone to see all of me and want me anyway. Then Titus waltzed back into my life, and he did. Even if he doesn't agree with my decisions, at least he accepts who I am. He doesn't try to get me to change. He doesn't try to control me. Not like Devon wants to. Devon wants the perfect little girlfriend who will morph into the perfect little wife and then the perfect little mother. I'll never be that and I never wanted to be.

My body sinks into the mattress as he sets me down. I want to ask him to stay. I don't want to wake up alone. Pleading with him would be pathetic. I roll onto my side, ignoring the urge to beg him to just be with me.

"Not pathetic, darling," he murmurs as his heat seeps into my back.

His arm wraps around my waist, holding me close to him. I don't know how long I doze, but he never moves. By the time I open my eyes, I feel pathetic. I'm not the type of person to beg someone to spend time with me. Devon said it was emotional manipulation when I asked him to bring me food. I never asked him for anything ever again. This feels dangerously close to that. Titus might not be easy to convince, but now that we've blurred the lines of our relationship, I'm afraid I'm using my pain as a way to control him.

"Don't," he mumbles, burying his nose into my hair.

"Don't what?" I whisper.

"Stop thinking. It's fucking annoying."

I roll my eyes. "It's annoying when I think?"

"Mhm. You fall down a rabbit hole and make up all sorts of shit that isn't true. So, don't." His fingers flex against my side. He's practically cupping my tit, his thumb between them.

"I wasn't going down a rabbit hole," I huff.

He sighs, then pushes his knee between my legs. "Then what were you thinking about? The weather? Perhaps the price of beef?"

"Who the hell thinks about the price of beef?"

"Farmers, asshole."

I wince, scrambling to come up with something when all I can think about is cows. "I was wondering why pterodactyl is spelled with a P instead of just a T. Shellie would probably know. She's an English major, so I assume she took a class or something."

"Try again," he murmurs as his thumb brushes across my skin, inching closer to my nipple with each stroke.

My breath catches in my throat and I silently cough. "Fine. I was thinking about pumpkins."

He chuckles, his chest rumbling behind me. "What about pumpkins?"

"Did you know sitars are made out of pumpkins? Well, more like a gourd, but that's in the pumpkin family. And to think we only carve them up or use them to decorate the dinner table. Not we as in you and me, obviously. We've never carved pumpkins."

"Is that your subtle way of asking to carve pumpkins with me?" His lips brush my neck and I shiver.

I clear my throat. "No."

"Of course you weren't. Because that's not what you were worrying about." He pinches my nipple and I jolt. "Tell me."

"I didn't think we were doing this anymore," I whisper, and he hums. "I shouldn't have asked you to stay."

He freezes, then props himself on his elbow. I refuse to look him in the eye. I didn't want to have this conversation in the first place. It's fucking embarrassing to admit I'm lonely. Especially to Titus. With his opinions of me, he'll probably tell me how ridiculous I'm being.

His fingers grip my chin and force my head to the side. "First of all, you barely asked me. You mumbled it in your sleep. And second of all, who said we were done?"

"Actions speak louder than words, Titus."

"Is that so?"

I should be worried, what with his raised brow and the glint in his eyes. I open my mouth to respond, but he swoops down. His lips crash into mine and I gasp. It only allows him to deepen the kiss, and his tongue tangles with mine.

He breaks away, leaving both of us panting. Seconds later, he's rolling me onto my stomach and ripping my panties from my body. A shiver of anticipation hits me as he tosses the covers aside. He grips my hips, forcing me onto my knees, my face smashed into the pillow.

A moan leaves me when he buries his tongue in my pussy. I push back when he sucks my clit between his lips and his fingers dig into my hips, probably leaving bruises behind. I don't care. He can mark me all he wants as long as he doesn't stop whatever the hell he's doing with his tongue. My legs tremble, my entire body vibrating as I inch closer to the edge. My orgasm is just out of reach when he pulls away, leaving me bereft and empty.

I cry out, cursing him, though he probably can't understand me. He nudges my legs apart, then slams into me. His grunts fill the room, mingling with my groans as he thrusts into me over and over.

"Is this clear enough for you, darling?" he grits out, and I whimper as ecstasy crashes over me.

My entire body shudders, yet he doesn't stop. My pussy spasms around him and his hand lands on my ass with a sharp crack. The burning pain turns to pleasure as he rubs the mark he's surely left behind.

"Answer the question," he growls. His hand comes down again on the other side and I come again, pleasure surging through me.

"Yes," I rasp.

"Yes, what?" He smacks me again, and I arch my back as I thrash underneath him.

"Yes, sir," I howl, flames sparking along my skin.

He surges into me, harder and faster than before. I don't know if I have it in me to come again. I'm spent, floating on a cloud of pleasure. I don't want him to stop, though. I want more. More of him. More of everything he's willing to give me. Hell, he could request anything and I'd probably give it to him.

He pulls out of me, and I yelp as he flips me on my back. My eyes fly open, gazing up at him as he grabs behind my knees and forces my legs up. He surges into me again, his jaw tight as he clenches his teeth.

His dark eyes meet mine, desire swimming in them. "Play with your clit. Make yourself come on my cock."

My fingers slip between my legs and find the sensitive bud. He watches as I circle it, my breath catching in my throat as a desperate need overtakes me. Another orgasm builds in me, and I glance down to watch his cock disappear into my pussy.

He drops one of my legs and wraps his hand around my throat. My gaze flies to his when he forces my chin up. It's not enough to cut off my air, thank fuck.

"Be a good girl and come for me," he growls, and I explode.

He follows me into oblivion, groaning as I quiver around him. Sparks ignite along my flesh as he runs his hands up and down my body, murmuring under his breath. I can't hear them over the roaring in my ears. He drops his forearms on either side of my head and presses kisses to my overheated skin wherever he can reach. He rolls his hips once, then twice, and my pussy responds, spasming around him.

"Was that clear enough?" he mumbles as he buries his face in my neck. A sigh is my only response.

Chapter 42

Titus

I'm completely fucked.

I knew it when I told Calvin he touched what was mine. I knew it when I had my fingers buried in Emma's cunt. I knew it when I tasted her. It wasn't solidified until I told her she belonged to me. She ignored my statement, probably not wanting to put any stock in my words since I'd just made her come. I didn't plan to say it, but I won't take the statement back. It took me a few days to process, but I'm determined to keep her in my life. It's probably the worst idea I've ever had and I won't be able to follow through.

Getting away from her apartment, from her, is exactly what I needed to clear my head. I don't like leaving her alone, but she's healed enough to deal with things if shit goes down. Helps that she promised not to open the door for Twitch.

The douchebag has been silent since I almost broke his nose. I haven't had to delete any text messages from her phone, and no one's called her except for Daisy. Emma refuses to tell me what the hell is going on with her friend and why she still hasn't left the hotel. She only said there was a delay, but not to worry about it. As if that ever fucking works.

I walk inside Joy's shop, then quickly flip the lock behind me. Only the grow lights illuminate the space and I spot Joy behind the counter. She lifts a hand without looking at me, her face buried in her phone.

"I could have been anyone. You shouldn't leave your door unlocked," I say in way of greeting.

"Except I was watching you on the cameras. You know you walk with a slight limp? I never noticed that before." She sets her phone on the counter and raises an eyebrow.

"Got shot," I grunt as I settle on the stool across from her. She waves her hand for me to continue. "Emma got taken when she was seventeen. I found her, brought her home, then went back to deal with the problem. Got shot in the process. It's fine except when the weather turns."

"You realize you're absolutely fucked, right?"

"Well aware. What did you find out?" Hopefully she'll stop prying into my business and give me the information she didn't want to say over the phone.

She flicks her lip ring over and over as she studies me. "At least you're admitting it now. Although, I'm sure actually telling *her* will be a long time off."

"Focus, Joy. We've got bigger fish to fry other than my relationship."

She straightens, delight splashing across her face. "Oh, we're calling it a relationship now, are we?"

I roll my eyes and pull my phone from my pocket. She snorts as I text Emma, and my leg jiggles until she replies with an alien emoji. I have no idea what the fuck that means, but at least I know it's her. I send back a ghost just to throw her off.

"You realize you're smiling, right?" Joy says, interrupting my thoughts.

"No, I'm not. Tell me what the fuck you called me down here for." I put my phone away, even though it vibrates as I slide it in my pocket.

"Don't go off on me like you do your woman, but I did some recon work. Most of the drop houses and the labs are abandoned. All the drugs are gone. The one warehouse they had didn't have a huge shipment of guns from the looks of it, but they're all gone too. Whoever is behind all this might be pulling out. I doubt it was because of you two. Doesn't make sense."

I cross my arms and glance out the window. "They didn't exactly have a smooth operation. It's almost as if they handed the town over to a spoiled mafia brat to play with. See if they'd be able to start shit on their own and run it."

"Well, that backfired," she retorts.

"I don't know about that. Emma said she'd been snooping around for a couple years. They were disorganized, but it's a small-ass town in comparison to Synd or even Harris. Not a lot of opportunities to grow here. Seems like an experiment, if you ask me." I shrug and she tilts her head. I don't have any evidence to support my theory. My phone vibrates again, but I leave it alone.

She taps her finger on the counter, contemplating what I said. "I suppose it's possible. Doesn't really matter, though."

"I think it does. If I'm right, they won't have as many resources at their disposal. They won't have many men. And those who are with them aren't loyal. They'll abandon the leaders at the first sign of trouble."

"Let's hope you're right. Otherwise, we'll have to call in the calvary and we both know how that shit will go down." She crosses her arms again. "There's a house, and I use that term very lightly, out on the edge of town. It's not as massive as the Kings or Byrns mansions, but it's not typical for around here. Been abandoned for a decade or so."

"I don't need a makeshift safe house. Not looking to visit a haunted house, either." If it's been abandoned, it's for sure haunted. I don't fuck with that shit.

She huffs, then snaps her mouth shut when my phone buzzes in rapid succession. "Do you need to get that?"

I pull it out and look at the preview. A mess of emojis that don't make sense greet me. Other than the eggplant. I know what that one means. I shove it back in my pocket. Whatever she needs can wait. She's just fucking bored and thinks I have nothing better to do than chitchat with her.

"Tell me about the house."

"Okay, don't come at me—"

"Holy fuck, Joy. Just tell me what the fuck is going on," I snarl.

She rolls her eyes. "There's been activity at this abandoned house."

"What kind?" I grip the back of my neck, waiting for the inevitable. She'll say there were lights and it'll turn out to be teenagers fucking around.

"I know what you're thinking. And yes, there's some lights and shit. But also some traffic. A fancy car pulled up less than a week ago and hasn't left the property. No one can find it now, though. The car vanished, yet never drove away."

I fight a smile, hiding it behind my hand, then rub my chin. "So you're saying it's haunted."

"Dammit, Titus. It's not fucking haunted. At least as far as I know. There are cameras hidden in the trees, but it doesn't seem like there's anyone there. No guards or anything." She gives me a look like I should take this seriously.

I trust Joy, but we haven't worked together much. I don't know who she's relying on or how she recons. But I trust her regardless. If she says it's something to check out, then I'll believe her. I'll have to bring Emma with me when I do. No way am I leaving her by herself for that long. Especially since I'll need backup if shit goes sideways.

We spend the next ten minutes going over everything. At least it's in the woods and will give us plenty of tree cover. Joy tried to insist on coming with. I need someone in Ridgewood in case something happens. Plus, she may say she's completely fine, but she keeps rubbing her temples. She refuses to go to the clinic, insisting she just needs pain meds.

"Call me if shit goes down. And don't go rogue," I say as I'm leaving. She waves me off, already buried in her phone.

I'm several blocks away when my phone buzzes again. Sighing, I check it, then read Emma's message again.

I need help.

My feet slow to a stop, and I text her back a question mark. The message could go so many different ways. She could need help with rearranging the living room or be begging for cock. Either one is completely plausible. I shake my head and start walking again. If it was an emergency, she wouldn't be sending a text. She'd be blowing up my phone.

I only make it two more blocks when the night sky lights up orange. Seconds later, a deafening blast rolls over me, and I spin around. My feet are moving before I've made a decision. Another explosion rumbles through the air, a cloud of smoke rising from the direction of the chop shop. Joy never said whether she was leaving and her apartment is over her store. If she's stuck in there...

Pulling my gun from my waist as I run, my breath saws in and out of my lungs. I skid to a stop a block away, making sure whoever blew the building isn't hanging around. I can't help Joy if I'm shot.

It might be a distraction, my mind whispers and I shove the thought away. Emma's capable of taking care of herself. If Joy is trapped inside, I can't let her die. Emma will have to deal with shit until I can get there. I race down the space between two buildings and approach the back of the chop shop cautiously. It's largely untouched so far, but that won't last long.

Shooting the lock off the back door takes three tries and the alarms blare as soon as I bust inside. Smoke curls through the large space, and I cover my face as I weave through the shells of cars half-stripped of anything valuable. We'll lose the entire place. Thank fuck we can afford to. I can't lose Joy, though.

I kick in the door leading to her shop, dashing to the side as the wood gives under my assault. Flames lick along the ceiling, eating at the walls.

"Joy," I yell, squinting into the dark interior. "Joy, where are you?"

I hesitate, pulling up her contact and calling her. If she's not here, I don't want to run straight into a blaze. A coughing fit takes over as the smoke thickens. I crouch, seeking the cooler air near the floor. Over the crackling of the fire destroying the structure, I make out the faint sound of her ringtone. She wouldn't leave her phone behind.

Bracing myself, I pull in a deep breath and hold it before rushing forward, following the jingle. I can't make out her store through the haze, and I wonder if I'm going to be able to find her at all. I search the back room and the air whooshes from my lungs. Coughing, I drop to my knees next to Joy's unconscious body. Blood coats her face along with soot, and I gather her in my arms. Assessing her injuries will have to wait until we're out.

I stumble back down the short hallway, flames licking at my heels. The fire has spread to the shop and it'll blow before long. Thankfully, most of the surrounding buildings are empty as far as I know. I don't have time to search them all, and Joy takes priority. Glancing behind me as I reach the back door, I wheeze out a curse.

As fast as I can without bashing her head on the doorframe, I make it outside to the blessedly cold night air. Seconds later, a series of pops echo through the warehouse as the fire finds the welding tanks. I knew we shouldn't have kept acetylene in the shop. I need to make it as far away as I can before the rest blow or we'll be swept up in the blast.

I gasp, my breath whistling as I duck into an alley. Collapsing against the hard brick, I clutch Joy's lifeless body against mine. I glance from left to right, making sure no one spotted us. My only goal is to get back to Emma's apartment without being seen. Then I can make sure she's okay. My arms tremble and my chest aches as I take off again. It'll be a miracle if I make it without passing out myself.

"Hold on, Joy," I plead under my breath.

I take the back way, avoiding the bright streetlights whenever possible. There's no back door to the apartment, and I peer from the shadows around the corner as a rumble of a motorcycle cuts through the night air. Closing my eyes, I listen for the familiar kick of Emma's bike, but it never comes. The engine cuts off out front, and nerves roll through my body. I swear to fuck if Helms showed up because of Ink, I'm going to fucking lose it. We don't need the president of the Reapers coming in to clean up the messes.

"Stop hiding, Titus," a familiar voice growls, and my shoulders slump.

I step into the light and Ink's eyebrows shoot up.

"Building exploded. She was inside."

"That's not Emma," he mutters, bringing a heavily tattooed hand to her face. "Let's get her inside. Can't fix her out here."

He lumbers inside, holding the door open for me before stomping to the elevator. I don't even fucking care at this point. Joy's been out too long, and I won't be able to carry her up the stairs. It takes longer than usual to reach the top, and I'm wheezing by the time the door slides open. Ink rushes forward and I wonder how he knows where Emma lives. When he punches in the code for the alarm, I wonder who the hell told him. If Ren did, then he'll be here soon.

"Put her on the couch," he grunts. "Then go grab my bag from my bike."

I set her down, my eyes fixed on her chest. It rises and falls shallowly. At least I think it is. It hits me then how quiet the house is. Glancing around, all I see is darkness.

"Emma?" I call, stomping toward the bedroom. It's empty, and I make my way to the bathroom, my heart pounding in my chest.

"Get my bag, Titus, and call Emma. She probably went to get food. You know that girl loves to eat." He doesn't bother to turn, expecting me to follow his directions.

He doesn't understand. I told Emma to stay put. I'm not even late. We came to an agreement. I wouldn't have been surprised at her skipping out before, but after our conversation earlier, she promised. If there's one thing Emma won't do, it's break a promise—even to me.

I take the stairs five at a time, my lungs burning the more I push myself. I'm panting by the time I get back to the apartment. Dropping his bag next to him, I cough. He glances at me while I brace my hands on my knees, trying to pull in a full breath.

"Don't fucking puke on me," he growls.

"Is she okay?" I gasp, pressing a fist to my chest.

"No, but she's not dead. Find Emma."

I reach into my pocket for my phone, but it's not there. When I pat myself down, I let out a curse. It's gone, lost to the fire by now. I run my hands through my hair, and ash floats around me. I stomp around the space, torn between staying here and going to find her. If she's in trouble, I can't sit around and wait. I'm supposed to protect her. Losing her...I won't accept it.

"Here," Ink says, tossing a phone on the coffee table he's shoved to the side while he cleans Joy up. "Her number's in there. So's mine. Go find her and bring her back. Now. She can't die. They'll fucking kill you if she does."

My head snaps up and our eyes meet. "They won't have to. I'll already be dead."

Chapter 43

Emma

"Shit," I mutter as I stumble over another branch. "Shit. Shit. Shit."

This is one of my worst ideas. I should have waited for Titus. Daisy's texts earlier became more and more frantic until she called. I've never heard terror in her voice before, and it sent me into action. She barely got out more than a few words about where they were headed. Then the line went dead. I don't even know what weapons I grabbed, but I'm wearing a veritable arsenal.

Daisy always wanted to come out to the abandoned house, thinking it was haunted. I doubt this is how she wanted to visit, though. I trip over another limb and curse again, desperately trying to keep my emotions in control. A vise wraps around my chest, squeezing tighter the closer I get to the house.

I stop on the edge of the property, the overgrown lawn stretching out in front of me. My nose wrinkles as I take in the place. I'm sure at one point it was grand and majestic. Now it's just a dilapidated three-story with a sagging wrap-around porch. Lights flicker behind the glass, muted and orange. Probably not the best idea to start a fire without knowing if it'll burn the place down. At least they look contained to fireplaces.

It's the silence that freaks me out the most. No guards roaming the perimeter. A few cameras are stuck in the trees, though I don't think they're on. Nothing moves except a door on the third level creaking slightly in the breeze. It doesn't even lead anywhere except a steep drop to the ground. I imagine there used to be a staircase leading up to it. Or maybe a small balcony. The remnants of either are lost to the tall weeds climbing up the siding.

I edge around the lawn to the back, wishing I could peek through the windows. They're dirty, but intact at least. I doubt I'd be able to slip through one without breaking the glass. I'll need another way in. Leaves crunch under my feet as I slink through the tall grass. Ducking into the shadows, I hold my breath, waiting for the shouts to begin. Still the world stays quiet. It's as if the night itself holds its breath, shushing the creatures hiding within the trees.

My phone vibrates and I jump, almost cracking my head on the broken banister surrounding the porch. I quickly silence it, then cup my hand around the screen and read a message from an unknown number. It must be a burner, though why Titus is texting me from one doesn't make sense. I roll my eyes at his demanding words, then sober when I realize I could really use his help. After texting back my location, I turn it off, then slide it back into the pocket on my thigh. Hopefully nothing went down with him because I need to find Daisy.

The stairs creak as I sneak up them and the wood squishes under my ballet flats. No light filters through the windows framing the back door. When I peek inside, nothing but darkness meets me. Part of me doesn't think Daisy is here. If they took her into the woods somewhere, I won't be able to find her. Calling her wouldn't be smart. I'm impressed she was able to get ahold of me in the first place. If we get out of this, I'm going to teach her some self-defense.

The knob comes off in my hand as I twist it and I whisper another curse. It's heavy and my lip slips between my teeth. Sam always said to use whatever weapons fate hands me, so I keep it in my grip as I ease the wood open. I slide inside, inching along the wall quietly. I don't know what the space was used for, but it's empty now.

Skipping over the floorboards, I keep my footsteps light. An old house like this will hopefully hide whatever loose pieces I hit. I peer around the large archway leading into a hallway. It's just as quiet as the rest of the house. Closed doors march into the distance—at least four on each side. I can't see what's beyond, and I fucking hate that.

Systematically, I search each of the rooms. Most of them are as empty as the last, though one or two have broken pieces of furniture scattered across the wooden floors. The house is old, like it paraded right out of another time with ornate carvings in the trim and fireplaces in almost every room. They're cold and black, long-since forgotten relics. The last one sends a shiver through me when I stare into the open maw of a lion. I hurry out before it can gobble me up.

"If she doesn't get here soon, we'll have to come up with another plan. You should call her," a man's low voice rumbles through the space, and I press my back against the wall.

Peeking around the archway, I try to figure out if they're sitting in the dark like creeps. I take in the sitting room, littered with several chairs and yet another fireplace. As I tiptoe into the room, another man mumbles something I can't make out.

"If I get fucked over because of this, I'm out. It's not fucking worth it," the first man snaps.

Two pairs of footsteps fade away, deeper into the house. My back slides along the wall until I'm deep in the shadows and I exhale quietly. A hand covers my mouth, another around my waist, and I flail. I slam an elbow into my attacker's stomach, earning a grunt.

"Stop it, Emma. It's me." Devon's harsh whisper filters slowly through the veil of panic, and I freeze. "Don't scream. I'm letting you go."

His hand drops, and I spin around. "What the fuck are you doing here?"

I glance behind me, making sure no one's around to hear us. When I look back, I can barely make out Devon's face. He's hiding in the shadows of what looks like an alcove. He's dressed much nicer than I'm used to, and I shake my head.

"I was following you. Emma, we need to get out."

He reaches for me, and I step back.

"I can't, Devon."

"Is this because of *him*?" he sneers, closing the gap between us, and frustration rolls across his features. It's only slightly obscured by the bruises around his eyes. "Because he's not going to come save you, Emma. There's only me."

I grit my teeth, wondering how the hell I can convince him to leave without me. "I can't leave yet. Daisy is here. I have to find her. You go out the back door and I'll find her. Then we can go back to town together."

"The hell I'm leaving you here. Daisy will find her way out."

He reaches for me again, and I skip backward, far out of his reach. "This isn't some foray into an abandoned house for shits and giggles, Devon. There are bad people here and I need to find Daisy. Now go before you get sucked into something you're not prepared for."

I narrow my gaze as he struggles to control his emotions. They flash across his face too quickly to decipher. He's probably just worried about me, but there's something else. It's not a normal thing to tail your ex-girlfriend. None of this is normal. I may not have a good grasp of average experiences, but I've gotten pretty good at blending in the last few years. I've seen how men react when a woman rejects them. Some of them fly off the handle, cinching the noose tighter as their control slips away. With Devon's behavior lately, I wouldn't put it past him to be exactly like them.

"We'll go together," he says finally, determination in his eyes.

"It's not safe." I want to tell him how unprepared he is, but I can't blow my cover. Not until this is done. "I'm capable of finding her and getting us both out. Wait at the edge of the woods."

His face turns stony. "I'm not leaving, Emma. Either I'm coming with you, or I'm dragging you out of here."

I glance toward the doorway, the faint glow from the fireplace gently lighting the next room. I don't want him trailing me. I'll have to protect him. But I'm wasting time and energy by arguing with him. If he gets in my way, I can just knock his ass out and come back for him. And if he has betrayed me in some way or gotten himself mixed up with these guys, I'd rather keep him close.

"Fine. But stay behind me."

A smirk pulls at the corner of his mouth. "Sure, baby doll. Whatever you say."

My nostrils flare and I pivot on my heel. His footsteps dog mine while I follow where the men disappeared. A small blaze flickers behind a grate, illuminating the sparse room in an eerie glow. Devon's fingers brush my wrist and I yank my arm away. I glare at him over my shoulder, and he holds up his hands in surrender.

"Why do you have a gun?" he whispers harshly, and I roll my eyes.

"Protection."

Leaning around the door frame, I scout out the next room. It's identical to the one we're standing in. Whoever designed this house clearly had a theme.

"Do you have an extra?" Excitement rolls through his tone as I lead the way across the room.

"Absolutely not," I hiss.

No fucking way am I handing him a weapon. I'd be half worried he'd shoot himself, but more concerned with catching a stray bullet. An enemy with a gun is bad. An inept man with a gun is worse.

A cold barrel presses against my temple, and I close my eyes.

"No problem. I have my own."

"What are you doing, Devon?" I whisper.

"I think it's about time you start respecting me, Emma. And that requires you to shut the fuck up."

He keeps the gun against my head, sliding his free hand to my own weapon. I force my fingers to unclench and he takes it from me. I should have seen this. I should have listened to Titus. He knew something was off about Devon. He was *adamant* there was something off, and I defended my ex every goddamn time. I didn't see what was right in front of me.

"Why?" I breathe as he pokes the barrel between my shoulders and urges me forward.

"Because I can. It wasn't supposed to be like this, baby doll," he murmurs, and my skin crawls at the nickname. "If you would have just listened to me, we wouldn't have had to resort to this."

I have no idea what he's talking about. Devon played the unassuming good guy so well. He bamboozled everyone. Who knew he'd snap? I wish I would have seen it earlier. Shame crashes down on me as he pushes me toward yet another room. We enter a hallway that splits off to either side, and I wonder if he'll lead me through the labyrinth. Hopefully, he'll take me to Daisy. Then I can formulate a plan to get out of this shitshow.

"I didn't love you," I say, and he grabs my arm, swinging me around. The doorknob slips from my fingers and hits the floor, then rolls away into the shadows.

He points the gun at my face, and I tip up my chin. The words tumbled out before I could stop them. I just needed to say something to get him to see why I couldn't continue with our relationship. It was a farce long before I ever broke up with him. If I can get him to see there's no future between us, maybe he'll see reason. I doubt it, but I have to try.

"You think that's what this was?" he sneers, then tips his head back and laughs.

I could take him out right now. Two moves and he'd be out cold on the dusty floor. Especially if I hit him in the nose. It's already swollen from Titus. I wish he would have punched Devon harder. I should have let Titus take the trash out the first time Devon showed up with fucking roses.

"If you don't care whether or not I loved you, then tell me what this was."

His lips tip up in the lopsided grin all my friends swooned over. He doesn't look evil or capable of threatening someone with a gun. Bastard looks like the boy next door who would compliment your mother when he picks you up for a date. He'd drop you off by curfew with a peck on the cheek. It's the perfect cover.

He gestures at me to walk, and I slowly turn. "You'll find out soon enough."

A chill runs up my spine and ice flows through my veins when I step into a large living area. Next to the front windows, tied to a chair, is Daisy. Tears stream down her face, soaking into the gag he's tied around her head. She struggles against the bonds when she sees me, and my heart clenches.

I spin around, knocking the gun from Devon's hand and kicking him in the side. His breath leaves him with a grunt as he doubles over. My fist connects with his broken nose and the bones crunch under my knuckles. He drops to the floor and writhes, moaning as I stand over him. Blood drips from his face, staining the light floorboards.

The click of a hammer being pulled back reverberates over his groans and my harsh panting. I freeze, then whip my head over my shoulder. An older man holds a gun to Daisy's head as she silently sobs.

"I suggest you stop beating my son. Unless this one is expendable? Devon told me she was important, but if she's not..." He raises an eyebrow, and I step away from Devon as he pushes to his hands and feet. "A wise choice. Now, why don't you sit down?"

He gestures with the gun, and I notice the chair set up next to Daisy. I take measured steps toward it, wondering if they'll tie me up as well. It's not the first time I've been kidnapped. This doesn't feel like the others. It's more of a trap I foolishly stumbled into. Yet another mistake Titus can give me shit for.

If I get out of this alive.

As I sink into the chair, I eye the older man. He's scolding Devon, demanding he get up. Eventually Devon grabs the gun I kicked away and gets to his feet. He glares at me, and I shrug.

"Why am I here?" I ask, and the older man swings around to face me.

He studies me for a minute, then tips his chin at me. I don't know what he wants, but apparently Devon can read his thoughts. The gun shakes as he points it at me. I refuse to cower. My only regret is dragging Daisy into this. I never should have befriended her. I should have accepted my fate to be friendless long before I got to Ridgewood.

"Weapons. All of them," Devon says, his voice thick and nasally from his broken nose.

I sigh before pulling out the various knives I've stashed away. It takes a minute and Daisy squeaks with each clang of metal. Finally, I drop the extra gun I grabbed on top of them and smirk.

"I think that's it, but I didn't count beforehand." They have no idea who they're dealing with.

It takes Devon longer than it should to gather them up and move them to the side. It's not far enough to stop me from getting to them, But my hands are tied until Daisy is safe.

"Well, now that we have that out of the way. Perhaps I should formally introduce myself. I thought we'd be meeting under better circumstances. As my son's fiancé, in fact. Alas, we'll have to settle for this. I am Leon Bradshaw, though I'm sure you've never heard of me."

"Devon said you were dead," I deadpan. Devon also said his last name was Smith, though I assume that was to throw me off if I ever searched him.

His eyebrows disappear under the thin hair on his forehead. "Did he now? A predictable cover, but a cover nonetheless. We don't have much time to finish up here, otherwise I'd tell you the whole story. Suffice it to say, your brother was not very receptive to my suggestions. Therefore, we're...finding another way." He spreads his arms wide, the same lopsided grin Devon has gracing his face.

"How long do I have to keep this farce up, Father?" Devon mutters, pain lacing his tone.

"As long as I tell you to," Leon grinds out. "You were perfectly content to play along while you were fucking her for what, three years?"

I flinch, though I cover it by glancing at Daisy. Silently, I try to lend her my strength. She nods, though I doubt she feels any better than she did ten seconds ago. Even if I don't make it out of here, I'll give her the best chance to run. Titus will find her. He'll take care of her. He knows how much she means to me. He'll be pissed I got myself killed, but he'll make sure she's safe.

I raise my hand and Leon glances at me, an incredulous look on his face.

"Are you expecting me to continue to date Devon? To what end?"

Devon snickers while Leon smiles indulgently.

"No, my dear. I expect you to marry him."

Well, fuck.

Chapter 44

Titus

As I tromp through the woods, I'm still not convinced I'm walking into a trap instead of a haunted house. I glance at Emma's text once more, though nothing has changed. The words didn't magically morph into an explanation. They're still merely a location. There's no way she snuck away to an abandoned house for an adventure. Couple this with the chop shop blowing up and it doesn't feel like a coincidence the world is falling apart around us.

The trees thin slightly, revealing a small clearing, and I skirt the edge. It'll take me longer to go around, but I'd rather stay hidden. The wind picks up, sending the remaining leaves shivering above me. My footsteps crunch over the ground and I attempt to lighten my steps. Joy may have said there wasn't any activity outside of the house, but I'm not taking any chances.

Once I reach the edge of the property, I scan the area. It's silent other than the breeze rushing through the trees. Dark clouds cover the moon, plunging the world into shadows. I grin, using the cover of darkness to rush through the tall weeds smothering the lawn. Several narrow windows grace the front of the house, orange flickering behind the panes.

Peering through the dirty glass, I grip my gun, hoping I won't have to use it. I'm not worried about Emma. She knows how to handle herself. If Daisy is here, though, Emma will put herself in danger to save her. Getting them both out won't be easy if there's a shit ton of men inside. Several blurred shadows move about the space, but I can't make out who it is. I crouch and move to the next one. Before I can peek inside, voices filter from around the corner and I freeze.

"Are we supposed to call for backup?" one man asks, not bothering to lower his voice.

"What backup?" another snorts.

I ease around the opposite corner, staying tight against the siding. If they're coming closer, I don't know. Their footsteps are swallowed by the wind. I glance behind me, making sure no one's sneaking up on me. The last thing I need is to be taken too. Hopefully, Emma is inside and formulating a plan to get Daisy out.

"We should bail. Bradshaw doesn't know what the fuck he's doing. Or if he does, he's not telling the rest of us," the second man says.

"At least we're getting paid. Besides, this isn't Bradshaw's operation. Not really. That little bitch is running things, or at least has been."

"How the fuck you know that?"

"Been here for months now. Plus, there's a big payout if Bradshaw's whelp marries the girl. Something about a big step up in operations."

Their voices fade away, but I can't move. I'd stake my life on Bradshaw being Twitch's father. It explains why Twitch was so persistent in getting Emma back. The bastard thought he could trick her, marry her, and probably give him an in to Synd. I shake my head, wondering at the audacity of them. It's a ridiculous plan. Even if he marries Emma, he won't get control of Synd. The others would float him before the ink dried on the certificate.

Unless she fell in love with him.

Thank fuck Emma didn't. Why they think this plan will still work since they've taken Daisy, I have no idea. Twitch really hasn't thought this through. And his father clearly hasn't either. I'll gloat later about being right. Joy thought I was way off point thinking Ridgewood was a test site. And Emma thought Twitch was just a good guy. He bamboozled everyone, most of all Emma.

I make my way to the back of the house, hoping I don't run into the two guards. At least they won't be calling in reinforcements. When I reach the back, the door swings in and out rhythmically with the wind. The men have disappeared, probably taking off before shit goes sideways. I sneak up the stairs and slip inside without a problem.

I'm halfway across the empty room when my heel goes through the floorboard, splintering around my boot. I freeze, waiting for someone to come investigate. After thirty seconds, no one appears and I pull myself free. Gritting my teeth, I make my way toward the light in the front of the house. Voices echo through the space, too low for me to decipher.

A small blaze in the fireplace lights my way through the last room, and I press my back against the wall. A large archway leads into the front area and I hesitate, hoping to figure out who is in there. I haven't found Emma and I wonder if she's in there already.

"Devon, this is insanity. You can't expect me to marry you." Emma's voice cuts through the air, and I tense.

"You will if you'd like your friend here to live," an older man says.

"And then what? Because we both know you'll kill her as soon as she's no longer useful. So, what's going to keep me from calling my brothers and having them take care of you, Leon?" she sneers.

Leon guffaws, the air wheezing from his lungs. "Your friend will be staying with us for quite some time. Once Devon gains access to your family, I regret to inform you, they'll die. You'll join them soon after, though."

"And you think our men will follow you? You think the rest of the leaders in Synd will allow it? You're more delusional than I imagined."

Twitch chuckles and my lip curls. "I'm sure you can be very convincing. We'll have to play the part of a happy couple until I've gained their trust. We'll have to get rid of your little...toy."

"Oh, I already took care of that, son."

I can't handle this anymore. Like hell is she going to marry him. They'd have to kill me if they expect to go anywhere with this plan. I don't understand why they think Emma isn't going to stab him in his sleep. What the hell were these people thinking?

I peer around the wall, taking in the scene. Daisy tied to a chair. Emma seated next to her. From the way she's gripping the arms, all that's holding her back is the gun trained on Daisy. The older man doesn't look like he'd be able to take on Daisy, much less Emma. He's stout, yet frail, his hand trembling with the weight of his weapon.

"How exactly did you take care of my 'toy'? Because Titus isn't easily distracted. Unless you've seen his dead body, I doubt you could stop him from coming for me. And even then, he'll probably haunt your ass." Emma crosses her arms, but her eye twitches. It's her tell and I realize she's worried they actually have killed me.

"No one's coming for you, Miss King. Let's get this over with." Leon gestures to Twitch. "Keep her here. I'm going to get the judge."

I duck around the corner and scan the space. There's nowhere for me to hide and a hasty plan forms in my mind. It's ridiculous and I fucking hate it, but I don't have another option other than jumping out the window. This entire thing is ridiculous. A foolish idea put in place by foolish men who don't know their ass from their elbow. How the fuck did Emma get involved in something so utterly asinine?

As soon as the older man shuffles into the room, I lift my weapon. He freezes, his watery eyes widening. When he opens his mouth to call for Twitch, I knock his gun from his grasp and it clatters to the floor. He looks vaguely familiar, but I can't place him. He might be the man who came to Emma's door after I first got here. That man had a lot more meat on him, though.

A croak leaves him and his face goes lax. I have no idea what the fuck is wrong with him until he clutches his chest. This fucking bastard is going to keel over from a goddamn heart attack. It's so fucking absurd I almost bust out laughing. Using the barrel, I push him and he stumbles, crashing into the moth-eaten couch.

"Father?" Twitch calls, and the sounds of a scuffle follow.

I leave Leon gasping for breath and step through the archway. Twitch yells, stumbling back and tripping over his own feet. His face is a mess. He skirts around the chairs. I expect him to threaten Emma, but he stops behind Daisy.

He holds his gun to her head, sputtering out demands for me to drop my weapon.

"Took you long enough," Emma says, and I roll my eyes.

"Shut the fuck up," I snap, pointing my gun at Twitch and shooting him between the eyes.

Daisy screams behind her gag as Twitch's body crumples to the ground. Emma sighs, pushing herself up to free her friend.

"Leave it to you to get yourself into this ridiculous bullshit," I mutter as I make my way to the pile of weapons in the corner.

"Rather deal with this than other shit. Getting shot isn't fun, if you'll recall." She shushes Daisy, whispering comfort to her. "Is Leon dead?"

"No idea. Pretty sure he was having a heart attack when I left him. Where you think they stashed the judge?"

"Seriously?" Daisy cries as she rips the gag from her mouth. "How are you two so goddamn calm? I was just *kidnapped*."

Emma wraps her arms around Daisy's shoulders from behind, murmuring in her ear. I'm not about to explain how this is the least amount of danger we've ever been in. Our enemies aren't usually so inept. As long as Leon didn't have any allies, this problem will die with him and his son. Emma will have to deal with the aftermath of knowing she slept with Twitch, but I imagine she's blocking that from her mind.

"Did you expect to have to fight an army when you came here?" I call as I dig through the various knives.

"Not like I knew what I was walking into. Where's your phone, by the way? I fucking texted you like an hour ago."

My heart skips a beat when I remember what I left behind when I came running after Emma. "Lost it in the fire."

"Fire? Tell me you didn't burn down my apartment building. You realize other people live there, right?"

"Why the fuck would I burn down your apartment?" I snap, glancing at her.

I'm so fucking over this. I want to get back to Joy. Ink will take care of her, but I'll feel better when I know she didn't die because of me. The next couple days are going to be hard. Cleaning up messes when I don't have the infrastructure in place isn't easy. I don't have men to deal with the bodies or someone to handle the bullshit with the chop shop. I wish we were back in Synd. The rules are set—easy to follow. Glancing at Emma, I realize we'll have to go back to being...nothing. Shane won't accept anything else.

"I wouldn't put it past you to burn my couch," Emma says, breaking me out of my thoughts.

"It's got soot and blood all over it now, so you'd better mourn the loss." My voice is devoid of emotion, and she tilts her head.

I turn back to the knives and start picking them up to busy my hands. No reason she needs to know what the hell is going on in my head. She'll either laugh in my face or convince me it'll be different. Either way, I'm not ready for that conversation. Especially in front of Daisy and the dead body of her ex-boyfriend.

She crouches next to me and snatches her dagger from the stack. I can't keep from watching her, attempting to read her mind. Life would be easier if there were guarantees. I've never experienced that, though. No one assured me the future would be bright. Not like Emma, who always knew she was wanted and loved. Her family would do anything for her. Which only sets us further apart.

Movement from the corner of my eye has me glancing toward the archway. A soft curse drops from my lips as Leon staggers into view, his fingers wrapped around his gun. Time slows as he lifts it—not at me or Emma, but at Daisy. I don't think as I launch myself at him. A sharp report rings in my ears and Daisy screams.

I don't even make it to Leon, crashing onto my side a foot from him. My head bounces off the floor and my vision wavers. Leon's body falls, Emma's dagger stuck in his throat. I groan, rolling to my back. Staring at the crumbling ceiling, I hope it doesn't fall on me. After all the shit tonight, I wouldn't be surprised. Glancing toward Daisy, I find her huddled on the floor, hands over her head.

Emma appears, concern splashed across her face. I have no idea what the hell her problem is. I practically saved her best friend. If she wants to bitch about it, she's going to have to wait because there's a burning in my shoulder from the fall.

"Titus?" she whispers, her voice distorting.

"What?" I squeeze my eyes shut, then open them, but it doesn't fix my ears.

Emma falls to her knees next to me and a tear slides down her cheek. My brows pull low as I try to lift my hand to brush it away. It doesn't move.

"Don't move," she says. "Just...don't move."

"Shit. He fucking shot me, didn't he?"

"Just don't move. I'll call..." A choked sob leaves her, and I huff.

"Call Ink. He's at your apartment."

"Why is he—no. Not important. Just don't move." She fumbles with her phone, hands trembling as she pulls up his number.

"Stop telling me what to do," I grunt.

"Fuck you," she whispers.

I close my eyes again, a grin on my face.

Chapter 45

Emma

Pacing the hallway in a hospital isn't new to me. I've been here many times before, waiting for news. I'm pretty sure every member of my family has been here at one point or another. Ink insisted we bring Joy and Titus to Synd, and I'm regretting it. I hate this place.

"Emmie?" Sam whispers.

I lace my fingers together before turning to her. "Yeah?"

She looks the same as when I saw her a few months ago, dark hair framing her face and dressed all in black. She shed her socialite persona years ago. I remember when she lost it on Alex, telling him she couldn't sit through another goddamn silent auction. That was about the time I started going with him instead.

She glances at my hands, then back to my face. "You okay?"

"I'm fine. Why wouldn't I be?" Trying to balance my worry for Titus while keeping from my family how I feel about him isn't as easy as I thought it would be. Actually, I knew it would be a fucking disaster.

"Because your friend and Titus are both in the hospital? Pretty fucking obvious, Emma." She crosses her arms, popping her hip out.

I wave away her concern. "Oh, they'll be fine. Ink said Joy will recover, and Titus just got shot."

"Just got shot. And you're not worried about him at all?"

I glance away from her knowing eyes. "He said he's fine."

"Then why are you pacing outside his room?"

I sigh, ignoring the turning in my stomach. "Is there a reason you're here? I thought you had a thing tonight?"

I'm not about to out her to the nurses and doctors filtering by. Being an assassin is supposed to be a secret. More people know these days that she's the Wraith, but the general public isn't on the list. Plus, she doesn't go out as often. Our families have fallen into what Alex called the sunset period. They have people in power who work with them instead of against them. Our enemies, if we have any, stay far away. Other than Leon and Devon, we haven't had trouble in years.

"I skipped it. No reason to shake down a mid-level gang leader right now. He'll keep. Are you going to tell me what happened?"

"You should get Titus to give you the report," I whisper. It's how we used to do things when he was my bodyguard. I tried to give my version of events, but no one really cared. They just wanted to hear what Titus had to say.

Sam latches onto my elbow and forces me into the chair across from Titus's door. "Start talking."

I suck in a deep breath and recount the recent events, leaving out most of what happened with Titus. She doesn't need to hear about how he lectured me. Or fucked me. Or how I fell straight back into the same heartache I experienced a decade ago. I don't know where Titus and I stand. Until I can talk to him, figure out where I fit into his life, I'll keep my mouth shut.

"I'm sorry I ghosted you guys." I turn away and wipe a tear from my cheek.

"You're an adult, Emma. We just wanted to know you were okay. Also, we wanted you to come home." She tucks her feet underneath her legs. "Ren knew you were dealing with things, so we weren't worried. Plus, we were putting out fires here."

"What happened?" I don't really have the right to ask. I ignored them for weeks, ashamed and avoiding their judgement. Part of me wouldn't be surprised if she didn't tell me. Most of the time I'm stuck on the outside of their conversations, anyway.

"You know, it was weird. There were some hits on our supply lines, but they weren't very good at it. I assume that was Bradshaw. Shane's pissed about that." Sam's eyes go wide when she spots my face. "Not because of you. Bradshaw came to Synd when you were like seventeen. He proposed an alliance between our families. Wanted Shane to marry you off to his son. Shane obviously told him to fuck off, but I guess Bradshaw didn't like that."

I snort, shaking my head. "He was in pretty bad shape at the end. I think he was sick. And Devon was..."

I don't have a way to explain my relationship with Devon. I can't tell her I dated him for so long without a clue who he actually was. It'll be a while before I can reconcile being with him. If I would have stayed in Synd, none of this would have happened.

"I know that look. Stop blaming yourself, Emma. It's not your fault."

I nod, my eyes fixed on the door. Titus hasn't woken up since he came back from surgery. The bullet was lodged in his shoulder and they thought he might lose his arm. If he did, there'd be no coming back from it. Shane wouldn't float him, but Titus would have blamed me. He barely spoke to me on the ride from Ridgewood. Granted, he was dozing in the backseat of a car Ink procured somehow while I was stuck in the front seat, but still. He didn't talk to me when we stumbled our way through the forest, either. Not a fucking word while I took care of Daisy. She'll probably never talk to me either, and I don't blame her.

I've fucked everything up and there's no coming back from it. "I was thinking of going away."

"Excuse me? You just got home."

"I know. I didn't mean right now. Just...later. After everything's settled down. I could go back to the mountains. Jasmine said I was always welcome. Thought it might be good to spend some time there during the winter." It's not true. I haven't been thinking of running away to the mountains. I didn't have a plan at all. If I stay here, though, I'll end up messing up again. Just like Titus said I would.

"Shane's not going to like it, but I'll put in a good word for you." Sam pats my leg, then pushes to her feet. "Try to get some rest. Ink said you didn't on the way here."

I swallow hard. "I will. I'm just waiting for Titus to wake up, then I'll sleep."

She doesn't look like she believes me, and I wait for her to scold me. Instead, she walks off down the hall and disappears around the corner. I don't know how long I sit there, staring at Titus's door and begging it to open. Which is ridiculous since there's no one inside. He's not going to come out and demand we talk. A nurse comes by, giving me a sympathetic smile before vanishing inside his room. My foot bounces, sending my leg into overdrive.

Ten minutes later, she reappears and gestures to me. "He's awake, but a little groggy from the meds he's on. Keep it brief."

I nod my thanks, then slip around her. She shuts the door softly and I brace myself. The steady beep of his heartbeat echoes around the space, bouncing off the cold walls. My palms break out in a sweat and I force my feet forward. Thankfully, he's not strung up with a bunch of wires. I don't know if I would be able to keep my shit together if that were the case.

I thought he'd be sleeping, but he's staring at the ceiling, his jaw clenched. Clearing my throat, I wait for him to acknowledge me. He doesn't. Because of course he doesn't. Bastard.

"How you feeling?" I ask, then clear my throat again.

"I feel like I had someone digging around in my bones," he growls. "Is Joy here?"

I'm not surprised she's the first thing he asked about. Still, my chest aches. "She's up in the burn unit. It wasn't too bad, and Ink was able to treat a lot of it. She had some wounds they think she got from the initial blast. Looks like something stabbed into her, but they did surgery to fix it."

He doesn't give me any indication he's heard me. Just stares at the ceiling as if he'll lose it if he catches even a glimpse of me. I knew shit would change when we got back to Synd. I didn't think it would be this bad, though. Chalking it up to him being injured would be the sane thing to do. Except it's my fault he's lying in a hospital bed.

"I'm sorry," I whisper. "You were right. I fucked up, and you got hurt because of it."

"Tell me something I don't already know," he sneers.

"I took care of the bodies. The chop shop is a loss. Alex isn't going to rebuild since I won't be going back. I'll cover whatever you lost from it." I don't have anything else I can do. I said I was sorry. It's not enough.

"Don't bother. We made enough over the years." The lie flows so easily from him, I wonder what else he's been fibbing about. Alex told me he was sending the profits to Aelia in Rima. I didn't know until earlier Titus was doing the same.

I wrap my arms around my stomach as a chill rolls through me. "Shane said when you're better, he expects you back."

"So I'm guessing you didn't tell him I fucked his little sister?"

I flinch at the bitterness in his tone. "No, I didn't. And I don't plan to."

"That's it?" He lets out a humorless laugh, then coughs, and my body sways toward him.

He doesn't want my comfort. He never did—not that he opened up enough for me to know when to offer it. Every time I've tried, he's shut me down. He's so set on being the outsider. Hopefully, with me gone, he'll finally find some peace. He'll concede he's home.

"I don't know what else you want from me. You want me to prostrate myself at your feet and lay out all my sins one by one? Would you like me to tell you every way I've fucked up? Or maybe I could offer for you to shoot me as retribution?" Now who's the bitter one? Fuck. I turn away, realizing this won't go anywhere. I'd rather leave with what little dignity I have left.

He snorts and I turn back. "Running away yet again, darling? I shouldn't be surprised. It's what you do when you fuck up."

"Running away and leaving aren't the same things, Titus." Numbness washes over me, cutting off the breaking of my heart.

He finally looks at me, emotions I can't name swirling in his eyes. "You brought this upon yourself. And now that shit's too hard, you're going to leave everyone else to clean up the mess. You're going to leave me with yet another goddamn scar. At this point, I've lost count of how many I have from you. Go ahead. Walk the fuck out. It's what you're good at."

I open my mouth to dispute him, to argue, to beg his forgiveness. Something to explain myself. Yet nothing comes out.

My breath whooshes out of me and I press my lips together to cut off the sound. I should have seen this coming from the beginning. We're nothing if not predictable. I believed we were friends before, and he set me straight. I thought I'd be more than just an easy fuck for him, and he's proving I wasn't worth the energy.

Titus only sees me as a one-night stand gone on too long. Devon only saw me as a wife—a means to an end. Apparently, that's all I'll ever be. Whatever future I foolishly imagined with Titus dissolves in front of me. The life I dreamed of wasn't meant to be. And I knew that. Logically, I knew it would end this way. My heart just didn't get the memo.

I gather the broken pieces of me and shove them deep, slamming the familiar mask I've worn so many times before over my features.

"I hope you find what you're searching for."

I pivot and take measured steps from the room, leaving my heart behind.

Chapter 46

Titus

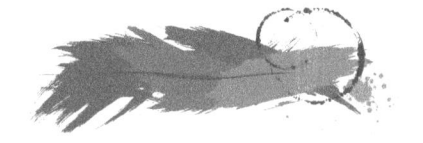

Voices outside my hospital room drag me from the restless sleep that's plagued me for the last few days. I'm due to go home today or tomorrow. I have no idea where I'm supposed to go. Alex, Ren, and Sam have been by, but Shane hasn't. None of them mentioned what would happen when I was released. I don't blame any of them.

"Well, you'd better fucking find her because I'm not doing this again," Shane growls from the hallway.

He stalks into the room, a scowl firmly on his face. I struggle upright, my shoulder aching. Shane crosses his arms while he waits for me to get my shit together. I grit my teeth as I settle against the pillows finally.

"Thank fuck it was your left shoulder. It's a pain in the ass to lift a gun when it's your dominant arm," he says, nodding at my injury.

"Yes, sir." There's no other response to his statement. He probably knows exactly what this is like.

He scoffs as he glances away. "Stop calling me sir. I fucking hate it. Especially coming from you."

I don't know what that means. I've been calling him sir or Mr. King for my entire adult life. Like hell am I going to call him Shane. The only reason I do is when I need to differentiate between the brothers. I don't have it in me to argue with him.

"Was there something you needed, s—" I clear my throat when he glares at me.

"We moved your room, so when you come home, you'll be on the third floor. Ink offered to come by and keep an eye on things. We've got Jay running the security team, so when you're up to it, he'll need some more direction. Since Bradshaw died, we haven't had any issues with the supply lines. Still a couple threats trickling in, but I talked to Ghost up in Harris. He thinks it was some trouble on his end. He's dealing with it. Turns out we may have jumped the gun on locking down." He runs his hand through his hair, then walks around the bed to collapse into the chair next to my bed.

"Jay will keep shit together. I trained him myself."

"I know. If you trust him, then I do, too. Don't fucking like it, though," he grumbles.

I've never seen this side of Shane. At least, not when it's just the two of us. I don't know if I'd call our relationship professional since he's the head of a mafia family. We don't chitchat or commiserate. He hands down orders and I follow through. Other than the occasional outburst or glimpse into their inner circle, I don't see this side of him.

"I'm fine staying in my current room. Unless you'd rather I move to one of the barracks," I say, and his gaze narrows. "Or not."

"Fuck. I told her she was wrong, and now I'm going to have to backtrack." He leans forward, propping his elbows on his knees. "You remember when you let Sam get away the first time she broke into my office?"

I bite my tongue, my muscles tensing. I don't like remembering how much I fucked up. Sam played my ass, pretending she was upset, and I didn't know what to do with a crying woman. She ended up shoving me into the office and barring the door with a knife so I couldn't follow her. Being freshly eighteen, I didn't know what the hell to do. Sam wasn't just a woman. She was a part of the Byrns mafia and therefore untouchable.

"I do," I say through clenched teeth.

He chuckles, shaking his head. "That was the moment. You let her get away. There was so much fear in your eyes. You didn't know how to hide that shit yet. It didn't occur to me until later, you weren't afraid of us killing you. Nope, it was losing your position."

"It was all I had, sir." The only thing I've ever had to live for was my position in their organization. I don't know what else I'd do if they dismissed me. I'd rather get floated, to be honest.

"Had being the key word there, Titus." He lifts his head, gaze piercing mine, and I brace myself.

I don't know what the fuck he's talking about. He made it clear he's expecting me to come back. He's moving me to the third floor where their bedrooms are—probably for more protection for them. So why is he speaking like I won't be coming back?

"It's still all I have. Despite the events of the last few weeks, I'm still capable of—" I snap my mouth shut when he lifts his hand.

"You're fucking stubborn, just like Sam. I told her it should be her, but she said it'd mean more coming from me. For fuck's sake, I hate this shit. Listen, apparently Emma mentioned to Sam you didn't think you were important to the family. And I'm supposed to assure you of your position or some shit." He sits back, his eyes closing. He seems tired, weighed down by life instead of enemies. I suppose it's the best outcome one could hope for when running an organization like this.

"I understand, sir. Emma has some strong opinions on where I fit in, but I know my place. You don't have to remind me."

"What the fuck," he breathes. "You think Emma doesn't see more than you?"

"I have no idea what Emma sees." My chest aches and I chalk it up to my injury. I reach for the button to up the meds, though I haven't touched it since I woke up.

He tracks my movements, a calculating look in his eyes. The last thing I need is for him to start probing into anything involving Emma and me. He may be saying I have a place when I'm better now, but if he finds out what happened between us, all that goes to shit. I won't make it out of the hospital. He won't even bother with a silencer, using me as an example for anyone else thinking of chasing his sister.

"Twitch...Devon was very good at hiding who he was," I mutter. "Even I didn't realize how involved he was in what was going on in Ridgewood."

"Are you defending her actions?" He raises an eyebrow.

I dig my fingers into the thin sheet covering my legs. "No, sir. Merely explaining what I saw. Devon was an expert at playing a part."

"I heard he was a douchebag."

I snort, glancing away. "Oh, he was. Bastard kept trying to drop off flowers and gifts, but nothing she'd like. I get the impression he was the safe choice."

Shane nods, and I realize I probably didn't do Emma any favors. If I defend her too fiercely, he'll suspect something else is going on. If I don't defend her at all, I'll be throwing her under the bus.

The words I threw at her the other night repeat in my head. I hate them. I hate that I said them. I hate that she believed me. It's the only way to protect her. And at the end of the day, that's what I need to do—protect her. I may be shielding her for different reasons now, but in the end, it doesn't matter. The result is still the same.

"When Emma was younger, I wanted to save her from this life. I held on too tightly, guarding her from the shadows of our world. And it didn't work. I pushed her straight into danger." He sighs, gripping the back of his neck.

"Hard to do when she was raised in the shadows. She's capable of living in them. In fact, I think she'll thrive in them if you give her a chance."

He smirks, then nods. "You just lost me a shit ton of money. I have half a mind to take it out of your salary."

He pushes to his feet, and I swallow, forcing the lump in my throat away. "Sir?"

"Doc said you can leave. Got a car out front, so get dressed and meet me out there."

He stalks to the door without another word, leaving me reeling. I have no fucking clue what any of that was about. It's probably the longest conversation we've ever had. At least he's not throwing my ass to the wolves. Then again, I'm walking straight back into the Kings' house, and I imagine the rumors will be flying, especially with the guards. Until things go back to normal, I'll be a ball of nerves, waiting for the other shoe to drop.

It takes me longer than I want to get dressed. I can't lift my arm over my head and almost give up. Going shirtless isn't really an option right now. A nurse comes in with paperwork, her hands trembling as she glances toward the door every few seconds. I want to reassure her, but I don't have it in me. She must be new. Most people in Synd know on some level they live in a world set apart from normalcy. They don't care since their lives go on without interference. Helps they never see the darkness underneath their perfect lives.

She rushes from the room, and I give her a minute before I follow. By the time I take the stairs to the first floor, I'm out of breath. I couldn't get myself to take the elevator, though. When I step outside, cold air weaves its way around me and thunder rumbles overhead. We'll be lucky to get back without getting caught in the deluge.

Sam leans against the hood of one of her fancy cars, fiddling with the keys. "Ready?"

"Yes." I glance around for any sign of the others. I won't admit it, but I thought Emma would be here. I haven't seen her since I accused her of running away.

"She's not here," Sam murmurs.

My spine straightens. "Who? I was looking for Shane."

"Sure you were." She pushes off the car and presses the keys in my hand. "She's at the train station. Go easy on her. She deserves to be happy."

She walks away before I can refute her words. I'm not surprised Emma's leaving, though where the hell she's going to run to I have no idea. She said she wasn't going back to Ridgewood. Maybe the training camp she's gone off to every summer. Like hell am I going up there. It's fucking cold and desolate. Plus, we'd probably get stuck there by a snowstorm.

Gritting my teeth, I slide into the driver's seat. I've never driven a car like this, and I'm slightly terrified I'll crash the thing. The train station isn't far. With each red light I hit, my stomach flips. Sam's words play on repeat in my head the entire time—*she deserves to be happy*. Why they think she'll be happy here is beyond me. The more I think on it, the more I wonder if Sam already knows about the shift in Emma's and my relationship.

As I weave through traffic, my heart pounds in my chest. I need to get to her before she leaves. I don't know what the hell I'm going to say, but she can't leave. Not alone. The train station comes into view and I pull up in front, not bothering to park. They can tow my ass if they want. Alex will take care of it if need be.

I always hated how open this space is. I hate it even more now as the skies open up. It isn't a soft pitter-patter of rain, either. More like a torrential downpour attempting to drown me before I've found her. Swiping my hand over my face, I search the covered benches for her. My feet slip as I rush toward the other end of the platform, and I grumble under my breath. Breaking my skull open on the ground after getting shot isn't my idea of a good time.

"Emma," I bellow when I spot her, and she whips her head around.

I stomp toward her, rage overtaking any anxiety I had on the drive over. She glances around as if worried I'll make a scene. There's no one else on this side, though. She stands, crossing her arms as she waits for me to reach her.

"What the hell are you doing?" I growl.

She rolls her eyes. "I could ask you the same damn thing. You're supposed to be in the hospital. Hell, you still have a goddamn sling."

I glance down at the contraption the nurse forced on me and rip it from my body. Pain shoots through my arm, but I ignore it as I toss the sling next to her backpack stuffed full of fuck knows what.

"Yes, because that's going to help," she snaps.

"Where the fuck are you going?"

She presses her lips together, probably contemplating whether she can lie her way through this. She can't. I know her too well for her to get away with it. Her throat bobs and I brace myself for her tears.

"Vacation. Always wanted to. Now seems like the perfect time. Did Shane send you?"

"Shane doesn't know you're here."

She sniffs, a rueful expression overtaking her face. "Sam. Of course, she sent *you* after me. What do you plan on doing? Throwing me over your shoulder and shoving me into a trunk? You'll have to tie me up first."

I grin, my cock hardening at the thought of her tied to my bed. "That can certainly be arranged, darling."

Chapter 47

Emma

"You insufferable bastard," I snarl.

Of course, Titus tracked me down. Of course, he couldn't just let me go without a word. Of course, he thinks he can just pretend he didn't rip my heart out. I'm not surprised Sam sent him after me. She always felt like our story wasn't done. She never said anything to me directly, but I knew.

He sobers, stepping out of the rain. "Why are you running?"

"I told you—"

"Bullshit. You're running and we both know it."

"You told me to go," I cry, throwing my hands in the air. "You told me this was all my fault, as if I didn't fucking know that already."

His nostrils flare as he pushes into my space, crowding me against the glass and keeping the rain at bay. His hand lands next to my head as he glares at me. I tip up my chin, daring him to deny it, all the while wishing I was anywhere but here. I can't have this conversation again. My heart can't take it. Every time I think we might have a chance at something more, I'm left devastated. And I refuse to show him how much he's hurt me. How much it kills me to walk away. But I have to walk away if only to protect myself. I'll fall apart when I'm alone like I did the other night.

"It wasn't your fault," he says, and I jerk away, my head thudding against the glass.

"So that's your play? Sam sends you to bring me back and you decide the only way to accomplish that is to lie. Great. Fine. I'll go back. Happy?"

"Not in the slightest. Sam didn't send me. She didn't tell me to bring you home."

"Then why the hell are you here?" I huff. "Why come all the way down here? To yell at me again?"

His jaw tics and he glances away. I need him to admit he's only here because of Shane. Or his job. I need him to confess he doesn't want to be here. It's the only way I'll be able to let him go. And if it's something more, I need to hear it from him. Not when we're in a post-sex haze or he's fucking me. Claiming me while he's making me come doesn't count.

"You are the most frustrating, infuriating woman I've ever met," he snarls.

"Gee, I love you, too, asshole."

As soon as the words pop out, I wish I could shove them back in. He looks like I've slapped him, and I open my mouth to take them back. Anything to salvage the situation. Then again, maybe he'll finally leave me be if I scare him off with my random declarations.

He drops his head, hiding his face, and tears fill my eyes. I bite my tongue, willing them away. He doesn't need to see my pain. No one does. Which is precisely why I'm leaving. If I stay here, I'll not only have to face him every day, but I'll just mess up again. And Titus won't stop stepping in to save me. It's not healthy. I need to leave so I stop fucking up everyone else's lives. They're better off without me.

I slide to the side and his free hand grips my hip, and I wince. Tipping his head back, he pulls in a deep breath before dropping his forehead to mine. I close my eyes, soaking in what will probably be the last time I'll be this close to him.

"Don't go," he whispers, and a shiver rolls through me, though I blame the rain.

"I have to," I whisper back. "If I stay, it never ends."

"What if I don't want it to end?"

I tuck my arms around my waist so I don't reach for him. "You want me to keep fucking up? To deal with me and the fucking mess I am?"

He chuckles and my lids flutter open. "You are a mess. Good thing you're the mess I want. Fuck up all you want, Emma. Make all the mistakes you could possibly make. I'll be right there to fix them. I'll be there to put the world back together for you. I'll catch you every time you fall."

He cups my face and wipes away the tears I didn't notice were falling. His lips brush mine as I silently cry, wondering where the hell we go from here. Something holds me back, keeping me from saying anything. What happens when we get home? What happens when I really do mess up? What happens when he gets shot again?

"What about my family?" It's more than them, but I can't force myself to bring it all up.

"Stop avoiding shit, Emma," he growls. "Tell me what you want."

"I don't want to live without you."

"Then let's go home." He leans away and grabs my backpack.

I shake my head, trying to realign my life with reality. I didn't expect him to come after me, but a sliver of my heart still hoped. Now that it's real, I don't know how to act. Butterflies erupt in my gut, though they're nothing like the ones I'm used to. They're more like angry bees about to sting the shit out of me. I'm already playing out the conversations with my family. None of them end well in my head.

Titus tangles our fingers together and tugs me into the rain. I shiver as the cold seeps into my bones. His arm is back in the sling and I wonder when he put it on again. I was so far into my own mind, I didn't notice. Shit. I'm going to be terrible at this. I'm not built to be in a relationship. The only reason the one with Devon worked was because he didn't care if I was present or not. He didn't give a shit about me. I could have completely ignored him and he would have stayed.

I stop, not caring about getting soaked. Titus glances over his shoulder at me, raising an eyebrow. How do I put my fears into words? How do I put my faith in him? His words don't mean much. Devon had pretty words, too. And I didn't care about him. If Titus lets me down, if he doesn't live up to his promises, it'll break me completely.

"Why did you do it?" I ask, blink the water from my lashes as thunder rumbles overhead.

He turns to me. "Do what?"

"When we were younger?" I wave my hand when he opens his mouth. "I know I was too young. But you didn't have to be a dick. You could have said I was too young, and we could have gone back to the way things were."

His brows pull low and he drops my hand. "That's why. We would have gone right back to the way things were. You would have pined for something..."

"Something that could never be?" My tears mingle with the rain, hiding my pain from him.

"No. I mean, yes. At that point, yes. You needed to move on. I couldn't have you hanging on to the possibility of something more. And I wasn't a creep, counting down the days until you were eighteen. We were friends back then, as much as we could be, but I didn't see you as anything other than someone I needed to protect."

I can understand his reasoning, even if I don't agree. Actually, he might have a point. I was a hormonal teenager with grand plans of us running off into the sunset. It wasn't based in reality, but I would have pined for him for years. Instead, I just got pissed and held a grudge against him.

"And when you got to Ridgewood? It couldn't be because of the pranks I played on you. They were harmless."

His mouth drops open. "You threw a brick through my window. You slashed my tires. And you smeared grease all over my goddamn bike. Those weren't fucking pranks, Emma."

"They were funny." I roll my eyes, and he scowls. "To me they were. But you were clearly pissed at me still. For what?"

"You sabotaged my place in the King organization. You were in Shane's ear, weaving all sorts of lies so I wouldn't advance. Which I'm willing to let go of since I created the situation in the first place."

"How kind of you. But I never told Shane a damn thing about you. I told Sam, but she didn't say anything. I'm sure he figured shit out when I asked for a new bodyguard. Blaming me for shit he decided to do isn't going to get you anywhere."

He runs his fingers through his wet hair as the rain tapers off. This is about the time he'll walk away. He never could finish a conversation with me. I hold out my hand, waiting for him to give me my backpack.

"What?" he snaps.

"I want my backpack before you storm off. My train will be here soon."

"What the fuck, Emma?" He turns his body as if I'll rip it away from him. "I'm not storming off. I'm not letting you leave. We're going home, and we're going to tell your family."

"Telling them what? What are we, Titus? Because from where I'm standing, we're two people screaming at each other in an empty train station."

I hold my breath while he works through what I've said. Or maybe figures out if I'm worth it. He could leave, take my ticket and go off to whatever random town I picked. I didn't even check, just closed my eyes and picked a place. It's not the smartest thing I've done, but I didn't want to know. I'd still be standing in front of the board, dithering about whether to stay or go.

He knocks my hand away, dropping my backpack, and steps into my space. His hand snakes around the back of my neck and pulls my face to his. My breath stutters in my chest, butterflies erupting in my belly. Actual butterflies this time.

"I'll tell them you're mine," he growls, then his eyes soften. "And I'm yours. We'll figure the rest of it out as we go."

"Later," I whisper.

He sighs, his fingers flexing on my neck. "Emma, do you really want to call me your boyfriend?"

My nose wrinkles. Even saying the words in my head doesn't sound right. I've never heard any of the others call each other boyfriends or girlfriends. I snort when I imagine Sam introducing people to my brothers—her three boyfriends.

"Fine. I concede."

He grins, then kisses me hard. When he pulls back, he rests his forehead against mine. "I win."

"Such an ass," I breathe.

His smile drops and he leans back. "I'm not going to fight with them, Emma. If they tell me to go..."

"Then I go, too," I rush out, and grooves appear between his eyes. "I've already got a ticket. And a bag packed."

I don't want to leave my family. I've missed Synd—my home. It wouldn't feel the same without Titus, though. He'd take a piece of me with him. He holds my heart in the palm of his hand. We may not be the same people we were, but we've grown into something more. Whether he knew it or not, he was always the one. And no one will take him from me. Even my family.

I tip up my chin. "They're not going to reject you, Titus. But on the very small chance they do, I'm going with you. Because if I have even the sliver of a chance at happiness, I'm taking it."

He kisses me again, then grabs my hand. "Let's go then. Here's hoping Sam's car didn't get towed."

Chapter 48

Titus

As soon as we step into the King's conference room, I put some space between Emma and me. Facing the Kings would be bad enough, but half the fucking leaders of Synd are posted up around the large table. My spine straightens as several sets of eyes land on me, and I stare over Shane's head. The energy in the room is different from when he visited me earlier. Thank fuck I dropped the sling in the backseat of the car. I'll take the pain in my shoulder over appearing weak. They need someone they can trust to keep her safe. Injured men don't inspire confidence.

Emma clears her throat, yet the sound barely carries over the rain lashing at the windows. It started up again as soon as we reached the house, soaking us both. I wasn't about to pull into the garage. If I need to make a quick getaway, I'm stealing their car. The ride over here was quiet while Emma picked at the skin on my knuckles. Neither of us mentioned the building tension. For all her words, she's just as nervous as I am.

"Well, this is fucking awkward," Alex mutters. Sam's hand shoots out, smacking him in the back of his head. He grins, unbothered as usual.

"Emma," Shane says, a warning in his voice. "There a reason you were at the train station?"

"What? No," Emma squeaks, and I close my eyes, only opening them when Sam hisses at him.

"We need to discuss what happened in Ridgewood, regardless of whether you're ready. Titus, I expect a report as soon as you're able. You can go." Shane glance down at a pile of papers spread across the table, dismissing me.

My body sways, muscle memory taking over. Emma pokes me in the side and I flinch. I glare at her and she glares back, then jerks her head at them. I don't want to be the one who tells them about our relationship. Where the hell am I even supposed to start? No way am I telling them it started in the forest with my fingers buried in her—

I cut off the thought before I get hard. I'm already struggling to keep my shit together. All it takes is a quick glance at Emma and my cock stands at attention. I hold my breath, willing my hard-on away.

"So, here's the thing…" Emma's voice trails off as Shane glances up. She steps closer, almost hiding behind me.

"Would you knock it off?" I mutter from the corner of my mouth.

"He's got that look," she whispers. Alex snorts, burying his face in his hands.

I glance over my shoulder at her. "He's not going to shoot you. You're his sister. Just spit it out."

"What exactly is she spitting out? Wait." Shane holds up his hand. "Please tell me you're not—"

"I'm not pregnant," Emma shouts, earning a groan from me.

Shane places his hands on the table and rises slowly. "Going back to Ridgewood. *Are* you pregnant? Is it his?"

Emma ducks completely behind me, twisting her fingers in my shirt. My muscles tense and I spin around. I raise an eyebrow, silently asking her if she actually is. If she was running off because she's pregnant and if it's mine…She furiously shakes her head.

"I'm on the shot. We talked about that," she whispers harshly as she glares.

"Birth control isn't infallible, Emma."

"I'm not pregnant. It was just the only thing Shane hammered into my head when I was younger, so I blurted it out. You really think I wouldn't tell you if I was?" Hurt flashes across her face.

"If you were pregnant, I doubt it'd be mine," I whisper, trying to not let my voice carry. "You wouldn't know this early."

Understanding dawns on her face. She leans closer. "It's been like six months. I mean, before you. I kept putting him off."

"You didn't sleep with him?"

"Do we have to have this conversation right now?" she snaps quietly, tilting her head toward the others.

I straighten and pivot. "She's not pregnant. We're...together, which I understand might come as a shock."

"Not really," Ren mutters, then passes Mason, the Byrns leader, a piece of paper.

Now that it's clear Emma isn't with child, Shane sits again and fixates on his phone. Sam nudges him, gesturing to us. He glares at her, then returns to his phone.

"Well, I, for one, am ecstatic," Sam proclaims. "Hurt her and I'll carve out your heart and make you eat it before you die."

"Oooh, can I help? I've been wanting to figure out how to remove body parts while keeping them alive," Lacey, Mason's wife, asks.

Sam nods eagerly and I press my fist to my chest as if that will protect me from them. Conversations pop up and Emma eases around me. Hurt flashes across her face before she turns to me. She forces a smile to her face.

"See? Easy. Let's go get cleaned up."

She turns and I grab her arm, swinging her back despite the surge of pain in my arm and down my back. Like hell are we walking away like this. She needs their approval, and they're acting like she's not even in the room. Like they haven't even heard her. It's not new. They're still treating her like the damsel in distress. Someone who needs to be coddled instead of deserving a seat at the table.

"Titus?" she murmurs.

Making up my mind, I drop my hold on her and slam my palms onto the table. Silence descends as everyone's eyes fix on me, but I'm only concerned with Shane King. He's the de facto leader. While Alex and Ren are in charge as well, Shane is the deciding factor. Plus, he's technically her older brother.

Shane leans back, crossing his arms over his chest. "Something you'd like to say?"

"Stop ignoring her. We're telling you we're together and you can't even bother to look up from your goddamn phone. You've spent enough time neglecting her. It's time to step the fuck up and give her your goddamn blessing. Now." I brace myself, expecting him to pull a gun or, at the least, tell me off.

He leans to the side to gaze at Emma. "Is that how you feel? Like we've neglected and ignored you?"

"I...I mean...yes. Sometimes. You were busy."

I glance over my shoulder and snarl, "Stop making excuses for them."

Her eyes bounce between mine and Shane's as she twists her hands together. She takes a deep breath and drops them to her sides. She steps next to me, focusing on her brother.

"I'm an afterthought. I know you were trying to protect me when I was younger. I know you wanted more for me than what our family business could offer. You forgot, though. You forgot I'm my own person with my own wants. You're still treating me like I'm thirteen and about to sneak out of the house. I fucked up when I was younger, but I'm not that girl anymore. I'm a grown-ass woman who wants to be a part of things here. I want a place. And I want him. And if you don't like that, you can fuck off."

I wince, muttering, "Not the way I'd end it."

"Shut up. I'm doing the best I can," she hisses. "You're the one who started it, anyway."

"You're the one who said we had to talk to them," I grumble.

Her mouth drops open and she faces me. "No, I wasn't. That was you, asshole. I was content to just let them figure it out on their own."

"Not the way I remember it," I mumble.

She throws up her hands. "What happened to the man who said, 'I'll tell them you're mine. And I'm yours.' Blah, blah, blah."

Shane clears his throat, and Emma's face falls. She turns slowly to him, pressing her lips together.

"Emma, clearly there are some things we need to work through. Which we can do later, when we don't have a bunch of people hovering around waiting to gossip." He glares at Lacey, who smiles innocently.

Sam leans in front of Shane and whispers, "Don't worry. I'll fill you in later."

"Not helping, Sam," he grits out. "Suffice it to say, there will be some transitions we'll have to deal with. I still need a head of security, and I'm not giving it to anyone other than Titus. So don't ask me to move him."

"Wasn't going to. This is his dream job," Emma says. I don't know if I told her that, though it's not really a secret.

Shane nods. "Fine. Welcome to the family, Titus."

"That went better than expected," Emma mutters as we enter my new bedroom.

"Are you fucking joking? That was a goddamn disaster." My head swims and I sway.

Emma huffs, then wraps her arm around my waist and helps me to the bed. I end up collapsing crosswise on the king-sized mattress, exhaustion overtaking me. She bumbles around the room as I dip in and out of unconsciousness.

I don't know how long I doze, but when I wake up, Emma's nowhere to be found and someone is pounding on the door. I stumble to my feet and tug on the knob. Alex's face splits into a grin, and I glance down. Someone—Emma—undressed me down to my underwear while I was sleeping. I have no idea how she accomplished that without me realizing.

Alex chuckles, shaking his head. "Emma sent me to check on you. She was talking to Shane and Sam."

"Yeah, I'm fine," I say groggily, running my hand through my hair. A bolt of pain hits me and I groan.

"Whoa there. Let's get you some pain meds and move your shit." He pushes past me into the room as I process his words.

I track him as he lumbers around the space, grabbing clothes from my closet, and shampoo from the bathroom. I didn't realize they'd moved everything up here. Somehow, the fact they went through all the trouble to put my things in here hits me harder than anything else.

"Wait, why am I moving?" Nerves bubble in my stomach.

"Emma's room is bigger. Plus, it's farther away from the rest of us. We love you guys, but no way in hell do any of us want to hear the other one's nighttime activities. Or in my case, all day activities."

"Gross, Alex," Emma says, slipping by me. She stands on her tiptoes, brushing her lips against mine, then smiling as she sweeps into the room.

She grabs a box from the closet and plops it on the bed. They fill it up, chatting as they do. I have no idea what's happening. I didn't expect us to move in together. Which is strange since we're living in the same house, but this place is huge.

"Emma," I croak, my shoulder still aching.

She glances at me, then shoos Alex away. He takes the box filled with most of my things with him.

I kick the door closed and sag against it. "What's going on?"

"Sorry. Doesn't make sense to sleep in different rooms when you're going to need help with your shoulder. I figured we could talk about it later."

I wave away her explanation as my head throbs. Too much has happened today and I need more sleep. She wraps her arms around me, and I hold her close.

"I need sleep. And I need you next to me," I mumble, and drop a kiss on her head.

She rests her chin on my chest and smiles. "This is going to be great. I just know it."

"As long as I don't have to let you go, then yeah. It's going to be great."

Epilogue

Emma

I close my eyes against the bright sun, pressing my phone to my ear. "I don't know what you're talking about, Ryker."

Titus's fingers run through my hair before he settles on the chair next to me. We've only been on vacation two days, but I swear I could move here. I'm sure I'd eventually get sick of the sun and the sand and the brightness. For now, I'm content to soak it all in. It's the first trip I've ever been on and I'm going to relish every moment of the next thirty days. Titus taps my arm and I turn.

"Why is Helms calling you on our time?" he asks quietly.

I smirk as Ryker continues to grumble on the other end of the line. "He seems to think I'm responsible for the hippo statue currently sitting in the middle of his headquarters."

Titus shakes his head, then rests against the back of his chair. Bastard won't back me up even though he helped me haul that shit into place. It wasn't easy, either. No fucking way I would have been able to do it by myself. But Ryker isn't calling up Titus to bitch about it. Nope, it's all my fault apparently.

"Emma, I'm not fucking around here. How the hell did you get it inside? It won't fit through the double doors with the bar in the middle. None of the windows are big enough. Did you burrow underground or some shit?" Ryker snarls, clearly at his wits' end.

"I don't know why you'd think I'd be able to get Tiernan in there in the first place. That thing is almost as tall as I am." I press my lips together so none of my laughter bubbles out.

The phone is plucked from my hand, and Titus glares at me. "Helms, we're trying to enjoy an actual vacation. I don't care if there's a golden hippo statue in your fucking living room. You've moved it before, you can move it again. Send that shit to Drake's new place or something. Now, respectfully, fuck off."

He tosses the phone on the table between us and closes his eyes once more. I stare at the device, waiting for it to chime again, but it stays silent.

"You realize Roman and Ember's new house is in Rima, right? Four hours away from Synd? He'd have to find a trailer to get it there," I murmur, then grin as the image of a hippo statue with a motorcycle guard around it rolling down the highway.

"Well aware. He already has one, though. It's sitting at Byrns's house right now."

"Are you shitting me? We could have just used theirs?"

He grins, and my heart skips a beat. I'm still not used to him not scowling at me most of the time. Somehow, I'm still caught off guard eight months later. One of these days I'm afraid I'll miss it.

"Except now Helms will be looking for the trailer since it isn't there. He'll find it at the Byrns place, and we'll be off the hook," he murmurs, snapping me out of my ogling.

I settle into my chair, listening to the waves lap at the shore. It's peaceful in a way I've never experienced before. Moving to a small college town after living my whole life in Synd was hard. I'd spent enough time in the mountains to understand what silence was, but I was always on edge there. Here I don't have to worry about anyone waking me up in the middle of the night to go on a run through the trees.

"I'm hungry," I huff, and he hums. Bastard isn't going to take the hint. I could order my own food, but that would require me to get up. And decide what to eat. Neither of which I want to do right now.

Silently, I grumble. Five minutes later, Titus pushes to his feet to make his way through the bungalow. I glance over my shoulder and fixate on his ass in the grey athletic shorts I slipped in his luggage. I'm not going to lie and say I'm not obsessed. He could wear them the rest of our lives and I'd salivate over him the entire time.

My stomach flips as I turn back to the ocean. While I don't question how I feel about Titus, the rest of our lives is a long time. I'm not even twenty-five yet. My birthday is only a few weeks away, but still. I've spent my entire life questioning who I am and whether I'm making the right decisions.

I want what Sam and my brothers have—what the others have. Standing on the sidelines and watching them fall in love was terrifying. What if I never found what they have? What if I messed up? And now that my future is laid out in front of me, it feels too good to be true. I keep waiting for Titus to wake up one morning and realize I'm not enough.

Titus returns and sets a plate in my lap and my mouth waters. Snatching up one of the fritters, I pop it in my mouth and moan. Titus chuckles as he grabs one.

"Keep making those noises and we won't make it to the waterfall later."

"After I devour all this, I doubt I'll be able to walk, much less climb a waterfall."

"I'll roll you up the hills," he says with a laugh.

We eat in silence, just the waves and breeze rustling the fronds around us. My mind wanders, thinking back to my conversation with Daisy before I left. She's slowly coming to grips with what happened. Her parents weren't exactly happy with me. I don't blame them. She never would have been in danger if it wasn't for me. I'm still dealing with the guilt, whether or not she thinks it's my fault.

Daisy was going to take the next semester off, worried someone from Devon's organization would find her again. Titus called in some favors and Daisy had a brand-new bodyguard. Actually, it was more like a shadow since she didn't want to know they were there.

"Have you talked to Wright?" I ask, hoping Titus hasn't fallen asleep. He's been doing that randomly the last couple days. I'd blame it on jetlag, but I'm pretty sure he's just enjoying not being on duty. Apparently, it's hard work to keep me alive.

"Last week. Why?"

"Did he follow Daisy home?" I don't want Daisy to be unprotected just because she's not at school.

"You make him sound like a stalker," Titus snickers. "Yeah, he's with her. He'll have to go back home soon, though. He's debating whether to tell her she has to come with him or find someone else to take over for a bit."

"He's going to let someone else watch her? Who?"

Titus sighs. "No one. I offered that solution, but he doesn't want to take it. You might need to convince her to go with him."

"You want me to tell my best friend to go off with a dude she doesn't know to a place she's never been before and I'm assuming stay with him just because he needs to go home even though she didn't want to know any of the details about any of this? But it's okay, because the other option is to get *another* complete stranger to take over and actually creep on her." I roll my eyes, hoping he didn't already talk to Daisy about this.

"First of all, anyone I pick won't be a creep. They'll know they'll get gutted. And then I'll get ahold of them. Second, I doubt Wright will abandon her. He's been following her for so long he's gotten attached to her."

I wrinkle my nose. "Why does he have to go back to Synd?"

"Because *someone* insisted on going on vacation." He smirks and I return it.

"Oh, so this is my fault?"

"Very much so," he murmurs.

"You fucker. You already put what's-his-face in charge. You're trying to orchestrate something, aren't you?"

"I don't know what the fuck you're talking about," he mumbles. "Besides, Wright might be needed if shit goes down."

I bust out laughing and push to my feet. "Sure, keep telling yourself that."

"Keep it up, darling," he murmurs as he pulls his phone from his pocket. I narrow my eyes at his screen.

"What are you doing?"

The screen goes dark, and he slips it back in his pocket. "Nothing."

I hum, lying back and closing my eyes. I wait until he's relaxed, then ease from my seat. He grunts when I straddle him and his hands land on my waist. I run my nails down his chest, leaving red marks in their wake. He shudders, his fingers digging into my skin. I play with the waistband of his shorts. He doesn't notice when I move on to his pocket and slip his phone out. I lean back slowly and catch his grin.

I scramble from his lap and dash into the bungalow. He races after me as I try to open his phone. He wraps his arm around my waist and my feet leave the floor. I kick, yelping as he spins me around.

"I just want to seeee," I squeal.

He snatches the phone from my hand and throws me on the bed. Every time I attempt to get up, he shoves me back down as he scrolls through.

"You want to see so badly? Fine." He holds it in front of my face, and I struggle to make sense of things.

"That's just a bunch of numbers. What the fuck?"

He leans down and presses his hips into mine. My breath hitches as warmth gathers between my legs. He grins and his lips brush my ear.

"Every time you sass me, I mark it down."

"What? Why?" I ask breathlessly as he rocks his hips against me.

"One orgasm for every time your attitude comes out. You've racked up quite a bit of them."

My mouth drops open, not sure how to respond. The audacity of this man to keep track of when *he* thinks I'm being sassy. I should start noting every time he does it, too. Sarcasm and cheeky responses are our love language. It's the way we've operated from the beginning.

"For fuck's sake, Titus," I grumble.

He leans back on his knees and holds up his phone. When I try to sit up, his fingers wrap around my throat, holding me down. He swipes at the screen, then turns it around.

"Brat points? Are you fucking kidding me? You're ridiculous. I can't come nine times, Titus. I'll fucking die."

He smirks, adding two more marks. I open my mouth, then snap it shut again when he raises an eyebrow. Pressing my lips together, I hold back the arguably impressive string of expletives begging to erupt from me.

He glances at the screen again, tilting his head as he contemplates things. "I'd split them up, but I'm pretty sure you'll keep being a brat, so it'll be a never-ending cycle."

"You don't look upset about that."

He grins, transforming his whole demeanor. He's smiled more in the last six months than ever before. I'd come to peace with it, knowing he didn't have much to grin about in our line of work. Alex can pull it off, but Titus still thinks he has to prove himself by being grumpy. Since we settled into a relationship, he's less tense—happier. I'm not naive enough to think it's because of me, but it's nice to imagine I'm the reason.

"What's that look for?" he asks, and I rearrange my face. It's not as easy to mask around him anymore.

"What look? I don't have a look. Are you going to do something about your hand around my throat or..."

His eyes narrow as he flexes his fingers, making my breath hitch. He leans down and brushes his nose along my jaw. If he starts something he doesn't intend to finish, we're going to have problems. I wiggle underneath him, and he grunts.

"Do you know how much I love you?" he murmurs, and I freeze. "So fucking much."

He drags his hand from my throat to my chest and plucks at the tie of my swimsuit. The fabric unravels, and he licks his lips before swooping down and capturing a nipple between his teeth. My back arches and my fingers spear into his hair. When he switches to the other one, a moan slips from me.

"Perfect fucking tits," he mutters into my flesh. His hand slides to my hip, and he unties the string there. He shoves my swimsuit away and cups my pussy. "Perfect fucking cunt."

I whimper as his lips skim down my stomach. He slides off the bed and lands on his knees. I catch his wolfish grin between my legs right before he yanks me toward him until my ass practically hangs off the mattress. When his teeth sink into my inner thigh, I jolt. My body quivers in anticipation as he skims his lips along my skin. Never where I need him, though.

"Please," I gasp when he leans back.

"You know I love it when you beg," he murmurs.

"Fu—" A moan takes over as he sucks on my clit.

My knees snap shut around his head, and he latches onto them, forcing them apart. He laps at my core and my eyes slam shut. He doesn't like when I don't watch him, but I can't help myself. I focus on his touch, then whimper when he pumps two fingers in and out of me. Heat builds in my stomach and spreads through my body. As his tongue flicks my clit, I moan, my pussy spasming. He chuckles, then kisses one thigh, then another as he slowly strokes me.

When he pulls out of me, my eyes fly open, and I find him grinning. "One."

I scowl, then shudder as he pulls his fingers out of me. He stands and shoves his shorts to his ankles, then kicks them aside. My gaze fixates on his hard cock, and I lick my lips. He grips my hips to move me back. Not enough to feel like I'm not about to tumble off the bed. A growl falls from his lips when he realizes the mattress isn't high enough for him to fuck me properly. At least not with him standing.

He grabs my hand and yanks me upright. My feet smack against the floor and my bikini bottoms drop. He fits his fingers in the crease of my ass and hauls me against his body. As my hands wind around his neck, he slams his lips to mine. My back hits the wall and I lock my ankles around his waist. When he lines himself up, I sink onto his cock, moaning as he fills me.

"Look at how well you take my cock," he murmurs, his eyes fixed on where we're joined.

My answer is a moan, and I try to force him deeper. He pulls out slowly, then surges into me again. My breath stutters as my orgasm dances just out of reach.

"Please," I whisper, and his hand returns to my throat.

"Be a good girl and come on my cock," he growls.

His command sends me over the edge and stars burst behind my eyelids. He grunts as I spasm around his length. My limbs become jelly and my legs fall from his waist. I expect him to finish, but he doesn't. His lips brush mine and he pulls out of me. I whine and he slams his mouth on mine. He devours me as he swings us around and marches through the bungalow. I rip my mouth away, panting as he steps outside.

"I'm naked," I squeal, burying my face into his chest. This place might be private, but that doesn't mean others couldn't walk in at any moment.

"Well aware, darling."

"Anyone could walk up," I growl. A shriek leaves me as he drops me onto the large, round bed situated on the porch. Titus has been eyeing it since we got here. I thought he just wanted to nap on it or something. Maybe a hot make out session. Not putting me on display for anyone to catch a peek.

"The chances are very low. I also know you like the idea of being caught." He strokes his length and my mouth waters. I am not one to get on my knees for anyone, but for this man? It happens more than I thought it would.

He chuckles as his gaze travels down my body. "You want to taste yourself on my cock?"

I scramble upright and my mouth drops open. I don't care if I look needy. He steps closer and his fingers slide into my hair, holding my head still. My lips close around the tip and I suck hard, earning a grunt from him.

I don't know if I can actually taste myself on him, but the idea has wetness gathering once more between my legs. My fingers dig into his thighs while he thrusts into my mouth and hits into the back of my throat. I cough and he eases off, wiping the tears from my cheek.

"You want me to come down your throat?" he asks slyly, knowing my answer.

I pull back and he pops from my mouth. "Fuck no. Gross."

His nostrils flare, and a calculating edge enters his eyes. "You were down to nine, but you fucked it up for yourself."

He tugs a chair closer to him and drops into it. He leans back as if he's clothed in the most expensive suit. My eyes catch on the tattoo wrapped around his side and my heart skips a beat. It's a morning glory, just like mine. I missed the small one he had hidden under his arm before he even came to Ridgewood. He never mentioned he got one to match mine. I'm not usually into matching tattoos, but his are different enough it doesn't seem intentional. Plus, he didn't even tell me he was expanding it until it was already done.

My eyes skip to his and he glares at me, then smirks. I don't know what the hell he expects me to do. No way am I putting my knees on the hard stones.

"Lie back and make yourself come," he says finally.

My eyes narrow, and he raises a brow in challenge. I glance around, making sure there's no one spying on us. Grumbling, I drop back, and he scoots closer until his knees force mine farther apart. I lift my head and glare at him.

"Got a good enough view?"

"I'm starting to think you're being a brat on purpose."

His fingers skim from my knee to my pussy, and he runs them along my folds. My back arches and he freezes at my entrance. I slide my hand to my clit, and he growls in approval. Fucking bastard. All thoughts fly from my head as he thrusts them into me. It doesn't take long for me to teeter on the edge of oblivion once more.

"Come," he snarls as my fingers work my clit, and I tumble into another orgasm. "That's three."

He doesn't wait for me to recover as he pulls away, then flips me onto my stomach. My arm gets trapped underneath me, but I'm too distracted to care. He yanks me onto my knees and slams into me. My muffled moan echoes in my ears. His movements are erratic as he pounds into me. His fingers find my clit and I explode around him. He slows, fucking me through another orgasm. He keeps pressure on the sensitive nub, and I shudder.

His chest presses to my back, and he whispers, "You're doing so fucking well. So fucking beautiful."

He thrusts harder, still murmuring praise, and I come again. Or maybe it's the same one as before. Either way, I don't care. I don't know how much more I can take.

"Six," I gasp, and he chuckles.

"Look at you counting for me."

He sits back and seizes my hips, then buries himself into me. I don't have it in me for more. Pleasure cascades through me and I grip the fabric lining the outdoor bed. A cry of protest falls from my lips as he pulls out of me. I don't know how the hell he's still going. He flips me around once more and my arms flop above my head. He chuckles, covering my body with his. His cock slides into me easily and he thrusts gently.

"I finally fucked the attitude out of you," he says.

I smile sleepily. "For now."

He kisses his way across my chest, running his teeth across my nipples. I groan as I pull my knees up. The move has him grunting as he slips deeper into me.

"You're going to give me one more. Then I'll let you rest," he murmurs.

I'm already shaking my head before he's finished speaking. He groans as I quiver around his shaft. I don't think he realizes how much my body is humming. His hips rock against mine, creating a new type of friction between us. My desire builds gradually. I swear if he coaxes one more orgasm from me, he's a fucking god. Or maybe he's just made for me.

"Fuck, I love you," I breathe as our eyes meet.

He swallows hard and his hands cup my cheeks. He kisses me softly. Tears gather in the corner of my eyes. Usually, we're ravenous, tearing at each other's clothes. This is different—sparking a warmth in me. He brushes the wetness from my face. I cling to him as he thrusts into me, wringing one more orgasm from my spent body.

I shudder in his hold, and he kisses me once more before pushing to his knees. I ride the wave of ecstasy as he buries himself into me over and over. He tenses, groaning my name as he comes. I wrap my arms around him when he collapses on top of me.

"I love you, Emma King. Never forget that," he murmurs into my neck.

I smile, happiness swelling inside of me as I drift off. No matter what happens in the future, at least I'll have Titus to catch me when I fall.

* * *

Thank You

Thank you so much for reading Titus and Emma's story!

Looking for extra scenes from Synd and Rima? Novellas?
Check out my newsletter:
https://subscribepage.io/emiliaabrahamspicynewsletter

Ready for another adventure?
Check out the other works by Emilia Abraham:
https://emiliaabraham.com

If you'd like to hear about the other stories that have been living in my head, sign up for my newsletter (including extra scenes & a novella), visit my website, or follow me on social media visit:
https://linktr.ee/emiliaabraham

Special Thanks:
K.B. Barrett Designs-Cover Artist and Formatter
Emily Michel-Editor
Emily Renee-Beta Reader
Krysten-Omega Reader

Other Books by E. Abraham

Shadows of Synd:

Under the Shadows-Book 1
Between the Shadows: Novella
Running From Shadows-Book 2
Becoming Shadows-Book 3
Shadows Within Us-Book 4
Beyond the Shadows-Book 5

Ruins of Rima:

Spin-off Series
Chasing Darkness-Book 1
Charmed by Darkness-Book

Also by Emilia Abraham:

Stuck at Sundown
The Cryptid Chronicles:
Bewitched by Bigfoot
Write on the Edge

About the Author

After many years of dreaming of becoming a full-time writer, Emilia Abraham took the leap, bringing her words to print. From sweet contemporary romance to spicy why choose and everything in between, she focuses on the happily ever after.

Emilia lives in the Upper Midwest with her husband (who's probably sick of listening to her expound on fictional men) and three kids (who try to steal her post-it notes). When she's not writing, she enjoys reading, playing video games, and consuming copious amounts of energy drinks.

Milton Keynes UK
Ingram Content Group UK Ltd.
UKHW030320090824
446663UK00001B/28